Praise for Michael Schiefelbein's *Vampire Vow*
Lambda Literary Award Finalist

"Michael Schiefelbein has employed the conventions of gothic fiction with wit, passion, and intelligence, a combination that will render his book a crossover success because these qualities will appeal to a wide range of readers, including those who would not normally read vampire novels... For most readers, perhaps, VAMPIRE VOW'S pleasures will be more concrete: Its action is tightly plotted, its characters completely and believably drawn, and its prose style simple but elegant. They will devour it–or let it devour them."

— *Lambda Book Report*

"[An] audacious, erotic and entertaining novel... Sexy, suspenseful and yes, spiritual, VAMPIRE VOW is a distinctive debut."

— *Philadelphia Gay News*

"[Schiefelbein's] take on vampirism is perhaps the most interesting... The theological concepts, the envisioning of a vampire heirarchy, the conflicting emotions of the protagonist, all conspire to render an absolutely fascinating book."

— *Gay People's Chronicle*

"VAMPIRE VOW is a literate, compelling, and original contribution to the horror fantasy genre, and strongly recommended, especially compelling reading for vampire buffs."

— *Midwest Book Review*

BOOKS BY MICHAEL SCHIFELBEIN

THE VAMPIRE SERIES
Vampire Vow
Vampire Thrall
Vampire Transgression
Vampire Maker

STANDALONE NOVELS
Blood Brothers
Body and Blood

All available as JABberwocky ebooks

VAMPIRE VOW
&
VAMPIRE THRALL

MICHAEL SCHIFELBEIN

Published by Jabberwocky Literary Agency, Inc.

For Gary

VAMPIRE VOW

Part I

BAPTISM INTO BLOOD

CHAPTER ONE

I wanted Jesus. That's how it started. Yes, the Jesus they built a religion on, the one they say rose from the dead. (I should be the last creature in the world to doubt that.)

There we were, on a quiet, stony hilltop overlooking the city, the stars above us like light through pinpricks in black velvet. Just he and I, years before the 12 dolts who formed his entourage. We huddled next to each other as we often did, and I finally asked him.

"Joshu," I whispered—that was my name for him. "Why resist this? You're always talking about the vanity of human law, about wanting to strike out against the old order."

He looked troubled, a young man of 23 still as idealistic as his disgustingly naive, dull Nazarene parents, who actually believed me when I told them I was a Jew—I, a Roman officer serving under Pilate!

"I'm troubled," he said. He leaned back on his hands. The moonlight washed over his lean form, his fine brow betraying his sensuality as much as it did his intelligence.

"What's to be troubled about? Love? That's what you rant about all the time, isn't it? Love must replace the legalism of the priests." I stroked his cheek, the smooth cheek of an unmarried Jew boy.

He took my hand and kissed it. "You know what place you have in my heart. You are the earth itself to me. But the earth is passing—"

"This is pious trash." I jerked my hand away. "The truth is you lack the boldness to act by your beliefs. You're not a man of action. You're a poet brainwashed by the Essene fanatics walled up in their caves. All this business about the end of this age, the plight of the complacent priests. Then when it comes to a radical move—"

"You're talking about forbidden relations."

"Forbidden to whom?" I asked. I could hear him weakening, see him eyeing my strong calves, my bulky thighs. It was hot and I had thrown off my tunic to tempt him. Nature had given me a square jaw, a cleft chin, a dark mane, eyes that could bring a vestal virgin to her knees—and a cock that could keep her there. My meaty physique came from years spent in the Emperor's training rooms.

"The point is," I said, "we've sworn allegiance to each other. We meet on this craggy hillside night after night. I listen to all these dreams of yours about a kingdom of god. Your god. The stuff of sedition, I might add. We race along the river, buck-naked. We even bathe each other! Ours is only the ultimate bond."

Right there, the Jew temple of Jerusalem beneath us, I swore to myself that I would finally enter him—the boy prophet, the ultimate challenge, my obsession. I would enter him the way I entered the Emperor's gates after a campaign: invincible, majestic. But hailed by his groans rather than by the cries of banner-waving masses.

I reached beneath his robe.

He pulled away. "No, Victor." His voice was not without regret. "I'm not ready to throw out the law of my fathers. This cannot happen."

This was the last time we met there.

Soon afterward I received a message from him: I must give myself *to no earthly man, only to my Father in heaven, for whose coming kingdom I must prepare. For the sake of this, we must meet no more.*

I persisted. I who had taken whomever I chose until that moment. I followed Joshu, hounded him until he fled to the desert to live as a hermit.

I had never hesitated to use force with other subjects of the Empire, to beat, to wrench them into submission. With this one, though, force could not be mustered.

CHAPTER TWO

I met him a week after arriving in Palestine. After military training in Rome, my birthplace, and commanding troops in Gaul, I received a commission to serve in Judaea under Pilate, who'd replaced the puppet king, Archelaus, when he'd proved incompetent. My head swelled with the honor of it—living at Pilate's palatial headquarters on the Mediterranean coast, parading through the rabble of Jerusalem to remind the Jews whose empire they belonged to, spending the day wrestling naked soldiers and training in the governor's gymnasium. Besides quelling riots now and then and presiding over executions, all I had to do was bark orders and look good.

My hopes were crushed, however, as I and a fellow officer surveyed Jerusalem for the first time from horseback. Beggars squatted at the city gates, pissed out in the open. The marketplace stank with overripe fruit and animal dung. Urchins ran naked through the streets, and toothless hags scrubbed linens at the wells.

Rome was not without its own squalor, but I had been exposed to little of it. I'd been raised outside the city in a magnificent villa with gardens, vineyards, and a superb view of the Apennines. The city drew me only after dark, when I needed a whore, when the lurid faces I passed in the night only excited my wild, drunken desires. In Rome, colossal buildings of marble overshadowed the ghettos. Fountains in enormous squares, mansions on the Palatine, the Circus Maximus, the baths of Caracalla, aristocrats draped in purple—the splendors of the city made up for its unpleasant corners.

While Jerusalem—aside from the temple (a shack by Roman standards), Herod's palace, and a few mansions—had nothing to offer but rank slums.

I got drunk every night the first week, depressed about being stationed in Judaea for three years. To hell with standards of Roman discipline, I thought. I needed an escape from that hole. After carousing one night after Pilate had left for councils in Rome, I shook off the clingy Egyptian whore who couldn't get enough of me and rode to the hills overlooking the city. A cool wind blew. The sky already burned pink on the eastern horizon. I dismounted, threw a blanket on a smooth rock, and passed out.

When I opened my eyes, the sun was setting. I'd spent a whole day sleeping off my stupor, but my head still pounded. A voice rose over a ridge just above me, a voice as smooth and sensuous as a wooden flute, a young man's voice. I scaled the rocks to peer over the ridge. A stark-naked boy, who seemed barely 20, cavorted on a bluff, throwing up his hands, swirling his head, all the while chanting an eerie Oriental tune. His eyes were closed and I watched him freely for several minutes before he stopped directly in front of me and gazed down at the ledge where I stood, without a hint of shame in his handsome face.

"What's wrong, haven't you ever seen one before?"

He'd caught me admiring his dark circumcised cock, thick as a rope used to hoist building stones. "Not like that," I said. "You're my first naked Jew."

"It's a sign of the covenant," he said with pride, continuing to stand unabashedly in front of me with his arms crossed.

"Covenant?" His Latin was crude and I thought I'd misunderstood him.

"Yes, the covenant between us and our God."

"Demanding son-of-a bitch, if you ask me."

He sized me up as though he might kick me in the face, then laughed instead, his taut belly quivering. He laughed until he coughed and wiped tears from his almond-shaped eyes.

"Help me up, damn it. I'm tired of balancing on this ledge."

Still smiling, he offered me his hand, and I scrambled up to the bluff. He handed me a skin of water, exactly what I needed after a night of liquor and a full day of sleeping in the sun. Then we hiked to a lower level, leading my thirsty horse to a pool of water that had collected in a cave. He seemed to know every niche of the mountain, stepping with confidence in his dusty sandals across gullies and jagged stones. Still naked. In the twilight shadows at the mouth of the cave, his sinewy form and his long, unkempt hair seemed to belong to a wild man who roamed the mountains.

"Are you one of the crazy Essene cave dwellers I've heard about?"

"What makes you ask?" He stroked the neck of my horse as it lapped the water.

"Don't tell me all Jews prance around on mountaintops with their peeled cocks flopping."

"No, just me."

"And why is that?"

"I'm strange, they say. I'm drawn to the mountains, up above Jerusalem. You can laugh, but I sense God here, even more than in the temple." He nodded in the direction of the city.

"Which god?"

"There's only one."

"Ah yes, a Jew idea. So you toss off your clothes when you feel the presence of your god?"

He smiled. "I go a little mad. Down there inside the temple walls, God seems confined. I know I feel confined."

"Watch out, Jew boy, you'll be stoned for heresy. I hear that's part of your religious code."

We secured my horse and climbed back to the summit where we'd met. It was too dark now to descend the mountain. We ate bread and lentils he'd brought in a pack, and stretched out on a homespun blanket to gaze at the lights in the city below. When the wind picked up, the boy slipped into his robe and lay close to me for warmth. He tantalized me more than any creature ever had, but I kept my hands to myself. Few, very few men could raise a sense of honor in me, but he—a Palestinian subject of the Empire, a Jew boy—managed somehow.

Over the next year, I became obsessed with him. We sailed on the Sea of Galilee, near his hometown, and hiked the rugged mountain terrain of Judaea. We feasted on roasted lamb, chugged his homemade wine until our vision blurred. Hot and drunk on the Mount of Olives, east of the city, we talked freely. He lampooned religious sects like the Pharisees and spun theories about the Elysian Fields, what he called the kingdom of Heaven.

In time he owned up to his heat for me—like I couldn't see it in his eyes. It frightened him. But it wasn't fear that kept him from grabbing my balls. He had religious qualms. He was destined to be some kind of eunuch for his god, a damned vestal of Palestine.

His power over me never relented. Not when I inspected with contempt the modest stone house of his family in a neighborhood of Nazarene artisans, not when I watched him join dirty swarms of Jews outside the temple, not when I nearly exploded in unrequited lust.

If he'd toyed with me, if he'd held me at bay to stir up my desire, I'd have taken him in an instant. But he didn't tease. Nor did he fear me. He wanted me but wouldn't succumb. And I wanted nothing less than his will.

Our last night together, I was horny as a satyr and thought, *To hell with it, I've been a Stoic long enough—and when he feels my cock inside him he'll forget his scruples.* When he refused me, and cut me off, my rage knew no bounds.

CHAPTER THREE

I'm sick of hearing of it, Lieutenant," Pilate said. He was flat on his stomach on his massage table, naked and glistening with oil. The man working his shoulder muscles was a barrel-chested Egyptian with braided black hair. The bath chamber was heavy with columns, gilded tiles, draperies. "It was one thing to beat the tax collector for cheating us above the usual amounts: He was an example. The defiant drunkard, too. But a woman with her baby? By the gods, man, we'll have a mob on our hands. We've got enough trouble the way it is."

These words from a man who loved bearbaiting.

"She was a prostitute, Your Excellency." I stood at attention above his bald head, my crotch level with his eyes. (I'd heard he liked to carry on with his soldiers, though he'd never summoned me to his chamber.) "The people might have stoned her tomorrow for all we know, and she refused to obey my commands."

The governor signaled for the Egyptian to stop. The servant did so and brought him a sheet. Pilate wrapped himself in it and strolled to his couch. He stretched out on his side, eyeing the insignia on my tunic. His dark eyes were bold and cunning.

"She did not realize your rank, your position here?"

"Of course the bitch knew."

"And what did you command her to do?" He didn't bother trying to hide his curiosity.

"The usual things. I wanted to enter her backside. I wanted her tongue inside me. I wanted to bind her."

"And she resisted?"

"She tried. I tied her down, forced myself into her, with the brat looking on, bawling in his own shit. I backhanded him."

"Yes, well you might have spared the child." He motioned to a ewer of wine on a table and the Egyptian brought him a cup. "The Jews won't tolerate beating one of their children, even one that belongs to a prostitute. I've met with two contingents of their priests today."

"I'll restrain myself, Your Excellency."

"If you're hungry for blood, I can make you head executioner, Lieutenant." He eyed me impatiently over his cup.

"I will restrain myself."

"See to it that you do. I won't have another riot outside my walls." He waved me away.

In my dark room in the barracks, I removed my uniform and sandals and stretched out on my cot. The arched window framed a moon round and white as a discus. I knew I had gone too far. But since Joshu had dismissed me, fury had driven me to madness. What Pilate didn't know was that I'd knocked around other whores, as well as two or three Jew boys who'd tried to guard their circumcised shafts the way witless maidens guard their own treasures.

I had never wanted anyone like I wanted Joshu, a superior specimen of manhood—not just in his taut, athletic physique, but also in his thinking. He challenged not only the inane Jewish laws of ritual purity but, at least in private, elements of Roman civilization—the Emperor's title of divinity, social classes, the possession of slaves.

I shared his disdain. The difference between us was that I at least pretended to abide by the rules and obey the commands of my superiors. Such adherence had won me my rank, and I believed I was destined for greater things, perhaps direct service under Tiberius himself.

Now, however, my ruthlessness had spiraled out of control. My downfall was imminent if I could not restrain my animal urges.

Chapter Four

Other officers had sworn by the tranquilizing potions of a seer named Tiresia. I'd resisted entering the cluttered slum along one of the city walls where she kept shop, but now I was desperate for an elixir that would temper my anger.

Made of stone blocks, all of its windows bricked up, the former inn was entered through a small portal leading to a long, cavernlike corridor built against the wall. I stumbled in the darkness past three or four cubicles toward a dull light. I found the wench staring into a mirror of polished metal, oil lamps glowing around her. She saw my reflection and smiled triumphantly.

"So, you've finally come, Lieutenant Victor Decimus. Welcome to my lair. Sit here." She patted a stool next to her. She wasn't the ancient hag I'd expected. She was not yet 40, her Ethiopian locks threaded with colored beads, her abundant bosom jiggling beneath her flowing robe with every movement she made.

"What, has another officer told you of me? Speak the truth, wench." I continued watching her in the mirror.

"The truth!" She laughed from deep in her chest. "I know nothing else. Nothing. If you please, my lieutenant, advance."

I approached the stool, removed my sword, and sat next to her.

"You're a handsome man, Lieutenant. You've a strong jaw, strong shoulders. Your eyes; they're bold, keen. You're a model client."

"I know what I look like. Enough of this prattle." I turned to her, but she averted her face from me.

"Please, my lord. Keep your eyes to the glass. If you want to be satisfied. Look only to the glass."

"If this is a game, I'll rip you apart, woman." I motioned to my sword and took a seat.

"You won't be sorry, my lord." Through the mirror, her heavy-lidded eyes again peered at me. She was a stunning beauty. "The remedy you seek, I have. I have something more, if you dare try it. However, it will stir up your passion rather than calm it."

"You must be a second-rate sorceress. The last thing I need is more of a temper."

"Ah, but what if you could be transported beyond the grounds of Pilate's headquarters? What if you could take whomever you pleased with no ill consequences?"

"Stop talking in riddles." I grabbed her arm, and she snapped her face away away from me.

"I promise, Lieutenant, I would not resort to tricks. What I offer is too grave for games. But you must not look at me."

"Why? I doubt you're afraid of a man's eyes, from the looks of you. Why do you hide from the sunlight? Why is the shop as dark as a prison? Why do you cower here like a rat?"

"You must trust me, my Lord. There is no other way." She continued to face the darkness.

"Proceed." I released her arm and turned back to the mirror.

Without loss of poise she resumed her attitude before the glass. "What I have for you, you shall receive with no small pleasure. But again, you must trust me. I've waited long for you. I have seen you coming for an eternity. You're the first in an age. Without you I would shrivel and die. Stop!" She raised her hand when she perceived my impatience. Rings of rubies and polished jade glistened on her fingers. "You will understand soon enough. First, drink this." She reached for a silver ewer on a table and poured from it into a cup, which she handed me.

I sniffed it.

"There is nothing magical about it," she said. "It's merely a strong liquor to relax your resistance to my words. I speak the truth. Drink."

I did as she bid and very soon breathed more easily. The flame of a lamp transfixed me and I felt as though I lay in the sun after a swimming race in the sea. She slipped off her robe to show me her black breasts, round and full as silky pouches of spring water, waiting to be tasted by a parched desert nomad. Then she stood and let her garment drop to the floor. Her ebony body gleamed. Her ringed fingers touched my cheeks, guided me to her belly, which smelled of musk and sweet oil.

"Ah, this is all, wench? You want me to hump you?" I pulled her to the dirt floor. She moaned when my swollen cock sank into her warm, moist cunt. She moaned more as I pumped her, first slow, then hard, then slow to heighten my pleasure. All the while she kept her face turned from me.

The ride affected me like the opium I'd once taken in Rome, producing a trancelike calm together with a keen, excited euphoria spreading from my loins through my body the way the heat of liquor in the stomach finally flushes the face.

She guided my mouth to her breast. My heart pounded as the brown nipple stiffened. At first I imagined that milk flowed from the breast, then I tasted something else, something warm and potent, something as rich and red as the wine of Capri, as exhilarating as a slash made by an opponent's dagger. When the liquid streamed down my chin, when I saw the stained breasts of the seer, I swallowed greedily. There was no stopping. The euphoria mounted.

I felt myself soar over the walls of the city on a moonlit night, over wells and courtyards, over crumbling stone dwellings wedged together on filthy streets. Below, lithe girls beckoned to me. Fair boys called for me to mount them. Amid them stood Joshu.

"So you see me, Victor!" he called from a rooftop garden. "You've discovered the power. But I promise, it will only trap you on the wrong side of eternity."

I soared round the roof, tried to light on its tiles, but could not descend. I was like a granule of chaff battling a whirlwind, while the palms below remained immobile in the silvered moonlight.

"You can't approach me, Victor. Believe me. Turn from her!" Joshu was as clear and distinct as a crow on white sand. None of the haziness of dreams obscured him, and I felt no awareness—as we often do in dreams—that what I saw would vanish if I willed myself awake. I was there, with him.

"Don't believe him, my lord." The seer's words burst into my mind, but I saw nothing of her as I soared, though the sensation of our coupling continued and I continued to taste blood in my mouth. "I am the way," she said. "Remember that. I am the truth."

"She mocks me. She mocks God," Joshu called.

"I will have you," I said. "I feel it. I feel it."

"You feel her."

"Enough for now, my lord." She pushed my lips from her breast. "More later if you like."

I was drenched with sweat, while she remained dry. The stain had disappeared from her breasts. I rolled off her to catch my breath.

"There's more, my lord. Why worry about your rage? You can find him whenever you like. And you can have much more besides. Much more." She propped her head on her elbow. In the shadows she had no need to turn her face away.

"What do you mean?"

"Come here again when you are ready to die."

"Are you raving mad, sorceress bitch?" I reached over and grabbed her throat. "I could strangle you now and leave you in this pit."

Suddenly a vise seemed to crush my hand, though I saw no culprit. I cried out in pain and tried, to no avail, to release myself.

"Remember what I've said, Lieutenant. I am the way. When you are willing to leave the world of the living I will take you to a place where you can be master of all. Even him."

My hand was freed from the invisible grip. Tiresia stood and, without moving toward her garments, was clothed.

"I want to see him again." I lay on the cold dirt, nursing my hand.

"You will not return here until you are prepared to stay."

She seated herself once again before the mirror and watched me stand and grope my way back through the dark corridor.

CHAPTER FIVE

For weeks I could not escape the vision of Joshu on the rooftop, the sweet, powerful sensation I'd felt. I became convinced that had I remained with him longer I could have reached him, embraced him. And that locked in my arms, he could not have resisted me. I wrestled with the officers in Pilate's game hall, I drank myself to oblivion, I worked the whores and the boys who attended me. At night I paced the labyrinth of Jerusalem's narrow streets. Nothing relieved the restlessness.

I approached Tiresia's shop several times, once intending to feign agreement with her demands, but always the force I had felt on my hand returned, causing me to wince and massage my fingers. Unable to shake the invisible grip, I retreated.

My temper flared again and again. When my secretary misplaced a scroll, I beat him until he wept. When I found my chamber pot unemptied after breakfast, I shoved my servant's face in it. I raised my sword to a harlot when I found bloody discharge draining from her slit and made her beg for her life before I retreated from her house.

As long as I vented my rage on servants and whores, I stayed in Pilate's graces. But my restlessness reached feverish heights, and finally, delirium obliterated good sense.

The boy was a Jew. I had spotted him during a military parade near Herod's palace. Long-limbed, like a gazelle, he sunned himself on a wall, captivated by the glinting silver and plumage of our uniforms.

"You called me, sir?" He had come to my chamber, brought by the soldier I'd sent to retrieve him.

"Approach me, boy." I lay on my couch, surveying his soft features framed by black ringlets. "Closer. That's right." I fondled his woolen cloak. "What are you called?"

"Benjamin, sir." He stared straight ahead, out the window, not daring to drop his eyes to mine.

"Take off your cloak."

"Sir?"

"It's warm enough in here with the fire. Remove your cloak. There, that's better."

He was lean but solid. His neck rose like a delicate pedestal from his robe.

"Are you breaking some religious edict by being here? Never mind. You shouldn't worry your conscience. You had no choice. If you hadn't come ... Do you have a family of some kind?"

"Sir?" He suddenly looked anxious.

"Oh, come now. I'm only asking from interest. I won't butcher them." I caressed his arm. My sense of protectiveness excited me.

"I have a mother, sir. A widow. She spends most of the day in prayer in the temple courts."

"Some kind of holy woman, I suppose."

"Yes, sir."

"Who looks after you? You can't be more than 14."

"I stay with my father's people, sir. They are potters."

"Ah, you've got good hands for that trade." I turned his hands over and examined the palms. "Sit here on my couch."

"Please, sir. I couldn't."

"But I command it." I pulled him to me. "Do you know what I want you for?"

"Do you want pottery, sir?"

"Look at me. Look at me, damn you!"

He looked at me as though I were going to recircumcise him.

"Do I look like I want pottery?"

"I don't know, sir."

Once he did know, he submitted like a lamb, stupidly following my directions without a sign of struggle. To break a boy in, to rob him of what most Jewish men never imagine surrendering, invigorated me more than a winter swim. When I was satisfied, I told him to dress and summoned my man.

"You'll breathe a word of this to no one, boy. For your family's sake. I warn you."

"Yes, sir." The boy stared blankly at me, as though stunned by days of exposure in the Judaean desert.

"Escort him to the gate," I said to my man, who had learned discretion from me the hard way.

The boy kept his word well. When his cousins tried to pry information from him, he kept silent. He lost his appetite, grew thin, stopped sleeping, ruined the pitchers and vases he was creating, burnt himself on the kiln. Then one day his cousin found him dangling from a tree, like an old woman's rug thrown up to dry. He'd hanged himself after his mother, the wise bitch of a prophetess, guessed his shameful secret.

A delegation from the Sanhedrin stood before Pilate the next day. The results, I knew, would be imprisonment for me in Pilate's clammy cells, reserved for debauched or inept officers, followed by demotion, which would mean marching with the foot soldiers during military parades—to the satisfaction of the slimy priests on the sidelines.

Unbearable? Not for some. But I knew punishment like that would ignite my fury. Like the baited cheetah in the Roman circus, I'd tear apart my tormentors, dooming myself to longer imprisonment.

I fled the palace before Pilate could send his guards for me.

CHAPTER SIX

In the whorehouse where I hid, incense burned night and day to camouflage the piss splattered in the corridors and courtyard by drunk patrons. The women painted their faces at night and floated up and down the halls in transparent silks, like ghosts, ghosts who returned to their grave beds by day. Not that customers did not demand service in the hours of sunlight—even pious Jews felt safe, knowing none of their kind ever showed his face in a neighborhood that would leave him ritually unclean. Then a ghost would be summoned from her grave by the shriveled mistress and display herself at the door, pale and naked, her eyes glassy and ringed by shadow.

The life of the night suited me to a degree. Hooded and cloaked, I wandered freely through the black city and returned each dawn to pleasures of a new whore. But I was an officer, accustomed to showing off my physique, my badges, accustomed to dramatic displays of homage from miserable peons, accustomed to taking what I liked. My agitation became unbearable, as though I were subjected to a shrill, incessant flute. I considered escaping to Egypt or stowing away on a boat to Rome. But now I was a wanted man. News would reach Egypt and Rome before I was halfway to either place. In hiding or on the run, I could never live the life I deserved.

My thoughts wandered often to Tiresia's proposal. One night, after working a whore to a sweat, I interrogated her about the seer.

"I know nothing about her, sir. She's not one of us. We know all the competition." The girl was 16 at most, but already possessed of the jaded, weary expression that marked all whores. She sat on the floor, her head resting in her arms on the foot of the cot, after performing her finale. Candlelight flickered on her alabaster back.

"Don't tell me you've never seen the woman. Ethiopian or something. Black as the bottom of a cooking pot. She lives less than half a league from here." I lay naked on the cot, my hands behind my head.

"I swear, sir."

"What about the others? Surely they've seen her. Talked of her."

"It's possible, but they tell me nothing. I'm too new to be included."

"Yes. I'll bet they make piles of denarii on you." I touched her cheek with the ball of my foot. "I want you to talk to them at any rate. Get the information from your mistress. Tell her there's money in it for her."

"Yes, sir." The girl said it as though approaching her mistress meant abuse for her, regardless of profit to the proprietress.

The next night, I got an answer I hadn't counted on—a contingent of Pilate's crew bearing shackles for me. Incensed at my inquiries about what she believed must have been a rival brothel, the mistress had arranged for my arrest. Fortunately the girl whore had taken a perverted liking to me. She flung open my door just after midnight.

"They're coming for you. Run, sir." Her chest heaved. Horror widened her normally listless eyes. She disappeared across the courtyard, a whirl of white.

Grabbing my tunic and a sack of gear, I climbed out the window and hurdled a low gate. Drawn by a force as strong as lust, I sprinted through alleys and back streets to the seer's house. This time I met no resistance to my entry.

"Welcome, Lieutenant." Tiresia sat enthroned in her place before the mirror, her reflection glimmering softly in lamplight.

"Who are you?" I demanded, panting at the doorway of the shadowy chamber.

Tiresia laughed and stroked the colored beads in her hair. "Oh, Lieutenant. Your nature will serve you well on this side of the night."

"Face me!" I flung down my bag and approached her, but thought better of clutching her after the hand-crushing I'd received before.

"You are prepared now to join the league of the night? You've destroyed hopes for success in a mortal life."

"I'm here to hide, wench, and nothing more." I sank onto a bench and wiped the sweat from my brow. A rat scurried along the wall and vanished behind broken furniture and piles of rags.

She raised her head and studied me from beneath her heavy eyelids. "When you emerge from this house, Lieutenant, you will never hide again. You've only tasted what I can give you. Wait until you feel the full pleasure of complete power over mortals, the ability to travel, to soar over continents at the speed of thought. Wait until you can crush whom you please with impunity, command anyone you will."

"What about him? The one I have wanted to taste as I have wanted no other."

"Why do you want him?" She seemed displeased.

"Why? If you know so much, you must know why."

"I know all about him. But do you?"

"More riddles." Impatient, I rose and peered down the corridor. Then I turned to her. "He's told me I'll never approach him. He's told me you lie."

"Of course. He wishes to keep you away."

"But I desire him. I want him as my beloved. And he desires me in return. I know it."

"Exactly, my dear Lieutenant. He sees you as a test of his faith."

"Damn this god he imagines. A moment with me will turn him into an apostate."

Tiresia smiled. She dropped the robe from her raven shoulders. Her breasts, nipples purple in the lamplight, rose and fell as she breathed, like floats on a calm sea. "Come to me."

Heated by her charms, I stripped, spread my cloak over the cold earthen floor for her to lie on, and mounted her. Once again she turned her face to the shadows.

"Why me?" I asked in the midst of her moans. "Why not the others, the officers who've come for your potions?"

"Oh, my lieutenant." She clutched my buttocks to drive me more deeply into her. "There were no others. The words ... were planted in their minds." Groaning with delight, she guided my lips to her breast. "Drink, my Victor. Drink."

The warm blood oozed from her nipple. The sight of it maddened me. I lapped it up like a starving dog. I sucked long and hard, until my whole body became as engorged with blood as my cock. The sensation I'd felt before returned, the strange sense of euphoria mixed with acute vision and heightened power. I could have strangled a bull with my bare hands.

"Yes, Victor. Keep drinking. You mustn't stop this time."

I had pulled away from her to get my breath, as though we'd been locked in a kiss of passion. She pulled me back to the wet teat.

"Drink and live."

Suddenly a pain shot through my skull and then concentrated in my eyes. They pounded. I thought they would explode in my head. But despite the torture, I clung to Tiresia's supple body. My loins continued to hammer against hers at a furious pace. Then, like a fountain, the seer's breast poured forth liquid that was no longer hot and salty, but cool and refreshing—blood still, but a chilled elixir that somehow dulled my pain.

My sense of strength redoubled. I felt like a man charged with superhuman energy in a time of disaster, mighty enough to lift a block of granite from a worker crushed beneath it. I soared as I had soared in our last encounter, above the tiled roofs, the palms and walls of Jerusalem. Higher and higher. Through clouds. Toward a sliver of moon. Toward blackness—not empty, but full of creatures, heads and hands and limbs. The beings peered at me from behind treelike shadows.

"You are approaching it, Victor." Tiresia whispered into my ear. "Ah, yes. You're almost there."

But where? By the gods, where?

The sweat that had soaked me as our mad coupling began suddenly evaporated. My skin tingled, cool and taut. I was aware of every inch of my body and at the same time attuned to the darkness around me as I soared.

Tiresia laughed. "This is the beginning of time, Lieutenant. My time, my birth into the night. You are returning me here to reign. I have proven myself. It has taken centuries, since the time of the great Sphinx, but it is finished. Now I join the court of darkness."

Lightning ripped through the night. I could see Tiresia distinctly next to me. Her garments fluttered in a whirlwind as she flew. Her beautiful face had become translucent. The beads in her hair shimmered like precious stones. Other figures, robed, crowned, surrounded her in the air. They caressed her face with long, tapered fingers. They deposited a crown upon her head and carried her away, fading into the blackness.

"Wait! Damn you, wait! What about me? What do I do?"

"Follow your instincts, Victor." Her cry rolled out in her wake. "Follow your instincts. You will know." The final word echoed through the dark vault, slowly fading.

Conscious of returning, in an instant, to Tiresia's shop, I rolled off her motionless, cold body. I lowered the oil lamp to examine her face. The shriveled features and sunken cheeks of a hag glowed in the light—the hideous face she had hidden from me. Before my eyes, her luscious breasts dried up and disintegrated.

That is how it began.

CHAPTER SEVEN

Behind a false wall in Tiresia's chamber, I found her sarcophagus, lined with hieroglyphics chiseled in ancient Egypt. There I slept by day for the next eight years, at night glutting my thirst on the blood of beggars and rich merchants, boys and maidens. I even rampaged Pilate's household, first unnerving his pathetic wife, who rambled about visions of black ghosts in her room, then sinking my fangs into the breasts of his best servant girls, their juice exploding in my mouth like plump fruit.

My cock swelled as I drank blood, and the sensation—the heat, the lusty ecstasy—transcended any erotic pleasure I'd ever had.

It didn't take long, however, for me to tire of satiating my thirst, of testing my new strength, of flight, and of preternatural vision. I, like all beings, craved company. But I existed in isolation. I knew others like me existed, but not in Jerusalem. We were assigned domains by the dark powers, and our provinces did not overlap. Strange voices told me this in dreams.

Whores and boys of the street entertained me at night, and vagabonds cast dice with me. I paid my debts to them with silver piled up in Tiresia's secret chamber, from what source I knew not.

But there was only one man I wanted.

After a month of refining my powers, I found Joshu bathing in the river after dusk. From behind the reeds, I watched his sinewy arms stretch as he scrubbed his back. I inspected his thighs, as strong as columns, his belly, taut as a drum. Light lingering on the horizon painted his angular features and left the shadow of his form on the shallow water.

"Who's there?" He scanned the shore as I rustled through the reeds.

"It is I, Joshu." I stepped into a clearing on the bank.

"I thought you were dead. Where have you been?"

For the first time the aura of strength about him, spiritual strength expressed in every firm muscle of his body, struck me as superhuman. For the first time a strange shudder of apprehension passed through me.

"Who are you, Joshu?"

"I have told you, Victor. I am my father's son."

I splashed through the water toward him. I stopped so close to him I could see the tiny scar on his temple that he'd told me about. A neighbor boy had struck him with a rock when he was six or seven. "Which god is your father?"

"I have told you. The only god." He stooped over and cupped his hands to drink.

I clutched his arm. "The Roman gods are much more powerful than this god of the Jews. They outnumber him after all."

"What have they done for you?" He straightened and faced me boldly. In the light of the rising moon, his eyes revealed his love for me.

"They've made me immortal."

"Have they?"

"It's what you always speak of, isn't it? An eternal realm. Well, I've found it."

He quietly contemplated my face.

I pressed my lips against his and for a moment he leaned toward me, but then drew back.

I snorted at his rebuff. "I thought you told me I could not approach you."

"When did I tell you that?"

"In the vision."

"I don't know of what you speak."

"Deny it if you like. But here's the truth. I've the power to take you. But why should I, Joshu, when you want me? Be my consort. I can grant you immortality."

"You can never possess me." Joshu started toward the shore.

I grabbed his arm and pulled his naked body to me. "I already possess you." I shoved him away and, with a flicker, sped through the night, as light and invisible as the wind.

Wherever he went, I hounded him. When he retreated to the desert like one of the crazy Essenes, I squatted next to his campfire. When he paced the temple courts beneath the starry sky, I blocked his path. When he slept at the homes of those who had begun to follow him, I boldly marched through their doors.

"Why are you doing this?" he screamed one night in the desert, where he'd gone to pray. I sensed I had not been the only devil to tempt him there in the darkness. "What do you want?"

"You know what I want." I stretched out on the blanket he had spread before the fire.

"Robbing my purity means that much to you? What if you did take my body? My soul would belong only to my Father." He looked weak and drawn in the rippling light.

"Save that pig fodder for the masses, Joshu. Piety means nothing to me. And as far as you're concerned—you want me too. I'll wage war on you until you weaken, my friend. You're body isn't enough for me. I can have any I choose. I want your soul."

He suddenly broke into a fit of laughter. "Oh, Victor, had you wanted my love, my company, my teaching.... But my soul?"

"Do you know who I am?" I sat up and glared at him.

"I know you belong to the night with the other demons. Except..."

"Except what?"

"For you there's still hope."

"Damn you!" I leaped up, ripped off his cloak, and threw him to the sand. I pinned back his arms and spread his legs with my knees. "Is there hope now?"

I tore at his throat with my fangs, but the second I tasted his blood a wave of nausea passed through me. I vomited the blood from my earlier victims into the sand.

"Who is protecting you? Who is keeping you from me?"

"I am free. No one commands my will. Not even my God. But I have surrendered to him." He sat up and rubbed his arms where I had gripped him. Then he reached for his cloak.

"They say you work miracles. Why don't you cast me away from you as you cast away the demons from the godforsaken creatures roaming the slums?"

His response was a prolonged gaze at me, as though he were actually considering using his powers. But his gaze also held compassion.

"You're a holy fool," I said, spitting out a remnant of the blood that had erupted from my throat. "You'll never rid yourself of me."

Indeed, I kept after him, hounding him until the very end of his divine crusade, when even his charisma couldn't save him. In the final days I nearly had him. Immortality in my company looked pretty good to someone condemned to die.

On the day when the sky darkened to the shade of midnight, I rose from my tomb and soared to Golgotha. Gazing lustfully at Joshu from the foot of his execution cross, fighting my urge to lap up the blood that dripped from his hands and feet, I invited him one last time. He listened to me but merely turned his eyes to the sky, invoked his god, and slipped into a death I will never know.

For two nights I ransacked Jerusalem's streets, torturing, murdering whoever came into my path, mangling limbs and tearing flesh with my teeth, without stopping to suck out the elixir after my first few victims.

Then, just before dawn that Sunday, as I hurried back to my refuge, it happened. I felt him.

"Joshu! What is this? What kind of spirit are you?"

I glanced around the street, gray in the harbinger glow of morning. "Show yourself to me."

He stood before me, naked and whole, not pale from death. The nail marks still on his feet and hands looked more like small tattoos than wounds.

"I am not a ghost, Victor. I live."

"As do I, my beloved." I stepped toward him, but the dawn was moments away and I had to flee. "Come with me, to safety."

But he stood immobile and I could not hesitate another second.

When I awoke later in the darkness, I felt as though I were the only being left on an annihilated earth. Joshu was gone from me. I knew this before his followers began babbling about a resurrection. He existed, was immortal, but not in a world of darkness like mine. I howled like a wolf who'd devastated a flock of sheep and was now left with nothing. It was only then that I believed in the god Joshu returned to, a god of light. And it was then that I vowed to avenge my loss on this pompous being who had deprived me of the only one I ever loved.

Part II

THE CLOISTER

CHAPTER EIGHT

Abbot Reginald of St. Sylvester speaks well of you, Brother Victor. He says you have much to offer us here at St. Thomas." Brother Matthew, a burly man, stood before a tall window in his office. He was abbot of St. Thomas, my new home, but he told me he didn't like titles. "Brother" suited him just fine.

The window looked out into the courtyard, where a gnarled old pine basked in the light of a full moon. The walls of the office bulged with thick, musty volumes. The oak floor and desk were blackened with age.

"I'm grateful for the abbot's recommendation, Brother Matthew." I assumed the tone of deference I'd perfected through centuries of monastery-hopping. Also robed in black, I sat across from him in a leather chair, venous with cracks.

"We Thomists have never accepted a monk from another order. But the accident was tragic—the demise of an ancient community stemming from the Dominicans, like ours. Order of the Divine Word—splendid name. What a pity." He shook his head.

"Yes." I studied the fat neck that rose from his black habit. His ripe jugular bulged as big as the infant snakes we ate as delicacies in Pilate's headquarters two millennia before.

"The fire was sudden?"

I nodded. "It was a medieval abbey, full of rotting wood. England is full of decrepit abbeys and convents. The unusually strong winds on the

English heath didn't help. When the fire started, everyone was asleep. They weren't due to rise for matins for another hour. And the fieldwork had been grueling that day, especially for the older monks. Most everyone died of smoke inhalation. Through God's mercy I was taking my usual walk on the heath, safe from the sun's rays. My skin condition won't cause inconvenience, will it?"

"Of course not, Brother Victor." The abbot seated himself in the leather chair behind his desk. The lamp cast a rosy glow on his smooth cheeks. His eyes were small and closely set and full of the disgusting charity I never grew tired of loathing. "It's a strange condition, I admit. What a misfortune to be intolerant of the sun. Though the night has its own beauty."

"Indeed."

"And you can work in the night? It will be good to have a sentinel of sorts."

"The underground cell is not a problem?"

"Not if you don't mind the damp rooms beneath the chapel. It's where we said our private masses in the old days—a network of dank little chapels and storage rooms. We've furnished a cell for you down there. I promise you you'll not see a single ray of sun."

"Excellent. The crypt is around there too, I suppose? The one you mentioned to Abbot Reginald?"

"Yes. I hope that won't bother you—sleeping among our faithfully departed. They're good old souls." He smiled benevolently.

"Indeed not. I can pray better in that environment, reminded of mortality." I mustered a smile, and he, predictably, reciprocated. "I have a trunk full of books. They're out in the car."

"I'll get a brother to help you." Brother Matthew picked up the phone. "I'm surprised Brother Cyril didn't bring it in already."

"That's my fault. I told him I'd get the porter to help me after I spoke to you. He did carry my other bags to my cell."

The abbot shifted the receiver and gave directions to the porter I'd glimpsed as old Brother Cyril had pulled into the parking lot, a willowy boy of 19 or 20 who blushed when I saw him peering out the window.

I rose when he knocked at the door and the abbot called for him to enter. He was indeed a specimen—full lips, limpid eyes, a shock of blond hair, the bangs curling over his eyebrows. He smiled bashfully at me, then turned his attention to the abbot to receive his instructions.

"Brother Victor," Brother Matthew called as we were leaving. "Why exactly did Abbot Reginald survive the fire? He wasn't clear in his letter or phone call."

"I think he was out of the building too, Brother. He suffered from insomnia."

"I see. And he really won't accept our hospitality?" The abbot squinted in the lamplight.

"He's very old. His community is gone. He wants to be with his family in Brighton." I tried to restrain my impatience at his irritating concern.

"I see. Welcome to America, Brother, and to the monastery of St. Thomas. We'll try to help you not miss England too much. Make yourself at home."

"Yes, Brother. Thank you."

How many times over the ages had I introduced myself to an unsuspecting abbot? It was in the late 13th century that I entered the first cloister, a Dominican fortress in the Apennines full of boys hardly old enough to shoot their loads. That's when I set out in earnest on a calculated campaign to destroy the harems of Joshu's god. I'd only begun to hear about monasteries, although apparently the communities of monks had spread from Egypt into Italy 200 years before.

But let me start at the beginning.

After the death of Joshu, I spent a dozen frustrating years waiting, searching for his spirit among the old Palestine haunts. Then, despondent, I made my way back to Rome, where I spent four centuries feasting on the rich blood of patricians and the exotic blood of slaves from every corner of the empire. The Germanic invasions began in the fifth century. At first I enjoyed the excitement, the chaos. I could smell blood from the battlefields when I emerged from my hiding places after sunset. But depression gradually set in as I watched the collapse of civilization as I'd known it.

I left Rome in the eighth century and wandered through the Far East until the Barbarian raids were long over. Then I returned. More than a millennium had passed since I'd beheld Joshu. A millennium. I caught wind of these idealistic followers of Joshu huddled together, renouncing the world as he had. It seemed too good to be true. My nocturnal wanderings, glutting my appetites, had begun to bore me. I lacked a purpose, stable companionship, things I thought I could dispense with on the dark side of existence. The challenge of the secluded abbeys where pietistic young males wrestled with their carnal desires, where Joshu's spirit perhaps lingered, where I could most injure his god ... that challenge baptized me into a new life. The night once again held promise.

The first millennium after Joshu's death was my adolescence as a predator, my youthful heyday. In the second millennium, as a monk, I enjoyed the fruits of experience: more finesse in my dealings with humans; more restraint over my cravings; more single-mindedness in my hunts; more concentration, hence ecstasy, in my feedings.

Between the 13th and 20th centuries, two dozen monasteries, in Italy, France, Spain, Germany, and the British Isles, harbored a creature of the grave unknowingly—until too late. With each abbey I left devastated, I cut a new notch in the belt squeezing my heart, the belt strapped there by Joshu. If I couldn't remove it, I could gloat over its defacement.

St. Thomas would make two dozen and one notches. And my first in the New World.

Leaving the abbot's office, I followed the boy monk, Brother Luke, down the dark hallway into the medieval-looking foyer of St. Thomas Abbey. Our feet thudded on heavy oak planks. High above us loomed thick rustic beams. The abbot had instructed the young porter to give me a tour of the buildings.

"Would you like to see the chapel first?"

Though I wasn't an expert on American accents, his drawl seemed rural. He pointed toward heavy doors surmounted by a carved image of Joshu on the abominable crucifix, the one I had stood before 2,000 years ago. In all that time I had not grown immune to the longing and bitterness the image evoked.

"Lead on, O Gabriel." I squeezed his shoulder when he beamed at the name of the angelic guide.

Lights from votive candles flickered before statues in side altars and near the sanctuary of the long, narrow chapel—an unimaginative variation on chapels since the beginning of monasticism. Choir stalls faced each other near the sanctuary, and pews lined the body of the church. The place smelled of incense and candle wax, old varnish and sickly-sweet flowers.

"You wanna offer a prayer?" The boy whispered as though the empty chapel were filled with meditating monks.

"Thank you. Please, come with me." I touched his back.

We walked side by side down the center aisle and knelt at the communion rail. The golden tabernacle doors were embossed with a predictable scene of the "last supper." The truth is, Joshu was sick during that final Passover and couldn't eat a thing. I teased him about it—and scoffed at the foot-washing ritual that embarrassed his foul-smelling men, their feet caked with filth. He had an irresistible penchant for degrading himself.

But he had enough sense to avoid ending up imprisoned in a bread box. The Blessed Sacrament indeed! And even if he was in the tabernacle, it wasn't as a wafer that I wanted to taste my Joshu.

Brother Luke amiably gabbed as he led me through the other buildings forming the sides of the large courtyard, thick with hedges and trees now dormant in the January cold: a high-vaulted library adjacent to the chapel was in one building; in another was a social hall, a kitchen, and a refectory with two long tables for the handful of monks who lived there; a third building contained a dormitory of tiny cells, administrative offices, and, adjacent to the foyer, a richly furnished parlor for receiving guests. A fairly new greenhouse had been constructed on the north side of the refectory, behind the buildings.

"There's a room of computers next to the library. But I ain't got the key." Boy Luke stood timidly behind a heavy chair. "They put in a lot of time in there, with their research and all."

"And you have no scholarly ambitions? I thought the Thomist order pledged to carry on the work of the great St. Thomas Aquinas." Through my research I had learned all about the 19th-century offshoot of the Dominicans. Most of the monks were scholars who did research at the monastery during extended university sabbaticals. Between the monastery's enormous library collections and its modern computer technology, they had all the resources a pinheaded professor could want. They would keep their noses buried in their books and stay well out of my way.

"Gotta have porters and groundskeepers, too." He smiled sheepishly.

"Ah, I see. You are responsible for the charming landscaping, then?"

"Me and Brother Michael. We tend the greenhouse, too."

"And is Brother Michael a stooped old farmer?"

Luke shook his head. "He ain't but five years older than me. Lot smarter though. Reads like a fiend. Just not interested in scholar stuff."

As the boy helped me unload my trunk from the car, I surveyed the landscape in the moonlight: the long dirt path to the monastery snaked through trees and down a hillside until it hit a country road, invisible from the promontory. Behind the buildings, acres of woods rose to the Appalachian peaks that now looked like bites taken from indigo paper. We were far from the city of Knoxville, from heavy settlement, but I smelled human blood in the cold night air, as I'd known I would.

My stay here would be short if I fed on monks again. This time I would resist the urge even longer than I had the last time. Once I started on monks—sick of feeding on drifters and prostitutes and other refuse no one missed—once I started on monks I couldn't control my appetite for their consecrated flesh, which carried me to orgiastic heights. I would grow careless, leaving trails of blood, missing the suppers I only pretended to eat anyway, missing compline—unable to stomach invocations of Joshu. In the bloody chaos, clues would point to me and I would have to flee once again, often destroying the monastery as I had recently done in England, when the good brothers of St. Sylvester discovered too much.

My cravings defeated my own purpose. I intended to steal the souls of devout boys, not their mortal lives. Controlling a boy thrilled me as terrifically as it had during my existence as a man. My cock still hardened. I could still take a boy, though it was the sight of him surrendering his will to me, not the friction of fucking, that triggered my orgasm.

I took no pleasure in barring the doors of St. Sylvester's, in torching the carpets and draperies, in razing the buildings that had given me security. But I had no choice, and no choice but to assume the identity of Abbot Reginald in order to make arrangements at St. Thomas. This time I would resist longer. I would stick to the indigenous food.

"People live in the mountains?" I asked, lugging one side of the trunk while Luke took the other.

"Some. Most is miners. But the mines done closed." Luke's breath steamed before him in the cold. "They get by on whatever they can shoot in the woods or pull out of the dirt. Michael takes them food and supplies."

"Indeed."

Inside the foyer, Luke unlocked a door that opened onto a dark and narrow stairway beneath the vestibule of the chapel. He flicked on the light and turned to take his side of the trunk.

"It'll be easier if I carry it myself." I picked up the trunk and he moved out of my way.

"My God, do you lift weights or something?"

I grinned, feeling his eyes admiring me from behind—for when I chose to I could feel any senses directed at me. "Natural, brute strength, my friend." He did not know the half of my powers.

Deep in the bowels of the church, we walked along a flagstone corridor, past alcoves made of brick, like burial niches in the Roman catacombs where I fed upon the neophyte Christians: the first martyrs—because of me, not the lions. The widely spaced incandescent bulbs along the walls shined upon marble altars within the alcoves.

"The ordained brothers used to say their masses down here." Luke was leading the way now. "Don't see how you can sleep so close to the graves. Gives me the creeps."

"With the Blessed Sacrament just above me? How can I be afraid, Luke?"

"Still ..."

"Ah, I see we're coming to the crypt." Engraved marble tablets spaced six feet apart lined the walls. Six names were engraved on each of the tablets, which were embedded in the wall above an iron door that was soldered shut. I'd seen this sort of mausoleum many times: the coffins inside the small chambers were sealed in vaults, stacked in pairs. "How long has it been since a brother died?"

"That'd be Brother Raymond, last year. Ninety-two years old. There he is." Luke pointed to one of the last mausoleums. The soldering was shiny still.

I deposited my trunk on the floor of my cell, a small storage room beyond the crypt, which had been furnished with a bed, a desk, shelves, and a chest of drawers. In a room across from mine, plumbing had been installed for the priests who said their masses near the crypt. A duct from the boiler room directed meager heat into the entire subterranean space.

It was after midnight, and I was growing ravenous, not having fed since the night before when I broke out of the coffin being shipped on a flight from London. When Luke offered me a fraternal embrace to welcome me, I wanted to pierce his supple throat and drink. I clutched him as I clutch my prey, willing him to immobility. Within his stunned body, I felt him succumbing. In that second I could have ordered him to do anything, he was so pliable. Latent homosexuals—a category that obviously fit him—were always the easiest to control in monasteries, where such creatures flourish. But there was no hurry. Young Luke could wait. I released the boy and he pulled away, embarrassed but not sure why.

Minutes after he had ascended to his cell, I was once again in the night air. The scent of blood drifted through the dense woods. I tore through branches, over frozen soil and brittle leaves, my preternatural sight steering me though the darkness in the direction of my prey.

The wooden shack, its porch sagging and windows boarded, nestled into the mountainside near a frozen brook. A doorless old refrigerator and a heap of rusty cans and other garbage littered the ground beside it. Light bled through the windows. Inside, a baby cried. I stood on the porch, listening to a husky-voiced woman singing. Before she could finish her lullaby, I charged through the door.

The woman, seated on a kitchen chair, cradling the baby in her arms, screamed. Of course my appearance was horrible, as always when I fed. My skin took on the jaundiced hue of a new corpse. My fangs grew in an instant to the length some stalactites take a century to reach. Fire burned in my eyes. I panted like a rabid dog.

"Oh God, please. No!" She clutched her baby to her breast when I reached for it.

I snatched the brat from her, raised it to my mouth, and, shaking off the blanket, sank my teeth into its soft belly. Its blood squirted like the juice of a plump tomato in my mouth.

Shrieking hysterically, the woman grabbed at the baby, but I held it firmly, draining it and dropping the corpse on the dingy linoleum floor. She scrambled from her chair and threw herself on her dead child. Snatching a handful of her oily hair, I pulled her to her feet and ripped off her sweatshirt. She reeked, as though she hadn't bathed in a month. Her face was pockmarked. But her breasts, swollen with milk, enticed me. My fangs sliced into them. Her eyes rolled back. Her head dropped and her body went limp. When I'd had my fill, I let her crumple to the floor beside her child.

I hauled their bodies to the heart of the dark woods and flung them into a ditch, rolling a fallen tree over them. Then I returned to the shack and wiped up stray drops of blood. Anyone searching for the victims in their remote dwelling—whoever supplied their food and fuel—would assume they'd vacated and trudged to the warmth of the city.

Shortly before dawn I raced back to my cell. Stuffing pillows under the blanket in case anyone should look in on me during the day, I left the cold cubicle and hurried to the crypt. The iron door of old Brother Raymond's mausoleum gave easily under my strength. I slipped into the dark, cramped chamber, where I had to stoop like a humpback, and pulled the gate firmly shut behind me. The lingering smell of decay, no longer detectable to a mortal, wafted to my nostrils, at once familiar and repugnant. Tracing the odor to the top vault of the third pair of tombs, the one farthest from the door, I pried it open. The plain pine casket was perfectly intact, probably the only one in the whole crypt in such a condition. I opened the lid, scooped out the skeleton, still dressed in a habit, dumped it on the floor to be discarded later, and climbed into the coffin. Within seconds of closing the lid, I drifted off, sated and exhausted.

CHAPTER NINE

I did not need to feed every night. Sometimes I could last a week or more if I'd imbibed enough blood. The woman and her baby had glutted me. I went for 10 days before killing again, this time a tramp who lived in a hovel of corrugated metal. In the first month at St. Thomas I fed on several more mountain people, careful to bury their remains in the woods to avoid raising alarm.

After centuries of inhabiting monasteries, I slipped easily into a routine. Rising just after sunset, I joined the brothers at table because it was expected of me, even though I always arranged to eat my own meals in the kitchen at times appropriate for a nocturnal schedule to keep hidden my inability to take normal food. While they swallowed their stew, the 23 men—most in their 50s and 60s with a few younger monks scattered about, all garbed in black, hooded robes—listened to readings from Thomas à Kempis's *Imitation of Christ* or from the works of their fat hero, Aquinas. (I'd never lived with that medieval scholar's community, but I had met many monks who confirmed rumors that a semicircle had been carved into the dining table to accommodate his piggish girth.)

After dinner came a period of recreation. The monks could gather in the social hall or exercise in the basement gymnasium. Compline was chanted at 8 in the dimly lit choir stalls. Then the monks filed to their wretched holes. Fortunately, the chanting of matins had long ago been abandoned by the group;

being in my assigned stall at 3 in the morning used to take some maneuvering, especially when my victims took me far from the grounds. I usually attended compline, as much as I loathed it—hearing Joshu's name again and again, the words about his blood, his body, at once a mockery of my own feedings and a reminder that I could not possess him. I was always half afraid that I would storm up to the altar and rip open the priest's throat.

But of course I did no such thing.

Instead, very easily, I exerted ever-increasing control over young Luke. I had him violating the Grand Silence within a few weeks. He would sneak down to my cell after compline, eager as a spaniel who wanted petting. He sobbed to me more than once about the mother who abandoned him after the death of his father, about the stern grandfather who raised him.

"Very sad," I said after one of his crying jags. "Come sit by me." I patted the cot I'd never slept in.

He rose from the desk chair and settled on the bed, nestling against my shoulder. His wet cheeks gleamed in the light of the candles burning on the bookshelves. I detested the overhead fluorescent tubes.

"That's better, isn't it?"

He nodded. "Victor...." He paused.

"Why have qualms?" I could hear his thoughts, like the confused voices of children on a playground. "What could be better? God has brought us together."

"Do you think so?" He sniffed.

I dug a handkerchief from my pocket. "Here, blow your nose."

He did as I directed, then said, "Brother Matthew talks about particular friendships. The *Imitation* says they're the work of the devil."

"Has the good abbot spoken to you about us?"

He avoided my eyes. "No. In his sermons, I mean."

"What about the others?" I glared at him. "Do they talk of you and me?"

"Not really." He lowered his eyes once again.

"Tell me the truth."

"Well, Mike has asked a thing or two," he finally admitted, sheepishly.

"Brother Michael wanted information about me?"

"Not information, really. Sometimes when we're working in the green-house he asks things."

"What kinds of things?"

"Well, he asked about your order."

"And what did you tell him?" I stood and walked to the desk.

"Nothing. I don't really know nothing but what Brother Matthew told us all. You was in some other kind of Dominican order in England, Order of the Divine Word, and the monastery burned down and the other brothers died. And it was our duty to take you into our community. You never told me nothing else."

I leaned against the desk with my arms crossed, examining his child-like face. "Tell me, if Brother Michael's as intelligent as you say, why is he content to spend the day doing mindless work in a greenhouse?"

Luke twisted his mouth to one side and contemplated the question. "I expect it's a spiritual thing. He's damn holy. God comes first in everything. Maybe working the soil is good for his soul."

I pondered the crucifix above the bed. I'd left it there to avoid rousing suspicion. "Why didn't you tell me about Michael's curiosity?"

"I ... I don't know. I never told him nothing, though. Not about breaking the Grand Silence or coming down here. I won't say nothing about you anymore."

"Never mind, Luke." I turned my eyes back on him. "Talk to him all you want about me. Now you'd better leave. It's nearly midnight."

Chapter Ten

From then on I paid special attention to young Brother Michael, whose good looks and intensity I'd already noticed during compline, when he sang the psalms with such fervor one would have thought he'd already entered the courts of paradise—or that he feared losing paradise altogether. I liked the latter possibility much better.

I'd seen many monks like Michael in my time: cocky, full of themselves, aware of their brawn and handsome features, of their intelligence and charisma. Yet at odds with themselves because of their strange ideas about religious perfection. Why in hell they did not stop resisting their gifts and make the most of them ... well, I didn't waste time puzzling over this question.

Such monks always posed the most intriguing challenge. I loved to watch them squirm against my magnetism, fasting, even flagellating their backs with cords until the flesh was raw and bleeding, and then inevitably succumbing to my powers. I possessed them—sexually, emotionally, spiritually. But when I considered making them like me—for I had come to understand this possibility—I despised them too much to have them as companions. Still, I never grew tired of seeking a companion or torturing my prey, especially those who were particularly unworthy of me.

Once I'd observed Michael long enough to know that invariably he lifted weights on Monday, Wednesday, and Friday evenings, I started showing up in the workout room at the same times. At first, I only nodded to him and went about my workout (a joke, really, since to me the free weights might have been made of cork rather than steel). But one night, after a couple of the other monks had finished their workouts and left the room, I spoke.

"You know," I said, turning my head from the bench press after replacing the barbell on its rest. "You should not worry so much about Luke. You can't keep him from worldly dangers."

Without looking at me, Michael continued working the leg lift, his calves bulging into balls of olive flesh. Though the basement was cool, he wore only shorts and a tank top, soaked with perspiration. His dark, normally unkempt hair was tied back, accentuating his noble forehead, classic nose, and sturdy chin. He reminded me of the best of the Roman gladiators, one fiercely flaring his nostrils, searing his gaze into the eyes of his opponent, and yet alert to sudden moves.

"I know you want to protect him," I persisted.

"Why should you care what I think?" He glanced coldly at me, then returned his attention to exercise.

His spiritedness only aroused my admiration. I looked him over as though he were a rare jeweled goblet, while he pretended to ignore my attention.

"None of us is above sin. True, good Brother?"

"None of us." He stopped, glaring at me. "I'm not pretending to be superior."

"Of course not."

"Some people are impressionable, that's all. They should be left alone."

"I think you do consider yourself superior." I sat up on the bench and faced him. "You're even above this kind of conversation, aren't you? I'll wager you've never had one quite like it within the walls of this monastery."

"I can't say that I have." He resumed his lifts, straining to speak as he raised the bar with his feet. "You don't care much for our Rule, do you? Surely, your own community had a similar one. How could you have made your peace with it?"

I laughed. "Now I see. You like me. You really do. Yes, Michael, I am worldly. But it doesn't mean I belong to the world. Oh, it sounds like a contradiction, I know. To crave things of the flesh, but to be above them. But that's exactly my position. And I relish it."

"You mock the spirit of monasticism. We're to live in the world, but not be of it. That doesn't mean giving in to bodily cravings, or believing we're above them." His emotion fueled an acceleration in his lifts.

"I didn't say I was above the cravings. I'm above this world."

He stopped, his chest heaving from the workout, and swiveled around on his bench to face me, his dark eyes intense. "You believe that, don't you? You're not just trying to scandalize me. But you're wrong, Brother Victor. You do belong to this world. So much so that you frighten me."

"Frighten you?" I grinned. "I'm flattered."

"Don't be. It says a lot more about me than you." Michael stood and grabbed a towel from a shelf above the weight bench and wiped his face and neck. "I have to shower before compline." He started toward the door.

I grabbed his wrist. "You're hard on yourself," I said. "But not by nature. That's why I like you." I smiled.

He studied me apprehensively and left the room.

That night, long after midnight, I crept down the dark dormitory corridor to his cell. The heavy door creaked on its hinges as I entered, but he did not stir in his bed. For several minutes I gazed at his form in a darkness that, in my gifted vision, borrowed the shades of dusk, not moonless night. He lay enshrouded in shadows, breathing with the regular rhythm of one whose conscience is clear. He lay on his side, his arm outside the wool blanket, his hair splashing the white sheets with black. Stooping and touching his shoulder, I entered the dream, which, though buried far beneath his consciousness, played as vividly before my eyes as my own memories.

"Come to me, Michael," I whispered, in spite of myself. "Don't fear the darkness. What kind of eternity awaits you in the light but one on bended knee? Would you fight your pride beyond the end of time?"

He moaned, opened his eyes and peered into mine, then slipped into a profound sleep.

Part III

COMMUNICATIONS

Chapter Eleven

Rivulets of blood from the thorns stream down his ashen face. He shifts his weight to his feet in order to breathe and, when his strength fails him, hangs from his hands once again, the nails tearing his flesh. I remember taking those hands in mine one day on a fishing boat. Then they were browned by the sun, calloused from what I called his quaint profession as a builder.

"Victor," he says, his head rolling until his pained gaze falls on me, "God can forgive you." This is the way he always begins our conversations, no matter what scene of our lives together we are revisiting.

"God be damned! What kind of god lets them do this to you? He delights in your torture." I am standing beneath the cross, alone, under a graphite sky, my cape whipped by the wind.

"No." He swallows and takes a breath, straining to support himself on his feet. "It's salvation. To give to the end. To give all, even your life."

"Why do you spew this rubbish at me, Joshu? You heard the rogue there next to you. Save yourself. Ask this god of yours for mercy, if that's what it takes. Don't pant and bleed here in front of me, with excrement running down your legs, telling me to ask for forgiveness from your god. Your god disgusts me. You disgust me."

"I ... I love you, Victor."

"Yes, so you say. Every time we speak. Every time, damn you. And for the millionth time I answer, 'Come to me then.' I know you have a power.

Not the power the mobs see, your flimsy healings and exorcisms. You know what I mean. The power derived from immortality. Power like mine. Why choose the world of light? What is its reward? Look what I have in the night. Eternity, mastery."

"Loneliness, longing."

"I satisfy my longings! Every one of them. And as for loneliness ... company be damned when it takes the form of sniveling humans or a tyrant god who can't stand to share his power. But you, Joshu," I press my lips against his bloody feet and savor his taste, "you are different. We could spend eternity together in the night, having all we want."

Joshu gasps for breath and collects his strength to stand once again. "If you want me, you want the God of light. My God, my God." His eyes roll toward the threatening sky, ripped by lightning.

"No!" I scream. "Not again." I pound the cross with my fist. "Curse your god and live!"

"This is my body ... body ... body." The words reverberate through darkness now. The winds cease. I feel myself spinning. I open my eyes and once again find myself in the choir stall. The fool priest is consecrating the wafer. "This is my body, which will be given up for you," he says, with gravity. I want to storm to the altar and rip the host from his hands. I want to tear open his throat. But I restrain myself, forced to take part in the mockery until the host is in my mouth. Then I defile it by swallowing, letting it mix in my stomach with the blood of my victims, and vomiting it up before climbing into my coffin.

CHAPTER TWELVE

My visions of Joshu were nothing new. They'd haunted me for 20 centuries. I hoped, though, as always upon moving into a new monastery, that they would cease. The crucifixion vision, especially, ripped at my heart. Although I had caused countless deaths, lapping up the blood that surfaced on taut flesh like vintage wine streaming from a cask, to see Joshu's death, Joshu's blood, was to relive my loss.

As much as I wished the visions would cease, I also feared this possibility. After all, the visions were all I had of Joshu. In them I felt that he was present, speaking, and not just a shadow created by my supernatural mind, felt that the risen Joshu communicated through this medium.

That there had to be such a medium at all exasperated me beyond endurance. It was like speaking through glass: The same cold matter that brought him near to me also, cruelly, formed an impenetrable barrier. The nearness to intimacy wrenched my heart.

The visions were induced by the chants and scents of Mass, and by feeding on the exceptionally rich blood of those who ate large quantities of meat—in the case of the mountain people, squirrel and porcupine and raccoon.

The visions also sometimes occurred while I studied volumes from my collection of ancient texts about Joshu: Some people called them the Apocrypha, but I knew from the lips of Joshu himself that much of the lore was true, tales about Joshu as a boy, breathing life into clay doves, striking down neighborhood bullies with a glance, healing wounded pets.

During our mountain hikes and sailing adventures Joshu would laugh over his youthful impetuosity. Not sure of what to make of his extraordinary powers at the time—whether he invented them or truly possessed them—but disinclined to reflect overly much, I would clap his naked back and say that he should use his powers. If he restrained his true nature, it would come out in one way or another.

Indeed, his power did come out, in the fire behind his words to temple officials, in his fury over injustices to toothless widows and snotty-nosed children. Compassion was his power, at the very core of his nature. This is what intrigued me about him: His compassion was not the result of pious submission to his god, but, in some inexplicable way, his very nature.

The visions also overcame me as I studied occult texts, which for many centuries were banned by the Church, though they could always be gotten from devious monks. Now such volumes were readily available in most monastic libraries. Mythology and satanism were now deemed legitimate fields of research by the new, sophisticated, incorruptible brand of monk.

I can't say how the authors of these volumes learned of the world of darkness, whether they were inspired by court members like Tiresia, whether they themselves were vampires like me. But I was convinced of their accuracy. From them, I pieced together the components of my world, my history, my fate.

Certain fallen angels, followers of Lucifer, had escaped hell and fled to a kingdom near the moon where they thrived on their lust for power. A hierarchy was established, the angel Principia becoming queen, Copulus and Demitria her consorts, and the others her court.

These beings were driven to extend their kingdom beyond themselves to the mortal world, created in time. Principia, assuming the form of a buxom wench, charmed an Aryan chieftain. As he lay on her, sucking at her breast, he was transformed as I was transformed by Tiresia.

The chieftain lived, solitary and hungry for blood, as I lived, foraging by night among robust villagers for his food, creeping by day into a burial chamber.

All the while the court above watched him from their dark realm, waiting for him to pass his gifts to another and enter their ranks, only to have the new creature of darkness join them in his turn—if he so chose. For there was a choice.

I knew this not only because of Joshu's words to me, but from the ancient writers' stories about weak vampires who caved into the demands of the possessive god of light. They had their tempting visions too, it seemed, long before Joshu. Which agents of the world of light appeared to them, I ever sought to discover in the books, though so far unsuccessfully. But I had learned much of the dark realm and delighted in discovering even more.

One fact in particular came to dominate my thoughts over the centuries. Bonds between members of the dark court were forged by mutual desire. When a vampire decided once and for all in favor of darkness, and created another soul of the night, he entered a world where he would no longer be alone. Long before I reached St. Thomas, I'd become determined to create my successor and move on to the dark realm, to be joined later, for eternity, by the vampire I'd created.

I had no delusions that Joshu could take that role. Once a spirit passed to the Kingdom of Light or the Kingdom of Darkness, the movement was final. So I lived for my communications with Joshu, as maddening as they were, until I could find one to replace him. Over the ages, as I toyed with pathetic young monks the way a cat cuffs and claws rodents, and as I defiled everything sacred with my lust and killings, I searched for a replica of Joshu—the one who obsessed me. Again and again my candidates disappointed me, as soon as they submitted to me. That ruined them, like a fissure ruins the blade of a sword.

Still, my obsession persisted.

CHAPTER THIRTEEN

One spring evening after compline, I willed young Luke to my cell. His blond shaggy locks had tumbled endearingly over his brow as he'd chanted the psalm. His pale face and hands had seemed almost translucent under the lights. The effort it took to summon him was nothing, barely the amount of concentration required for lacing a shoe. Fifteen minutes after the Grand Silence began, he tapped on my door.

"Enter." Having pulled off my robe, I lay stretched out on the bed.

The lamplight threw his lean shadow on the wall as he closed the door behind him. With an impatient wave I bid him come to me. He timidly approached the bed.

"What took you so long, boy?"

"I came as fast as I could, Victor. Brother Matthew was walking up and down the dormitory hallway. I had to wait."

"Why are you lying?" I pulled him to the bed by his cowl and brought his face inches from mine.

"I'm not."

"Get out." I released his robe.

"No, please, Victor." He touched my cheek. "Don't make me go again. We ain't done nothing for weeks."

"Why is that, Luke?" I eyed the cowering boy with disgust. "Well?"

"My confession," he admitted. He lowered his eyes and then turned them imploringly on me. "But I told you, it's the guilt. When you sin against celibacy, it's like you're unfaithful to the Lord. I can't help confessing. The guilt just eats away at me. Old Brother Joseph ain't gonna tell anyone anyway. He'd never break the confessional seal. Besides, he's heard it all before."

"From your friends Peter and Gerard, no doubt." I'd written off the effete pair of monks as not worth raping the moment I set eyes on them.

"It's just common here, that's all."

"You've whored ever since you set foot in this place, haven't you, boy?"

"It was different. It was never like this."

"Like what?"

Luke's eyes gleamed and he smiled like a child dying to share a secret. He sat on the edge of the bed. I leaned back, my hands behind my head.

"I always knew I was different, Victor. When I was little, there was this farmhand of ours. He'd work in the field and come back all sweaty. He'd take his shirt off and wash himself down at the pump outside. I'd stand inside the screen door and look at him, my heart pumping away like an engine. I didn't know anything about what I was feeling except it was good. He'd bring me a stick of gum or some licorice. Sometimes he'd skip rocks with me across the creek on our place. My grandaddy was too old to do much with me and all my brothers was raised and married." Luke lifted my legs and, scooting back against the wall, laid them in his lap.

"So anyway. I took a shining to Bud—that was his name. Used to dream he was holding me in his big ol' hairy arms, kissing me. I knew that wasn't right. But I woke up feeling good all the same. Then he got work down at Chattanooga. Left us after harvest.

"I tell you, Victor, I liked to have died. Was sick to my stomach. Couldn't eat. My grandaddy sent me into town to see the doctor. He said there wasn't nothing wrong with me. Granddaddy about beat me senseless for pretending. Course I couldn't say nothing to nobody.

"I got over Bud in time, but the whole thing started me seeing things different. Here I was, 14 years old and never had no interest in girls. I noticed how good the other field hands started looking. Played around with one in the barn. Knew it couldn't be right so I went to confession."

"Your first mistake." The story was starting to bore me, but since he was working up to his paean to me, I humored him.

Luke sighed and shook his head. He rested it against the wall and stared at the ceiling. "Man, that priest gave it to me bad. Told me sleepin' with another man was worse than murder. Said if you died with that on your soul, you'd go to the deepest part of hell. Gave me a penance that would have worn out a saint."

"And you took it to heart, of course."

"Yes, sir, I took it to heart. Started praying that I'd shake off these feelings for men. Started going to morning Mass in town—had to walk two miles to get there, sometimes in snow and ice. Started talking to the priest about living a holy life. Before you knew it, I was in the novitiate here at St. Thomas—right out of high school. Then ..." He hesitated and lowered his eyes as though saddened by what came next.

"Then you saw that the feelings got even stronger here. You were surrounded by beautiful men and thought you were in heaven." I had heard this confession many times.

"I got desperate. I ended up going to bed with a couple monks. But I fasted, prayed. Mike helped me."

"Brother Michael?" The boy had my attention now.

Luke nodded his head. "When I told him about the temptations, he said he had 'em too. Said we could help each other out."

"Yes, I'll bet."

"No, Victor. It wasn't like that. I thought he was good-looking, but we never fooled around. He was too strong. We'd pray together. We'd talk while we worked on the grounds and in the greenhouse. I dunno, it was like I could keep the feelings down then. Like they were channeled into a new path."

"Touching," I said.

"It was all going OK until you showed up. I wanted you bad. You was so confident and good-looking. You didn't seem to give a damn about rules. I never thought of things the way you did. Questioning, I mean. I never rebelled against the Church. It's like, when I'm with you, it don't seem like my feelings are bad. It's like God sent you for me."

I chuckled at this. "So that's why you run off to confession regularly."

Luke's face grew serious. "I ain't saying I've got it all under control. I ain't completely changed. It's mostly when we're apart, afterwards. Then I start worrying that maybe I have sinned."

"Maybe you have."

"What do you mean?"

I smiled at the panic in Luke's voice. "Maybe it is a sin. Maybe you'll wind up in hell."

"You don't really believe that, Victor. I know you don't."

"Think what you like. It's getting late. You better go." I wanted to feed and it was nearly midnight.

"Not yet." Luke grinned, got up on his hands and knees and buried his face in my crotch.

My cock hardened. Although I stopped ejaculating after my night existence began, sex gave me great pleasure, mostly the pleasure of having power over the human kneeling to lick my balls or take me in his ass. My whole body still shuddered with orgasms, but now it was my mind that exploded—in a dizzying euphoria of colors and sounds.

I stripped Luke of his clothes. I inspected his slight body, hairless and soft, his long slender cock protruding from a mass of blond fur. Throwing him face down on the rug, I mounted him. But I had barely entered him when I suddenly lost interest in the white body splayed before me. It was too easy. He wanted me too much. I felt no resistance in his will.

"Go to bed," I said, getting up and throwing on my robe.

"What's the matter, Victor?" He rolled over, still erect and badly wanting me.

"Another time, not tonight."

"Did I say something wrong? Do you want something else?" He clutched my arm like a beggar.

"Leave me."

Crestfallen, he dressed. I let him kiss my lips before he left the cell.

By now I was weak with hunger. In the heavy rain, I squished through the muddy grounds of the monastery toward the trees, invisible in the darkness to mortals, but to me a line of grayish branches, still leafless. Just inside the woods, I froze in place. I sensed a human within a stone's throw from me. My fangs instantly grew. My breathing became as excited and loud as that of a bull ready to charge. Someone lurked among the trees. I could stalk him, but as famished as I was it could only be to feed, and if the spy was a monk, I would endanger my position at St. Thomas. While I still had some power of discernment, I sped through the forest, as fast as my thoughts could carry me. My legs moved not at all now, but with the velocity of a jet I was carried bodily through the woods, my body dodging trees and brambles as though it carried its own radar system.

My senses guided me to a shack, like those of all my other victims in the mountains. The windows were dark, but the chimney smoked. The rotting door gave with a slight tug. Inside, the uneven floor moaned beneath my weight. The light from the fire painted the sticks of furniture orange. The room smelled of cat urine and damp upholstery.

"Who's out there?" an old woman demanded from the bedroom. "I got a gun in here, and I ain't afraid to use it."

Her delicious scent overwhelmed me. My nostrils dilated to catch her flavor. When I entered her door, she was standing near the bed, aiming a shotgun at me.

"Hello, Granny." I advanced, and she started trembling.

"Get out of my house else I'll blow you out."

"Now, that wouldn't do."

Before I could take another step, she fired. The bullet passed through my stomach and out my back, stunning me only momentarily. In an instant the pain dissipated, the wound closing as though my flesh were liquid and the projectile had only briefly parted the waters.

"Please!" She dropped the gun and sank to her knees. "Oh, please leave me be."

I approached her, lifting her chin to look into her rheumy eyes. "Good night, Granny." With a quick twist, I snapped her neck, a merciful gesture as I saw it, and picked her up to sink my fangs into her throat. It is only a myth that vampires cannot drink from corpses; they can, as long as the blood stays warm. Her loose skin tore easily and I fed on her rich old blood for nearly a quarter of an hour, I was so hungry.

After disposing of her body beneath a pair of fallen trees, I trekked up the mountainside to a clearing for a view of the valley. Below, the monastery rested in darkness, except for a few faint lights. Who was up at this time of night? Who had been watching me in the woods? Perhaps only Luke, who couldn't bear to leave me. But the presence I felt there was a stronger one than his, one I did not sense again as I crossed the monastery grounds but one I would attune myself to in the future.

CHAPTER FOURTEEN

The balmy nights of May brought with them a keen loneliness, for during the whole month I was bereft of contact with Joshu. Luke, who had amused me for a while, now satisfied me less and less. Still, he proved useful for learning more about the monk who did intrigue me.

One night when I did not find Michael in the weight room I wandered to the greenhouse. The lights there annoyed me, but I shaded my eyes and strolled quietly toward voices that rose above the rows of plants grown to raise money for the monastery. (The plants were transported to a market in Knoxville.) Concealed behind a wall of tall ficus, I listened to the conversation between Michael and Luke.

"It is different, Mike. God, I can't explain it. It's not like the other times. Why don't you just lay off!"

"What are we about here, Luke? You can argue for that kind of love all you want. For the sake of argument, let's say you're right. Homosexual love is legitimate. Even so, you're a monk. You took a vow of celibacy."

"That's when I thought I'd go straight to hell if I didn't kill the urges. Hell, Mike, I don't wanna kill 'em when I'm with him. It's like it's a sign from God or something."

One of the two took a few steps, and I drew back behind the foliage.

"You want to know what a sign from God is?" Michael sounded impatient. "Good fruit. Remember when Jesus says you'll know them by their fruit?"

"Hell, yes. And that's exactly right. God is love, right? That's what we have, Victor and me. Where two or three are gathered and all that, you know. I understand it now."

"Attractions are deceptive, Luke. Attractions don't mean love. Why do you think you still feel guilty? You think if this little affair were such a good thing, you'd be heading to confession all the time?"

"You're pissing me off."

"I'm telling you the truth."

"It's just the old shit." Luke nearly shouted, but he seemed to collect himself, lowering his voice. "God don't send guilt trips. Brother Matthew said so himself. Lotsa times, they're from the devil. He gets a person all tied up in knots to do his dirty work."

"If he were good," Michael implored, "if he were good and if the love were pure ... Luke, don't you see this is exactly how Satan works, not through what seems grotesque and repulsive, but through what seduces us. That's what I'm trying to tell you: The man has seduced you. He has no love to give you."

"You'd take away the only joy I ever had, wouldn't you?" Luke sounded choked-up now. "Here I thought you was my friend."

"He doesn't give a damn about you. Open your eyes." Michael's voice quivered, perhaps as he shook Luke by the shoulders—the plants blocked my view.

"He wants me. Don't look at me like that, damn you. I ain't crazy. Don't you think I know when someone wants me?"

"For what, Luke? For what? It's some power game he's playing. He likes to have people under his thumb."

"You know what I think? I think you're as jealous as all get out. Someone else takes a shine to me, and you go bananas. That's what it is. You like to play like some high and mighty judge. But you're in the game too."

A definite hit on the part of young Luke, I thought. I waited for Michael to go on the defensive. His response was a pleasant surprise.

"Maybe I am jealous." He spoke softly, seriously. "Maybe I envy this intimacy you feel, the physical affection. Maybe I feel Victor's power myself. But that only confirms what I'm saying to you. You don't seduce someone you love. This is his mode of operating."

"So that makes him Satan? Maybe it's the only way he knows."

Michael sighed, defeated. "Maybe it is."

That night after compline, Michael remained kneeling in the dark. I remained, too. A cross-breeze from the opened windows carried in sweet smells of lilacs and irises blooming in the courtyard.

I willed him to cross the chapel to me, but he resisted. His own will pressed upon my chest like hands keeping me at bay. But his bowed head, his kneeling form betrayed no hint of struggle, he was so composed. Suddenly he looked up, recognized me in the shadows, and spoke.

"Where are you from?"

"Many places. England was the last place. Brother Matthew told the community all about me, didn't he?"

"Why did you become a monk?"

I smiled. "If it's a heart-to-heart you want, Michael, perhaps we should adjourn to my cell, if you don't mind violating the Grand Silence."

"Did you listen to the reading tonight? 'The Lord has given an opportunity of repentance to all who would return to him.'"

"Yes, Clement of Rome waxes on, doesn't he?"

"The words didn't faze you."

I crossed the aisle and stood before him where he knelt. "You're not a prig, Michael. And you're not as self-righteous as you sound. So why are you preaching to me? What is it that possesses you? Surely it's more than the love for your friend." I touched his hand. He pulled it away and stood. We were so close I could smell the wine from dinner on his breath.

"I have a responsibility to Luke. If he won't listen to reason, I'll have to go to the abbot. It's my duty. I'm telling you so you'll back off."

"He's like a brother to you, eh?"

"He is my brother. So are you."

"Funny, I don't feel like your brother."

He started to turn away, but I grabbed his firm arm. "You're intelligent, Michael. Surely you don't take all this too seriously." I waved toward the chapel, as though it were a world rather than a room. "Dogmatism, I mean. Human rules, penances, busy rituals. Surely for you spirituality is something more ... how should I put it ... elastic, expansive, spontaneous. God speaks to each soul in a different way, don't you think?"

"Yes, he does. And I know his voice when I hear it." He jerked his arm away.

"Ah. One of the fortunate ones. The chosen few. You can discern good from evil, like hot and cold. No warm for you. Perhaps my first assessment of you was wrong after all. Perhaps you are self-righteous." As he walked away from me, I called after him, "If you run into Luke, tell him I'll be waiting for him in my cell."

CHAPTER FIFTEEN

My father was a true paterfamilias. As a Roman patriarch, he ruled his sons and his sons' families by the laws of practicality, reserving sentiment for private moments with my mother. Embedded in my memory is the sight of my youngest brother, Justin, sick with fever after serving in a provincial regiment. Moaning in pain, he lay naked on his cot, his youthful body still firm and muscular but writhing now, his eyes glazed, his face pallid as the linens. My father, a senator, was involved at the time with some important state matters that required careful attention. My mother, exhausted from attending Justin, was in danger of nervous collapse. I was home on leave from Palestine, but family business occupied my time. My other brothers, both officers, were stationed abroad.

"What are his chances?" My father had taken the physician and me outside my brother's room, away from my mother. Still fit and straight of carriage at the age of 60, my father was a fierce-looking man. His cold blue eyes, focused on the physician, gazed intensely from beneath a wide brow.

The old physician, a bald curmudgeon with a great beak of a nose and thin lips, scratched his chin. "I have seen this fever before in those returning from the provinces in the far south. If he survives it, his mind will be touched. If not, he will die within the week."

My father hesitated not one second. "In that case, it must end. Today, no later. Take care of the matter in haste. Let my wife learn nothing of it."

The physician bowed and disappeared. Immediately my mother, who'd been eavesdropping, rushed to the corridor and fell in hysterics at my father's feet, a bundle of white robes.

"No, Lucretius, I beg of you. Let him live. Do not take him from me." Justin, who had her fine features and high cheekbones, was her favorite son.

"What would you have, woman?" My father's face remained immobile. "Unbearable pain for him, madness if he's unlucky enough to live?"

"I will tend to him myself," she said, grabbing his legs, her reddened eyes turned up to him. "You needn't waste one moment here."

"You have duties, Lydia." Her emotion only made my father speak more sternly. "Now release me."

Mother collapsed into a heap, sobbing violently.

Following my father's lead, I ignored her and accompanied him to his rooms to discuss business matters needing urgent attention.

"She will recover," he said as we crossed the courtyard, which was gleaming in the midday sun. "And so shall we."

Recover he might, but for three days and three nights after my brother's funeral rites he locked himself in his rooms. As for myself, though I shed not a single tear in public, though I reprimanded my mother for her tears, I knew for the first time the emptiness that a final death, a mortal's death, brings. Especially when it is your own flesh and blood whom Charon ferries across the river Styx to the Underworld—a boy you taught to ride, to handle a sword, to swear admirably.

For some reason, after my chapel interview with Michael, my mind returned to the scene of my brother's fever and my father's pragmatic decision. Cold blood guaranteed survival, not only of an individual, but of a people. Certainly a vampire needed it.

I was not given to brooding, but in certain periods the isolation that was the fruit of such coldness, the isolation of centuries, came over me like a blanket of darkness that even my sight could not pierce. In moments like these, I rallied my spirit by dreaming of the time when, after entering the realm of night, I would be joined by whomever I had chosen on earth, a beloved who would wipe away all thoughts of Joshu.

In the meantime, I took comfort where I could. That night I willed Luke to my cell. With a flashlight to guide us—for Luke's sake—we hiked out to the woods, to a spot cleared by mountain dwellers, and rested against a stump overgrown with vines. Along the way he asked me questions about the Church with an interest, an ebullience, of one who never previously conceived of the possibility of questioning.

"What do you mean the Church's power is arbitrary?" he asked, cradling my head in his lap. Around us a warm breeze rustled the branches and cicadas whirred.

"I mean the Pope's a foolish old man who invents laws."

"But he's the Vicar of Christ."

"He's nothing. He knows nothing of Christ but the wives' tales passed on about him by ignorant fishermen and tent-makers."

"But didn't Christ call Peter to feed his sheep?"

"Your Christ, the Church's Christ, is a god made in the image of effete men who've never had a good fuck in their lives, or if they have, who've thrashed themselves with whips to relieve their guilt. They hate their own cocks so much they'd light votive candles to make them fall off, if it would do the trick. Good old Origen, revered Church Father that he was, castrated himself. Did you know that?"

"Shit!" Luke winced.

"Virgins. Celibates. What kind of god makes bodies and forbids you to use them? And makes you feel holy and superior when you do manage to turn into gutless, passionless stone?"

"But Jesus didn't—"

"He worshiped a demented god. He was deluded." I stood. "Let's get off this subject. Before I tear off someone's head."

"If you feel this way, Victor," Luke timidly pursued, "how come you ended up in a monastery?"

I picked up a fallen branch and cracked it against the stump with such force that the sound reported like shotgun fire. "It is my mission, damn you! We hear the gospel every day. Well, I have my own gospel, the true gospel. Not the one that serves a possessive, tyrannical god, but one that frees us from submission to him. I live it. Daily. Why grovel at his feet for eternity? Do you want an eternity on your goddamned knees?"

"Jesus said God is our father." The boy was frightened by my outburst. For all his delight in unorthodox talk, I had gone too far.

"I am your father." I fell on the boy, worked up his habit, and with only the dew for lubrication, forced myself into him. He groaned in pain at first, then in pleasure as I rode him.

In that moment I wanted his blood more than ever. Nuzzling my face against his throat, I heard the blood pumping through his jugular as loud as a bass drum. My fangs descended. I bared them. They grazed his soft skin, barely scratching its surface, before I jerked my head away, just as my thrusting body brought him to his climax.

"God, I love you, Victor." He panted the words.

"Go back. I need to walk. Alone." I got up and disappeared into the woods before he had time to protest. My urge for food had suddenly driven me to near-insanity. Spotting a raccoon nosing the carcass of an animal, I rushed to it, grasped its furry throat, and sank my fangs into its tough hide. I sucked every drop of gamy blood from its veins and hurled the hairy mass against a tree.

Just before dawn, tired from aimless tramping about the woods, I crawled into the mausoleum and settled into my pine bed. Exhausted, I drifted toward a welcome sleep, when my eyes snapped open. Someone lurked outside the tomb, someone strong and unafraid—I felt such a presence within my bowels. Then I smiled and closed my eyes.

Part IV

CLEARING THE PATH

CHAPTER SIXTEEN

Brother Matthew stood before the communion rail, the saints in all their glory inspecting the crown of his balding head from their niches in the high altar. He removed his wire-frame spectacles and rubbed his close-set eyes. "This isn't the best time of day for serious news," he said, "but it is one of the few times we're all gathered together."

All 23 monks had remained in their stalls after compline, which had been moved to 10 o'clock to accommodate me during the summer months when the shadows of dusk didn't collect until after 9. A couple of the older bastards regularly nodded off before the final blessing, and they had to be nudged now.

"It looks like there've been some break-ins up in the hills. The police aren't sure what the motive is. As you know, the folks up there have no valuables to speak of. They're also as isolated as can be, so we're not even sure why anyone would wander around up there." Matthew replaced his glasses, clasped his hands, and rocked nervously back and forth. "It seems some people have abandoned their houses. Brother George and Brother Michael first noticed that several months ago."

I glanced across the aisle at Michael, whose dark hair, pulled back into a ponytail, gleamed after his post-workout shower. He was all intensity, scratching his new goatee, studying the abbot as though he were pondering metaphysics rather than the disappearance of hillbillies.

"As you know, it's nothing new for people to move down to the city's shelters during the winter months to get out of the cold, so at first no one was alarmed. Then relatives put in missing person reports. And the disappearances continued when the weather warmed up. The county police started to investigate. Of course you can imagine how seriously they pursued trudging through mountain thickets to investigate the cases of missing indigent people."

Several of the monks shook their heads or mumbled something about the shame of it.

"However," Brother Matthew continued, "earlier this week they found a body."

A rumble of voices echoed through the chapel.

"Brother George, perhaps you would like to take it from here." The abbot turned to Brother George, a short, middle-aged man who managed the community's finances and was second in command after Matthew. His silver hair, clipped close to his skull, fuzzed the outline of his squarish head. He stood to address the group, and the abbot rested against the communion rail.

"You all know that the monastery regularly sends food to some of the mountain folks." His voice was a deep, gravelly smoker's voice. "Well, Michael and I got worried when one of our regulars disappeared without a trace—an older woman with no family, practically lame in one foot and with no transportation. We searched the woods ourselves, thinking maybe she fell and hurt herself. At first we didn't see any sign of her. Then we noticed a trail of something—it could have been blood—leading up to a fallen tree, a big oak about five feet around. It was strange since how could she have gotten under it? But we got the police out here a couple days ago. They sent for a crew of workers with a crane. They found her body under it. Molly Spaker was her name. Nice old woman. Husband died last year. He was a miner from up in Kentucky."

"How did she get under the tree?" Brother Alfred asked the question, a swarthy man at St. Thomas to complete a book on some drivel in Aquinas's *Summa Theologiae.*

"They don't have a clue," George answered. "But evidently her neck was broken. And, well, I might as well say it—her blood was drained."

The chapel buzzed with murmurs.

The abbot stood, looking grave. "The concern here is that some psychopath is on the loose in the woods. The police are continuing their search for the missing folks, with the help of our information about them. And they're hunting for the killer of Mrs. Spaker. In the meantime, we've got to tighten our own security measures since we're obviously sitting ducks for a killer at large."

"That means all outside doors stay locked," Brother George threw in. "Please use your keys. And keep windows facing the exterior of the monastery shut. If you open your transoms, the interior courtyard windows should keep your rooms cool."

"We probably have nothing to worry about," the abbot continued. "If someone had wanted one of us, they could have had him by now. Probably, we're talking about someone smart enough to pick victims who wouldn't be missed."

The monks for the most part were not gossips—scholars rarely are, content to keep the world at bay while they bury themselves in their studies—but several of the monks did whisper together in the foyer after we had prayed for the deceased and for the apprehension of the murderer, apparently feeling the Grand Silence warranted violation under the circumstances. The shadows of the robed men rose like spirits on the walls.

I retraced my steps through the chapel to get to the library, where I could bury myself in books and stew over the matters at hand. The antechamber to the stacks was a large room whose beamed ceiling rose to a height of 40 feet, the vast space corresponding to five levels of stacks on the other side of one wall. Against tall wainscoting, study desks of darkened oak were arranged around a block of reference shelves in the center of the room.

I took a seat at one of the desks against an external wall where two arched windows framed the woods and distant mountaintops in the daylight, but in the darkness formed two blank eyes. Yellow lamplight fell upon the volume I'd left on the desk, a study of the historical Jesus, the result of some ambitious theology professor's drive for tenure, and for me, the opportunity to dream of Joshu.

The words blurred as I read, the page becoming like a theater curtain of transparent gauze that melts away when the lights behind it reveal a set and movement on the stage. I saw the mangled old woman crumpled on the linoleum. *Nothing can be linked to me, I said to myself. The woman's body, the blood, the superhuman effort to move the tree—none of these points a finger to me. But I must find new grounds for feedings. Down in the city perhaps, among Knoxville's poor neighborhoods, in the prison outside the town's limits. Less convenient of course, especially now when my lust for the blood of young Luke makes it hard to resist sinking my fangs into his throat. But necessary all the same.*

"Good evening, Brother Victor." The voice of the abbot broke through my thoughts. He looked a bit uncomfortable. "I hate to break the Grand Silence, but I do have something important to discuss with you, something I've been putting off, and with all this horrible stuff going on—well, there's not much silence right now anyway. May I?" He nodded to a chair near the desk.

"Please."

"What is it you're reading?"

"Nothing of interest. What's on your mind?"

He shifted and removed his glasses, studying them as he spoke. "Something's been brought to my attention, regarding you and Brother Luke."

"What's that?"

"At the risk of taking our friend Thomas à Kempis too seriously"—he looked up now as though to say I ought not take him too seriously either—"it's about particular friendship."

"Becoming too close to one person in the community."

"Yes. It's an old-fashioned idea of course. But there's something to be said for it." Perhaps detecting the disdain in my voice, he became emboldened enough to look me in the eye.

"I'm all for old-fashioned ideas, Brother Matthew."

"That's good, because I do believe this is a serious matter. Luke is ... what can I say. He's naive in the extreme. He's not bright either—very impressionable. You, well, I take it you've seen some of the world."

"What makes you think so?"

"Oh, I'm not sure. The way you carry yourself. The way you speak. I guess it's just an impression."

"I see."

"But at any rate, you're older. He's hardly out of his teens. Luke needs to be handled delicately."

"Protected, you mean? From more experienced people?"

Frustrated, the abbot rubbed his cheek. "Of course experienced people have a lot to teach a boy like Luke. That wisdom, the right way to handle feelings, etcetera, that's something he should learn about."

"The boy's infatuated, Brother. He's young. It happens. I'll take care of it."

"Very good." He stood to go, but turned back to me as though a bit dissatisfied with the turn our conversation had taken. "I hope you'll take my advice in the right spirit. I don't want to seem inhospitable to a brother who's been through a tragedy. I can see why you would reach out for a friend."

"You're kind, Brother. Good night." I turned my attention to my book. He hesitated a second, then left the room.

So Michael had carried out his threat. Of course, since our talk in the chapel, I had continued summoning Luke to my cell and we'd gone on with our nocturnal romps through the woods. For the most part young Luke's company amused me, took the edge off the solitude of the night. Granted, he offered me no challenge and never had. But before it got tedious, his kind of wide-eyed fawning entertained me for an hour or so. Besides, our liaison won me Michael's attention. Perhaps now, however, my strategy should change.

Later that week I made my move, after sucking on his tender cock in the woods—so excited by its engorgement that I would have pierced the nearly transparent membrane keeping me from the blood if I'd possessed an ounce less restraint. The full moon had already reached a western point in its arc back to the earth. Patches of its faint light lay on the rocks, vines, and bare earth the color of coffee grounds. Luke and I had thrown off our habits and, guided by a flashlight, treaded naked to the familiar clearing where we conducted our rendezvous. In the hollow of a tree he'd stashed a bottle of wine he'd filched from the dusty collection in the cellar—the daring boy he'd now become. He'd chugged a good amount of it before our playing began. Now his face was the shade of the wine, but instead of breaking his energy the drink pumped it through him. His slim, naked form paced restlessly as he rambled on and on about the stalker roaming the mountainside.

"You think he escaped from a loony bin? I believe there's one in

Knoxville, or maybe it's Nashville. Wherever the hell. You know, it's a damn scary thing. Someone sucking out blood like that. That's what the coroner guy said, ain't it?"

I shrugged, bored with the topic, and lay my head back against the stump. I imagined the dim moon, bright to my sight, was the sun and that once again I was basking in its heat.

"That ol' gal musta died from shock before he even started sucking. You think? Tell you what, I wouldn't want to be the detective that's gotta go poking around for the rest of the bodies."

"Maybe there are no other bodies."

"Hell, where there's one, I'll lay odds there's a dozen. Like rats in a barn. Yessir, betcha anything some crazy man read too many vampire stories. Got hisself some spikey teeth and ripped into her." He finally stopped pacing, peering through the trees as though on the watch for the killer, and sprawled out next to me after he tossed the drained bottle into the thicket.

"You've got a morbid imagination tonight."

"I expect so." He had calmed himself now and laid his head on my shoulder, his blonde locks soft against my cheek. "Anyway, with you here, I feel pretty damn safe."

"The abbot spoke to me the other night, Luke. About us."

"What about us?" He spoke drowsily now.

"He said our liaison had to end. The man could make trouble, weakling that he is."

It took a moment before Luke could register the news. Then he lifted his head, his spirit rallied by the threat. "To hell with him. To hell with St. Thomas. It's time for us to get out of this place, Victor. We could get out of this hick state and head to a big city. San Francisco maybe. Hell, half the city's gay, according to a magazine I read. We could get us a house. You might could teach. I could tend to lawns and such." The pupils of his blue eyes dilated with his excitement.

"Like a dream come true, eh?"

"Yessir. Exactly."

"I'm afraid you'll have to live your dream with someone else."

"What? What do you mean?" His forehead wrinkled as though he were trying to discern whether I was joking or not.

"This is the end, that's all. You'll get over me." I got up and put on my robe. As I started to walk away, Luke sprang up and grabbed my arm.

"Damn, Victor, you're serious, ain't you? Why? What use have you got for this place? You hate the fucking Church. Jesus, Victor, you can't just pitch me like garbage. I love you."

I stared coldly into his panic-stricken eyes, jerked my arm free, and resumed walking.

"Don't you love me, Victor?" He called after me. "Don't you love me?" His voice broke into a sob. "You bastard! Goddamn you. You hear me? Goddamn you!"

As usual, my appetite for blood overpowered me after coming so close to Luke's veins—one reason for my abruptness, which was perhaps more severe than usual. But I couldn't hunt in the mountains, not now with county police scouting the area, so I headed west toward the city. Attuned to the scent of blood, my body lifted and soared through the humid June night to a farmhouse several miles down the road, still far outside the city. The two-story abode rose on a hill, above fields of tobacco, a weather-beaten but sturdy structure. Inside a screened porch, I found the back door unlocked. A large calico cat, lounging on a dresser stripped of its drawers, watched me with curiosity as I entered.

The back door opened into a kitchen, where pots and pans lay piled on a drainboard and a table covered with a checkered cloth held a bowl of plastic fruit. Through a dining room, and a living room where a grandfather clock's pendulum ticked noisily, I followed the scent of blood. It became especially strong in the entrance hall. I mounted a staircase there, pausing at the top before a partially open door where I inhaled the rich odor of what I needed. But I advanced toward a second door where the smell was even stronger, more concentrated.

Bunk beds and another bed held three boys. The youngest, in the bottom bunk, couldn't have been more than three. The boy in the top bunk, his long lashes curling up against his cheeks, was probably 5 or 6. An older boy lay in the large bed, his sheet crumpled up at the foot, his tanned arms and legs dark against the linens. Through the open window, cicadas buzzed, but no breeze stirred the heavy summer air.

My chest was heaving now I needed blood so badly. My fangs were ready to tear flesh. But which child should I take? The youngest and most tender? The oldest and biggest portion? A pity it would have been to have two brothers awaken in the morning to find the third drained of life. I could take all three; they were small enough. But the parents in the next room would be left with nothing. I cursed the speck of human softness surfacing now. "Worry be damned," I muttered, clapping my hand over the oldest boy's mouth. His eyes flashed open. He tried to scream, and flapped against the mattress like a fish in the bottom of a boat. Within seconds I had pierced his throat and, draining most of his blood, I quickly twisted his neck to end any lingering misery.

The youngest boy stirred, and for several seconds I remained frozen, inhaling the sweaty odor of my victim, the wet-dog scent that children get when they play outdoors. The child in the bottom bunk suddenly started to cry. I rushed to him and snapped his neck. With no time to drink in case the parents had stirred, and with my thirst already slaked, I bolted out the window and rode the thick, warm air back to the monastery.

CHAPTER SEVENTEEN

Restless and sullen, and now lonelier than ever, I cursed Joshu again and again during the next month when he continued to not appear in a vision. I was sick of the inescapable fate of my feedings, sick of preying on drug addicts and prostitutes, people living on the streets in Knoxville. I resented being deprived of Luke, even though a better trophy required this sacrifice. I hadn't the patience for calculating ingenious ways to win Michael, and since he had kept a distance from me, I feared that my desire for an equal would go forever unmet.

Over the weeks Luke's reactions to my dismissal of him fluctuated as much as the whims of a Roman aristocrat's spoiled child. Initially, he slumped at the long dining room table with lowered eyes, mechanically moving his spoon but eating little. In the chapel he held his breviary in front of his face so no one could see that his lips weren't moving to the psalms. When we filed into the corridor after compline, he dragged his feet despondently.

Then several times he rallied himself to plead his case. The first time I was lying on my cot, turning the brittle pages of an ancient tome on the Dark Kingdom—a book I'd discovered half a millennium before. Some ambitious vampire had written the Latin text, I was sure of that. I'd lit a few candles to rest my eyes from what for me was the painful light of the chapel. Before Luke could knock, I felt his weak presence outside the door.

"Come in, Luke," I called. I was lying on my side, my elbow against the bed, my head propped on my hand.

The door opened. His eyes were red. He wore his habit, but his feet were in slippers.

"Well, don't stand there. Come in and shut the door."

He followed my orders but continued to hover sheepishly near the door. "I couldn't sleep."

"How unfortunate." I turned the page to a drawing of a voluptuous woman swathed in an ermine mantle, high priestess of the Dark Kingdom.

"Victor, if you're tired of me, I could try some new things. To make you feel really good. I know I ain't that experienced. But hell, I'd be willing to take a shot at anything. You're a temperamental type. Just like a horse I had once. Wouldn't let you near him for days and then would eat out of your hand like a puppy." He forced a smile. "I know that's all there is to it. The abbot ... hell, you have him under your thumb. He ain't gonna do nothing if you wanna stick around here. Maybe sometime, though, you'll wanna go. We could go anywhere, right? Sky's the limit."

"Come here, Luke." I patted the mattress.

He eagerly obeyed, sitting down on the bed. His body left my book in shadow. I could smell tobacco on his habit. He'd started smoking, apparently to ease his misery.

"You're right. I am temperamental. I am weary of you. It can't be helped. There's nothing you can do. The best thing for you is to stop dreaming. Open your eyes. You're young. If you want to find love, get out of this perverse monastery and get yourself a lover. But don't expect anything from me. Now go to bed."

He started to tremble. His eyes welled and the tears tumbled down his face. "Damn, Victor. I can't put you out of my mind like you was some impure thought." He sobbed and then took a deep breath to collect himself. "I ain't never loved someone. I'd rather die than be without you." He grabbed my wrist.

"Then you'd better die, Luke. I'm telling you once and for all, you're a fool to hope."

He nodded his head dejectedly, rose, and slowly walked to the door.

"It's the best thing," I called after him.

There were a few more scenes like this one, then long letters blotched with tear stains, then angry outbursts during evening recreation, when in my boredom I would gravitate toward the common room. During one of those times he deliberately spilled his drink on me as I sat on the sofa, joking with one of the younger, better-looking brothers.

"Oh, I'm sorry, Brother," he said, with exaggerated remorse. "Hell, I'm clumsier than a blind old cat." He mopped my habit with his handkerchief.

"Never mind, Luke." I grabbed the handkerchief from him.

"Never mind? Hell no. I'm a damned good brother. I'm here to serve."

Two brothers seated near the piano interrupted their conversation at Luke's loud declaration, made, as best I could tell, with the help of a few glasses of wine. Michael, playing a board game with Brother George, the administrator, also glanced up and comprehended the situation at once. When Luke tried to tug the handkerchief away from me, his eyes filling with angry tears, Michael came over and reasoned with him.

"Luke, why don't you come help me a minute in the greenhouse."

"To hell with the greenhouse." Luke's blue eyes stood out against his flushed cheeks. "To hell with you." He turned, stumbling against a chair, and charged out of the room.

"Maybe you should go help him," I said to Michael.

His dark eyes peered at me with uncertainty and reserve, but also with something more. "No, he's best left alone for now."

After another similar scene, and after the abbot counseled Luke that the end of our intimacy was for his good, Luke rebelled again, calling me a cocksucker in chapel. When he ventured to my cell later that night, drunkenly remorseful and eager to plead for my affection, I clutched him by his slender throat. His eyes widened in horror. The acne on his cheeks stood out like blue match heads against his white face.

"Listen to me, damn you. I'll kill you if you don't shut your mouth and stay out of my way." I flung him to the floor.

"Kill me then!" he sobbed, rubbing his neck.

When I lifted my foot to kick him, I felt a twinge of conscience, even pity. I stepped over him and left my cell.

CHAPTER EIGHTEEN

The sheriff and his men found the remains of two more bodies, and their investigation turned up another 15 missing people. Although it had been a couple of months since I'd preyed on the mountain dwellers, the new findings alarmed the monks. The sheriff asked us to assemble so he could warn us to stay in after dark, when a culprit could lurk about with less danger of detection, and not to wander in the woods alone, even though no recent victims had been discovered.

That night I was taking some air at the edge of the woods, deliberating whether I should feed in the city or wait until the next night when the monks might be less alert. It was August, still warm, though I smelled rain in the heavy air and a breeze stirred the branches. A circle of light suddenly glowed near the monastery and grew larger as it approached me.

"Who's out there?" Michael called when he heard me snap a limb. He scanned the trees with his flashlight.

The darkness that shielded me from him did not, of course, shield him from me. I watched his athletic form, dressed like me in jeans and a T-shirt, hike with determined strides toward the forest.

As he neared, he inadvertently shined the torturous light in my eyes.

"You're blinding me, for God's sake," I said.

"Brother Victor?" He lowered the light. "What are you doing here?"

"Taking a walk. My usual midnight stroll."

"I see. You're not afraid of the lunatic roaming the mountainside." His tone was lighter, more agreeable than it had ever been with me.

"I'll take my chances. Where are you going?"

"I'm worried about a couple of kids up there. Their father went to the city to find work. They're alone. He called from Knoxville just before compline. Said people were talking about the new bodies and he got worried. I told him I'd check in on his kids."

"I thought the bodies they found had been there for quite a while. The killer probably has disappeared now."

"Most likely. But he's worried all the same." Michael switched off the flashlight. His eyes had evidently grown accustomed to the darkness. He gazed at me in the meager light of the moon, his eyes bold but no longer full of loathing.

"Do you plan to stay up there with them?" I asked.

He shook his head. "No. Just to walk them to a house about half a mile from theirs so they can stay with someone. The man there's a big guy with a lot of guns."

"I'll go with you."

"It's quite a trek. Up by that radio tower." He pointed to the north, maybe three miles from the spot.

"Good exercise," I said.

We wound through the thicket, tree frogs and cicadas clamoring, probably in anticipation of the coming shower. Lightning seared the sky in the direction we were heading, followed by a crack of thunder.

"Looks like we'll be soaked," Michael said, stopping to catch his breath. Guided by the flashlight's beam, we'd been steadily climbing toward a footpath.

Once we reached the path the hiking was easier, though we continued to move up the incline, through heavy growth. Big drops of rain sifted through the branches and then poured from the sky. Even under the partial shelter of the foliage we got drenched. But Michael forged on, not the least bit hindered by the storm. His stride was big, his muscular arms steadily swinging. I thought he could wrestle his god if he wanted, like Jacob of the Hebrews.

It took an hour and a half to reach our destination, a shack nestled in the thicket, not far from the path. No lights glowed in the house. The screenless windows beneath the shaky roof of the porch were wide open.

"Watch your step," Michael said, whisking his light across gaps in the rotting planks of the porch. He hammered on the door with his fist.

The white face of a little girl appeared at the window.

"It's Brother Michael, Dora Anne," he said.

"Ginny, Brother Michael's here!" The girl disappeared from the window and the door swung open. She was 5 or 6, with a missing front tooth, limp blond hair, and a pale face splattered with freckles. She hugged Michael's legs excitedly.

"Brother Michael?" A girl of 16 or 17 appeared in a T-shirt and cut-off jeans, folding her arms as though she were cold. Her short hair was tousled from sleeping. "What's a matter? Something wrong with Daddy?"

"No, no." Michael entered the cramped living room and I followed him. "He's just worried about you. He thinks you'd be safer staying with the Jacksons."

"They ain't found another body, have they?" Ginny said.

"I'm afraid so."

Ginny shivered and lit an oil lamp on a shelf. The pale light washed over a table with mismatched chairs, a sagging armchair, and two mattresses on the plywood floor, where water had puddled from our shoes. "Gives me the willies," she said. "We thought that crazy man done took off. Sheriff and his men been patrolling the woods."

"Did he cut off their heads?" Dora Anne looked up earnestly at Michael. "Ralph Jackson says he did. Then he stuck little needles into their body so they looked like porcupines."

"Ralph Jackson's just trying to scare you, Dora Anne. You just don't pay him any mind." Ginny turned to me, suspicion in her eyes. "You a brother too?"

"Yes. Brother Victor."

She nodded as though she had her doubts. "We'll be just fine, Brother Michael. Ain't no need to bother the Jacksons this time a night. I got Daddy's shotgun here and I can use it."

"How come you ain't never come up to see us before?" Dora Anne said to me.

"I'm new at the monastery." The little girl roused my appetite. Perhaps I would go down to the city to feed, I thought. If enough time remained.

"You wanna see a snake?" Dora said to me. "I got it in a jar."

"You can show him another time." Ginny grabbed Dora Anne's arm as she started toward the back door.

"Your father wants you to go to the Jacksons'," Brother Michael said to Ginny. "I think it's a good idea."

Ginny nodded. "Well, if you say so, Brother. Just hate to put 'em out. And Dora Anne ain't got nothing but flip-flops for walkin' in."

"I'll carry her," I said.

Michael looked at me with curiosity, as though I continued to surprise him by my benevolence.

"Yaaay! A piggyback ride!" Dora Anne jumped up and down, clapping her hands.

We waited until the rain slackened before heading for the Jacksons'. Dora Anne chattered the whole way, tugging at tree branches, squirming excitedly against my back, despite her sister's reprimands. Once we delivered them to the family, at nearly 2 in the morning, we tramped back to the monastery.

As I followed Michael, in answer to my question, he explained that many of the destitute mountain people chose to remain so far from civilization after the mines closed because of ignorance and fear of the city. And because of incestuous relationships they wanted to safeguard from the authorities. "I know one girl with three babies by her father," he said.

"Surely the sheriff must know about it?" Following Michael's lead, I stepped across a large puddle.

"He knows. But he also knows how life is here. The girl wouldn't leave her father if you paid her. And if they took her by force, she'd probably kill herself."

"That's a pity."

Michael reeled around. "You don't really mean that, do you?"

"No, I don't. Do you think it's a pity?"

Michael looked hard at me, despite the darkness. He could not make out my expression, but I could his, a gaze of recognition of an affinity between us. "There are worse things," he said and turned away.

We made the rest of the trek in silence, me savoring our new intimacy, Michael no doubt pondering it. We spoke only to warn each other of a treacherous limb or gully. But when we reached the fringe of the forest, where we could walk side by side, he spoke again.

"Thank you for being stern with Luke. I'm sorry if I misjudged you." He kept his eyes forward.

"And what if you didn't misjudge me?"

"Then you deserve even more credit for cutting him free."

I smiled in the darkness, though he had spoken quite seriously. "Have you talked to him? Is he still desperate?"

"He'll get over it. It's just infatuation."

"You sound as though you speak from experience."

Michael stopped. We were on the monastery property now. Our sneakers were sopping wet from the marshy ground. Michael steadied himself on my arm to remove his shoes. "It's no secret that monastic life attracts homosexuals. Men get to live with men, with impunity, with praise, at least from the Catholic world. I've had my share of attractions. Thanks." His eyes turned to mine when he straightened up and then darted away in discomfort.

"But you are dedicated to celibacy?" The opportunity seemed ripe for pressing him.

"I'm dedicated to God."

"And what does that mean, to be dedicated to God?"

"I discover it, day to day, like everybody else."

I grabbed Michael by the arm and stopped in my tracks, turning him toward me. "Let's stop playing games now, Michael. The intensity between us is as palpable as this flesh." I squeezed his firm arms. "You accused me of seducing Luke, but I wouldn't even attempt to seduce you, I desire you far too much for that. I can see you struggling, not against me but against yourself."

"Does this amuse you?"

"It gives me hope. May I hope?"

"Do you know why I struggle? It's not against my attraction to you. It's against the evil I find in my soul, the same evil I see reflected in your eyes. Both of us are proud, rebellious, but it's not just that. It's a coldness, like the ice trapping Satan at the bottom of Dante's inferno. A coldness that cuts us off from everyone."

"You've cared for Luke."

"I have a duty toward him. That's different."

"We're not sentimental types. Our hearts bother with nothing short of passion."

He continued gazing steadily into my eyes. I pulled him to me and kissed him. His full lips responded, his body pressed against mine. For a moment we merged with the loftiest mountain peak behind us, now star-crowned in the clearing skies.

"We can leave this place," I whispered in his ear as I embraced him.

He made no answer.

We kissed again in the dark entrance hall of the monastery and separated. My soul blazed for him. I longed for blood to calm myself, but dawn was too close now and I retreated to my cell. A figure sat wrapped in shadows outside the door.

"What are you doing here, Luke?" I nudged him with my foot to awaken him.

He shook off his sleep and got to his feet. "Where did y'all go?" he said accusingly.

"Go to bed." I opened my door and he followed me into the dark chamber.

"You was with Mike. I seen him going out to you."

He grabbed my arm. His eyes were filled with desperation.

I shook off his grip. "I said go to bed."

"No, Victor, you ain't gonna get away with this. No sir, you traitor. Both of you. You ain't gonna do this to me. Know what I'll do?" He was nearly hysterical now, his voice trembling, his hands making fists at his sides. "I'll go to the abbot with everything. Hell, I'll confess everything about you and me. I'll tell him 'bout every time we fucked, every time you sucked my dick. You'll be outta here so fast you won't know what hit you."

I grabbed him by the shoulders. "Listen to me, boy. You'll keep your mouth shut or you'll be out of here too."

"No!" He tried to free himself from my grip. "I'll tell him, you bastard. You think I care what happens to me?"

I had no choice now. As Luke struggled in my hands, in the darkness of my cell, I plunged my fangs into his throat. For a moment, he melted into my arms, as though once again I were mounting him, and I felt his desire for me flare. But as I siphoned the warm, young blood, he collapsed, unconscious. I continued drinking until his heart, whose rhythm had moved from a frantic speed to the tempo of a solemn war drum, sounded a final beat.

Deep into the woods I carried his body, hiding it in the underbrush. I made it back to the monastery just as faint light rimmed the mountains. Quietly, I slipped into my tomb, as filled with dread as with the blood of my victim.

Part V

THE BELOVED

CHAPTER NINETEEN

Tolling, tolling, tolling. Throughout my fitful sleep in the close coffin, the bass voice of a bell, like an ancient prophet's lament, intruded into the dreams that followed my killing of Luke. When my nerves finally registered the sinking of the sun, my eyes flashed open in the dark chamber and I thought I heard the bell still. But silence prevailed. Around me the dusty skeletons lay, complacent, I thought, in their immobility, their finality. There were brief moments when I envied them.

The taste of Luke's blood was in my mouth. I thought I would retch. To kill a stranger, in the heat of lust for blood, in dire need of it, was like running a sword through an enemy during combat. No matter how young, how beautiful, how brave the opponent, I plunged the sword up under the ribs as a matter of survival. But to kill a boy who fawned on me, though he hung like a stone around my neck, made me realize the darkness, the suffocating darkness of my life. The tight dimensions of the pine box, the close vault that held it, trapping awful shadows: How many times did I awake that night to see the chamber as a symbol of what I carried with me when, like a rodent, I crawled from its confines? But when upon my mind's screen were projected Michael's eyes, dark and intense, solemn and keen as a winter night's stormy sky, the darkness held hope, life that mocked the pious, insipid light of day.

I rose, eager to find Michael, stripping off my blood-splattered T-shirt and stuffing it under the mattress in my cell until I could bury it later. In a fresh habit, I ascended the stairs to the entry hall of the monastery. There, to my irritation, I found the sober-faced abbot awaiting me.

He greeted me with a nod. "Would you come into my office a moment, Brother Victor?"

I followed him, taking a seat in the leather chair across from his desk, where he seated himself. A pair of dim lamps glowed, leaving unbroken the shadows stretched across the books and high corners of the room.

"What is it, Brother Matthew?"

"Brother Luke has disappeared."

His unusual directness amused me. I imagined that, determined to overcome his intimidation of me, he had rehearsed this confrontation.

"He did not show up for lauds this morning, and when one of the brothers went to check on him, he found Luke's bed still made. We searched the greenhouse, the grounds, finally the whole monastery. There was no sign of him."

"You think he ran away?" I asked. I leaned back and crossed my legs.

"What do you think, Brother Victor?" The abbot removed his glasses and managed to look directly into my eyes.

"How should I know, Brother Matthew? After our conversation in the library I did exactly as I promised. I ended my association with Brother Luke."

"He made no attempt to keep up your friendship?"

"Of course he tried. As I told you, he was infatuated. But I insisted. Did he leave a note?" In the brief time I'd had to dispose of Luke's body there was no opportunity to scribble an explanation. Besides, I couldn't forge his hand, nor could I print something from a computer since he didn't have access to one and therefore couldn't have done that himself.

"No. Nothing. I hoped he might have said something to you about his whereabouts. I thought he must have run away out of anger or desperation, and that he might have warned you."

I shook my head. "I'm sorry. I know nothing."

Brother Matthew searched the wall behind me, his brow furrowed in distress, his delicate finger pressing his lips. Then he leveled his troubled gaze at me.

"Did you hear or see anything last night, any unusual noises inside the monastery, or outside? Did you go outside at all last night?"

I knew this was a test. Only in that second did I understand how little the abbot trusted me. "Yes, I took a walk. I know the sheriff told us to stay in, but I can't stay cooped up. I ran into Brother Michael. I'm surprised he didn't say anything to you. He was worried about some children left alone. I went up with him to take them to a safer place."

"Brother Michael did mention it." The abbot's eyes fell for a moment and then turned back on me after he'd composed himself. "I assembled the brothers, except for you, of course, because it was daylight, to explain the situation and to ask if they heard or saw anything last night. Brother Michael told me you'd gone up the mountain and didn't see anything unusual. I just wondered if you had noticed anything before or after your trip."

"I see." I gazed at him until he lowered his eyes again. "No, I didn't notice anything. So you're concerned that Luke might have been attacked by the crazy man roaming the mountains?"

"It's a possibility we have to consider." He stood and went to the window. "Brother Luke took nothing with him, as far as we can tell. He had no means of transportation. To hitchhike into town in the middle of the night, on a country road ... well, that seems pretty unlikely. At least the sheriff thinks so. He's had men searching the road into Knoxville all day."

"Are they searching the woods too?"

The abbot turned and rested his hands on the back of his chair. "Yes. If Luke did wander into the woods. Well, just pray for him, Brother."

I nodded.

"Sheriff Johnson will be here shortly to question you. He's already spoken to the others."

"I don't see that I can help him."

"Still, he wants to cover all the bases."

When the sheriff arrived, the abbot left us alone in his office. The stocky, 50ish man sat on the edge of a wing-back chair and, resting his elbows on his knees, wrote my responses on a page in a clipboard. He looked exhausted, straining to see his own notes through his bifocals. He wore a khaki uniform with short sleeves and two buttons open at the neck in the heat. His reddish beard needed trimming.

"Now, Brother," he drawled, glancing up at me with steady gray eyes. "You say you was outside last night till what time?"

"Nearly dawn. It took us that long to get back from the Jacksons' house. Didn't Brother Michael tell you all this?" I made little attempt to hide my impatience.

"All a formality, Brother. Bear with me here." He jotted down something. "And you saw or heard nothing suspicious?"

"It was raining. We were talking. I didn't notice anything."

"Mmm-hmm." He scribbled again.

"You think there was foul play?"

"Too early to know." He straightened up to yawn, sat back in the chair, and crossed his legs as though we were having a very amiable conversation. "You and Brother Luke was pretty close, I hear." He removed his bifocals and put them in his shirt pocket.

"You could say that, I suppose." I stared steadily at him.

"You suppose? Were y'all on the outs?" He tapped his pen against a gold cap on a bottom tooth as he peered at me with interest.

"Luke was making a pest of himself. He followed me around like a dog. I told him to find another hero. I'm sure the abbot told you he advised me to talk to Luke. He probably also told you Luke was upset with me. Which explains why he ran away."

"If he did run away."

"Yes."

"You don't seem too bent out of shape about Brother Luke. I guess it's probably good to keep a level head when there's nothing you can do." He continued to eye me with interest.

"Exactly. If there is something I can do—"

"Well, in fact there is one thing you might help me with. You mind if I take a peek at your bedroom? Abbot said it was down in the cellar under the church."

"Yes. I have a skin condition. I can't take any amount of sunlight. Why do you want to see my cell?" Civility had never come natural to me, and I made little effort to hide my resentment now.

"Oh, just a formality. You know. Got to poke around the whole place."

The sheriff followed me down the dark stairs. When we got to the crypt he stopped to examine the tablets on the walls.

"Well, look at that. This 'un died pert near 100 years ago." He had put on his glasses to read the dates on the middle tablet. "I guess the one down here's the newest dearly departed." He advanced toward my tomb.

"Yes." I stepped forward. "Do you mind if we get this inspection over? I have some work to do."

"'Course, Brother. 'Course. Lead on."

He looked around my cell, under the bed, under the desk. "You mind?" He pointed to the dresser and opened each drawer.

He approached the bed again and my heart stirred. Under the mattress lay the bloody T-shirt. Boring into his mind with my glance, I willed him away from it. He stopped in his tracks, scratched his head as though he'd forgotten what he was doing, and glanced at his clipboard. "Well, that'll do her," he said.

After nosing around in the boiler room and the storage areas, he departed.

Compline was already over, and the monks had retired. I grabbed the bloody T-shirt and tossed it into my tomb. I went out into the night for air, but the humid atmosphere weighed me down as if the ocean itself pressed me to its depths.

CHAPTER TWENTY

After 2,000 years, I found mystery in few things. But Michael proved to be an enigma. After feeling our eyes, our souls connect, speaking without words as we traipsed through the woods, as we crossed the grounds behind the monastery the night I sucked the life from Luke, I expected to see him nightly, to hold secret rendezvous of sweet passion, to lead him away from St. Thomas, ultimately to the Kingdom of Darkness. But I walked the grounds, the woods, alone for more than a week. I saw no sign of him under the September moon.

In chapel he gazed steadily from his breviary to the high altar, as though he conducted telepathic communications with one of the plaster saints in the niches. He knelt when the others knelt, but not meekly with his head bowed. Even as he knelt, his keen eyes bore into some private apparition. I frequently drew his gaze to me with my own bold stare, and for many seconds we would survey one another as though we placidly watched our reflections in a mirror. But he did not linger after prayers, and I did not pursue him.

Until finally I noticed a change in his expression. His contemplation of me across the aisle warmed to desire, and I felt in an instant how much he craved me. That night I found him in the greenhouse, dark except for a lone bulb in the far corner. Outside, branches brushed wistfully against the glass roof. Passing tables of ivy twisting down to the slate floor and row upon row of bright annuals, I found Michael bent over a cart of herbs divided into small white cartons. He wore gym trunks and a tank top. His shoulders and arms were brown from the sun, his hair gathered into a ponytail. He glanced up as I approached, and then continued removing the herbs from their containers and inserting them into trays of dirt.

"You haven't come to me," I said. Humidifiers made the air practically unbearable even though I had changed out of my habit after the sheriff left and slipped into light clothing.

"I needed time." With a small trowel, he loosened a sprig of parsley from its container and planted it in the earth.

"Time? For what? To confirm my desire for you or yours for me?"

"Neither." He glanced up as he continued transplanting the herbs. "A very wise woman once taught me to wait, to listen."

"Listen? To what? To God?" I folded my arms.

"To the night, to the wind, to my fantasies, my nightmares. To spirits, too." He looked up again.

"And what kind of spirits speak to you?" I wasn't sure if he was playing with me.

"All kinds. Evil. Good. Spirits of ages past. Spirits speaking through the pages of books. The old woman, Jana, was my grandmother, my mother's mother, a Creole in New Orleans, where I grew up. She ran a tarot shop in the French Quarter, voodoo dolls on the walls, and crucifixes, altars for saints, candles burning everywhere. She had quite a clientele. Sometimes I sat in the corner while she read their tarot cards."

"Your grandmother raised you?"

"No. My father. A thick-headed Italian drunk. My mother died when I was a baby. But I spoke to her, through Jana. She burned spices at her mausoleum in St. Louis Cemetery."

"You are serious."

He looked up as though surprised I had doubted.

"Come walk with me, in the woods. Tell me about this sorceress grandmother of yours."

"Let me finish these first. I'll meet you on the grounds in half an hour."

Thirty minutes later, he strode up the incline from the buildings, cutting a confident, athletic silhouette in the moonlight. I led the way to a familiar path. When we reached it, I turned to him.

"Not a stickler about the Grand Silence, are you?"

"The Sabbath is made for man, not man for the Sabbath." He stooped to inspect a glittering stone, then hurled it into the trees.

"Tell me more about your adventures in spiritualism." I longed to take him in my arms, but his reserve stopped me.

He shrugged. "What's to tell? I spoke to my mother. I've done it more than once. I've spoken to Jana too, now that she's gone. I learned quite a bit from her."

"Such as?"

"Such as discerning forces at work around me, attuning myself to them." He spoke as though he referred to a power no more unusual than the ability to tell whether the moon was full.

"Forces? You mean evil spirits or some such thing?"

He looked at me with curiosity. "Evil and good."

"Not a very monklike thing, is it? Why enter a monastery if you want to tell fortunes in the French Quarter?"

"Why did I enter? I don't want to bore you with all of that."

I grabbed his arm. "You know nothing you could say would bore me."

"Yes, I know."

"Then tell me."

We had steadily climbed the hillside to the clearing where Luke and I used to come, about 100 meters from where I had disposed of his body. Michael's eyes had adjusted to the dark, and during our walk he'd turned off the flashlight he carried. But now he turned it back on and scanned the clearing.

"What are you looking for?"

"Just a place to sit. Over there." He pointed to the fallen tree.

We sat on the dew-dampened ground, leaning against the tree. Michael folded his legs yoga-style and leaned his head back to view the stars.

"This is my fifth year in these mountains," he said. "The life of a monk has fascinated me since childhood. The ritual, the silence, the solitude. Working with the earth. Poring through volumes on philosophy and mysticism. The sublime chants."

"And celibacy?"

"As a discipline, it has its place. It strengthens the soul."

"For what purpose? To overcome evil, I suppose."

He smiled at my cynical tone. "Wasn't it idealism that brought you to the monastery?"

"No. It was anger. Survival, too, and power."

He registered the passion in my words but made no response, only turning his eyes back to the sky. "I used to think I had to fight evil. But Jana corrected me. Evil, she said, lurks everywhere, even in your own soul—especially there. Never underestimate it. Don't pretend to banish it. Respect it. Listen to it, and even evil will speak to you."

"Don't tell me you have a closet full of voodoo dolls."

Michael laughed and slapped my leg.

I grasped his hand, shoved him gently to the ground, and, lying over him, kissed him. The heat of desire flashed through my veins. His heart pounded too, through his meaty chest. I felt him stiffen against my loins. So much blood, so close to my thirsty soul, pumping so mightily, like the raging waters behind a dam.

"No, not now," he said.

"I want you."

"Not now!" He pushed me off him.

I was furious. I wanted to shout, *Do you know who I am?* The words echoed through my head, discipline alone restraining my tongue from speaking them.

But Michael's eyes told me he knew what I was thinking anyway. And his unspoken response, as clear and firm as his own voice, sounded in my brain: "The link between body and soul—it confuses me, Victor. I'm learning."

CHAPTER TWENTY-ONE

A utumn came and vanished, the oak tree in the courtyard surrendering its last leaves in mid-November when, by day, I knew, the sky grew ashen and more intrusive through the naked branches of the woods. With the passing months fire raged through my veins and my spirit marched toward the trophy I'd coveted for two millennia: life with an eternal comrade.

I met Michael every night, and while the others wasted their hours in mortal sleep, we trod the woods under skies moonlit or black. We discussed occult and mystical volumes in the shadows of the library's stacks, and embraced in the humid jungle of the greenhouse.

Yet both of us guarded our secrets: I, my predatory and preternatural nature; he, the reason for his caution, his reluctance to yield his body to me despite the passion he could not hide.

I longed to take him, wholly, lustfully, his soul along with his body. But a companion worthy of me must surrender freely. His strength, his mysterious mind, raised him higher and higher in my estimation. Still, as the energy between our souls intensified like the friction of pistons in an engine, my restraint threatened to explode.

In the meantime, after our nocturnal rendezvous, I continued to feed on undesirables in the city—prostitutes, vagrants, drug addicts holed up in condemned shacks. Driven by my desire for Michael, I tore at jugulars with a fury, lapped up warm blood from full breasts, sated myself to the point of drunkenness on a slew of victims in one night. The headlines of the newspaper flashed my rampages to the whole city—terrified though I had restricted my prey to undesirables. The police had established that the murders took place between midnight and dawn. They kept surveillance not only in the red light district and the projects, but in the other urban neighborhoods, where half their fleet of cars patrolled the streets through the night.

The vast number of murders brought in federal agents to investigate—not only the killings in the city, but those in the mountains too. The whole cursed area, yet again in my long life, became the notorious central subject of the local and also wider-ranging media. I knew as technology advanced investigators could easily trace my path of destruction across the globe. It was only a matter of time before they linked the blood feasts in Knoxville with those in the English village I'd escaped.

A group of monks gathered around the television one night to watch a national report on the massacres.

The expressionless newscaster, unnaturally tan, peered into the camera. "Federal agents still search for leads in what has now become an international crime. Scotland Yard believes a cult could be at work in the killings, most of which involved the draining of the victim's blood, usually through the jugular vein, vampire-style. In fact, U.S. investigators believe a satanic cult steeped in vampire lore is behind the massacres. We interviewed FBI Director Walter Searling today in Washington."

Here the camera flashed to a hallway in the FBI building. A lanky blond reporter held a microphone in front of the neat, mustachioed director.

"We have followed the pattern of killings," he said, "and we're certain that a series of murders in Boyshire, England, were committed by the same group as those in Knoxville. We've been working closely with Scotland Yard, and we are certain we will find the perpetrators."

"So you're certain that a group of people are responsible for the crimes?" The reporter took the microphone away from the director's lips just long enough to ask her question.

"No, we are not, although it would be more feasible considering the widespread nature of the killings. We might be trailing someone like the Boston Strangler or Jack the Ripper, but psychologists tell us that serial killers usually restrict themselves to specific geographical areas."

"What about Ted Bundy?"

"There are always exceptions. We're considering the possibility that one person is acting alone, but it's most likely a group."

"Any clues at all about the identity of the killer or killers?"

"We're putting together a profile of the perpetrators. It's just a matter of time. In the meantime, local police have increased surveillance in the Knoxville area."

Following the interview several residents of Knoxville recounted to another reporter the grisly scenes I'd left behind. The brothers leaned forward on their chairs or shook their heads.

"What a god-awful thing." Brother Raymond took a drink from a bottle of beer and wiped his lips.

"They shouldn't show this gruesome stuff on television." Brother Herbert, a big-jowled professor on sabbatical from a university in Europe, frowned as the camera panned across a bloody bed.

The others sighed and moaned, and for the rest of the social hour the killings formed the topic of conversations around the coffee table and the bar. Michael had watched the news program intensely, but I saw nothing in his expression suggesting he suspected the truth.

How long, I wondered, until the investigators found monasteries at the center of both massacres? How long before they came to hunt me down in the crypt of St. Thomas?

The moment was ripe for claiming a place in the Dark Kingdom. Once I'd secured my consort, I could leave the detestable life of feedings and tombs and flights from those who hunted me.

The silence of Joshu over the summer and autumn months went unbroken, a sign that I had finally found his replacement. But though no visions of Joshu visited me, other apparitions did. Often, as I slumbered in the dank mausoleum, Tiresia's eyes, full of malice and sensuality, teased me in my dreams. "What are you waiting for, Victor?" she would say. "Your world awaits you. The time has come." Her ebony limbs and breasts cut a silhouette into a full white moon. A sleek mare galloped across the sky and Tiresia's creator and consort, a barrel-chested, hairy soldier, dismounted and wrapped her in his embrace.

Horrible apparitions haunted me too, apparitions of Luke. As I slept in the coffin or became entranced by a demonic book, he would moan and call my name from the woods. His voice would come closer and closer and finally he would stand naked before me, the gash in his throat oozing blood that streamed down his pallid chest. His listless eyes would fall on me and, panting for air, he would speak:

"Let me be your consort, Victor. Take me from this hell."

"What hell?" I would demand.

"It's cold here. Like ice, Victor, like ice. I'm freezing." He would futilely rub his arms. "Take me up."

"You've passed to another world. It's too late. Go back, damn you."

During the vision I would will Luke to vanish, the way the dreamer tries to alter a nightmare just as the demon's hand reaches for him, but my mind had no effect. Plaintive Luke remained, gasping for air, repeating his speech, until I reached out to kill him once again, when he would bare his teeth at me and fade into nothing.

Michael, on the other hand, appeared to enjoy more comforting visits from the supernatural world. When he'd first told me of Jana and his dabblings in spiritualism, I was amused. Not that I doubted the communications he received: Every human has a sixth sense, as they say, though in most it goes undiscovered or ignored. However, the magnitude of his experiences and the identity of his visitor roused my interest and envy.

The first time I witnessed his ecstatic seizure was a December night during Advent, when purple cloths draped the altar and pulpit. When Michael failed to show up in the crypt at the appointed hour, I searched for him and found him in the dark chapel, kneeling before the crucifix on the high altar, completely naked, his hands stretched out as though he were crucified. Light from the vigil lamp suspended by a chain near the tabernacle cast a red glow across his face.

"Michael, what are you doing?"

I touched his shoulder but he gave no sign of recognizing me. His eyes, like the eyes of a corpse, stared ahead as though they focused on nothing at all. His body was as cold as a corpse, too. Giving up my attempt to shake him from this reverie, I sat on the sanctuary steps to observe him and, if I could, to enter into his strange communion with the world beyond.

For a quarter of an hour his muscular arms stayed frozen in place, his body as immobile as the statues above him. Then, as though riding a mighty jet of air, he rose, locked into the same position, until he was level with the crucifix mounted on the gabled apex of the reredos.

Then he chanted over and over "O Crux, ave spes unica," words from a hymn I particularly despised—the damned "placing hope in the cross." His clear voice reached a crescendo and then faded. Finally he struck his breast and muttered, "Eripe me, Domine, ab homine malo." *Who was the evil man he sought refuge from?* I wondered. *I who could give him what heaven only pretended to give?*

Suddenly the pallor of the marble corpus of the crucifix melted away like a coat of paint, revealing the brown flesh, the true features of Joshu himself.

"Joshu!" I yelled, jumping to my feet. Levitating myself to the pair floating near the vaulted ceiling, I tried to grasp first Joshu, then Michael, but what seemed to be a wall of glass prevented me from making contact. I remained a spectator.

Now Michael's body relaxed and spun around toward me. His cock was erect. He licked his lips and sensuously caressed his chest. Joshu approached him and, flinging his arms around his waist, kissed his neck. In that moment I thought I beheld twin Joshus, their sinewy bodies, their strong features and dark coloring were so alike. Michael panted, Joshu's hands remaining fixed around him, and he finally moaned as though climaxing. But though his cock remained stiffened by the blood of passion, nothing spewed forth at the moment of orgasm.

Joshu released him and resumed his place on the reredos.

"No, Joshu!" I cried. "Come back, damn you!"

His placid face showed no sign of hearing my demand. The human color faded from his flesh and he solidified once again into the corpus that resembled a pious artist's fantasy, not the man who smelled of Hebrew wine and spices, of labor's musky sweat, of the desert and the sea.

Michael floated back to the sanctuary and landed in a heap near his crumpled habit. Descending to him, I crouched to touch his forehead, before like ice, now burning with fever. Unconscious and trembling, he moaned and called out Joshu's name. I scooped his naked body in my arms, along with his clothes, and carried him to his cell by way of the corridor along the library, a safer route than past the abbot's rooms. I lay him upon his narrow bed and, checking the dark corridor before closing the door, rinsed a washcloth with cool water from the basin in the corner and mopped his face and neck.

For more than an hour I sat next to his bed in the darkness, bathing his flesh, until finally the fever broke and his limbs calmed. Color filled his wan face again, as it had the marble cheeks of Joshu's corpus, and he breathed quietly in a sound sleep. Near dawn, while I sat lost in thought, his eyes opened and he turned his face toward me.

"Victor? Is that you?"

I leaned over and touched his cheek.

"Did I ... was there an apparition? Where did you find me?"

"In the chapel. Raving like a lunatic. Do you remember what you saw?"

He shook his head and kissed my hand.

"What do the others think of your raptures?"

"No one knows. Not now. Luke did. He found me a couple of times, outside, near the woods. I told him it was epilepsy."

"Maybe it is."

"You know it's not. You know." He gazed at me admiringly.

"Victor ..." He brushed my arm with his lips.

I crawled into the bed next to him and found his lips, heated now but not with fever. His kiss stirred my desire for him, the desire I'd struggled to restrain until his will moved, until now, when its motion surged like a flooded stream. I stripped off my clothes and into that stream cast my soul, taking him in my arms, kissing his neck, his chest, taking in my mouth his engorged cock as though I were a hungry infant at the breast.

When he moaned in pleasure, his chest rising and falling, not with the regularity I had seen in the weight room but with urgency and a quickening, erratic rhythm, with an abandonment of predictability and control, I entered him. The warm passage expanded without a hint of resistance, as though my full cock belonged there, wrapped in the warm, bloody membrane. I drilled into that blood, pumped seconds ago from the excited heart of my beloved. I felt the blood there, and smelled blood on his lips. I felt blood coursing through his every vein and artery, bearing in its red tide his very soul—to me, to me. I longed for the blood, longed to drink of that soul. My fangs, now extended to their full length, sought it, but as the spasms of consummation shook his sweaty body, I turned my head away. He must be my lover, not my victim.

Part Six

THE PROPOSAL

CHAPTER TWENTY-TWO

On Christmas, fresh snow piled three inches on the branches and drifted against the stone walls on the east side of St. Thomas. Irrationally or not, I breathed more easily, thinking that by shrouding the ground, the snow would trap the ghost of Luke, who continued to haunt me. But it was no use. As dried as it now was, I could smell Luke's blood on the shirt I'd deposited in my tomb. Destroying it or burying it in the woods was out of the question now that federal agents were searching the area with renewed vigor. News reports only speculated as to why the agents had returned to the woods above the monastery, since the director would reveal nothing about the agency's motives. I knew it was because they needed Luke's body to link the crimes to St. Thomas. Even someone without my keen perceptions would sense the sheriff had suspected me, and the drill I was subjected to by one of the agents only confirmed this impression.

"Now, Brother Victor," he said, sitting behind the abbot's desk with a pad and an expensive fountain pen. "How would you classify your relationship with Brother Luke?" His arrogant manner heightened his attractiveness. He had a boyish face but a stocky, well-built frame. His collar fit tight around his thick neck.

"I've been over this with the sheriff." I stared straight into his eyes, but he betrayed no intimidation.

"Formality, Brother. When we need to go over the same ground, we do. Right now, I need for you to answer me."

"We were friends." I crossed my legs and tried to keep myself calm. "He was young, looking for a mentor. I was the mentor."

"Just a mentor?"

"What are you asking?"

"Are you a homosexual, Brother?" His eyes remained leveled with mine. The agency had chosen well when they hired this cold, direct official.

"No."

"I've heard different."

"So? It's not true. I'm a monk. Celibate, Mr. Andrews. What kind of a monastery do you think we have here?"

He recapped his fountain pen. "That's the exact question we're working on, Brother. When we piece it together, you'll be the first to know."

I left him in the office when he'd finished his interrogation. Which of the monks had reported my unnatural liaison with Luke, I wondered. The pathetic abbot? One of the head-in-the-clouds scholars who'd for once noticed something outside his own esoteric world? It didn't matter. Even if I did covet my monastic refuge, I never sought to please my foolish companions. No witch-hunts would be held within the sacred walls now anyway, no matter who in the monastery observed my movements. Creating a scandal in the world without could injure the reputation of the order, could result in the abbot's demotion. Perhaps the arrogant agent himself had surmised the truth. So be it. My time was coming.

A freak blizzard stopped the FBI's search for a whole day. That night, the wind howling in my ears, I sped through the air to the spot where I'd buried Luke's remains. A downed tree sank into the ravine where I'd dug a grave with one hand while I lifted the trunk with the other. Snow filled the entire ditch and camouflaged even the tree itself beneath a drift.

I'd no choice now. If the agents discovered Luke's remains, I'd have to flee, and flee without Michael. The time was close. Between us, close as the dawn, lay the pact, itself a dawn whose bright rays even I could bask in.

The icy flakes coated my brows, my hair by now. The cold stung my hands as I clawed beneath the tree, which I'd shifted with some difficulty, laden as it was with snow. Blinking in the storm, I kept an eye out for ambitious FBI interlopers while my hand groped for the remnants of my prey. I felt a shock of brittle hair, then pulled up Luke's skull, skinless now after all these months, and dropped it into the garbage bag I'd brought with me. His habit, his loose bones, his shoes came next, all embedded in the frozen earth, which seemed to tighten its grip the more I dug and pulled. But at last I had every scrap of him. I replaced the tree, scooped snow back into the ravine, and, pitting myself against the storm, flew back to the monastery.

Nightmares or not, the skeleton could be concealed in only one place: the mausoleum. The stream was frozen and would be dragged when it thawed—soon, given the usually mild Tennessee winters. Transporting the bones to another location, to a farm or beyond the city, involved the risk of being seen. Besides, I believed the key to conquering my nightmares was to face the ghost who haunted me. What had I to fear from a cluster of bones, I who had slept in the midst of bones for 2,000 years?

I trod quietly through the dark entryway with my treasure and stole down the stone stairs to the crypt. The mausoleum's gate whined as I opened it. I ducked into the tomb and jerked the lid from one of the vaults. On the neat skeleton of a monk, clad in the tatters of his habit, I dumped the new, jumbled bones and the habit and shoes of a youth who, if not for his idiocy, would still live.

When day arrived I slept like a baby.

CHAPTER TWENTY-THREE

Twice more I witnessed Michael's strange seizures. The first time, he repeated his conference with the transformed marble corpus of Joshu, chanting the same hymn, muttering the same Latin injunction about an evil man. Again I carried him to his cell and we made passionate love. The second fit overcame him in the woods in early February, after the agents had given up their futile search for Luke's remains. The snow had long ago melted. In the prematurely balmy air we were hiking along the path through the woods when Michael launched into a sprint. At first I thought he was playing.

"Just try to get away!" I called after him.

Waiting until he had disappeared beyond a slope, I flew at the speed of my thoughts, arriving at a place where the path divided, part of it disappearing into the trees and winding around an abandoned shack. After standing against an oak for a good time, I called to him.

"Is this a challenge? All right then, I accept." I laughed, believing he hid from me in the woods.

But as I tramped up the hill, a light caught my eye, fire blazing through the trees. I found him, a glimmering cloak draped around his naked shoulders, his eyes raised to a limb where an old woman rested. A turban like the headdresses worn by American slaves wrapped her small, dark head. A large, bold print splashed her robe with purple and green, visible to me despite the darkness.

"This is Jana, Victor." Michael threw his arm around me.

His eyes were glazed, as though he spoke in his sleep.

"Yes." I studied the shriveled hag.

"We meet at last, good Victor," she said. "The World of Darkness bids you greetings." She spoke with a heavy accent—Creole, I assumed. Her eyes were full of mischief.

"The Dark Kingdom? You reside there?"

"I reside nowhere. I flit about in the darkness."

"What kind of apparition are you?" I asked, doubtful.

"One conjured by this one." She glanced at Michael, who continued looking on in a daze.

"Ah, only a shadow then," I said.

"A projection of the shadow within Michael's own soul. He would know evil."

"For what purpose?"

"To reckon with it, to understand its power."

I laughed. "Understand it? Vanish, hag, there's nothing you can teach."

Her eyes returned to Michael. "Witness the power of evil, boy." She faded to a transparent image and then vanished altogether.

Michael collapsed. The cloak had disappeared along with the apparition, leaving him naked. His body could have been a corpse, it was so cold. I dressed him and lay with him near the fallen tree until he opened his eyes and inhaled deeply the balmy air, spiced with the clean scent of firs.

"It's very dark, Victor."

"Yes." I stroked his hair. "I've learned to love the night. With my illness, I have no choice. Do you remember your apparition?"

He shook his head. "Something sad. That's all I know."

After he regained his sense of orientation, we relaxed together against the fallen tree, and I asked him about his mystical experiences.

He stared thoughtfully toward the stars. "I'm not sure what to say. I've had them ever since I can remember. I know when they come. I wake up naked and confused. Sometimes I remember the content exactly. Sometimes it's just a feeling of doom or lightness, depending."

"What about this time?" I said, grasping his hand. "What did you feel?"

He shrugged. "Fear."

"Of what?"

"I don't know. Who can make sense of dreams?"

"But you take these spells to heart." I paused. "Do you fear me?"

"You asked me that before. In the weight room. Should I fear you, Victor?"

"No, I would never harm you. In fact, what I want ..."

I turned my head to consider whether the moment was ripe for opening the door, at least an inch. "What I want is to give you something."

"What?" His dark eyes gazed at me intensely.

I released his hand and got up. I paced for a few moments with my hands behind my back and then I faced him. He had drawn up his legs to hug his knees.

"I want you to think of an image."

"An image?"

"Anything, a broom, a car, anything. Only focus on it as though you were projecting it on a screen in your mind. Go ahead."

Michael closed his eyes. Within seconds of concentrating on his thoughts, the image of a skull reproduced itself in my mind.

"Why a skull?" I demanded.

"You see it?" Michael opened his eyes in surprise.

"No." I sat down next to him. "Close your eyes again. Imagine the skull. That's right. Now watch." I once again directed my will to Michael's mind, where blood now streamed from the skull's eyes. "See the blood?"

"Yes."

"Keep focused on it. Move toward it. Do you feel it?"

His breathing grew more rapid. "Yes," he said, excitedly.

"Feel it. Feel the power, the strength. Feel the lust, the hunger."

"Yes."

I shook him at the height of his pleasure and he opened his eyes, still panting.

"I want to give you this passion as often as you want."

The pleasure vanished from his face and he glared at me in indignation. "How is it yours to give, Victor?"

"I can't tell you now."

"You can't tell me?" He jerked his hand away from me and stood. "You ask me about intimate visions, but you can't tell me how you get inside my head?"

I climbed to my feet and faced him. "Don't push me. Strong chains are forged slowly. Like the bond between us."

"You think I withhold secrets from you?"

"You've no reason to." I grabbed his arm when he shook his head in exasperation and started to walk away. "Wait, please. I have a long past, Michael. You've got to let me unfold it slowly. You've got to trust me. You're the one who believes in waiting, remember?"

He gazed steadily into my eyes as though he were trying to read my thoughts. Then he relaxed in resignation. "All right, Victor. I'll leave it to you."

He remained true to his word, his discipline taking over when his pride reared its head, no small feat since his ego matched my own. It was my own impatience that worried me. I burned for our consummation; had I followed my impulses, I would have revealed everything in an instant, but at the risk of taxing even Michael's courage to hear the truth. A gradual disclosure alone would ensure our future.

One night in the library's reading room, as we pored over so-called "apocryphal" volumes on the life of Joshu, Michael went to retrieve another book from the stacks. When he arrived at the fifth level, reached only by the flights of narrow stairs he'd climbed, I was waiting for him there, having willed myself to the spot. His gaze absorbed the significance of the accomplishment, but without a word he walked to the shelves for his book.

At other times I heaved a fallen tree from the forest path or crushed a stone into powder. In the refectory one night, I caught his eye during the reading and made a sign for him to watch while my eyes seared into the mind of fat Brother Athanasius as he read from the Lives of the Saints. Suddenly confused, Athanasius stopped and returned to the beginning of the passage. After he stopped and started twice more at my prompting, the abbot motioned for him to take a seat.

Michael registered my powers with gravity, but stayed true to his promise, demanding no explanation.

One night during Lent I decided to broach the subject of the Kingdom of Darkness. Michael had spent the day spreading mulch around trees on the property and we inspected the hedges near the buildings to determine how much more was needed. When we returned to my cell, he sprawled out on the bed, exhausted. I straddled the desk chair, facing him. The tired lines around his eyes showed up even in the soft lamplight. We chatted awhile about trivial matters, and after a long pause in the conversation I spoke.

"What do you think heaven is like?"

"It's 3 in the morning, Victor. I'm not in the mood for a catechism lesson."

"This isn't catechism."

The seriousness of my tone got his attention. He rolled over and propped his head on his hand. "Go on."

"I think people are goaded toward it by some strange lofty ideas. Blessed union with the creator. Eternal blessedness. What is that?"

"What happens in eternity is anybody's guess."

"Guessing's not the problem. It's spelled out by Scriptures. The Book of Revelation paints a nice picture—the masses kneeling at the throne of God, singing, praising. For eternity. Frozen forever on their knees. Sounds like hell to me."

"What about Dante? Paradise is contemplating God, according to him."

"Contemplation be damned. We're made for action, life, movement, pleasure." I pounded the back of the chair with my fist.

"From the way Dante describes hell, I don't think we'll find much pleasure there." He yawned.

"What if there were another option, Michael?" I got up and sat next to him on the bed, my elbows on my knees. "What if you could spend eternity laughing, making love, feasting, living like a god yourself?"

He rolled onto his back and clasped his hands behind his head. "That's what Lucifer was after, if I remember the story."

I shook my head. "Lucifer wanted to rule the same damned heaven. He lost the war, that's all."

"What are you saying? A third realm exists? We've all been brainwashed into being good so we can go to heaven?"

"It's true. The Dark Kingdom is a place for the elect, bold souls. A realm of gods." I paused. "It's the source of my powers. I can give you a glimpse of it."

The adrenaline pumped through him now. His eyes were keen, every nerve of his body ready to receive. But I had said enough for the time being.

"Stay patient," I said. "I'll show you everything soon." I kissed him good night and asked him to leave, despite his curiosity.

How did I know I could enter the Kingdom of Darkness? It was like an animal's instinct to mate, latent until the right moment, when it flared into the single impulse of its existence. My movements in the night, despite centuries of my own ignorance, had not been directionless, I now sensed. My mating dance had begun—the time to carry my prospective consort across the boundary of darkness for a taste of what awaited him once he served his term as a nocturnal predator.

After he left I rushed so rapidly through the night that my cheeks stung and my ears rang when I lighted on a dark Knoxville street to feed. Ravenous, I forced myself to move with caution since the police still patrolled the streets. Sweet, rich blood hung in the March air, so much that for a moment I felt disoriented, as though pulled in a hundred directions. "Focus, focus," I urged myself, and when I obeyed my own command the route to take traced itself in my mind, as vivid and red as the blood I sought.

A porch wrapped around a modest frame house, meticulously painted and adorned with shutters and lacy trim along the gable. I scanned the rest of the houses in the quiet cul-de-sac. Every window was dark. Still, to play it safe, I walked around back and through the gate of a picket fence. A decal on the back door announced "Proud to Be a Vietnam Vet" over an unfurled American flag. I pulled the knob of the locked door slowly and as quietly as possible until the bolt tore through the door frame.

The snug kitchen smelled of bay leaves. In the living room, afghans draped sagging armchairs. From a photo above the antiquated television gazed a shiny-faced young man in a dress Marine jacket and white cap. The boards squeaked under my step as I followed a scent down a hallway. I paused, listened. Someone turned in a bed and sighed.

The first door I came to was slightly ajar. I crept in toward a large four-poster bed in the center of the room, where I could discern a woman's weathered face. Snatching her robe from the foot of the bed, I pressed it over her mouth. Her eyes opened; she struggled and moaned; her flailing arm knocked a glass to the floor.

"Mama! You all right?" The man's voice came from the adjacent room.

I twisted the old woman's neck until it snapped, and hid behind the door as the hall light came on.

"You OK, Mama?"

When no response came from the bed, a man in a wheelchair rolled into the room, his long ponytail jiggling as he worked the wheels. "Mama?"

Before he could discover my deed, I grabbed his shoulders and plunged my fangs into his bearded throat. He clutched my hair as blood spurted from his jugular until he lost consciousness. I drank greedily for almost ten minutes, emptying every vein of his tobacco-laced blood.

After feeding, I surveyed the scene before me: one body slumped over in the wheelchair, the other still staring toward the door, arms stretched out like a cross. "Soon, now," I said to myself. "Soon I will stop creeping in the night, desperate for prey."

I sped back to the edge of the woods and walked across the grounds to the monastery. As I came around to the front of the building, I caught a glimpse of a white car disappearing down the drive without its lights. I was sure it stopped behind a cluster of trees, but with dawn only half an hour away I couldn't investigate.

My sleep was fitful. I dreamed that blood gushed again from my victim's throat, but every time I stooped to drink from the red jet, it ceased. When I sucked the musty, hairy throat, it yielded nothing. Thirst maddened me. I stalked victim after victim, but each time I caught my prey it turned into a half-familiar corpse I had drained long ago.

The scene changed then. A golden throne rose from the midst of four six-winged creatures bulging with eyes in front and back. In the throne glowed a translucent figure whose crown of jasper and carnelian seemed an extension of the throne itself. The ruler lifted a scroll, the creatures fell to their knees, a man approached. In a white robe, his skin now alabaster, his hair like bleached fleece, the man accepted the scroll.

"Joshu!" I screamed from the midst of a throng of people. But he did not hear.

"Worthy is the lamb that was slain!" The crowd chanted.

"Damn you, Joshu!" I screamed, immobilized by the bodies pressing around me. "Damn you then! Rehearse your coronation for eternity. I will live!"

Chapter Twenty-four

The night after I'd preyed on the crippled man, Michael approached me after vespers and said to meet him in the weight room during the recreation period. When I asked why it couldn't wait until our usual meeting time in my cell he shook his head gravely and whispered, "We can't. I'll explain."

"Shut the door," he said, straining to lift a bar loaded with weights.

"They'll be suspicious." I nodded to the locker room, where several of the monks were undressing.

"Close it, damnit!" The biceps of his fully extended arms swelled under the weight. Sweat plastered the hair on his naked chest and abdomen. "Take this."

I placed the barbell on its rest and sat on a plastic chair, scuffed from use. Michael sat up and wiped his face with a white towel. I could smell the bleach in it, used heavily by the pathetic monk who did the laundry.

"The federal agent talked to me today." Michael spoke in a hushed voice despite the private room.

"Andrews?"

"Yes. He had all kinds of questions about you, and about the two of us."

"Why should he care about two homosexual monks? Isn't finding a serial killer enough for him?" Nonchalant, I hoisted my feet up on the other bench.

"It's got something to do with finding Luke. He apparently knows about your relationship with him."

"Yes, he asked me about it."

"He wanted to know if there was anything unusual about you."

"Unusual? In what way?"

Michael shrugged. "Seems like he wanted to know if you indulge in some form of sadism. He seems to suspect you."

"Of scaring Luke away from the monastery? I know that. Good agent Andrews made that clear in our chat."

"It's more than that." Michael scooted down the bench, closer to me. He leaned over on his knees. "This is incredible, but I think he suspects you of killing Luke."

"What!"

"He made me show him my arms and back to prove you'd never abused me. He asked about your weird ideas, about your occult beliefs. Victor, I think he bugged your cell. That's why I wanted to talk here."

My face and manner remained calm, while fury welled in me like electricity in a stormy sky ready to burst forth in lightning. The news confirmed my fears about the car I'd seen slip behind the trees. Michael and I were under surveillance.

"Victor, I want the truth." Michael's eyes were unflinching in their intensity. "Did you hurt Luke more than emotionally?"

"Why don't you ask your real question?" I shouted. "Did I kill Luke and cut him up in pieces? You think I'm the killer stalking the woods?"

Michael remained unintimidated by my rage. "I don't think anything. I only want to hear from your own lips that you didn't harm Luke."

I glared at him. "I thought you loved me. Do you?"

"Yes, God help me. But I understand you, the extremes of your passions. You're capable of anything. That's what drew me to you. And your strength."

I broke into a laugh. "I see what this is all about. I've always known it. You got Luke out of your way, just to have me for yourself. Now you have qualms of conscience. That's very unbecoming of you, Michael. I thought you were above petty scrupulosity."

My words hit my mark, as I knew they would. He calmly studied me. "I'm not above shame."

"Relax, Michael." I slapped his arm. "I'm not a psychopath. Unless my own life were at stake, I wouldn't waste my time killing anyone."

Brooding, Michael stood, pulled on his T-shirt, and opened the door.

I laughed again.

"What?" he said, irritated.

"You look like Judas Iscariot."

He dismissed me with a glance and walked out.

"It's not worth hanging yourself over," I shouted after him and broke into a fit of laughter.

Back in my cell, I turned over the bed and pulled the books from their shelves in search of the listening device. I stood on a chair to inspect the painted pipe that ran the length of the ceiling and rummaged through the desk drawers. I was just about to fling the crucifix down after searching the back of it when I noticed the tiny case behind the bent knees of the corpus.

The irony of my enemy's means of spying did not escape me. Not only had Joshu fled from me, but his image assisted my would-be captors.

In that moment I craved the blood of the arrogant agent, who even now listened to my excited breathing. My fangs shot forth in anticipation as I stormed up the crypt stairs and down the winding drive. The white sedan was exactly where I expected it to be. In wrinkled starched shirts, Andrews and another agent got out of the car when they saw me approaching, both with their hands near the guns on their hips.

"Evening, Brother Victor. Can we help you with something?" Andrews had been eating a sandwich. He dabbed his lips with a handkerchief.

Andrew's partner was 40ish and balding, but a large, well-built man. I could have lunged at them in an instant, their blood titillated me so.

"You've invaded my privacy, Mr. Andrews." I held out the recorder, then hurled it off into the trees. "If you want excitement, go get yourselves fucked."

"Something right up your alley, isn't it, Brother?" Andrews sneered at me.

His neck, rising firm and thick from his loosened collar, beckoned to me in that moment. My fangs, which had retracted, inched forward again, and only through enormous concentration could I control their growth. As I turned to avoid any more temptation, Andrews called me back.

"Where are you from, Brother Victor?" He emphasized the word "Brother" in a mocking tone.

I stopped and faced him.

"You think you'll hide your tracks long?" He leaned against the car now. The other agent had relaxed too.

"The abbot has my records. I'm sure you've already seen them."

"Records from a monastery that no longer exists? A letter from a dead abbot?"

I smiled at the cockiness behind his transparent ploy to goad me into desperation now that the FBI was on my trail. I swore to myself that I would have that man eventually, then retraced my steps to the monastery.

The next day the evening news covered my most recent slayings, neighbors only that day having discovered the bodies of the crippled man and his mother. Cameras scanned the scene, the empty bed and wheelchair, the bodies being carried out in black bags. The elderly couple who had found the corpses explained that when the son hadn't emerged for his usual spins around the block, they'd knocked on the door. That failing, they'd tried without luck to reach him by phone. Then, finding the broken door in back, they ventured in.

At this point the old woman, wearing a sweatshirt stamped with the words "Proud to be a Grandma," broke into tears. "Oh, sweet Jesus! I never seen such a thing in my life."

Her husband, pushing up a pair of thick glasses, wrapped his arm around her.

The lanky blond reporter asked him how long they had known the victims.

The old man shook his head. "Mr. and Mrs. Sanders lived here when we bought the house back in '48. Jimmy came along a couple years later. Always playing soldier out in the yard here. A good boy. Took care of his mama after his daddy died." The man was too choked up to go on.

The maudlin curiosity of the monks annoyed me, and I had no desire to watch the rest of the coverage. But to leave now, with the abbot entertaining fears about me because of the FBI's probings, would have drawn unnecessary attention to myself.

A shot of the man's Marine photograph flashed on the screen, followed by an interview of a Paris Island officer, who attested to the soldier's dedication in boot camp and then in Vietnam, where an exploding land mine left him a paraplegic.

When the reporter interviewed Andrews, I swore he was looking directly at me.

"Yes, we are following some leads," he said in response to the reporter's question. He wore a navy-blue suit and a tie with neat rows of print—straight and controlled. "But we are not at liberty to discuss our suspects. We want to assure the community that we are doing everything within our power to get this fiend."

"Is it true, Lieutenant Andrews, that the blood was drained from these victims? That the killer is a member of a vampire cult?"

"We are not at liberty to discuss details of the investigation." Andrews's boyish face remained expressionless, his tone official.

"Could you tell us anything about the monk from St. Thomas Monastery, Brother Luke McMahan? A missing person's report has been filed with the police. Do you suspect foul play in this case?" The eager reporter tucked her straight hair behind her ear.

Andrews started looking impatient now. "The local police are handling that case. There is no evidence of foul play at this point."

The subject stirred the monks to comment and sigh and chat over their cocktails. Two younger monks appeared to take out their frustration over Luke on a ping-pong ball, which they knocked mercilessly back and forth across the net. Michael glanced at me from the open window, where he'd been musing over an illuminated fountain of John the Baptist in the Jordan.

I wanted air. Before evening prayer I strolled out to the courtyard. Daffodils had already bloomed and hedges of forsythia clustered around the oak, which had started to bud. I sat on a stone bench, closed my eyes, and inhaled the cool air stirring the skirts of my habit. No moon glowed, but even so I felt its magnetic power upon my immortal blood and reveled in the vision of the realm ever bathed in its illumination.

This was the last time I'd be forced into a corner, waging battle against human enemies that snapped at me like dogs. I was weary of it. From Jerusalem to Athens to Nampo; from Mozambique to Brindisi in the heel of Italy to the villages of Alsace-Lorraine and the hamlets of England; I'd traveled across the globe for 2,000 years, powerful but hunted, and I was now ready for my eternal reward. This time I would not flee the region, but the mortal sphere itself.

CHAPTER TWENTY-FIVE

Holy Week nauseated me. The scripture readings about Joshu's triumphant entry into Jerusalem (if you call 20 beggars and a handful of religious fanatics fluttering palm branches triumphant); his romanticized last supper with 12 laborers who reeked of fish; him sweating blood in Gethsemane (more palatable than saying he was ready to soil himself from fear). The early Christian movement had spun the whole train of mundane events into a myth surpassing the epic of Aeneas.

But Good Friday revolted me the most. The rituals and readings reveling in the gore dripping from Joshu's face, hands, and feet because with it flowed his life, the prerequisite of redemption; this maudlin sentimentality perverted real passion for the sinewy man, wasting the blood that should have been lapped up as the fuel of orgasm.

Who on this damnable earth, millennia after his death, could lust for the man Joshu?

When I crept from my tomb the night of Good Friday, the chapel above seemed to press like a weight on my back. On their knees, amidst clouds of incense, the monks had observed the sacred hours from noon to 3—when Joshu expired—loading the vaulted space with, for me, a tangible perversion of my love.

Now, tested and watched, I had to ascend and join their desecrating rituals.

Purple cloth swathed every statue in the dimly lit chapel. The tabernacle door stood wide open, the ciborium of communion wafers removed to commemorate Joshu's arrest and removal from Gethsemane. The marble altar had been stripped of its linen.

When evening service began the monks rose, black figures in the shadows. Swinging a censer by its chain, Michael led the procession down the center aisle. His bleached surplice set off his dark brows and hair, his olive complexion. His face showed his absorption in the ritual.

The abbot brought up the rear of the procession, lifting a crucifix that was three feet tall and shrouded in purple.

"Behold the wood of the cross," he chanted, "on which is hung our salvation."

"Come, let us adore," responded the monks, dropping to their knees.

The invocation and refrain were repeated twice more, each time the abbot exposing another arm or leg of the plaster corpus until, upon reaching the sanctuary, he hoisted up a crucifix completely bared.

When the monks filed from the stalls to kiss the feet of the corpus, I fought the impulse to rush forward and crush the plaster figure. When my turn came to genuflect before the cross, while the abbot held it on the sanctuary step, I shot a glance at Michael. He stood by with a linen napkin to wipe the feet after each kiss.

"Yes, Victor," his eyes said to me. Was he directing me to offer the ritual kiss, or was he expressing assent? If so, to what?

I took a breath and brushed my lips against the cold feet. By the time I returned to my stall, I knew the moment had come. Michael must tour the Dark Kingdom.

When he came to my cell just before midnight, I was sitting in the soft illumination of candles burning in all four corners of the room. Michael closed the door softly behind him and glanced around. The bed was stripped, my books packed back in the trunk. The crucifix rose from the wastebasket.

"What's going on, Victor?" Michael wore a black sweatshirt and black jeans, a modernized habit of sorts.

"I want to take you to the place now." I'd tipped back the chair to rest my feet on the bed.

"The Dark Kingdom?" Michael leaned against the desk. "Why now?"

"It's the right moment. Will you go?"

He paused and studied the wall. "Strange. I feel exactly the way I did the day I entered the monastery. A step into the unknown."

"Very appropriate." I lowered my feet and leaned forward to take his hands in mine. "Believe me, once you see it, your life will change. Immortality will mean something. Not pious garbage about eternal peace. You weren't made for peace and neither was I. Our souls are strong, violent, passionate."

"And evil?"

"Evil. What does that mean?" The word disgusted me. "Rebellion against the Christian god, who rules with an iron hand, twists souls into his own image and likeness, demands from them unyielding devotion to no one but him? Is that evil? What about black skies scorned by sailors as they approach the rocks, winds that strip a field of grain? Are they evil, or are they simply power? Why moralize about strength and passion?"

"Take me," Michael said in a whisper, his dark eyes willful, excited.

I stood and stripped off my T-shirt and sweatpants. "Come here."

I pulled off his shirt, caressed his exquisite pectorals and biceps. Our heated lips met, our tongues pressing past each other's lips like impatient serpents entering their lairs. Then I pulled him to the bed and directed his mouth to my nipple, as Tiresia had directed me to hers centuries before monks came into being. He sucked, tenderly at first, and then as blood squirted down his throat, greedily, wantonly.

My head spun. I abandoned myself to the movement, which took an upward turn, like the takeoff of a plane, gracefully piercing an ebony sky. Michael's position had changed now. From behind me he hugged my waist, his face against my neck, as I rocketed moonward. He moaned in delight, gasped for air.

When we entered a sea of silver light, our momentum slowed. We floated now, over a wall, over tiled roofs gleaming under the dreamy light.

"It's Rome," I cried. "Rome restored."

Below us the Tiber snaked through the spires and domes, past the round Castel San Angelo, its crenellated tower near the riverbank, where pines swayed in the warm current above the river. Along the water, lovers embraced, their nude bodies perfectly proportional, strong, supple.

The marble facing of the Coliseum, torn away by the invading Visigoths, again covered it like shiny pink armor, and the noble buildings and columns and squares of the Forum were risen from the melancholy rubble. Medieval churches were restored too, their facades shimmering in the moonlight along the narrow streets. Crowds of spectators roared over gladiators in the Circus Maximus, whose sculpted muscles were as beautiful as their movements when they dodged and thrust the sword. And from the Pantheon, the sphere of perfection, haunting mantras to the gods rippled across the Piazza Navona, whose elliptical perimeter enclosed sword-eaters, lute-players, men at game tables, boys splashing through the waters of Bernini's fountain, women laughing with abandon as they inspected jewels on display in canvas-covered booths.

The colossal structures, the marble columns and Egyptian obelisks claimed as battle trophies, the noble shapes and movements of bare human forms, as breathtaking as statues and yet as flexible and rapid as the Tiber as it empties into the Ostian harbor, the eerie light cast on the city and its vital inhabitants by a white moon, round and precious as a giant jewel lying on velvet—all these things lent an awesome sublimity to the world we surveyed as we glided through space.

"Did you know this?" Michael yelled into the wind, panting, sweating against my body. "Did you know it would be like this?"

I shook my head. "It's beyond my wildest dreams."

Laughter caught my ear and when I turned, Tiresia moved through the air next to me, her dark skin spangled with jewels, a crown of rubies and emeralds glittering on her head. "Yes, Victor, it's time. What more could you want?" She stretched her hands, arched her smooth back, and dove down to a courtyard, where she mounted a boy stretched out on the ground and soon convulsed in pleasure as she rode him.

"I've waited centuries for this!" I shouted. "Now, with you, I can take my rightful reward. Laughter, sensuality, beauty, action. Action, Michael, action. For eternity."

He tightened his grip around me as his body trembled spasmodically against mine.

A moment later, we lay entwined once again in my cell, our chests heaving as though we'd run a race and collapsed beyond the finish line.

Part VII

REVELATION

Chapter Twenty-six

Two millennia?" Michael strained to comprehend the length of my history.

"Since the reign of Caesar Augustus, yes."

It was the night following our journey, the first chance to discuss an experience that had exhausted us both. We walked through the woods, where buds swelled on the oaks and maples stretching their arms after winter's dormancy into the sweet air of spring.

For the first time in my nocturnal existence, I unfolded the entire story of my origins, earthly and supernatural—Rome, Jerusalem, Tiresia, the roaming of the world's monasteries and the obsession that took me within their walls until that very moment. My means of nourishment I left for later.

"Joshu," he said. "Because it's closer to the Hebrew." He had listened silently as we hiked, until now.

"I wanted him as much as a soul can want."

"In love with Jesus of Nazareth." Michael mused over the idea. "The Christ."

"That's what history has called him. I knew the boy, the man of flesh and blood. The man who laughed at my crude jokes. The man who raced me across the Jordan. The man with pimples on his back. It's taken me 2,000 years to replace him."

"Incarnation. Incarnation." Michael murmured the word.

"What? What are you talking about?" I grabbed his arm to stop him.

"Nothing. I don't know. This is too much to take in."

Impatient with his musings, I leveled my eyes with his. "The point, Michael, is that you must inherit my existence. Wander here a brief time, then join me in that kingdom we've inspected. That's all that matters. Our eternity together."

"What do you mean inherit your existence?" He seemed to snap out of his contemplation, his eyes now sharp as a lawyer's.

"I mean this." I raised my hands. "The night. To live in the night until it's time to join me."

"Never see the sun again?"

"No. To hell with the sun!" I let go of him and took a few steps away to cool myself before turning back to him. "You want mortality when you can live forever? You'll have the power to take what you want. Anything. Then you'll go on living, really living, for eternity."

"But I wouldn't be mortal here. I'd become ... whatever kind of being you are. Those are the terms?"

"Yes. You would have my powers. You could communicate with me."

"You're not telling me everything."

"What!"

"Everything, Victor." He drew close to me and clasped my arms, his eyes inches from mine. "There's still a closed door. Once again, you expect me to surrender, but you put up a wall. I'll take nothing less than everything, or there's nothing more to discuss."

I pushed him away. "Damn you. You want to know what it's taken me centuries to learn, is that it? A shortcut? I'm telling you, you can't under-stand it all now. Not until you are what I am. I can only promise you a free-dom and power you've never known. Isn't that enough?"

"It's you I want, only you."

I laughed deeply and kissed him hard on the lips.

Over the next week, I made arrangements for Michael's new existence. His affection for New Orleans directed my search for lodgings there, not far from the above-ground tombs of St. Louis Cemetery, where his beloved Jana was buried and where he could easily claim the coffin of a new corpse and a forgotten mausoleum as his sleeping chamber. From a Swiss account, I transferred funds to a local bank in the French Quarter. Over the centuries I'd added to Tiresia's treasure through robbery and investment.

As for monastery life, that was up to Michael. He wouldn't share my initial motive for seeking cloisters, though he was drawn to the secluded life and would find in them companionship of sorts, as I had.

How would he take the life of predator, ripping into throats of children, women, crippled war veterans? He would adjust. Survival was survival, wherever you stood in the food chain. I counted on his supernatural cravings, his philosophical perspective, his passionate nature—these could obliterate mortal sensibility, which focused on the petty, the particular. I counted on his union with my soul to stir a sublime storm whose winds would devastate the oppressive claims of conscience. But for now, he must know nothing of my bloody nourishment. Before its strangulation, his conscience could misguide him, shrinking into a narrow chink his mind's all-encompassing window.

CHAPTER TWENTY-SEVEN

Easter lilies around the altar, the moist, clean smell of the season of love—it was the first time in a monastery that I'd caught the excitement of resurrection. Not Joshu's, which I'd cursed over the centuries, but stirrings, nonetheless, that only he had raised in me before now. A longing deep in my immortal core, echoed by warm wind when it rushed over the mountains and through the pines and maples, by spring rain falling like Chopin's melodies. A longing that promised completion, though it could never be truly completed.

We prolonged the time before my departure, the days before his death and new existence. If centuries should pass before he joined me, we wanted to spend them anticipating a continuation of an interrupted love affair. In balmy air or thunderstorms, under moonlit or raven skies, we haunted the woods together, laughed as we pitched stones at bats spilling from hillside caves, made heated love in abandoned shacks.

One night in early May, Michael challenged me to a race on the footpath where he'd disappeared before. The moon, directly overhead, washed the ground with pale light.

"Don't make me laugh," I said. "What are your chances against me?"

He surveyed me arrogantly. "Let's just see." He pulled off his shirt and deposited a stick on the path. "That's the starting line. Are you ready?"

We positioned ourselves, and at the count of three, shot forward.

At first I held back, giving him a chance to gain ground so I could pass him more impressively. His arms pumped furiously, his feet kicked up high behind him, his dark ponytail bounced.

When he'd covered a good half-mile, I launched forward, speeding past the trees, reaching the apex of the hill in a matter of seconds. But when I got to where Michael should have been, I spotted him in the distance, at a curve in the path. Then he vanished behind the foliage.

Accelerating to my full speed, I gained the bend in seconds and intended to tug his ponytail, but once again he was relentlessly sprinting far ahead of me.

When I reached a rocky ledge, he was sitting on the ground, waiting for me. Winded, I dropped down beside him.

"Is this a trick Jana taught you?" I asked when I'd finally caught my breath.

"How did you guess?" He grinned and leaned back on his elbows. "I've got a surprise for you, another trick. Watch the sky."

The sweep of the wooded gray valley rolling to the horizon was magnificent. The river glinted through the branches. The monastery buildings huddled in a clearing and to the south, a black train threaded in and out of the trees, its lonely whistle piercing the silence.

Suddenly the pale sky brightened, as though the sun rose from the west, just beyond the horizon. "What!" I shot to my feet, ready to fly back to my dark refuge.

"Wait!" Michael grabbed my hand. "It's not real. Come on, sit down and enjoy something you haven't seen in a few centuries."

Light suffused the sky now, a sky bluer and clearer than I had remembered. Birds twittered in the false morning light.

"Now look there." Michael pointed to the eastern sky, where a ball of light blazed, my enemy in all his glory. Heat bathed my face, my arms and hands, as though I were on a beach near Positano rather than a mountainside at midnight.

The flaming sun shrank and the blue sky changed to indigo and then to silver as the moon resumed her post.

"Impressive," I said.

"It's my pledge to you, Victor. I have to admit, no one has ever affected me like you do. I've always been a detached spirit, drawing what I could from every circle I found myself in. I don't want to call it coldness or fear. It's just that I felt satisfied—working with the soil, studying philosophical discourses, drinking in the waters of mysticism. But now," he hesitated, lowering his eyes, "now I breath you like air. You're Patroclus to me."

"So you're Achilles? I like that." I grinned, and then clasped both his hands. "I've waited for this moment, night after night, century after century."

On the rocky ledge, the moon falling to the west, we entwined ourselves more like wrestlers than lovers, heaving, pressing, squeezing, and grunting, more primitive than the animals populating the woods around us. More than once, Michael's lips found my nipple, and each time the ecstasy his mouth brought to me almost numbed me to the danger of letting him drink too much of my blood.

"No," I finally said, each time, pushing his head away. "I'm not ready to leave you yet."

We stayed in the spot until the light of dawn bled into the sky above the mountains. I'd lost track of the time and now every cell in my body was alert to the imminent danger. His head on my chest, Michael had fallen asleep. I shook him.

"We've got to hurry. It's almost dawn." Scooping him up in my arms, I willed us to the monastery grounds. Branches gave way to us, the air formed a vacuum with the velocity of our movement.

As we raced to the entrance, Andrews's white sedan pulled up. He got out and motioned for us to wait for him.

"Go ahead," Michael said. "I'll talk to him."

With no other choice, I hurried to the crypt, my skin stinging from exposure to the predawn radiation.

CHAPTER TWENTY-EIGHT

Because Andrews watched my every move—as he emphasized to Michael the night of the sun show—my feedings required caution, mostly to prevent him from knowing when I left the grounds. I had to initiate my flight from within the courtyard, where I also returned at the end of my hunts. I could give him no grounds for linking me to the crime scenes investigated day after day in a city frozen by fear.

One night in late April, I stole through a poorly lit neighborhood of housing projects in the city. Ducking into shadows whenever a patrol car whirled its searchlight, I sniffed for a large concentration of blood to keep me satisfied for a number of days, reducing the number of risky trips. Just when I caught the scent of a mass of blood in one of the dilapidated apartments, a searchlight shot out from a police car hidden behind a tree in an empty lot. I moaned in pain at the intensity of light, too stunned to move.

"Police! Put your hands up!" an officer shouted from the car.

I couldn't see him for the light, but I heard footsteps and voices on the street. The smell of blood laced with alcohol wafted from his direction. I waited with my hands raised as he'd commanded.

By the time he started frisking me, while his partner pointed his gun at me, my pain had subsided and I was able to concentrate. I had no choice now that they'd seen me. In two moves I'd flung them both to the ground. I'd snapped the neck of the first officer when the second recovered his gun and fired, hitting me in the shoulder. Before he could shoot again I grabbed the gun from him and snapped his neck. Between the two of them, both hefty men, I could drain more than enough blood. But the shot had roused the neighborhood. A siren wailed only streets away.

I reached the opposite end of town in seconds, lighting near a park. A colonial home across the street emitted the sanguinary scent of at least two people. With no time for a more leisurely hunt, I broke into a side door hidden by a trellis and found myself in a richly furnished parlor dominated by a grand piano. Before proceeding to the bedrooms, I sank into a white sofa to rest while I healed. The bullet wound of a vampire closes in minutes, the missile itself disintegrating as soon as it penetrates the skin.

The floor was littered with wrapping paper. Empty drink glasses cluttered the tables. I picked up a greeting card from a stack on the coffee table, wishing Diane and Paul a happy 25th wedding anniversary. I could exhibit mercy, but under the circumstances I needed to feed and flee the city. Once I'd recovered, I crept down a carpeted hallway and up a staircase. The scent of blood swelled as I approached the last door, which was shut. With my ear against the door, I listened to gentle groaning and squeaking springs within. At the moment of climax, I opened the door.

The man's white body covered his wife's. Her legs were wrapped around his. He couldn't make me out in the pitch-black room, though of course I could discern his panicked expression as he glanced toward the door.

"Jimmy? Wait a minute, son." He rolled off his wife and grabbed his robe. She pulled the sheets up.

Now the pungent scent of semen and female secretions joined the smell of blood. My fangs shot forth and I lunged greedily at his throat.

"No!" The woman screamed. Scampering naked from the bed, she bolted out the door. I cut her off at the bottom of the staircase, where I had willed myself.

"Please!" she sobbed, dropping to her knees. "Oh, God, please!"

Although she was probably in her late 40s, she was quite alluring. I stroked her long, soft hair and raised her chin to me, as her body continued to convulse. Her breasts were large and round, the nipples unusually large. I pulled her up by the arms and dragged her to the open hallway, where I fell upon her breasts as she cried for me to stop. Licking the nipples gently for a moment, I finally pierced through the tender flesh and lapped up the blood. Then I turned to her throat, but before I could drink, footsteps pounded down the stairs.

"Mom, where are you?" a boy called in the darkness. When he reached the hallway, he flicked on the light. He was 15 or 16, in a sweatshirt and shorts. "My God!" He disappeared into the sitting room and came out brandishing a fireplace poker.

"Get off her!" He drew back the poker as though he would run it through me. "Mom, are you all right?" His body trembled.

The unconscious woman remained motionless. I stood and stepped toward the boy. "She's just asleep."

When he jabbed at me with the poker, I wrenched it from his hands. I gripped his shoulders and drew his face up to mine and inhaled his luscious scent. His eyes were wide with horror.

"You're quite a specimen," I said. I kissed his full lips and sank my fangs into his neck. He instantly went limp.

When I had drunk every drop in his body, I returned to his mother to drain her. Between the two of them I was more than satiated. Even if the man upstairs had not already chilled to a dangerous point for drinking blood I wouldn't have touched him.

I left them all where they had died and exited through the same door I'd entered. Sirens howled throughout the city. Searchlights flashed up the street and scanned the park. Just as a patrol car turned the corner, I rose into the air and sped across the miles between Knoxville and the monastery.

It was nearly 3 o'clock when I returned. I crossed through the dark chapel on my way to the crypt. Exhausted from the killings, bloated with blood, I wanted to sleep though dawn was still a few hours away. But when I crawled into my coffin in the close, dark mausoleum, I lay awake for a long time, disturbed by something—not the killings, but a presence, like the presence I had felt once before outside my tomb, a presence that had amused me then. Now it threatened my dreams.

CHAPTER TWENTY-NINE

At dusk, as though electricity surged through me, my furious heart awakened me. He waited for me outside the tomb. The iron door squealed like a rat as I pushed it open to face Michael, who watched as intensely as the Roman sentinels outside the tomb of Joshu.

"Exactly dusk," he said as I emerged. He sat on the cold floor, against a stone pillar. The meager incandescent lights lacked the strength to wipe the shadow from his face.

"So, you know?" I stretched and rubbed my eyes.

"I watched you come in, just after Andrews sped into town. I couldn't sleep. I was out walking. He and the other agent had apparently been searching for you here. But they didn't look long before they gave up and took off down the drive. I waited until you got back. I knew you'd be coming."

"Michael, I've put off explaining—"

He raised his hand to interrupt me. "Everything was confirmed this evening on the news. Three corpses, two drained of blood. A patrol car cruising the area spotted a suspicious man, then checked the houses on the street."

I squinted to see his eyes. "Come to my cell. Let me explain it from the beginning."

"We can't miss dinner and vespers, Victor. The last thing you need is to stir up any more suspicion here. We can talk later."

I grabbed his arm as he started to get up. "You don't blame me, then."

"Nature is nature."

"I adore you, Michael." I shook his arm.

The evening dragged. We chanted the longest, dreariest psalms at vespers. At dinner, the reading from *Lives of the Saints* detailed the martyrdom of St. Lawrence, who praised God while he was grilled to death. Talk of the killings dominated the social hour. Neighbors of the victims were interviewed on the news and Andrews once again assured the city that the murderer would be apprehended. When the reporter pressed him about the killer's identity, Andrews refused to share the details he claimed to have.

As much as Andrews suspected me in Luke's disappearance, surely by now he'd given up trying to pin the mountain and Knoxville murders on me. After all, he'd never seen me leave the monastery grounds. Or maybe he thought I had a partner in the city. But none of that mattered. I focused on setting things right with Michael and preparing for his baptism into the night.

Grave, intense, Michael fired question after question at me when we met in the library's stacks after the Grand Silence had begun. We sat on the age-darkened plank floor between shelves of books, the humid air full of their smell. Thunder rumbled above us.

"This author traces vampires to Satan." Michael picked up one of the volumes piled next to him. "Is it true?"

"Satan, the fallen angel? No, he took a different route than the founder of the Dark Kingdom. He wanted to usurp the role of heaven's god. He wanted an eternity of adoration—static, lifeless worship. The Dark Kingdom is a place of activity, as you've seen."

"Heaven's god? There's more than one?"

"Many powers rule the universe. Nations take their pick—Isis, Zeus, the Hebrew god. I'm no enemy of the gods. They are simply not relevant to me. They exist in spheres not accessible to me, just as mine is not accessible to them."

"Your food, Victor. All these people. The killings in the mountains too, I suppose. What is it like?" He spoke with the burning interest underlying all his quests for knowledge.

I shrugged. "Sometimes exhilarating, sometimes ... sometimes unpleasant."

"You killed Luke, didn't you?"

"It was unavoidable. He threatened to expose me, to have me expelled. It was a matter of survival."

He looked away for a moment before speaking again, in nearly a whisper. "And you drank his blood?"

"Yes. It's how I live. How you will live, Michael. As you say, nature is nature. If you give in to petty scruples, see through mortal eyes, it's abhorrent. But look at the wolves. Look at human's killing for meat. Vampires live on blood."

"Vampires." Michael pondered the word. "Jana spoke of creatures of the night. Are there others? Do you have enemies, allies?"

He'd asked the question I dreaded most. To condemn him to a life of solitude, the most torturous aspect of my existence, how could he understand?

"Yes, there are others. But we operate alone, until we create a successor." I paused, then said, "What are decades or centuries, though, when compared to eternity?" I leaned forward and clasped his shoulders. "Besides, in the interim you can live on our passion, Michael. I lived without it all this time on earth. Now I think I could stay another 2,000 years, if I knew I would be joining you."

"Will I be able to communicate with you?"

"I can make no promises. I don't know enough."

"What if we both stay here? What if we leave this place and make a life somewhere else?"

"You mean until you die?"

"Yes. Can't I share your existence now? These books talk about large numbers of vampires."

"Forget the books!" I pounded a shelf with my fist. "I'm telling you it's not a choice. Other vampires exist, but all rule their own domains. We never come into contact. We can't. There's a barrier."

Michael gazed at me steadily, despite the excitement and fear I detected pulsing through him. "How can I live without you for centuries?"

"You are strong enough to do it. And there's no choice."

"And feeding on people—"

"You'll do it. We all do it. The blood: There's nothing like it, the sense of elation, the power. To think the life of a man is pouring into you. Think of communion, for God's sake. The hunger for blood takes people there. The blood of a victim. Remember the taste of my blood, Michael?"

"But you weren't a victim."

I laughed. "You're wrong. You held complete power over my soul."

As the thunder rolled and exploded, rain pelted the roof. Our niche among the books was a snug refuge that, in light of our impending separation, took on the romance of a dark bedroom the day before a battle.

Aware of our alliance in subversion, united in blood and the dark longings of our souls, we fell into each other's arms. I stripped off his shorts and T-shirt and buried my face in his musky crotch, licking the dark sack, the thick cock. My tongue traced the line of dark fur from that sweet meat to his chest, where it densely swirled. Our lips met, then our tongues. We wrestled playfully. He finally sat upon my belly, pinning back my arms, and impaled himself upon my rigid cock. Massaging his own, he groaned in his motion, and I, panting in the scent of his racing blood, groaned too, until we both exploded in orgasm.

CHAPTER THIRTY

In the midst of the relentless media coverage of the devastation wrought by the "vampire killer," as I was dubbed by the press, Luke's grandfather visited the monastery. The dotard had to see where his boy last lived, had to search the woods himself. Apparently, Brother Matthew had discouraged his coming, but to no avail.

During compline, he sat in Luke's choir stall, glum and distracted, not bothering to follow the psalms in his grandson's breviary, which he caressed as though it were a child. He was a tall, rawboned man in his mid-60s, with deep grooves in his tanned cheeks and close-cropped gray hair. He wore a short-sleeved plaid shirt and blue jeans—a farmer through and through. From dawn to dusk he'd trekked through the woods, Michael told me, without stopping to eat, and had only picked at his food during dinner.

When the moment came for petitions, he spoke up wearily, in what I by now recognized as a country accent.

"I wanna ask the Lord to lead me to my boy. If he's dead, I just wanna know. But I pray he's alive. He ain't never hurt nobody. Looks like a killer wouldn't have no use for him, but I don't guess that matters to a pervert. I know it ain't right to wish evil on nobody, but I ask the Lord to strike that monster down in his tracks, afore he can kill another soul."

After compline, Michael spoke to him, briefly clasping his shoulder. It was a mistake to allow this compassion. Why stir the waters? A general could not weep over the slain soldiers on the field, whether his own men or those of the enemy. He must harden himself against future losses, future massacres. But I knew for now it was asking too much. With time Michael would see the necessity of leaving uncompromised the detachment natural to him.

What concerned me more was the incredible susceptibility of Michael's soul to supernatural interference. When he failed to show up at my cell that night at the appointed hour, I ventured to his. Flames encased in red glass flickered throughout his room and sweet incense smoked densely. Michael lay naked on the floor, his arms outstretched. The shadow of the crucifix suspended in midair above him fell across his face. His cock was swollen with blood. As before, he invoked the cross, instrument of torture, as a source of hope.

"O crux, ave spes unica." His tone was insistent, as if he were leading a war cry, and he repeated the pronouncement again and again as though accompanied by a battle drum.

I wanted to interrupt the spell, shake him from his vision, but once again I could not penetrate the invisible wall between us. Frustrated, I stood near the door.

The chant quickened, gaining urgency, and then stopped abruptly, as though the enemies now stood eye to eye, ready to charge across the battlefield. He got up on his knees, extending his arms before the crucifix, apparently receiving from it a burden. Straining under the invisible weight he stood and approached the door, which swung open of its own accord when I stepped aside. I followed him down the dark corridor, alert to any movements behind the closed doors, particularly the door of the abbot's cell.

I followed him all the way down the stairs to the crypt and through the long, dank passage to my tomb, where he stopped.

He grimaced as if in great pain, sweat beading on his forehead. He moaned like a frustrated dumb man trying to communicate. It was the iron gate, I knew; he wanted it opened and I obliged him. That calmed him. Standing naked before the black mouth of the mausoleum, his arms still extended, he appeared to wait for someone to relieve him of his heavy treasure. I followed his cue, pantomiming a transfer of the burden from his arms to mine.

When he motioned to the tomb, I pretended to lay what must have been a corpse inside. Tears streamed down his face. Then he opened his eyes and the weeping ceased.

"He's here, Victor." He whispered, his eyes on the gaping tomb.

"Yes."

"He called out to me. Then I found him in the woods, white as chalk."

"This is a temptation, Michael." I laid my hand on his shoulder. "Joshu wants you for himself. But for what? So you can kneel with him before his father's throne for all eternity?"

He turned his head slowly until our eyes met. "Yes. There was something in the vision about Jesus. At first there were colors—red, yellow, black splashed against a white screen, and then a cross, a writhing body, and then Luke lay before me in the woods."

Securing the iron gate, I led Michael to my cell, where I directed him to wait until I could retrieve his clothes. When I returned with his shorts and T-shirt, he was rolling his head as if to relieve tension from his neck and shoulders.

"Let's take a walk," I said.

He nodded, alert now after the long trance.

The grass, taller after a week of rain, formed a soft carpet beneath our feet. Light-green leaves budded on the trees scattered across the grounds. The sour smell of mulch wafted on a warm breeze cascading over the mountains.

Once secure inside the woods, I took Michael's hand as we climbed through the leafing oaks, over stumps and fallen trunks. Only a slice of moon jeweled the sky, so it was up to me to guide him through the black thicket to our clearing.

"Your gloom's because of our parting," I said when we had settled on the ground against the log. "And once you're transformed the visions will stop."

"How do you know? How do you know these things?"

"Don't question me," I said firmly. "Give yourself over. A divided soul can't survive."

"Yes, I know." He laid his head back against the log and studied the sky. "This has to happen soon, Victor. I won't permit my soul to be used as a battleground for invisible forces. But there is one thing." He turned to me. "I want to sleep with you."

"Sleep?"

"Next to your coffin. I want to spend our final hours together. At dusk when we wake up this thing has to happen."

I studied his keen eyes, in search of ulterior motives, but without success. "Is this a test run? Do you want to make sure you can survive sleeping among the dead?"

"I've told you what I want."

"All right. At dawn we sleep."

When the sky lightened behind the mountains, we climbed down to the crypt. I entered the tomb first and made space for him near my coffin. He lay calmly, quietly, while I shut the gate. I loosened a brick in the back wall to let in air from a narrow channel between the mausoleums and the outer wall of the foundation. Then I climbed into my bed.

"How are you?" I asked.

"Fine. The dead don't frighten me."

"You know, in some medieval monasteries monks had to build their own coffins and sleep in them every night."

"Yes, I know, to remind them of their mortality."

"For you it's a promise of eternity."

I squeezed his hand and fell into the most peaceful sleep I'd had in two centuries.

Just before dusk, though, I dreamed of Luke. He stood over us in the tomb, naked, pale. He sobbed. Putrid blood dripped from his throat onto Michael's face. Michael's eyes snapped open. In a feverous delirium he struggled to escape from the tomb. I awoke and realized that it was no dream. Kneeling over my coffin, he pummeled my chest.

I seized his wrists. "Wake up. It's a dream."

"I am awake. I am." He stopped struggling against me and took a deep breath.

"Don't let Luke haunt you."

"It's not Luke. It's something else. I dreamed of heaven."

"What? Some fantasy?"

"No. I don't know." He settled back on his haunches. "I can't do it, Victor."

"What! What do you mean?"

"I can't."

"You're babbling like an idiot. Get out in the air and calm yourself."

"It won't help. My sense is strong. This can't be done."

"What, is your Jana putting crazy ideas in your head? Fuck her. You love me. That's what matters. A magnificent life is ahead of us. You won't back out, not if you listen to your own desires instead of a spirit's black magic."

But his gaze was one of resolution, not fear.

"It's useless to discuss it now," I said. "Get out. We'll talk tomorrow."

He said nothing as he crawled from the tomb.

Part VIII

THE STORM

CHAPTER THIRTY-ONE

That night was the darkest, longest I'd known in my centuries of flight from the sun. Restless to the point of madness, I heard the subtlest movements in the woods, smelled the decay of animals lying dead miles away. The nerves in my body formed a network of live wires, exposed, popping, near the point of conflagration. If now, with all my hopes, now when the moment to act announced itself like a giant bell tolling over the land, if now this partner who'd freely entered into a pact with me betrayed me, I knew not what heights my fury would reach. His flesh would rip, flesh as abhorrent to me in that moment as it had been enthralling for the past year. How could I bear to let him live? Impossible. And he knew it. He knew it but spoke still.

Yet couldn't he have been under the old woman's spell, as he'd been that night in the woods? Perhaps she, not he, spoke. Perhaps she was in league with Luke's spirit. Damn them both. Cowards of seduction.

When Michael met me in the shadows outside the crypt the following night, I already knew his position, even without reading his thoughts. Erect, determined, silent, he approached. He did not play up the pain he felt. All the same, I despised him as he uttered the words I expected to hear.

"I can't do it, Victor," he said solemnly. "I can't."

"Damn you!" I pinned him to the wall. "It was a test, sleeping in the tomb. You refused to trust me. I'll kill you, I swear."

"I'm not stopping you."

"Stop me!" I gripped his throat and would have broken his neck, but footsteps sounded on the stairs. I covered his mouth and pulled him behind a column. The intruder stopped, then retreated. I slammed Michael against the wall.

"So you want to ruin my plans, my happiness! When I can almost taste it, like blood?" My chest heaved with fury. "You like power, do you? You like to experiment with the forces of darkness?"

"No, Victor. I love you." His face was still red from the pressure of my hands on his throat.

I backhanded him. The sting brought tears to his eyes. "Traitor. I'll kill you here and now. No, wait. I'll have some amusement first. You want power? I'll show you power."

Gripping him by the arm, I took him outside and rose into the night while he clung to me. We lighted near a corner grocery store in Knoxville, just as the owner was locking the doors. I knocked on the glass, clutching Michael still. When the owner mouthed the word "closed," I shoved open the door.

"Hey, Mister, I said I'm closed." The man was 70 or so, with a widow's peak and a bulbous nose sprouting black hairs.

"So you are." I advanced a step, my fangs now protruding, and he ran to the counter. Before he could grab his gun, my arm was around his neck like a vise. "Behold power, Michael."

"Let him go, Victor, for God's sake." Michael pounded on the counter.

"For whose sake?" I grabbed a shock of gray hair, pulled the man's head back, and pierced his throat. Then I sucked slowly, so he would struggle a long while under Michael's gaze.

Michael came around the table and tried to tear the man away from me.

With one thrust, I hurled him into a shelf loaded with wine. Bottles crashed to the floor, staining the white linoleum as red as the blood I drank. As soon as he stood up, I bared my dripping fangs at him.

"Nature is nature," I said. "Here, try it." I reached for his arm and pulled his lips to the old man's throat.

He strained against my grip to move his face, now smeared with blood, away from the man's neck.

The old man, his eyes stretched wide in terror, groaned and struggled to breathe. Blood had drained down the collar of his shirt and collected around his pocket protector full of pens. Holding Michael with one hand and my victim with the other, I lunged at the old man's throat, sucking greedily until he collapsed behind the counter. Michael darted toward the door, but I intercepted him.

"I could use your help now." I slammed him into shelf after shelf of canned goods and cereals and laundry soap until the quaint market was as devastated as an earthquake would have left it. Then, pulling him to his feet, I licked the blood from a gash in his forehead. "The night's just begun."

Waiting inside the store until a patrol car sped down the street, I dragged Michael, bruised and limping, across an alley into a large Victorian home, now shabby and divided into apartments. The unlocked back door opened onto a long, poorly lit hallway flanked by several doors. The scent was strongest from an apartment at the front of the building.

"Don't do this, Victor. Just kill me now." His dark eyes were filled with scorn.

"You're asking me for mercy?" I laughed. "No, come with me, my beloved."

The flimsy door gave way with a firm shove. A small dog scampered to the entrance and yapped hysterically.

"What's wrong, Nipper?" A woman called from down the hall. "Come see Mommy."

When the dog continued to bark, I scooped him up by the throat, strangled him with one hand, and flung him on the rug. Michael looked away.

"Nipper? Whatsa matter, girl? Come see me."

Submissive under my grip, Michael accompanied me down the hallway to the steamy room at the end. By the time the woman heard us, it was too late to run. Young and shapely, she stood in an old-fashioned tub with claw feet, reaching for a towel. She screamed at the sight of us. I jerked the towel away from her and stuffed it into her mouth. Wrapping her in one arm and Michael in the other, I carried them both into a room with a canopy bed. Like those of a mad dog, my teeth tore at her throat, her naked breasts, until blood gushed from the wounds and she lost consciousness. When Michael vomited, I shoved him to the floor and dropped her on the bed.

"What do you think—should I let her bleed to death?"

"Feed on her, damn you!" He lay on his side, deathly pale. "Put her out of her misery, for chrissake."

"Not yet." I picked up her body and laid it next to him.

"She would have been a fine catch for someone, don't you think?" I got down on my haunches and stroked her chestnut hair. Her blood trailed down the uneven oak floor toward Michael and he tried to get away from it but I held him down until the blood saturated his shirt and he vomited again.

"So, you like to play with evil forces? But you didn't bargain for this, did you."

"Kill me, Victor." As he looked up his eyes started to roll back and he collapsed in his own vomit.

"No! I'm not through with you yet." I carried him to the bathroom and dunked his head in the tub until he came to. Then I dragged him to his feet and back to the bedroom for my finale. I gulped the blood spurting from the woman's throat and breasts and lapped up the floor. My lips now dripping, I kissed Michael, thrusting my tongue down his throat until he gagged and vomited once again.

"Damn you." Michael was exhausted and ill. I nearly had to carry him to the house next door toward the scent of more blood.

Just as I tried the door a police car stopped in the alley. An officer got out and shouted for us to raise our hands. In the time it takes me to break a neck, I rose, my arm wrapped around Michael. The officer fired several shots. I winced when one struck my shoulder blade, but continued on. By the time I cleared the treetops, I felt blood oozing from Michael's stomach.

"You've been hit!" I shouted against the force of the wind.

Grimacing in pain, he did not respond.

I landed with my burden in the forest clearing, laid him on the ground, and stripped off his soaked shirt to inspect the wound. The bullet had plunged deep into his bowels. With every beat of his heart, blood spurted. Blood which, linked as it was with jeopardy to his existence, gave me no delight. Wadding his shirt into a tourniquet, I pressed it against his stomach. His rib cage heaved as he struggled for breath. His skin was as hot as summer pavement.

"Michael, don't slip away. Fight this." I shook his shoulders gently until he opened his eyes. "There's still time. You can still drink." Holding the tourniquet in place, I stripped off my shirt and positioned my nipple near his mouth. "Drink, damn it!"

He shook his head, slowly but deliberately.

"Why? Why let yourself die when you can suck life from me? Power, eternity. Eternity with me, damn you." I brought his lips to my chest, but he would not suck.

I leaned down and spoke directly into his ear as he fought for consciousness. "This god that draws you, doesn't he command you to love? Isn't that what the Gospels teach? Then do this for love. I need you, do you hear me?"

He labored more and more to take in air as he struggled to speak. "I love you, Victor."

"Then come with me!" I whispered the words forcefully into his ear.

Desperate ideas to save him flashed through my mind—whisking him away to an emergency room, retrieving bandages to bind him, tearing out the bullet with my own hand. But only moments remained for him.

"What is this heaven you have seen—that you'd sacrifice eternal freedom for? Freedom and me. What can it offer that I can't? Tell me! If it's worth eternity, I'll follow you, by God!"

Michael turned his head. He worked to focus his listless eyes on me, as though he wanted to speak. He inhaled and released a shaky breath. He did not inhale again. His gaze froze on me.

"No!" I knelt over him and shook him violently. "No, damn you. You can't leave me alone. I'm through with the night. I want my reward." Hot tears ran from my eyes. I lifted his face and kissed his lips.

"Are you satisfied, Joshu?" I called into the night sky, whose dazzling stars seemed to mock me. "What else do you want from me? Another two millennia of torture, is that it? You won't have it. I swear you won't!"

Casting a last look on the eyes no longer mysterious and penetrating, I got up and sprinted into the woods, bounding over fallen trees, snapping branches, splashing through the brook, until I reached the ledge where Michael had shown me the sun after 2,000 years of darkness. I howled like a wild animal, howled until I thought I would explode in anger. The sound resonated in the valley below and was answered by the cries of wolves deep in the thicket.

Then I tore at my hair, and clawed my face until it bled. I rolled on the rocky ground and beat it until my fists were crimson with blood. I longed to kill now, but the night was far gone and the streets of Knoxville were infested with police. So I remained brooding on the ledge until just before dawn, when I fled back to the shelter of my tomb—the tomb where only a day before Michael had slept with me.

CHAPTER THIRTY-TWO

My sleep was fitful that day. Several times I awoke to Michael's voice and called out to him. In dreams I reenacted the killings I'd staged for him while he pleaded with me to stop. The old store-owner's face reddened as my arm tightened around his throat. The woman's white breasts spewed blood.

Late in the day voices awakened me, first distant but gradually louder until the speakers stood outside my grave.

"Here's where the blood stops." Andrews spoke. "Shit. He's in there."

I heard the sound of guns whisked from holsters.

"Don't kill him." Brother Matthew cried from a distance. "How can we be sure?"

"Get back up to your office, Brother. We'll handle this."

The abbot's footsteps grew more faint as he retreated from the crypt.

"All right, Brother Victor," Andrews shouted toward the mausoleum, "come out with your hands up, nice and slow."

For a moment I considered surrendering. When they took me up into the sunlight, I would disintegrate instantly. No more wandering, hiding, feeding. No more searching for a companion to make eternity worthwhile. But the temptation evaporated as suddenly as it had formed.

"You win, Andrews," I called. "Here I come."

I kicked open the iron gate. Facing me under the dim lights were

Andrews and three other agents, all pointing revolvers at me. I approached one of the agents, a neophyte with smooth cheeks.

He backed up. "Don't take another step!"

When I did, he fired. Stunned only momentarily, I grabbed the gun from his hand and crashed it against his skull. As they fired on me, I slammed the other two agents against the wall.

Andrews hit me several times while I handled the two, but I only flinched and the wounds closed immediately.

"You finally got what you wanted, Andrews." I faced him, smiling. "The serial killer. The vampire of Knoxville. Big accomplishment for you."

Andrews continued pointing his gun at me, but he looked worried. Sweat beaded on his forehead. "Reinforcements are on the way," he said as I stepped toward him.

"Too bad for them."

I took another step and he fired.

I didn't wince. "How many more bullets? One?" I couldn't resist laughing.

"What kind of a monster are you?" He backed away toward the open mausoleum. Now his gun trembled.

"Let me show you." After he fired his final bullet, I grabbed the weapon from him and tossed it on the stone floor. He tried to run, but I clutched him by the neck, flinging him to the floor. Straddling him, I pinned back his arms and lowered my face until our eyes were inches away. His were full of terror.

"Don't kill me. Please. I've got a family."

"That's a pity." I nuzzled his throat for a moment and then plunged my fangs into his jugular vein. He struggled against me longer than any of my prey ever had. Even his blood seemed to resist the force of my lips, barely trickling from his throat. But when he eventually succumbed, the blood gushed into my mouth, as robust as fine wine.

Since the other agents were still breathing, I snapped their necks. Then I waited in the dank crypt until the sun set, itching to leave, energized by Andrews' blood.

When I finally opened the door to the foyer, all was quiet, the abbot nowhere to be seen. Like a submissive lamb, he'd followed orders perfectly.

He must not have heard the gunshots through the thick stone walls of the monastery. I stood outside his office door and heard him explaining everything to Brother George, who responded in gravelly monosyllables. When I opened the door, they looked up, stunned.

"Brother Victor." The abbot stood behind his desk. The blood drained from his face. He glanced at Brother George, who sat in an armchair with his legs crossed, smoking as usual.

"Mr. Andrews sent me up. He asked me to give you something."

Brother Matthew stared in horror as I approached his desk. My clothes were covered with blood and my fury, no doubt, fired my glance. Brother Matthew backed away from me toward the window. Brother George put out his cigarette and got up to rescue him.

"Now, Victor," Brother George said in his gravelly voice. "They're on to you. There's no escape. If this is a mental illness—"

The moment he touched my sleeve, I grabbed his throat, my eyes still searing into the abbot's, and squeezed the breath out of him while he thrashed about. When I released him he slumped to the floor.

"Oh God, God." The abbot frantically surveyed the room for a means to escape. Beads of sweat formed on his pink scalp. "Please, please, Victor. In the name of God," he said as I moved around the desk.

I pressed him against the window, both hands on what little neck emerged from his habit. He pounded my chest as I strangled him until his eyes rolled back in his head.

"So much for the power of your damned god!"

Rather than satisfying me, the killings only fueled my desire to strike out against the god who stole from me the only two creatures I had ever loved. I stormed to the recreation room, where the handful of monks who were not away at universities gathered for the social hour. Four old monks watched the blaring television in a corner of the large room. Two monks played pool, while another looked on from the bar. Not a single head turned when I entered; evidently they knew nothing about my crimes or the FBI's chase.

"Like a drink, Victor?" the scrawny bald monk at the bar said. Then he noticed my bloody clothes and his mouth gaped. In an instant I grasped him by the throat and snapped his spine.

The brothers playing pool had been too absorbed in their game to notice anything. While one, short and olive-skinned, leaned over the table to make a shot, I pounded his head against it with such force that he was dead in an instant. Dazed, his curly-headed opponent tried to fend me off with his pool cue. I snatched it from him, knocked him down, and punctured his heart with it. Blood rushed from his black robe like a geyser.

The monks near the television stared at me in horror, frozen in their chairs. Silver-haired Brother Augustine stood and, gathering his courage, reasoned with me, his frightened eyes darting to the bodies on the floor as he spoke. The other three rose. Two edged toward the door. I grabbed them by the throat and strangled them. When Augustine came at me I did the same to him, before turning to the last monk, the obese cook. His face pale, he backed away, clutching his chest as though his heart was failing. His eyes widened as I squeezed his throat, and he tore at my hands until I crushed his windpipe and he went limp.

I was met at the door by a new young monk, Brother Stephen, who saw the carnage and tried to flee.

"You don't think you can get away, do you?"

His terrified blue eyes looked past me at the door. Barely 20, he'd grown a soft reddish moustache after the monks teased him about his youth.

I brushed it with my fingers. Then I tore off his habit and flung his naked body to the floor.

"Oh God. Let me go, Brother Victor. Don't do this."

But without mercy, I rammed my cock into him, while he screamed in pain. When I was through, I bit into his tender throat and guzzled his blood, sweet as honey.

Maddened by a rage that had only gained momentum with the massacre, I rushed to the chapel, leaped onto the high altar and flung statues from their niches. When piles of plaster lay on the floor, fine white dust sifting down, painted hands and heads scattered over the marble, I wrenched out the tabernacle itself and hurled it into the sanctuary. The bronze doors flew open and released the ciborium, which spilled its store of wafers.

Like a wild ape, I scrambled up the reredos, tore off the crucifix that had taken possession of Michael, and hurled it across the chapel. In that moment, the room shook as though the crash had caused an earthquake.

I dropped to the floor and searched the darkness, struggling to keep my balance in the trembling room.

I sensed a presence. "Who is it?" I shouted. "Who is it?" The corpus from the crucifix moved, becoming supple, taking on the color of flesh.

"Joshu! So now you come to me. To hell with you!"

"It's not too late, Victor." The man who rose before me, though radiating an eerie, unnatural light, was the Joshu I had known from life. Wrapped in the loincloth he wore at his execution, blood streaming from the thorns digging into his scalp, he stood before me in all his strength and beauty. "Heaven is not beyond you. I am not beyond you."

"So you haunt me?" I blurted. "You torture souls to bring them to salvation?"

"There's still hope, Victor."

"To hell with you, Joshu. You're a traitor!"

He looked at me as he had once looked at me, not in piety, not in pity, but in devotion, attachment. Then he turned and started back to the cross.

"Joshu, no!"

I ran to him, but my hands passed through his form, as though he were vapor. He mounted the cross and solidified once more into the immobile figure who embodied a sentimental artist's conception of him.

He had jabbed my heart again. He had betrayed me with full knowledge. How many times would we repeat this scene? I would never accept his conditions. To show him, to rebel against his god ... that vow I renewed then and there.

Part IX

NIGHT AGAIN

EPILOGUE

My view of the above-ground tombs was partially obstructed by the tall magnolia in the front yard of the mansion. But through the second-story window I could discern a row of the white mausoleums across the street, protruding like teeth from a black mouth. A crowd near the iron cemetery gates gathered around a bearded tour guide dressed in a turtleneck and jeans, who gestured toward the cemetery. I knew he was giving the speech he gave every night at the same hour. The day after my arrival in New Orleans I'd gone down to listen, hearing him explain the process of "falling through," whereby the decaying body, baked to ashes in the brick grave—in which the internal temperature often exceeded 200 degrees from the intense southern sun—gradually sifted through the stacked racks to the bottom of the grave, where it mingled with the dust of its ancestors. The skull and any bones still intact on the top shelf were swept to the floor when it came time to bury the next corpse. "Falling through" was the passage to an eternal family reunion of sorts.

I had risen an hour before from the mausoleum I had claimed in the cemetery, one belonging to a family whose line had died out, indicated by the last burial date (1935) engraved in the white door. No one would disturb my slumbers in that resting place in New Orleans's Garden District. But the hot chamber had made my sleep fitful, haunted by nightmares of Michael. Upon waking, rather than crossing to the antebellum mansion I'd purchased, I often strolled the streets of the District, brooding as I passed the grand porticos, the cypresses and oaks of other old estates.

Only a week had passed since my flight from the monastery, and I continued to replay in my mind the final scenes there—Michael's death, the massacre of monks, the demolition of the chapel's sanctuary. And of course, the apparition of Joshu, pale and bleeding, once again ready to comfort and to torture my soul.

Excited by his appearance, infuriated by the promise of renewed torment, I set out to conclude the ravage I had begun. With gasoline from the storeroom, I doused the volumes in the library and trailed a stream along the wooden floors throughout the buildings. Then I set the monastery ablaze. From the grounds I watched the flames shoot from exploding windows and lick the roof. Before long, the old rafters and supports burned and the structures, one by one, collapsed. The inferno heated the grounds like a desert sun.

Then, once more, I fled to a new grave, new nights, knowing not what cloister I would next find myself in, or even if I would seek another. But I swore to myself I would not abandon a predator's life until a companion promised me his eternity.

Having had enough of morbid ruminating, I wandered downstairs, out to the street, past the crowd touring the cemetery, and took the streetcar to the French Quarter. Although it was still early, Bourbon Street already reeked of piss and beer. Sleazy barkers beckoned to prospective customers outside the strip clubs. Dixieland and blues blared through open doors of restaurants and bars.

To escape the growing crowd and neon lights, I turned down a dark side street. A row of renovated shotgun houses with colorful shutters gave way to shabby brick buildings whose galleries cast shadows over the cracked, garbage-lined walks. The smell of the river rode on a breeze through the Quarter's maze of brick and wrought iron.

"Got a light?" A shirtless boy in low-waisted jeans stepped out of a doorway. His bleached hair fell to his shoulders. His smooth face, his lustrous, innocent eyes belied his profession.

I lit his cigarette. Then I took him around the corner, far from the nearest streetlight.

VAMPIRE THRALL

ROME

When a call
From a land
Far away
Draws your ear,
GO.
You may find
HOME.

CHAPTER ONE

Four monks clamped my arms and legs to keep me from thrashing—my naked, sweat-soaked body spread-eagled on the mattress. They liked what they saw. I felt their eyes scanning my broad chest and shoulders.

"Jesus!" I shouted. "You really need it, don't you? Well, you can all go to hell... goddamn you!" The more I yelled the more my head pounded and my vision blurred.

A thick-necked monk with a massive chest tightened his hold on my arm, leaned over the bed, and nosed my crotch. Suddenly my vision sharpened. I saw him look up and grin at me. His black eyes flashed. Dark beard dotted his jaw. A rip down the front of his habit exposed a nest of black hair. A crucifix on a chain around his throat dangled against my scrotum. My dick stiffened. I wanted him to take me then and there.

"We have to perform an exorcism," he said.

As he drew his face away from my groin, I shouted, "What's wrong? Don't you have the nerve?"

Pinning my arm with his knee, he traced the sign of the cross on my forehead and mumbled something in Latin. The monk holding my other arm knelt on it and grabbed my head so I couldn't turn away. He was pock-faced and squinty-eyed. His breath smelled like garlic.

The scent, part of my usual aura, always announced my seizures, but its intensity now scared me—garlic reeked like this only before a grand mal. What if this religious mumbo jumbo was making me seize? "Goddamn you," I said to the sexy monk who had nosed my crotch—but I choked on my words.

As he prayed, my body went into spasms and the monks tightened their grip.

This is payback for inducing seizures. See if you do it again, Paul. Just see.

The monks chanted: *Excede Satanas! Excede Satanas! Excede Satanas!*

Like mercury in a thermometer, a bulb of heat rushed up to my head. The pressure mounted behind my eyes until I thought my face would explode. White light blurred the monks. I gasped for air. Froth bubbled from my lips.

Suddenly I floated out-of-body and found myself looking down upon the scene with complete visual clarity. The chanting monks restrained the naked, jerking body I'd left on the mattress. The squinty-eyed monk grabbed a spoon from the bed table and stuck it into the epileptic's mouth.

No! I wanted to shout. *He won't swallow his tongue. Seizures call for space. Leave him alone. Let the attack play out. Keep away from his mouth.*

Then it occurred to me: Why was I seeing this? I never observe my seizures as if they're happening to someone else.

Maybe I really was dying.

The squinty-eyed monk abandoned the spoon and stuck his fingers in the man's mouth, *my* mouth. The ignorant bastard grabbed my tongue. Even out-of-body, I tasted the salt and nicotine on his fingers. When I bit down, he screamed and tore his hand away, raising the bloody stump of his index finger.

In a rush, I was sucked back into my body. The monk's finger felt like a raw chicken neck in my mouth. I chewed it. Blood dripped down my chin. Grimacing, the wounded monk clamped the stump with his other hand. His friends ignored him, their blank gazes fixed on me, the chant escaping their mouths like breath: *Excede Satanas. Excede Satanas. Excede Satanas.* I spat the gnawed finger at a young curly-headed monk, who winced in disgust but continued chanting.

Then I sensed a presence. *His* presence. The vampire. My heart beat to the rhythm of the chant. My nipples hardened. My dick stiffened again. My throat constricted. I salivated. *I am bringing on the seizure*, I thought. *I'm summoning the vampire, like all the other times.*

A dangerous game—to mess with seizures. But the vampire visions, as I called them, were worth the risk.

The monks sensed him too, their eyes darting toward the door. They edged away from the bed, but there was no place to run. He blocked the exit. I recognized him now as the sexy monk with the ripped habit. He must have been posing as one of the exorcists. With a cocky smirk, he stood—legs spread, arms folded, the little crucifix gone.

The vampire shut and locked the door. He strolled to the squinty-eyed monk, who flattened himself against the wall—his pitted cheeks white as milk. He grabbed the monk's crotch like he was ready to rip off his testicles, and when the monk winced, he bit into his skinny throat and sucked. The monk fought back for a second or two before collapsing. By now, the other two monks were pounding the door, shouting for help. The vampire shoved the curly-headed one against the door. He pressed his powerful torso against the monk's slight body and kissed his cheek, smearing it with blood. Then he twisted the monk's head until his neck snapped.

The last monk—gaunt, bearded, and wearing a surplice—had frozen during the attacks. He stared at the ceiling now, as though turning his soul over to God. The vampire untied the cord from his own waist and wound it around the monk's throat. The monk's face turned red as sunburned flesh. His tongue stuck through his bearded lips like a little pink animal trying to escape the doomed body—and he sank to the floor.

The vampire turned. The hunger in his dark eyes scared and excited me. My chest tightened, and I sucked in air as I waited for him, supine and hard. He leaned over me, emitting a strangely feral odor, and brushed his lips against my belly. They were cold as ice. His grainy chin scraped my tender flesh. My dick pulsed as though my heart had moved to my groin. He brought his mouth to my throat. I closed my eyes and waited. With the first prick of his fangs, I exploded in orgasm...

"Oh! I'm sorry. Excuse me."

Pain shot through my elbow, and I opened my eyes to see the pear-shaped flight attendant continuing down the aisle with the beverage cart that must have hit me. My briefs were damp with precome. No climax after all. The chubby woman in the window seat glanced up from her magazine. Was I imagining the suspicious look in her eyes? I got up and dug my travel kit from my bag in the overhead compartment.

In the plane's tiny rest room, I inspected my face in the mirror. Did I look like a freak? Would the monks in Rome know they'd hired a vampire-loving epileptic?

I washed my face, brushed my teeth, and took a doubledose of phenobarbital to ward off a real seizure. What I'd just experienced couldn't have been real. I had to remind myself of that. I'd only dreamed about a seizure, probably because for the past week I'd been worrying about convulsing in front of the monks. If that ever happened they'd tear up my contract.

Yet the dream-seizure had been more real than real—the aura, the spasms, the frothing at the mouth. And the fatigue and dizziness I felt now were the usual aftereffects.

But during real grand mals I drift in a kind of half-consciousness. Sometimes I remember nothing.

I returned to my seat. On the monitor attached to the cabin ceiling a little icon airplane moved across a map of central France toward Switzerland. From the window, the green countryside below seemed to ripple toward the Alps. We'd be in Rome in an hour.

I closed my eyes and remembered the vampire. This was the first time he'd ever noticed me. The first time I'd ever felt his lips. It was also the first time he'd ever appeared apart from a real seizure—in a dream, if that's what it was.

For the past year, I'd stare at the flickering flame of a candle or a street light to induce a mild attack. As perverted as it sounds, I longed to see the vampire. His laser gaze, his methodical, decisive movements, even his compulsions changed a merely handsome, well-built man into a fierce protector of anybody he chose to love rather than kill. When he fed, the victim—man, woman, or child—wasn't a victim any more than a duck or a deer is when my brother Al goes hunting. The Law of Nature applies. The food chain.

Besides, the scenes were just fantasies. And, after all, I didn't *know* the victims. I didn't feel what they felt, not the way I felt what the vampire felt—his arousal, his urges, his excitement—even his solitude. I was hooked on the sensual vampire. Sometimes I even came from watching him.

The seizure that led to my first vampire vision wasn't self-induced. It had hit me when I stared out my bedroom window at the moon above the snow-covered rooftops—a stupid thing to do, since staring at any kind of light can bring on a seizure. Add to that my exhaustion and the fact that I'd skipped my meds for several days, and you have a recipe for trouble. First the usual smell of garlic wafted to my nose. Then came another familiar part of my aura: blood splattering on a white canvas that sinks into oblivion. The vampire sat in a boat, waiting for someone. Despite the darkness around him I could just make out his features. Maybe a moon glowed or maybe a lantern was hidden somewhere inside the boat. His eyes bored into the night like lasers, focusing on a point across the water. He breathed harder and harder. Yet for all his intensity, he emitted an icy chill. He was poised to pounce. The scene blurred, then refocused on the vampire as he approached a building. He grabbed a hefty man in a uniform by the scruff of the neck. The man's cap slipped to one side as he tried to free himself. The vampire—my sensual vampire—bit into the man's throat and sucked.

The seat belt sign flashed and the flight attendant directed us to raise our tray tables and seat backs as we prepared for landing. Rome appeared below us, a labyrinth of ochre walls and tile roofs bright with sunlight. When the Colosseum came into view, a strange thing happened. My testicles buzzed. What was it about the oval structure, full of broken brick and stone? Did it summon the thought of sweaty gladiators fighting? Or maybe some kind of Freudian association—a bruised sphincter? Who knows?

When we landed, I tightened the laces of my black suede shoes and carefully hoisted down a leather satchel from the overhead compartment. The satchel held my new burnisher, jars of pigment, brushes, and a portfolio of sketches I wanted to show Father Rossi, who said he'd be waiting for me outside of Customs.

CHAPTER TWO

Q uid est? I asked myself, wondering what or who was stroking my navel. After all these centuries I still sometimes think in my native tongue.

I panicked for an instant until I glanced at the clock on the bed table and saw dawn was still hours away. I had only dozed off. I looked down at the monk, Brother Andrea. His heavy head was pressing my bladder. The old sensation returned, but I had no need to piss. A vampire's body absorbs all the blood he swallows. As Andrea tongued my belly and crotch, I drew my hands behind my head and closed my eyes again. *Ah.*

Andrea raised his head. "Something this good can't be sinful, can it?" he said with a strong Italian accent. I'd lived in more than one Italian monastery over the centuries and spoke the language of Dante fluently. But he believed I was American and he liked to practice his English.

"You're asking my opinion?" I'd had him every night since I'd arrived at San Benedetto a month before, in August.

"Yes, I know," he said, tugging on my cock. "You have no conscience. Very bad for a Benedictine monk. That's what you are, remember."

I pushed him off me, rolled him onto his back, and climbed on top of him, straddling his short, solid torso and pinning back his arms. His olive skin was smooth as a boy's though he was 32—a year younger than I claimed to be. His black hair grew so thick and curly it could have been a wig. In the lamplight his gray eyes, flecked with blue, reminded me of a wolf's, soft but dangerous. His nose was Roman, appropriate since he, like me, came from the capital.

"Do I hump like a Benedictine?" I said.

"How would I know?" he said demurely.

"That's right. You were a true celibate until you met me."

"Victor!" he said, turning his head. Then he gazed at me, taking in my broad shoulders, chest, and arms, brawny as the day I entered Pontius Pilate's service two millennia ago. My meaty physique and my swarthy, military looks had conquered more men and women over the centuries than I could count. But I never forgot that not all succumbed. Not all.

"You never get tired of it, do you?" I leaned forward and brushed his face with my stubbled cheeks.

I had met him at a monastery in nearby Subiaco, 30 miles east of Rome, a medieval fortress built into a rocky mountainside. I'd been posing as a pilgrim looking for a retreat from the rat race of the city, and the monks let me stay with them for six weeks. Andrea arrived to computerize the backward monastery office. An easy target, he belonged to me before he'd been there 10 days.

His position back at San Benedetto was too good to be true. As right-hand man to San Benedetto's doddering abbot, he arranged for me to reside there as a Benedictine monk who'd transferred from the States. I'd told him I was a wealthy drifter in Europe without a work permit and just one step ahead of the authorities. I needed a place to "lay low" for a while. He risked little since San Benedetto's abbot had no reason to question him. As for my need to retreat from daylight, Andrea accepted the explanation I offered at every monastery I'd ever inhabited: a skin disease that could kill me.

Bald, middle-aged, and dull as they were, most of the monks at San Benedetto didn't interest me. And the few young ones weren't much to look at—except for Giorgio, a sweet-faced boy who reminded me of an infatuated monk I'd finally had to kill at the last monastery—Luke was his name. I steered clear of Giorgio. The trouble Luke had caused me far outweighed the pleasure of being fawned over and sucked at command. This time, in this monastery, I would stay out of trouble. No biting the proverbial hand. No feeding within cloister walls, no killing, no rousing the interest of local authorities.

After the obligatory servicing, Andrea crept back to his cell. I slipped into jeans, a T-shirt, and a pair of sneakers—no need for the heavy black habit now that the monks were asleep. I strolled out to the larger of San Benedetto's two courtyards and peered through an archway of the cloister at Rome below. The September moonlight fell on the clutter of terra cotta roofs and ochre stucco and the dome of St. Peters Basilica, barely a mile away. The monastery stood on the Gianicolo, one of the seven hills of the Eternal City.

Cluttered with buildings, dense in population, Rome was the perfect place for feeding anonymously. My father's villa, destroyed by the Visigoth invaders in the fifth century, had stood only 30 miles away, where the broad campagna rose to the Appenines. After the toll my recent rampages had taken on me, I wanted to go home, where my father's spirit continued to walk, where I had learned to fight, to compete with the best officers in the Roman army.

Where I had learned to survive.

I strolled down the Gianicolo and across the Tiber and disappeared into a labyrinth of alleys that cut through the heart of ancient Rome. In a dark, narrow passage outside a trattoria, a beautiful boy in a waiter's white apron smoked a cigarette. I wanted to choose someone else, someone old or ugly, but he was the first solitary person I'd come across and I was trembling with hunger. Waiting for a crowd of German tourists to turn the corner, I crossed the narrow street to the edge of the building. To draw him away from the plate window of the trattoria, I dropped a pocketful of change and began scooping it up. He flicked his cigarette away and stepped into the shadows to assist me. I gripped his wrist, covered his mouth, and pulled him to the side of the building.

He bit my hand and clawed my arm like a girl. His heart pounded in his neck, and I pressed the location of his pulse against my lips in a kiss before piercing it with my fangs. His warm, nicotine-laced blood rushed down my throat, calming me. I emptied him, lapping up the elixir that had spilled down his neck and onto the cologne-laden collar of his white shirt. His beautiful, lifeless body hung limp in my grip. I lowered it to the ground and hurried away through a warren of dark streets.

My appetite appeased but my soul empty after destroying such a beautiful creature, I wandered past closed palazzos and the ochre facades of Renaissance churches, hugging walls when motor scooters and cars sped by. I'd had no choice about killing the boy: I needed most of his blood. Vampires can appease themselves over several small courses, but surviving victims tell tales. Besides, stopping myself in the heat of a feeding is harder than pulling out at the moment of climax.

After an hour of brooding, I turned toward the accordion music and laughter echoing through the streets from the Piazza Navona, center of Roman nightlife. Vendors selling jewelry and trinkets packed the huge ellipse of brick and stone. Tourists in shorts and T-shirts and jogging shoes crowded around the merchandise and took photographs of Bernini's gushing fountains. A gypsy boy of 7 or 8 pumped an accordion for a group of American women, and a shirtless fire-eater performed for a crowd of teenagers. The cafés around the piazza buzzed with customers under sidewalk umbrellas. Beggars worked the crowds. An old woman in a checked scarf approached me with her hand extended for coins.

"*Cinque-cento lire?*" she whined. Then she caught sight of my T-shirt in the light from a booth and backed away, making a hasty sign of the cross.

After killing the boy, I hadn't checked my white T-shirt. Blood had splashed on it, drying to brown blotches in the warm air.

I stripped my shirt off and stuffed it into an overflowing garbage container at the edge of the piazza. Suddenly a gust of arctic air hit my back. Customers at the booth near me continued inspecting lace tablecloths as though they'd felt nothing. I turned to look for the source of the chill and found nothing but a portrait artist sketching a woman with close-cropped hair and large hoops in her ears. The pair sat beneath a high-intensity lamp so hot I could feel it from three feet away. Yet the cold blast continued.

Then a strange, strong presence came.

I glanced around, finding nothing. I must have mumbled something. The pale artist looked up at me—his silver nose-stud bright in the light—then turned back to his work.

The cold wind ceased. The force departed.

Who was this spirit? An enemy? What enemies did I have besides my powerless victims over the centuries? Even if their ghosts haunted the earth, their eternities were separate from mine. Other vampires roam the earth, but we avoid one another. No predator loves a mirror. Besides, the abundance of prey makes turf wars unnecessary, and anyway no vampire can check the power of another. The sorceress Tiresia instilled in me this knowledge when she created me. And occult volumes written over the centuries by vampires and human sages confirm what she taught.

Whatever the force, it angered me by choosing cowardly harassment over direct confrontation. The taste of blood lingering on my tongue grew more metallic with my anger. I spit and sauntered to the central fountain. A group of hustlers lingered there. A skinny, frazzled looking hustler eyed my bare chest, but I ignored him, knowing that he would end up dead if he approached me. Someone touched my elbow. I turned to find a middle-aged prostitute with heavy-lidded eyes and bleached hair chopped into uneven tufts. The nipples of her heavy breasts poked her pink halter top.

"*Ti piace?*" she said, stroking my back.

"Yes, I like," I answered.

She motioned for me to follow her and led me away from the piazza up a side street to a dilapidated palazzo probably built by a 16th-century merchant or magistrate. It was an inn now, divided into cubicles as small as a monk's cell. At the end of a dark hallway, she unlocked a door, flicked on the light, turned, and touched my hip pocket.

"*Cinquanta mille,*" she said.

I pulled out my wallet and gave her one of the bills I'd taken from a wealthy old crone the week before.

Inside the room, she stripped and started to turn off the light, but I stopped her. She smiled knowingly and turned to exhibit herself. She dropped to her knees and unzipped my jeans, taking me in her mouth. For a second, she looked up, as though she were puzzled by something. I knew it was the taste of the boy's blood, absorbed by now into my skin. Lifting her by the wrists, I turned her back to my chest and entered her from behind. She moaned, at first to please me, then in earnest. Squeezing her full breasts, I continued pumping, ramming her until she screamed in pain and I covered her mouth. When I reached the point of climax, I withdrew myself, whipped her around, and threw her on the bed. She beat my chest with her fists as I leaned over her, her scream vibrating against my fingers as I continued to clasp her mouth. Her eyes widened when my fangs descended. As I slashed her breast her body jerked and she hammered my back. Though I had fed less than two hours before, I sucked her blood as if I was starving. Still hard with excitement, I finally shuddered the vampire's dry orgasm. Her eyes had rolled back. Clutching her head with both hands, I snapped her neck.

When I left the building, a patch of clouds hid the moon. The black sky enveloped me as I walked back to San Benedetto. The blood from my feedings swished in my bowels and dulled my mind. Better that I couldn't think. Violent feedings left me wishing for a comrade who could understand my brand of pleasure. In my lover Michael, I'd had the promise of someone like that. Someone who could eventually join me in the Dark Kingdom. But Michael had failed me, choosing death and a dull heaven over the world of a predator.

As I trudged up the Gianicolo thinking of Michael, I felt the strange presence again. An image formed in my mind, so sharp it could have been digitally manufactured. It was a woman as dark and tough as a Brazil nut, her face lined but still hinting of hard beauty. I recognized the spirit of Michael's Creole grandmother, who'd once taught Michael her voodoo tricks. Her black eyes glared with purpose. Her rage pushed against my chest like a fist.

"Michael's gone, Jana," I said. "Don't blame me."

The pressure on my chest intensified and then subsided, like the final surge of the day's tide.

CHAPTER THREE

The priest wasn't hard to spot as I exited the cordoned-off customs area. In his black habit, the short, stocky man stood out in the crowd of people waving to passengers, calling out in Italian, and holding up signs for tour groups. Would he see? Would he detect epilepsy in my face? The thought came to my mind whenever I met someone new.

"Father Rossi?" I said.

He smiled big—his friendly brown eyes almost incongruous on his rugged mug with its heavy blue shadow of beard—and motioned for me to follow him away from the crowd.

"It's nice to meet you, Mr. Lewis." He gripped my hand and shook it just once—European style. He was probably in his mid 50s, but his hair, oiled and neatly parted, was still thick—and black as licorice. He stood a good head shorter than me, so the dandruff on his dark habit was especially noticeable.

"Call me Paul," I said, satisfied that he noticed nothing.

"OK, Paul." He winked. "How was the flight?"

"Great."

"Very long, though, right? And cramped. Especially for someone with those legs." He patted my thigh. "Let's get your luggage. Let me carry that."

He took the satchel from me and led the way to the baggage carousel to collect my suitcase. Father Rossi was very impressed that I'd checked only one bag. I told him I'd never been a clotheshorse. The suitcase contained a pair of jeans, underwear and socks, a pair of hiking shoes, two button-up shirts, two jerseys, two sweaters, and a toiletry kit. I'd left my worn coat at home, figuring I could buy a new one and anything else I needed in Rome.

The drive to the monastery was a real adventure. Father Rossi wove his old model Fiat in and out of traffic on the freeway, coming within inches of bumpers as I slammed an imaginary brake on the passenger side. But he stayed as calm as can be, gesturing with one hand while he told me about his years in America.

"Seven years at our college in San Francisco—teaching the art of calligraphy," he said, "then five restoring documents in our monastery outside Chicago, and eight more teaching in upstate New York."

Without showing the slightest impatience, he tapped the horn when a guy on a motor scooter cut in front of us.

"Do any of the other monks speak English?"

Father Rossi wiggled his hand to indicate a mixed answer. "The abbot can fumble along if you don't go beyond the weather. His assistant, Father Andrea, is a little better. A few of the others can get by. Oh, and the new monk is American. Brother Victor."

I felt relieved. "What's an American doing at San Benedetto?"

"He's translating some documents for his own community in California."

We exited the freeway and entered Rome. I couldn't believe it. The Corso Vittorio Emanuele, a wide avenue lined with Renaissance buildings, bustled with pedestrians in suits and sleeveless dresses. At open squares, palm trees jutted above rooftops and fountains gushed. Traffic was heavy. Big green buses, motorbikes, and small European cars whizzed along merrily, darting in and out of traffic, oblivious to lanes.

"That's Castel Sant'Angelo," Father Rossi said, pointing to a round, crenellated fortress as we crossed the bridge. "It was built as Emperor Hadrian's mausoleum in 139 A.D. But it was used as a citadel. And a prison."

The same strangely erotic sensation I'd had on seeing the Colosseum struck me now. I could almost hear military drums pounding within the fortress as sweaty, brawny-armed men gathered their armor.

We climbed the steep Gianicolo Hill, passing grand gated buildings with tile roofs, and within a few minutes the monastery bell tower appeared. A fat man in a booth buzzed open the iron gate. Father Rossi waved to him, followed the pine-lined drive around to the entrance, and parked in a paved area near several other small cars.

In the front of the medieval monastery a series of central arches joined two long brick buildings, the whole facade roofed in tile. Tall pines, like stern sentinels, cast their shadows over the structure. The sight made me nervous. I hoped Father Rossi didn't notice my sweaty hands when he took my canvas bag and satchel from me. We passed through the arches, stood on a brick walkway, and looked through another set of arches at the monastery church rising before us. The Romanesque building looked exactly like the photo I'd seen on the monastery's Web site, but the photo hadn't unsettled me the way the real building now did. The two sides of the plain facade flanked a taller section that rose to a peak with a round window in the center. Behind the building, the narrow brick campanile loomed above the church. The two windows positioned high on the tower stared out like eyes beneath a monk's hood.

Father Rossi set the bag and satchel on the walkway. "Leave your suitcase here," he said softly, glancing cautiously toward the door of the adjacent building. He motioned for me to follow him.

Crossing a stone courtyard, we entered the church. In the dark vestibule, Rossi stopped and explained. "The abbot is expecting us, but I wanted you to see the church before you meet him."

We stepped in and Rossi stuck his hand in a bowl of holy water. He crossed himself, mumbling a prayer.

A cool draft hit me. The sense of foreboding I'd been feeling shot up several notches. I stopped.

"Paul?" Father Rossi said. "Are you coming?"

I nodded and forced myself to follow him. The dark, cool space smelled sweet and smoky. The ceiling, supported by triangular wooden trusses, soared above us, and tall columns dividing the church into three sections supported lofty Roman arches. Dim light sifted through the narrow windows on either side of the church.

The reason for my anxiety suddenly dawned on me. I recognized this place and the weird sense of impending danger I felt in it. It was as though the silent, sacred chamber masked an invisible force waiting to rear up like a whirlwind and suck my breath away. I'd stood on these flagstones and breathed in this exact aroma of incense. I'd gazed at the life-size crucifix suspended by two long chains from the beam at the front of the church. I knew the forlorn expression on the plaster face. But how? The Web site included no photos of the interior of the church. Maybe I'd dreamed about a place like this.

We traveled up the stone aisle, past worn pews.

"This is the choir," Father whispered as we stood under the crucifix. "The monks pray the office here." He pointed to several rows of carved choir stalls facing one another across the aisle.

"The office?" I said, distracted. The massive granite altar ahead was one more disturbing landmark in my memory.

"Prayers that punctuate the day. Matins, vespers, compline. The psalms mostly. Chanted. Prayer is the core of the Benedictine life."

I followed him to a side altar that held a box with two bronze doors. Near it glowed a large candle in an ornate fixture.

"This is the tabernacle," he explained. "It contains the Blessed Sacrament, the consecrated host. We believe it is the real presence of our Lord." He genuflected, knelt on a prie-dieu, and motioned for me to kneel on the other prie-dieu, which I did. He crossed himself, folded his hands, and bowed his head.

"Oh, Lord, bless this visitor. Keep him safely in your care. Bless his work, performed for your glory. Bless the work of your scribes, who write the word of God for the salvation of all men." He paused.

I hoped he wasn't expecting me to say anything. I'd never prayed aloud in my life. After a few seconds of silence, he crossed himself again and got up.

When we stepped out of the church, St. Peter's dome appeared through the cloister arches. It sat against the blue sky like an embroidered cap. My tension eased.

"How far are we from St. Peter's?" I said.

Father Rossi shrugged. "Maybe a mile. Just down the hill and a 15-minute walk."

We passed my suitcase and satchel in the entrance cloister and walked through a set of double doors that led to a parlor with a high ceiling and clean white walls. A couch and two armchairs were arranged around a table. Father Rossi knocked on a half-closed door.

Out came a young olive-skinned monk who reminded me of a short version of Joaquin Phoenix. He said something in Italian to Rossi and glanced at me.

"This is our illuminator, Paul Lewis," Father Rossi said. "Paul, this is Father Andrea, Abbot Anselmo's assistant."

"Nice to meet you," I said and stuck out my hand.

Father Andrea grinned as though he got a kick out of the gesture and was humoring me by clasping my hand.

"The pleasure is mine," he said with a thick accent. "We are happy to have you with us. We have much work for you."

"I'm looking forward to it."

He turned and said something in Italian to Father Rossi. Thanks to my language tapes, I understood the word *dispiace*, sorry.

"The abbot isn't feeling well," Father Rossi explained. "He'll welcome you later."

I nodded stupidly. Father Andrea made me self-conscious. A monk. Go figure.

"I will show you your cell," he said, smiling. His teeth were perfect, even and white against his dark skin.

"*Bene.*" Father Rossi patted my shoulder. "You go get settled in. When you're ready to see the scriptorium, come and get me. I'll be in the church."

He left the parlor, then Father Andrea and I walked around the interior grounds before we collected my stuff from the entrance cloister. He pointed out the front building that contained the dining hall, the side and back dormitories, and of course the library where I'd be working.

All the orangey-brown brick structures and their tile roofs were in good repair. And the grounds around the church were neatly landscaped with junipers, cypresses, palms, shrubs, and flower beds bordering stone pathways. A garden, tucked behind the church, formed a little cloister. In the center, a fountain splashed at the feet of the Virgin Mary. Nearby, a stone bench sat beneath a pine, and in a sunny patch roses basked and herbs too, marked with little name tags attached to sticks.

"We like to pray here," Father Andrea said. "It's quiet." He grinned and added, "You can pray here too."

"Thanks, but no thanks," I said, grinning back.

Glancing at the church, I felt the weird sensation again. I almost asked the priest if the Web site had ever contained a photo of the church's interior. But I didn't want to expose myself.

My room was on the first floor of the two-story building flanking the church. Father Andrea lugged my bags and I rolled the suitcase down the corridor to the last door. Arched windows in alcoves along the hallway let in a good amount of light. A little card with my name in calligraphy was taped to the door at the end of the hall.

I waited for Father Andrea to pull out a key, but the door wasn't locked. I must have looked surprised.

"No keys," he said, then winked. "Monks have nothing to steal."

My "cell," as it was called, was about 10 by 12 feet, but the high ceiling and sparse furnishings made it seem bigger. A twin bed covered with a gray wool blanket sat in one corner, a wooden night table next to it. A small wooden desk and chair were in the opposite corner. Behind the door was a sink. The tawny plaster walls were bare except for a crucifix above the bed. Light streamed in through the single window, which had a marble sill and no curtains, and fell on clean terra cotta tiles.

"You can put your clothes in here," Father Andrea said, opening the doors of a built-in cupboard. On one side was a clothes rack and on the other shelves and drawers.

"You are tired? You would like to sleep?" He nodded toward the bed.

He held up his hand like he wanted to show me something and lowered a shutter stored inside the wall above the window. The room went black.

"See?" he said. I felt his hand on my arm.

"Thanks," I said. "I think I'll go meet Father Rossi."

"*Molto bene.*" Brother Andrea raised the shutter. "Pranzo is at 2 o'clock. That is dinner. Here." He picked up a sheet of paper from the desk. It was the monastery schedule. He pointed to *pranzo.* "See." He looked at his watch. "One hour."

"Great. I'm hungry."

"And the bathroom is down here." He walked out into the hall and pointed. Then he nodded and left, closing the door behind him.

I read the schedule. Hopefully I wouldn't be expected to observe the routine that started at 5:30 with matins (morning prayers) followed by

Mass and ended at 9:30 with compline (night prayers) followed by the Grand Silence. I imagined 50 hooded monks filing out of their choir stalls, their mouths taped shut.

A whole damn year of this, I thought. Incense, chanting, silence, a day broken into periods of work and prayer. San Benedetto adhered to a regimen tighter than the Army's, with the added burden of pious eyes scrutinizing my every move. Not that I kept the three gay bars of Lawrence, Kansas, in business, but I wasn't a stranger to them. Let's just say my longest stretch of celibacy lasted about a month, long enough for a nasty cold sore to heal. And I wasn't always safe—"reckless" is what my ex Rick called me. In a moment of passion, I'd open wide enough for three men—a favorite fantasy of mine.

What would the holy monks of San Benedetto think about having a heathen homo in their midst? Maybe I could live on my mental file of fantasies for a year. Maybe the illuminations would consume me. It wasn't every day an artist got to illustrate a hand-written vellum Bible. The first in over 500 years.

I went back to the church looking for Father Rossi, and I found him on his knees in front of the bronze tabernacle. We resumed our tour and he showed me the library, which had big, well-lit, open areas and several levels of books on each of its two floors. The calligraphers and I would work in the second floor area on huge, old, oak drafting tables. I met a hefty calligrapher named Brother Roberto, who was arranging some cabinets, and then walked over to the dining hall with Father Rossi.

For an hour, silverware clanged against dishes as an old monk at a podium read a religious treatise in Italian. Four tables of robed men ate without a word, not even looking up from their plates unless it was to signal for bread or condiments. I scanned the faces for other monks who were as hot as Andrea. One young, blondish monk stood out among the geezers, but he didn't look up at me even once.

At the end of the meal, Father Andrea, at the head table with 10 other monks, stood and introduced me to the group. I followed Father Rossi's cues as he translated the little speech—standing, nodding thanks, saying I was glad to be working on the project—so self-conscious I couldn't look anyone in the eye.

That afternoon, after I unpacked, I climbed into my narrow bed and fell asleep. When I woke up it was dusk. I looked out at the dusty purple light in the distance and wondered how Alice was doing. My mother. I started calling her by her given name sometime in high school. I think I got the idea from a movie or novel about some hip kid. I don't remember exactly. I just started calling her Alice, and she humored me. Then we both got used to it.

The crucifix above the bed marked the sparse room with sadness, the way a wreath does when it's placed along the road where someone has died in an accident.

I wished for a vampire vision.

Minutes passed as I stared out the window at the fiery sunset. But nothing happened. Was I still scared by the seizure or dream—or whatever it was—from the flight?

Jet lag was kicking in. I had no desire to join the gloomy monks for supper, so I lowered the shutter, got undressed, and climbed back into bed. Not a thread of light shined in the black room. I fell asleep right away, waking only once before morning, briefly, when the strains of chanting drifted in from the church. I thought of the strange experience I'd had in the church, the familiar sense of danger that almost took my breath away. The music conjured a haunting image: moonlit roses strewn across a patch of dark earth, their petals quivering in the breeze.

Chapter Four

So is the old abbot going to die?" I said, sitting up in the bed where Andrea assumed I slept during daylight hours. He'd cleared a n-by-12 storage closet for me in the windowless crypt, a corner room originally intended for more graves. The room contained a bed and the usual sparse furniture found in a monk's cell. My real resting place was the tomb of a Frater Anastasius, about 20 feet from the room. According to the slab that had sealed his grave, Anastasius died Anno Domini 1648. On my arrival, I'd pried off the slab, brushed aside the brittle skeleton buried without a coffin, and claimed the space as my own.

"He's weak," I said to Andrea. "The doctor's worried about his heart."

Naked, Andrea was cleaning himself at the corner sink. Thanks to him, not me, the room smelled like sex.

"If he dies, they'll make you abbot," I added.

"I doubt it. The community resents me. No one voted me Anselmo's assistant. It was his choice. I wouldn't win an election."

"Who would?"

"Why?" he said, throwing me an accusatory glance. "Plan to fuck him too?"

I laughed. "You're kidding, right?"

"They're not all old and toothless." Andrea walked over to the foot of the bed.

"Yes, but Giorgio's not in the running, is he?" I playfully nudged his prick with my foot.

He eyed me tolerantly. "The American got here today."

"The American?"

"The illuminator. Paul Lewis. We had a nice chat."

"That's nice."

"He's attractive. Looks like a model. Skinny, though." Andrea returned to the sink and ran his fingers through his rumpled mop of hair. "I'm sure you two will be great friends."

"Introduce us." I looked at my wristwatch, the only thing I was wearing. It was 10:30. "We can go find him now It's still early"

Andrea smirked. "Rossi will probably do the honors. He's watching over him like a hawk."

"Why?" I said.

"Don't ask me. I'm going to bed." Andrea put on his briefs and habit, then slipped into his sandals.

I got up, put my arms around him, and kissed his ear. "You don't want to take a walk with me? We could change into jeans and go to the Piazza Navona."

"I have to check on Anselmo." Andrea kissed my lips and started for the door.

"Has Rossi been asking about me?" I said.

Andrea stopped and turned around. "Rossi?"

"He seemed very interested in my translating work when I talked to him."

For the sake of appearances, Andrea and I had concocted a reason for my residence at San Benedetto: I was translating a manuscript entitled *De Cristo*, recently discovered among the rare documents in the library. The book was a meditation on the sufferings of Christ by a 19th-century monk, Angelo Ferravi, currently being considered for sainthood by the Vatican.

"He didn't say anything to me," Andrea said, adding facetiously, "How's it coming, by the way?"

"I'm thinking I should do it if he plans to poke his nose into my business."

"It's a monk's way. Brotherly interest."

"When does this project of his begin, anyway?" I said, pulling on a pair of briefs.

"He's already put the calligraphers to work on the Gospel of Matthew. With four of them, they'll be finished with it by the first of the year."

"I thought there were three scribes—Rossi and the two queers." The two queer monks Roberto and Ricardo were inseparable, within the limits of monastic life. They spent the recreation period arranging flowers together on the altar and prayed the rosary side by side during their private devotion time—as a monk or two had mentioned to me. (Who knew or cared what the ugly pair did during the hour set aside for siesta?) Andrea disregarded the gibe.

"Rossi is making your boy Giorgio an apprentice," he said. "He might as well. He's too stupid to do much of anything else but copy script."

"Rossi says it's an art, I hear." I lifted a pair of jeans from a drawer.

"Where are you going?" Andrea said.

"I told you. A walk in the city."

Andrea looked perturbed. "If the monks see you in jeans, they'll cause problems. It's bad enough you don't keep the monastic schedule."

"They're all in bed." I had a feeling he was worried about what I might do in the city without a sacred habit to discourage trysts. "Why don't you come with me?" I said, to appease him. "I'll wait for you to check on Anselmo."

He dismissed the invitation with a wave of his hand. "Good night."

The air was cool in the city, a sign that the torrid Roman summer had finally run out of steam. I walked south along the dark Tiber, thinking I'd feed on one of the streetwalkers who take their clients into the bank's thick foliage. Seeing no activity among the trees, I cut through the tight, smelly streets of Trastevere, a cluttered, working-class neighborhood with laundry hanging from windows. Full of bohemian cafés and shops, the area had become popular with beautiful people who got off on slumming. As I passed a medieval Franciscan church, I thought I heard someone following me and stepped around the side of the building to wait. No one passed by. This happened two more times. I finally fed on a teenage boy pissing in an alley near a noisy café. His throat was soft as a breast in my mouth. He struggled, clawing my hands. His blood was like vinegary Chianti. I gagged on it but drank half a liter anyway so I wouldn't have to find another victim that night. When I released him, he crumpled to the ground like a marionette. He wasn't dead. Maybe he would live, but he'd never be able to explain what happened to him. And if he did, who would believe it?

When I returned to the monastery, I retrieved Angelo Ferravi's book from the dark library and translated a few pages in my cell. When I couldn't take another minute of pious shit about Christ's sufferings on the way to Calvary, I put the book down and thought about the American visitor. Andrea's snide comments about the illuminator had only aroused my curiosity. How could Andrea not realize that his petty insecurities worked against him?

At any rate, I wanted to take a look at the newcomer. I climbed the stairs, crossed through the dark church, and entered the rear building. This was where visiting monks usually stayed. A typed list of monks and their cell numbers was posted at the end of the hall on the floor above the recreation area. Not finding the American's name, I walked to the lateral dormitory On the first floor list, his name had been scribbled next to the number 2. I went to the end of the corridor and listened outside his door before turning the latch and entering. I stopped when he moved, concentrating on his mind until I could feel its energy and will him to continue sleeping.

With a vampire's vision, I saw him through the darkness and approached the bed. Andrea was right. He was a handsome boy with a gentle, open face. His long, sandy-brown hair spread softly on the pillow. His wide shoulders and lean, smooth torso rose above the sheets. I touched his hand and sensed a quiet strength rising from his flesh.

Then I sensed something else and jerked my hand away. His body held some sort of illness or disorder. Why it should matter to me, I did not know. Vampires never get sick. In a medieval French monastery I once inhabited, the plague took every monk within a six-week period. Not worried anymore about ruining my cover, I had fed on the sick brothers as they died in their beds. Their contaminated blood tasted acidic, but it didn't harm me.

I left the room and paced the cloister for an hour, contemplating the handsome boy before going to my rest.

A week passed before I met him. He came to dinner every night, nodded sheepishly to the monks at his table, and ate with his eyes on his food while the reader droned on in Italian. He disappeared during the recreation hour. I couldn't blame him. I felt sorry for him, unable to communicate with anyone but Rossi. I wondered about his disease and wanted to probe him. But the abbot recovered, leaving Andrea free to hang on me all night. Then we had a fight about something. I don't even remember what. Pouting, Andrea avoided me for a couple of days, giving me the chance to officially meet the newcomer.

When I saw lights in the upper floor of the library one night after the monks had retired, I climbed the stairs.

He sat at one of the five drafting tables in the big, open room, which also contained a long table covered with completed vellum pages spread to dry and a computer station against one of the white plaster walls. Heavy lamps, suspended from beamed trusses, glowed softly, and light from a gooseneck lamp on the boy's table flooded the page he was working on. He didn't look up when I entered.

"Interesting interpretation," I said, looking over his shoulder. The script on the page framed a painting of the Annunciation. The Virgin was not the standard European maiden found on hundreds of Christmas cards. She had dark hair and Middle-Eastern features. A vague defiance tempered her tender face, and she clutched her belly as though fearful of her imminent pregnancy. The angel—golden-haired and serene—stood behind her and appeared to whisper his message into her ear.

Flashing his bright hazel eyes at me, Paul smiled shyly. A thin scar left a gap in his left eyebrow and his nose was on the big side. The flaws somehow transformed a pretty face into a sexy one. He turned back to the picture, dipped his brush into a jar of russet paint, and applied it to the Virgin's cloak.

"I'm Victor," I said.

"Father Rossi told me about you. Nice to meet you. I'm Paul Lewis." This time his gaze connected solidly with mine. His clear eyes hinted of talent, if that's possible, a quiet perceptiveness and creativity His shyness had more to do with awareness of what his gaze revealed than it did with insecurity—though that too played a role. His sandy hair fell to his wide shoulders, bony under his gray turtleneck sweater—the sleeves of which he'd pushed up on his strong forearms. His hands were large, with long fingers and knobby knuckles, but dexterous, his left hand (I noticed he wore no wedding ring) wielding the brush without the least tension. I shook his free hand.

"You're freezing," I said, rubbing his hand between my palms. "You need to ask for a space heater. The boiler isn't big enough for the building."

"I don't think we better risk a space heater—if you know what I mean." He nodded toward the vellum pages on the long table.

"How long have you been here now?" I said, pulling up a chair. "Has it been a week?"

"A week today" he said. He deposited his brush in a little jar of water, which clouded to brown, and moved his chair to face me.

"What do you think?"

"Of the monastery?"

I shrugged, not caring what this delightful boy talked about as long as he talked. "Sure."

"Big," he said, his lips stretching into a grin.

"And cold."

"And cold," he agreed. "It's beautiful. The church, the grounds, the view of St. Peter's."

"Have you been down to see it?"

He shook his head, looking embarrassed. "No, believe it or not."

"Have you seen any of Rome?"

"Not much. The Trevi Fountain. The Spanish Steps."

"Want a tour? I can go change out of this and come back for you." I tugged on the scapular of my habit. "Or maybe you need to work."

"No. I'd love a tour. Don't you have to get permission or something?"

I laughed. "To hell with the rules," I said, then patted his knee when he looked surprised. "Don't worry, I've got a dispensation."

Dressed in jeans, a pullover sweater, and a leather jacket, I met him in the dark entrance cloister. He was inspecting the illuminated facade of the church.

"The original Abbey of San Benedetto was built in the 12th century," I said, "but 200 years later a fire destroyed every building in the enclosure—except the Romanesque church. A miracle, according to the holy monks."

Paul looked at me, once again surprised at my irreverence. "So they started all over?" he said.

"With the help of wealthy benefactors, the brick structures were soon rebuilt in the original design. Come on."

I led the way out of the enclosure and we started down the Gianicolo. The light from street lamps glowed softly on the sidewalk. The road was more or less deserted. Only the occasional scooter zipped by—down from the park up the hill that was a popular make-out point.

"How many monks live at San Benedetto?" Paul said.

"Over 50. Quite a few teach at Benedictine schools in the city or serve in local parishes. The rest work in the monastery, maintaining the buildings. And the library, of course. Your territory" I smiled at him. "Are you impressed with our illuminated manuscripts?"

"They're wonderful," he said sincerely. He seemed incredibly innocent.

"But nothing like what you're working on. How did Rossi find you anyway?"

Paul smiled. I was happy to see no sign of annoying self-effacement. "My boss, Derek," he said. "He was the head calligrapher of a Bible manuscript commissioned by a Benedictine Abbey. I was an illuminator. The team of scribes was about halfway through the Old Testament when Derek said he wanted to take me out to lunch one Friday afternoon. He seemed really serious, so I thought he wanted to fire me or something."

"Why? Were you a bad boy?" I threw him a playful glance. Why not flirt for once with someone who really got my attention, instead of pathetic Andrea?

His eyes showed he liked the attention. "I'd ruined my share of pages."

I clicked my tongue. "Go on."

"Well, we drove to a Taco Bell. It was really hot out. The place was packed with sweaty football players." Paul's glance seemed to test my appreciation for the erotic image, and mine reassured him of it. "We found a table outside. Derek unwraps his fajita like the paper's full of explosives. I mean, it was so slow, and I just sat there staring at his wonky plaid shirt, his pocket protector with its two pencils... anyway, he takes a bite, chews—again *very slowly*, then he asks me if I'm curious."

"And you're probably ready to tear his head off?"

"I was *relieved*. He says, 'Take a look at this,' and hands me a typed plan for an illuminated manuscript of the Gospels. A one-year project, 200 pages of sheepskin vellum, one-half meter long by about one-third meter wide. An honest to goodness hand-written book of the four Gospels. A half-page illumination to head each Gospel. Another 50 illuminations of major parables scattered through the manuscript: the Prodigal Son, the Good Samaritan..."

Paul's eyes gleamed as he described the project. His soft voice lilted with animation.

"Then he reaches across the table, thumps me on the chest, and says, They want you.' He'd sent them copies of my work. I was floored. I asked him about our own project—we had three years of work left. He shrugged and told me I couldn't pass up the opportunity."

"So here you are," I said, patting his back and keeping my hand there. "You must be a pretty good artist."

Paul's back stiffened slightly, and I removed my hand.

"I owe everything to Derek," he said. "The only illuminating I'd ever done was for a senior project in college. I painted figures of Madame Eglantine for a manuscript of *The Canterbury Tales.* Derek showed me how to grind lapis lazuli and vermilion for incredibly vivid blue and red pigment. And he showed me how to blow through a reed straw on gilt. Which makes condensation, so gold leaf will adhere to the gesso. He also showed me how to burnish the gilt so it would last 1,000 years."

"That long?" I admired Paul's passion as he described the technicalities of illumination. Two thousand years of residence in monasteries packed with paintings and sculpture had numbed me to their beauty.

At the bottom of the Gianicolo, the dark river just ahead of us, we turned north and walked along the hulking Hospital of Santo Spirito, just a few blocks from St. Peter's.

"This is Rome's oldest hospital," I said. "Pope Innocent the Third built it for orphans in the nth century after he had a nightmare about abandoned babies bobbing in the Tiber. Take a look at this." I led him to a little window near the hospital's quiet entrance. "It's called the rota. Women stuck their unwanted babies in it. There's a little barrel inside that revolves."

As Paul touched the bronze grill over the window, a breeze fluttered strands of his hair. I fought the impulse to brush them back from his face.

"According to Martin Luther, the pope fathered the babies," I said.

"You think he was right?"

"Absolutely."

We cut through a side street to Via della Conciliazione, the avenue leading into St. Peter's Square. Shops were closed and the area was quiet. Paul seemed intrigued by the tacky religious goods displayed in the shop windows. In one window, we saw a framed hologram in which a crucified Jesus opened and closed his eyes.

"He's winking at you," I said.

Paul studied me. "You know," he finally said, "you don't seem like a monk."

"No? Well, maybe I'm not the typical monk."

"Did you join the order here?"

I shook my head. "The States. My community sent me here to translate St. Angelo's meditations.

"Meditations on what?"

"The sufferings of Christ. Real and imagined."

"Seems pretty sadistic."

"It is sadistic. Self-flagellation. Saints being grilled alive. St. Lucy proudly displaying in her hands her own eyes, which have been plucked out because she guarded her precious virtue. It's all sadistic. But you have to admit, there's something alluring about blood and pain."

He didn't answer. I wondered if he was thinking of his disease. He obviously liked men; maybe he was infected with HIV.

We walked through St. Peter's colonnades, which reached around the piazza like two arms snatching the faithful from the sinful world. The majestic Renaissance facade of the Basilica was dimly lit.

"Here we are," I said, "the center of Roman Catholicism. Michelangelo's masterpiece."

We crossed the vast piazza, dotted with tourists futilely snapping pictures in the dark and chattering in English, Portuguese, and Japanese. Three off-duty Swiss guards in their medieval striped uniforms joked with one another near the portico. They nodded at us as we approached the enormous columns.

"My God," Paul said, touching one of the pillars.

"The interior is even more impressive."

"We'll have to come back when it's open."

"You'll have to do that without me," I said. I told him about my skin disease, going into the technicalities of the epidermis, the immune system, and the effect of solar radiation. I spoke matter-of-factly, to clearly communicate the conditions of our future dealings without arousing sympathy. It seemed to work. Paul attended to the explanation with an expression of understanding, not pity.

"So you have to stay out of direct sunlight completely?" he said.

"Even indirect sunlight. I can't risk it. So I lock myself up in a special little cell in the crypt and stay there until sundown. Like a vampire."

The word seemed to take him off guard. He puzzled over it for an instant. Then he looked away, scanning the dim piazza.

I waited for *his* confession. But it was not forthcoming.

"Have you always had the condition?" he finally said.

No, I imagined answering *him, just for 2,000 years.* But I told him the disease was congenital, active since birth and worsening—requiring more severe measures—in my adulthood. There was no cure and no treatment apart from avoiding sunlight. Only a handful of people around the world had documented cases. And from what experts knew, the disease was not fatal as long as the correct precautions were taken.

"So what do you know about the eternal city?" I said as we headed away from the Basilica.

"Just what I learned in the guidebooks. Seven hills. The Tiber. Founded by twins Romulus and Remus, who were nursed by a wolf. The Republic, the Empire, the Barbarians, the Vatican. Sophia Loren."

I laughed. "The old city is what matters. The Vatican is back there, behind St. Peter's." I pointed over my shoulder. "Then just to the south the Gianicolo area, with old Trastevere to the south of it. The rest is in front of us, to the East. The landmarks are the Spanish Steps and a huge park called the Villa Borghese to the north, the Colosseum, Forum, and Baths of Caracalla to the south. The Piazza Navona, the Pantheon, and the Trevi Fountain in the center. You could hike around the entire ancient center in one morning."

"Or evening," Paul said, smiling warmly.

I could see that Paul's shyness had nothing to do with reserve. He spoke without self-consciousness. His glances, his tone showed his attraction to me, his willingness to trust.

We crossed the river at the Castel Sant'Angelo and walked the mile east to the Piazza Navona, chatting about this and that as we strolled through the dark, narrow streets, breathing the crisp air that heralded October. Rome in autumn was toasty by day, like a ripe apple basking in light filtered through branches. By night the sweetness of the apple crystallized in the cool air, infusing the stucco buildings and cobbled back streets with an innocence and charm that belied centuries of toil, violence, and political machination.

As usual, even at the late hour, the Piazza buzzed with activity The vendors, tourists, and gypsy performers filled the elliptical space, and customers crowded the cafés on the perimeter. We found an outside table near a gas heat lamp and ordered coffee. I gave Paul my jacket when I noticed him shivering, joking that I was warm-blooded. In that moment, he looked at me as though he wanted to kiss me. I wanted to kiss him.

As we trudged up the Gianicolo on the way home, he asked me why I became a monk.

"Passion," I said, without thinking.

"For God?"

"I suppose so." The god of the monks, Joshu's god, certainly aroused a passion that had ruled me for centuries, the passion for revenge that no one but a being like me could begin to understand. What better place to find it than in his sacred monasteries?

"I've never been religious," he said, reflectively. "It's ironic, isn't it? Here I am, illustrating a Bible for a bunch of monks."

"The soul and religion are two different things," I said. "Religion confines, unless you call the shots."

"Call the shots?"

"Let religion serve your purpose. People have done it for centuries."

"You mean serve the soul's purpose?"

"I guess you could say that."

"What is the soul's purpose?"

"To create," I said, squeezing his arm. "The way you create with your art. Truthfully. Without the pious bullshit. Remind people they're made of flesh and blood."

He smiled gratefully. "What about inspiration? Aren't artists supposed to remind people that there's something more?"

"You mean heaven?" I shook my head. "Leave that to the pope."

"You don't believe in heaven?" he said, amazed.

"Not the one for only pious souls."

"I didn't know there was another one."

"There is." I was thinking of an eternity in the Dark Kingdom, an eternity that would become available to me once I left behind a vampire's life. The Kingdom where people remained themselves, with all their passions. Where they laughed and lusted and felt cool water on their flesh and the warmth of a new, transformed sun, whose rays could never kill.

The night I transported Michael to the Dark Kingdom, I believed he would succumb. Clinging to my bare back as we flew, he pointed excitedly to arches and towers and massive palaces in the pristine New Rome. I felt his heart race as we soared above beautiful boys hurling javelins in green fields and lying in one another's arms on rooftops. Parades, games, lovemaking unfolded beneath us in the glittering city. Barrel-chested men raced boats along the Tiber, and on the banks danced men and women and children, all decked in scarlet, green, and shimmering gold. Among them was Tiresia, the Ethiopian sorceress whose blood had transformed me into a predator. "A brief period as a vampire," I said to Michael, "and all of this is yours and mine. Forever."

I could escape the nocturnal life only by finding a replacement, and Michael could have done the same after the required years had passed, joining me in a place where daylight couldn't hurt us anymore.

But in the end Michael refused. It had been too much to ask.

At 2 in the morning, I reluctantly said good night to Paul and, feeling more restless than hungry, walked back down the Gianicolo to the city. I paced the overgrown field near the Colosseum, where the magnificent Circus Maximus once stood. The stadium around the elliptical track had roared with a crowd of 300,000 as chariots flew past the bronze dolphins in the center. Nearby, the forum and the palaces of the Palatine Hill—now pathetic rubble—had once surged with the energy of politics and trade and intrigue. Rome's lifeblood.

Lions tore Christians to shreds in the Circus Maximus, not in the Colosseum. I'd seen a man throw himself to the ground and stretch his arms as if nailed to a cross. When they released the lions, one of them galloped to the ready meal and bit a chunk from his leg.

The sky glowed from the city lights. Traffic whirred along the Corso, half a mile away. But the field and the ruins around it were dark and vacant.

After an hour, hunger gnawed my gut. I wandered to a bar for men in Trastevere. The beefy attendant eyed me with admiration when I paid the cover charge at the door. I thought he'd make a nice meal, but his public position discouraged an attack; and anyway I wanted to examine the goods inside. The dark, crowded room smelled of tobacco and cologne—like every gay bar I'd ever entered. American rock blasted over voices, the bass vibrating my teeth. The small dance floor gyrated with sweaty bodies. Most of the men clustering around the tall tables were friends, but plenty of singles preened near the dance floor. Several eyed me, but none suited my taste. I descended a narrow staircase to what had once probably been a wine cellar and strolled through a damp, dimlit network of corridors perfect for sex. I passed several heads bobbing at crotches but found no one alone.

On my way back up the stairs, I met a boy on his way down. He had long, bleach-blond hair, and black eyebrows, an open shirt exposing pierced nipples, and drug-glazed eyes that managed to retain their seductiveness. He could see I wanted him. He brushed against me and motioned for me to follow him down.

I shook my head. "Too crowded," I shouted over the music.

He looked me over and nodded. "*Bene,*" he said, cupping his mouth with his hand to amplify the sound, "you come home with me." He thumped his chest like a self-important monkey. I kissed him hard to keep him excited.

As we strolled through the narrow back streets to his apartment, he frequently stumbled and clutched my arm to steady himself. I didn't much like the idea of his drugged blood, but he was easy prey and I had to feed.

Stiff towels dangled on a clothesline strung between his dark apartment building and the one across the brick alley. On both buildings, the usual shutters found on most Roman buildings covered the windows. *Good,* I thought. *No nosy neighbors to remember me later.*

The floors and walls in the lobby of his building were made of Travertine marble—as cheap and common in Italy as plywood in America. Years of grime and soap scum had dulled them. The dim overhead light of this depressing chamber reminded me of a public rest room, and because the odor of urine wafted in from the alley, the place smelled like one too.

The boy led me by the hand up two flights of marble stairs to his door. He squeezed his hand into the pocket of his tight jeans and fished out a ring of keys.

The neatness of the apartment surprised me. The marble floors sparkled in the lamplight. The plaster walls were spotless. While he used the bathroom, I wandered through the large living room and dining room. A modern Italian sofa and two matching chairs upholstered in fake tiger skin created a sitting area. Movie magazines were stacked neatly on the glass and chrome tables. On the largest wall hung a huge silk-screened image of Marilyn Monroe. In the dining room six black high-backed chairs sat around a glass table with a bowl of ceramic fruit as a centerpiece. Behind a cotton curtain, I found a neat kitchenette. A hot plate and microwave sat on the countertop. A dishcloth lay folded over the faucet in the tiny porcelain sink, indelibly yellowed.

"You want something to eat?" the boy said as I peered into the kitchenette.

"Yes. You." I pulled him to me and sucked the salty skin of his neck. His body relaxed in my arms. My fangs descended. But I took in a breath to control myself. I wanted to make my pleasure last. "Let's go to bed."

He smiled a drunken smile, exposing straight, white teeth. Taking me by the hand once again, he led me to his bedroom, where he clicked on a lamp. The large chamber was as neat as the rest of the apartment. The bureau and night table shined, dust-free and uncluttered. The lime-green bedspread, printed with large geometrical shapes, draped the mattress without a wrinkle.

I stripped off his shirt and then his jeans, finding a bulging black jockstrap underneath them.

He threw his arms around me and whispered in my ear, "I'm Marco."

"*Molto piacere*, Marco," I said. Kissing his smooth cheek, I felt that sweet *piacere* in my loins. "I'm Victor." I saw no reason to lie about my name. He would never reveal it to a soul once I'd finished with him.

As trusting as a bride, he opened his legs to me. The drugs and alcohol might have explained his lack of inhibition, but I sensed he gave himself easily to strong men, as the movie star on his wall once had. He sucked my tongue hungrily, spat in my hand at my command, and moaned when I rammed myself through his sphincter. He smiled dreamily, too high to be hard. But I was hard as steel.

As I merged with him I saw Paul in my mind. I imagined those shy eyes, and the lean, smooth torso I'd inspected in the dark cell. I imagined burying my face in his long hair and feeling his knobby, dexterous fingers on my back.

By the time I'd withdrawn myself, he was asleep. I could feed without fighting him. He would go quickly, peacefully, maybe dreaming that I continued my lovemaking. But I couldn't bring myself to end his life.

Quickly dressing, I let myself out of his apartment. At each door down the hall I paused, listened, and inhaled the aroma of blood. At the door farthest from Marco's, the aroma was faint, which indicated perhaps only one inhabitant, much safer for me. I slowly pushed the door until the deadbolt broke through the frame. I stopped, listening for any response to the noise, but heard nothing.

I eased open the door and closed it behind me. Light from an aquarium in the corner of the living room revealed a piano, heavy furniture, and a cluttered floor. A cat stood and stretched on the back of the sofa, hopped down, and brushed against my leg before sauntering off toward what looked like the kitchen. I proceeded down a dark hallway with two closed doors on each side and a partially open door at the end. The smell of blood came from the room with the open door. Slipping off my boots, I crept down the cool marble floor to the dark room. Inside it rosewater perfume hung in the air. I clutched my nose to keep from sneezing, but it was too late.

"Who's there?" a woman cried out.

As she reached for the lamp on the night table, I jumped on the bed, clasped her mouth with my hand, sank my fangs into her warm, fat throat, and gulped her blood. When she went limp I removed my hand from her mouth and continued drinking. Then I snapped her neck.

There was no reason to turn on the light. Better to leave without any memory of my victim's face. But I wanted to see her and turned it on all the same.

She was a heavy woman in her 50s with a mole the size of a marble above her thin lips. Melon-sized breasts rose under a white cotton nightgown. Her nails gleamed with bright red polish. Her almond-shaped eyes, vestiges of former beauty, stared at me. I closed them, turned out the light, and went to the front door. Finding the corridor empty, I hurried out into the night.

* * *

Back in my cell, bloated and lonely, I thought about going to Andrea's bed, but I couldn't take his need for reassurance. Only the day before he'd approached my choir stall with a hurt expression.

"You were looking at him," he'd whispered, glancing at two monks who were kneeling in their stalls.

I'd nodded toward the sacristy and he'd followed me across the stone floor, both of us bowing to the altar before slipping into the room off the sanctuary. The place smelled of wax and incense. Tall cabinets lined the walls with thin drawers for vestments and closets for altar linens, candles, and other liturgical paraphernalia.

"What's this about?" I said. My low voice reverberated against the vault.

"You were staring at Giorgio during vespers."

"Dressing like a monk doesn't make you one, you know." I touched his cheek.

"Maybe this is a bad idea after all. I have responsibilities."

"So?" I said. "Take care of them. You don't have to worry about me."

"You can't stay here forever." He seemed to be reminding himself more than me.

"I'll stay as long as you let me," I said. His body relaxed as I took him in my arms and kissed him.

I resented playing his little games and was glad to have the scene over with. I didn't want another encounter with him now. I stuffed my pillow under the blanket in case Andrea looked in—though he'd promised not to disturb me by day—then went to my tomb.

The crypt resembled the church itself. Columns, which supported arches, divided the chamber into three sections. Alcoves lined both sides of the chamber, and each alcove housed six tombs, three behind each lateral wall of the niche. Votive candles on stone altars in the alcoves cast their meager light on the flagstones. I slid into my shelf, pulling the slab into place by means of spikes I'd pounded into the back.

As usual on settling into sleep, my mind returned to *him*, the one who'd haunted my existence for 2,000 years:

Joshu.

After 2,000 years, desire for Joshu still tore at me. After 2,000 years, he remained the sinewy boy I had discovered dancing naked on a ridge above Jerusalem. I had changed. Victor Decimus, proven officer under Pontius Pilate, had become predator of the night, immortal stalker of mortal prey. But the sensuous Jesus of Nazareth survived crucifixion by Roman soldiers and deification by two millennia of pious followers looking for a sterile god. To me, he would always be flesh and blood. The thought of his solid, chiseled pectorals, his delicate throat, his circumcised flesh still made me hard. His gaze, half-arrogant, half-playful still teased me to the point of insanity.

With my lover Michael lost to me forever, and the Dark Kingdom no longer tempting without an eternal companion, how could I keep my thoughts from Joshu, who lived on? Maybe if I'd ever mounted him, as I ached to, he would have lost his power over me. Maybe if I'd ever thrust my prick through his lips. But that had never happened, and it never would. How could it? A kind of membrane divided our eternal spheres. I could see him, feel him, even taste him through it, but I could never possess him.

And he still pursued me in apparitions. In some he hung once again from a cross, dripping warm blood on my face. In others he pressed his taut belly against me and whispered in my ear. His message never changed: "It's not too late, Victor. Come to me. Come to heaven." His heaven—an eternity of static worship in a court of castrated angels.

I remembered seeing him in New Orleans, where I'd fled after the events recorded in *Vampire Vow*. I'd just snapped the neck of a hustler in the French Quarter. I was bloated with his drug-laced blood and still hard with excitement after ramming his soft, tattooed buttocks. The Quarter's streets reeked of piss. In need of fresh air, I strolled along the riverwalk. Ten feet from me, Joshu stood under a streetlamp. Wearing only a loincloth, he stretched out his arms as though they were nailed again to the cross. A breeze from the river rustled his dark hair. Knowing he would bring only frustration, I tried to flee, but couldn't. I ran to him, dropped to my knees, and embraced his waist. The scent of his rich blood made the hustler's blood churn inside me, and I retched.

"Follow me," he said.

"Where?" My head was spinning or I wouldn't have asked a question with such a predictable answer. But his response was new.

"Home," he said.

"Home?"

"Galilee. The Sea of Galilee."

"What are you up to?" I shouted, squinting to sharpen my blurry vision.

His pale body brightened, as though the streetlamp had become a flood-light. The wind gathered force. The river lapped fiercely against the pilings. A garbage can on the walk overturned and paper and bottles whirled across the boards and down into the street. A ship's foghorn blared nearby in the darkness. When the noise grew as loud as a siren, I clapped my hands over my ears. The light intensified until I was blinded by it. Then in an instant there descended around me a darkness and silence so profound, I might have been at the bottom of an ocean. Joshu's name formed on my lips, but no sound emerged.

For days afterward I slept fitfully in the crypt I'd occupied in a ceme-tery near my New Orleans mansion in the stately Garden District. Joshu's words echoed in the chamber, "Follow me... Follow me..." In a state of half-sleep, I believed he was actually there and awoke in a sweat, expecting to see him. But I found only darkness.

As I now began to doze, my belly full of warm blood, whispers echoed in the alcove. At first I thought of Jana, whose angry presence I had felt at the Piazza Navona. Then I recognized the voices. They belonged to Joshu and Michael, together now in Joshu's heaven. I shoved the slab. The crash it made when it hit the floor must have echoed through the church above.

The votive candles flickering on the little altar in the alcove revealed no one.

"Cowards!" I shouted, not giving a damn if anyone had heard the slab or me. My fangs descended as they do when I feed. I wanted to tear into their throats.

The crypt was still. I lay in the silence for a moment before again hoist-ing up the slab and falling into an uneasy sleep.

Love

They say opposites attract.
The sun loves to gleam on ice (before destroying it).

CHAPTER FIVE

PAUL

Alice's phone rang eight times. I waited nervously for her to answer. I stood at the end of the dim corridor in the monks' dormitory. It was after midnight Rome time, 5 P.M. in Kansas. She should have been home from work by now.

My mind flashed back to the sight of her in the hospital: Normally, she was a nice-looking woman—with high cheekbones and the same bright hazel eyes as me. But that day in the hospital bed, with no makeup, she'd looked skeletal. They'd removed her dentures and her lips had caved in. Her frail, spotted hands lay at her sides, an IV tube taped to one of them. When I smoothed her short gray hair and kissed her forehead, she'd opened her eyes, blinked a few times, then shut them again. Her room reeked of the damn tobacco that had probably put her there.

Nine rings. Ten. As I waited for my mother to answer, I imagined her crumpled on the living room floor, her chihuahua Emilio frantically nosing her face. Finally she picked up.

"Hey Alice." I kept my voice down. "What took you so long?"

"I was outside with Emilio. How are you, honey?" She sounded happy and maybe a little teary.

Almost a month had passed at San Benedetto. I'd settled in. The work was exciting. I was in love. Of course, I didn't tell Alice that. She'd be happy if I met someone—especially after Rick—just not another monk.

"So have you been feeling OK?" I said. "What did the doctor say?"

"Everything's just great."

"What about the smoking?"

"Oh, honey. I'm trying."

"Mom, you've gotta stop. It'll kill you."

"I will."

I knew she wouldn't. She had no discipline. The two or three times she'd tried—once when she had pneumonia—she lasted all of two days.

"Why don't you try the patch again?"

"All right," she said to appease me. "I miss you, Paul. I'm worried about you over there, with everything that's going on in the world."

"There aren't any terrorists in Rome," I said, clueless about the state of Italian security.

"Foreigners just hate Americans."

"The monks are great." I hesitated before adding, "One's even an American."

"Well, that's nice. Where's he from?"

"New Orleans."

"Oh," she said. For her New Orleans was almost as foreign as Rome, and anything foreign didn't suit her. "Well, just watch yourself when you're out and about."

Another monk...

I'd had crushes in the past, especially on guys who didn't know I existed. The first was in seventh grade, when hormones suddenly alerted me to every shirtless actor on TV. Over the summer, a nerdy kid in class had developed into a witty, suave heartthrob. His new bass voice made my groin tingle when he sat next to me in the lunchroom. His neck thickened, his body filled out, his hair waved, and his new glasses heightened his sophistication. Giving myself over to the fantasy of his lips on my neck, belly, scrotum, I rested in his protection. I was safe. And desirable.

Nothing came of that crush or the crushes on straight boys in high school. But at the University of Kansas I had a couple of real boyfriends, both athletic and assertive. I broke with the second guy a year before I met Rick. Rick with the soft-brown eyes flecked with amber. Rick, the solemn, disciplined, guilt-ridden Catholic who channeled his struggles into sexual energy. My luck.

We'd make out in his dorm at night and he'd run to confession in the morning, undaunted by the humiliation of admitting the same sin day after day. I guess I was relieved when we finally broke up and Rick joined the Benedictines.

Several months later he called me out of the blue. Just hearing his voice again turned me on.

"How you doing?" he said. He seemed to miss me. "How's teaching?"

"Fine." I doubted he'd want to hear about the farting contests conducted by the fifth-grade boys in my art classes. Such was my life after graduating with a fine arts degree from the University of Kansas: moving every day like a gypsy from middle school to middle school, teaching drawing and painting in converted storage rooms and closets—most without windows.

"You working on any projects?"

I glanced at an empty canvas leaning against the wall of my bedroom, under a poster of Venus di Milo. "No," I said. "The kids take all my energy."

"Want one?"

He told me about the Bible project coming to the university.

"What about you?" I said. "You draw better. And you're a monk."

"Not my thing anymore. Besides, you've done this. Derek loves your work."

"You showed him?" I'd given Rick a page depicting the dainty Madame Eglantine, dressed in a blue habit and riding a horse.

"He was impressed," Rick said.

"It's a full-time job, isn't it?" I said. "I'd have to quit teaching."

"The manuscript will be around for a thousand years."

I suddenly felt sad, wishing I could kiss him. He was a great kisser. "So you're happy now?"

"Yes," he said quietly.

That had been our last conversation.

*   *   *

My feelings for Rick had been tender; but those for Victor were intense. I had never been so consumed with a man. For two weeks now, I'd woken up and fallen asleep with a strange sense of his presence. In the scriptorium, I worked merrily away, hour after hour, imagining what he would say that evening when I showed him the widow of Naim's expression or my take on the loaves and the fishes. I lived for our evening strolls through Rome: As Victor pointed out Bernini's fountains, explained Roman history, and helped me practice Italian, I imagined myself in his strong arms, pressed against his chest and groin, inhaling the musky scent on his throat.

He reminded me of a gladiator, with his sturdy neck and square jaw, his blatant arrogance. But physical attraction alone couldn't explain his power over me. As strange as it sounds, his body was shaped by his soul. Some kind of deep-dwelling insistence or determination controlled his facial muscles, the movements of his limbs, and even his posture. He was beyond alert. He was attuned to something silent and invisible. He was waiting and watching. And the weirdest thing—his intensity was somehow a matter of pride. And survival.

But even when his glances and touches made his attraction to me unmistakable, I held back. *He's taken his vows*, I told myself. *He is consecrated.*

Another monk.

After spending time with Father Rossi and the four calligraphers and getting to know a few of the other guys, I came to understand the monks' brand of reserve. As friendly as he was, Father Rossi spoke to me mostly about the work or about his religion. Roberto and Ricardo, the two portly scribes, joked with me in bad English but left me out of their conversations and even out of the silence they somehow shared. When it was time for prayer before dinner they disappeared from the scriptorium without a word. Even Giorgio, as young as he was, had already learned to keep his distance, nodding politely as he came and went. The language barrier might have explained some of this. But mostly a different world explained it, a world with ideals, loyalties, and a history that didn't include me.

Victor possessed their sense of superiority, but to the nth degree. People seemed to exist for him. Even the other monks aroused his contempt. His attitude confused me. He was like a monk, but not like a monk.

His sense of superiority, his sophistication despite his unworldly calling as a monk made me keep certain information from him. For starters, I guarded facts about my hometown and my family. In Topeka, the meager little downtown skyline had only two prominent features: the capitol dome (a thinner, missile-like version of the national rotunda) and the twin steeples of St. Joseph Catholic Church. The skinny brown Kansas River snaked through the north part of the city. Along it, the Santa Fe railroad yards sprawled their clutter of boxcars, giant spools of cable, corrugated storage sheds, and heaped metal parts that gleamed in the relentless sun. Warehouses, grain elevators, and dingy factories lined the river too, near neighborhoods of simple frame homes built by German immigrants and even more modest, brightly painted homes where Mexicans had settled.

Our little ranch-style house was north of that section of the city, in a rural area with mailboxes along the roads. Rusted pickups perched on cinder blocks in gravel driveways. Double-wide trailers sat on lots overgrown with weeds. Vegetation was scruffy, itchy, vining along dilapidated picket fences and into drainage ditches along the roads. Even the trees seemed inferior, growing only half as high in the Kansas prairie as they seemed to grow in the rest of the country.

I guess I always dreamed of living somewhere else, in a cosmopolitan city on the East Coast—Washington or New York—but my family had a hold on me. Despite my clipped answers to questions about them, Victor seemed to sense their power over me. He seemed curious to know why they possessed such power, like it was some kind of novelty to be so attached to a family. The truth is they embarrassed me a little, and my shame for feeling this way wasn't strong enough to overcome my reserve about them.

My redneck father, who died when I was 7, repaired roofs for a local contractor. Every night he settled into his recliner and downed a six-pack of beer as he watched TV. My mother served food in a cafeteria. My sister, Becky, was a single parent who seemed destined to go on welfare. My older brother, Al, ran a second-rate hardware store and spoke in grunts.

None of them cared much for books or culture. They didn't understand me. But they loved me. And I loved them. I owed them too, or at least I owed my mother. Alice had protected me against my father, who couldn't stand to have a son so obviously destined to be queer.

Once when I was 5 or 6, Dad walked into my room and found me playing with Becky's Barbie doll. I was dressing her in her wildest outfits—a tiger-skin bathing suit, a sequined evening dress. He saw me on the floor with the doll in my hand and looked wounded, like he could hardly stand the shame. Then he cussed and went for the board he liked to use on me, a slat from an old rolltop desk. As his striped overalls disappeared through the door, I flew under the bed. He came back, dragged me out by the arm, and laid into me.

Alice ran in and yelled for him to stop. She beat him on the head with her fist and pulled me away from him, getting her forearm smacked by the board in the process. The welt lingered for a week. Red-faced, Dad eyed me with disgust, stamped out of the house, climbed into his pickup, and tore off down the road. Alice picked up the board, trudged out to an old dried-up well on our property, and dropped it in. Dad came back drunk and feeling sorry for himself, expecting us to pity him for having it so bad.

When Dad died, she found a new reason to protect me: epileptic seizures.

The first one hit me in a grocery store where Alice had stopped after picking me up from school. She had pointed the shopping cart in the direction of the cereal aisle when I told her we were out of my favorite brand, but I was 9 and had just gotten a new pair of sneakers and ran ahead of her, making them squeak on the linoleum. A box of Trix in my hands, I was waiting for her when she turned down the aisle. She'd just finished her shift at the cafeteria and wore a white uniform and white tennis shoes. For an instant under the fluorescent light she blurred into a radiant angel.

The store's Muzak suddenly blared, and I smelled garlic and heard a sound like a spoon clinking against glass. The next thing I knew, Alice was kneeling over me, yelling my name. Panic seemed to tighten everything about her—her face, her shoulders, even her hair, which was pulled back under a hairnet. Her chest was heaving, and her nicotine breath made me so queasy I turned my head and found three pair of shoes near me—black oxfords, sneakers, and hush puppies.

Someone, the man in the oxfords I thought, said, "Well, the ambulance is on the way." He sounded irritated, as though he shouldn't have bothered.

"Are you OK, Paul?" Alice said. She felt my cheek, which was wet with drool.

"I'm just tired," I said, closing my eyes. I'd never felt so tired.

The ambulance ended up taking me to the hospital, though Alice had no insurance to cover the cost. The ER doctor shone a light in my eyes, listened to my heart, took my pulse, and asked Alice if I was taking any medication or if I'd been sick. She said no. Then he asked her to describe exactly what had happened.

"He just went into convulsions," she said. "He was flopping on the floor like a fish. His teeth were chattering. And he was drooling."

"And nothing like this has ever happened before?"

"No," she said.

The doctor stroked the little peninsula of brown hair above his forehead. "What happened just before the seizure?" he asked her.

She frowned and shrugged. "Nothing. He ran to the cereal aisle, and then it started."

"Did you notice anything beforehand?" he said to me. "Any strange sounds or smells?"

I told him about the garlic and the sound of the spoon against the glass.

He nodded, as though the sensations made perfect sense. I later learned that they were part of my aura, the warning epileptics often get that a seizure is imminent. Before severe seizures I sometimes saw blood dripping down a canvas.

The doctor told Alice the convulsion might mean epilepsy, that I should have an EEG and an MRI to check for any brain problems. She looked worried and asked how soon I could get tested—pretty good of her since the insurance problem loomed. She asked the doctor what caused seizures like mine.

"Disorderly brain activity," he said.

I imagined little gremlins running around in my head.

"It can be caused by a tumor or brain damage," he said. "But in 70% of cases, no cause is found."

Alice just stared at him, apparently imagining the possibilities. Later, when she read that lack of oxygen at birth can cause epilepsy, she beat herself up for smoking, somehow figuring that it deprived me of air.

"Don't worry," the doctor said. "Seizures can't cause brain damage. And they can't kill." He winked at me.

So I had the tests. They showed no abnormalities. After two more seizures, I was officially pronounced an epileptic at the age of 9.

Phenobarbital controlled the attacks, but if I lost sleep or stared at sunlight on water or through branches as I drove, the drug actually caused a weird seizure that left me half-conscious. Visions came to me.

The first one occurred on Thanksgiving Day when I was 11. The night before I'd stayed up late in the kitchen drawing faces in a sketchpad. An art teacher at school had suggested I cut in half magazine photos of movie stars and try to sketch the other side of their faces. The kitchen was cozy and smelled of the pumpkin pies Alice had baked for the next day, and I was absorbed in the drawings. When I finally looked up at the clock it was 2:30. I went to bed. At 6:30 Emilio started yapping outside my door to be taken out, so I got up and stayed up.

We loaded the food in the car and headed for Grandma's. In the backseat of our mildewy 1964 Chevelle Malibu, I stared out at the sunlight flashing through the trees along our road.

Before I knew it, I was mesmerized, half-asleep and yet strangely perceptive, my senses sharp. The garlic smell wafted around me as though I was in an Italian restaurant. The spoon tinkled on glass.

A vivid scene played before my eyes.

Dad was balanced about five feet away from a dormer on a steep roof, a hammer in his hand. He wore a red stocking cap, a plaid flannel shirt, jeans, and a puffy, down-filled vest that allowed his arms free movement. Squinting in the bright sunlight, he turned his angular features toward me. He could see me, I could tell. He seemed sad. I imagined he was sorry that he didn't much care for me, that he wished he did.

His hammer slipped from his hand. As it slid down the roof, lodging near the gutter, he crouched to retrieve it and lost his footing. I shouted, "Hold on, Dad. Hold on." He seemed to fall in slow motion, like a sheet of paper drifting on a current of air, his legs and arms outstretched.

The next thing I knew my head was in Alice's lap on the back seat. She was crying. She'd pulled the car off to the shoulder of the road.

My father had died in exactly the way I'd seen it happen, only I wasn't anywhere near the scene of the accident at the time. Maybe my imagination had just reconstructed the scene from details I'd overheard, but what I had seen was incredibly real.

Over the next couple of years, more old incidents replayed during the trances, none of which I had witnessed, all pretty bland—my brother Al's winning free throw in a high school basketball game, Becky's wipeout on her bicycle. But then the trances changed.

First there was the vision of Alice's toy poodle getting hit by a truck one Sunday afternoon. He spun off the wheel of a red pickup, landing in the drainage ditch by our road. I snapped out of the trance. When I came to, I went out and found him, his little skull bashed in. We buried him in the backyard.

And on the Fourth of July big fountains of blue and yellow and red against the black sky above our property prompted a scary trance. I saw Becky hoist a Roman candle and strike a pose like the Statue of Liberty. She was at a cousin's pool party at the time. The candle fired twice and then backfired into her bare stomach. I yelled "Becky," Alice shook me from the trance, and the phone rang inside. My aunt confirmed everything.

Some trances scared me even more. I saw strangers being beaten and stabbed. I saw several drownings. The worst involved a little girl trapped under a dock at a nearby reservoir, her hair floating up like the sepals of a sea anemone.

Sometimes the local news corroborated the visions. Sometimes no confirmation came. And what could I do to help people I didn't recognize or know how to find?

Alice took me to the doctor, made me explain everything, and drilled him about my meds, as though the wrong ones could bring on clairvoyance. He told her epilepsy doesn't give people a sixth sense and reminded her I'd probably outgrow the seizures altogether. Eventually.

I didn't want Victor to know about the epilepsy or the freakish visions. I didn't want him to know I was defective. I don't know what I expected from him. I only knew I wanted him and had to screen out whatever might ruin my chances of getting him. So I kept the phenobarbital out of sight.

The evening after my phone call to Alice, Victor and I had planned to meet in the weight room that was adjacent to the recreation hall where the monks sometimes spent their evenings socializing. Of course the prospect of stripping down to athletic shorts with him thrilled me, and I hoped he felt the same. He arrived in a white tank top and black nylon shorts. When he sat on the bench to tie his sneakers, I took in his powerful arms and thighs. They were covered with dark hair. He noticed my body too, candidly scanning my crotch when I straddled the weight bench.

As we lifted, we discussed the Gospel project. I said it was off to a great start, that I admired the dedication of the scribes and the precision of their calligraphy, partly due to Rossi's high standards. He inspected every word with a magnifying glass. He'd thrown out several vellum pages that contained just one or two less-than-perfect characters. Victor seemed less-than-impressed by Rossi—especially when I relayed to him the priest's detailed explanations of Catholic dogma.

"What kind of shit is he feeding you?" he said, adding weights to a bar.

"He just invited me to come to Mass. I've never been to a Mass." I lay on my back, ready to do a few bench presses.

"He wants to convert you." Victor heaved the bar to his chest. His bare arms bulged, but there wasn't a trace of sweat on his face.

"Shouldn't that make you happy?"

Victor exhaled, lowering the weight. "He lives in his own pious world. He's a self-righteous bastard."

After our workout, when I noticed Victor looking me over as I mopped my chest with my T-shirt, I couldn't hold back anymore, and I kissed him on the lips. I could tell it made him hot. But he stared at me without moving a muscle.

"I'm a monk," he said.

I felt too foolish to reply.

After we showered—in tense silence—he became as friendly as ever. We strolled to Giolitti's, a café famous for its gelato, and found a table in the quaint turn-of-the-century salon. The arches and ornate molding glowed in the yellow light of chandeliers. Customers filled the room with chatter and laughter. Victor wore his leather jacket over a black T-shirt. His beard was heavy and bluish. "So," he said. "How's Alice?"

"It's hard to say," I said, still confused by his earlier behavior—and cautious. "She sounded tired on the phone. She doesn't take care of herself. She was on death's door, and she's still smoking."

"What exactly happened?"

"She reached over to turn off her alarm clock one morning and a pain shot through her arm and chest. She couldn't sit up or get her breath. Luckily, her car was in the shop and my sister, Becky, stopped by to take her to work and was able to call an ambulance."

"What kind of work does she do?"

My face suddenly felt warm. I considered lying but didn't see the use of it. "She works behind the counter in a cafeteria downtown. White uniform, varicose veins, says 'ain't' a lot, and 'I seen this' and 'I done that'—the whole nine yards."

"It's nothing to be ashamed of." He seemed to be amused by my discomfort, as though he detected my concern with his opinion and liked it. "So she'll be OK?"

"If she takes care of herself."

He nodded and played with his ice cream for a while before looking up and asking, "Did your old man die of a heart attack?"

What was he getting at? Did he think I came from a family of inferior physical specimens, all with puny, ineffective hearts?

"He was a roofer," I said. "He fell off a roof. I was 7."

He stared at me, his dark, lucid eyes so intense they seemed capable of reading my thoughts. And his question seemed to confirm that they could: "You saw him fall, didn't you?"

"No," I said, goose bumps rising on my neck. "I just dreamed about it."

I finished my ice cream. Victor sat back in his chair, studying me. He hadn't taken a single bite from his dish, and his ice cream had turned to soup.

*   *   *

That Sunday afternoon when I got up from a nap, I found a note from Father Rossi taped to the door of my cell. He asked me to come find him in the church when I woke up. I ran a brush through my hair and walked over to the church. The aroma of olive oil and chicken from the midday meal lingered in the cool, sharp air.

In the silent church, sweet smoke hung on shafts of light. The monks knelt in their choir stalls near the apse. On the altar between two candles stood a gold vessel shaped like a big daisy with a little window in the center. Father Rossi turned his head when he heard my heavy rubber soles on the stone aisle and knew they didn't belong to a monk's sandals. Father Andrea looked up too, and stared at me. I wondered if I was breaking some kind of rule forbidding outsiders to attend a service. Father Rossi got up, dropped to his knees, bowed his head to the gold flower, and met me halfway down the nave. He motioned for me to enter a pew, then sat beside me. Smelling garlic, I worried that an aura was forming. But then Father Rossi belched.

"This is Eucharistic adoration," he whispered. "We're worshiping the Blessed Sacrament." He pointed to the golden vessel. "It's in the monstrance. The host contains the real presence of our Lord."

He could see I was clueless.

"Christ is truly present in the host, which is reserved for worship," he explained. "It may look like bread and taste like bread, but it is Christ himself, under the appearance of bread." The words sounded like something memorized from his childhood.

"It was in the tabernacle, right?" I noticed the open bronze tabernacle doors.

"Exactly. We take it out to venerate it."

"Why not just venerate it in the tabernacle?"

He touched his heart and smiled. "Intimacy," he said. "Special communion with Christ. To see him. To lift him up in the monstrance. It's a time of grace, of benediction. Would you like to kneel and worship?"

"I'm not Catholic," I said, feeling cornered.

"It doesn't matter. Just for a moment." He lowered a kneeler and slid off the pew to his knees. "Please," he whispered.

I humored him, and we knelt side by side on the unpadded board.

"Close your eyes," he said. "Try to feel his presence. It's Christ himself. The Son of God. The divine king."

Feeling self-conscious, I closed my eyes and a strange thought came: My resistance was evil. My own sinful ego wouldn't allow me to worship God. People like me burned in hell. I imagined the fiendish laughter of cartoon characters.

After a few moments of silence, Father Rossi made the sign of the cross and signaled for me to follow him. We went to the library. The empty building was as still as the church. The big tables in the reference room on the first floor shined with polish applied by the monks during their morning work detail. The smell of lemon oil mixed with the smell of old books in the spacious, high-vaulted room. We climbed to the scriptorium and Father Rossi directed me to sit at my desk, which held a stack of manuscript pages. He pulled up a chair and sat next to me.

"These are my finished paintings," I said, thumbing through the vellum sheets normally stored in the thin drawers of a cabinet in the scriptorium.

"I wanted to show you something."

"Is there a problem with my work?"

"Look at this painting," he said, gingerly pulling out the second page. My picture of John baptizing Jesus occupied one half of the page. It was the leading illumination for the Gospel of Mark. In this painting, a naked, dark-skinned Jesus stood in profile, the water of the Jordan up to his waist. A bearded, wild-haired John the Baptist faced him, gripping his shoulders, ready to plunge him into the river. "Do you see a contradiction?" Father Rossi said, his brown eyes bright and eager.

I stared at him. Clueless.

"A contradiction of the Christ we were just discussing. In the Blessed Sacrament. The Son of God. When you paint him this way, you distract people from his true nature."

"You mean because he's naked?"

"It's not just that. This is a sensual image of him—with St. John like this. It's almost..." He hesitated, as if hating to pronounce something shameful. "It's almost pornographic."

"Their privates are covered."

He shook his head. "See the way they look at each other?"

I saw trust in their faces, maybe a sense of bigger and better things ahead. John was turning the show over to Jesus.

"I don't like it," Father Rossi said. "I get the same feeling from some of the other illuminations. In the Annunciation the Blessed Virgin touches her body. In the illumination from Matthew, King David stands over the manger with his hand on the infant's belly." He sifted through the pages to point out these illuminations. "These won't guide people to our Lord. The other illuminations have the same problem."

"Why didn't you say something sooner, Father? Before I finished 10 of these?"

He smiled. "You're very talented, Paul. I didn't want to stifle your creativity." He glanced at the manger scene. "Can you let yourself be guided by the holiness of Christ?"

I wanted to tell him to go to hell. But if I lost my job I might also lose Victor. "I can try," I said.

Father Rossi brightened, slapping my shoulder. "Good," he said.

"Will the calligraphers need to redo these pages?"

"Ten pages are nothing to them." He winked.

After he left, I sat there looking at the paintings. I liked all of them. I liked how they felt. I didn't want to paint scenes that did nothing for me, pious boilerplate. But I'd play his game. On the time clock, I'd regurgitate illuminations I'd seen in the monastery's manuscript collection. On my own time, I'd paint what I wanted.

CHAPTER SIX

VICTOR

The last time I lived in a Roman monastery was in 1850, before the reunification of Italy. Along with the rest of the Catholic Church, the Dominicans I'd joined fiercely opposed the Republican cause, blasting the insurgents from the pulpit, leading parades of peasants down the Corso to St. Peter's for daylong prayer vigils. Politics distracted the community from my comings and goings through the abbey gate. And the tense atmosphere gave me pleasure. Reading about the unification campaign in newspapers revived the pride of empire I felt as a Roman officer. Of course the modern capitol would never return to its glory as ruler of provinces from Spain to Palestine. But to restore Rome's status as capitol counted for something.

And how satisfying to watch the Vatican shrivel like the prostate gland of a castrated choirboy. Joshu's Church had now become an impotent spiritual institution confined to 100 acres of land. I half-hoped for the Church's complete disintegration in an encroaching secular world. But without monasteries I might lose my convenient shelter. More frightening was the possibility that a constant reminder of Joshu's presence would become lost to me.

What kept my longing for him alive for 2,000 years? The answer is easy. You love until you find a replacement. And I hadn't done that. After losing Michael I thought I never would. Paul raised the old hopes. But I resisted them. What were the odds anyone could accept my terms? Maybe the apprehension I felt around him was no more than my own keen sense of self-defense in the face of another refusal.

Still, I couldn't stay away from him. We frequently burned the midnight oil in the scriptorium. He worked on illuminations while I translated the *Meditations*. I'd join him at half past 10, after reaming Andrea and tucking him in. The task annoyed me more and more as Andrea's suspicions about Giorgio shifted to Paul: "We're both American," I told him one night. Andrea sat on the edge of his bed while I massaged his bare shoulders. "Naturally we spend time together."

"Is that what you call it? Spending time together?"

"He's skinny. Why would he interest me?"

Andrea shrugged.

I slapped his smooth, meaty back. "There," I said, settling back against the wall. "You know, maybe I should go."

Andrea's back tensed. He raised his head.

"Do you agree?" I said.

"You can do whatever you want," he said. "You're free."

"Why do you care, Andrea? What do you expect? You think you and I are going to run off together?"

"Maybe you *should* go."

I smiled at his bluff.

"How's the translation going?" he said, introducing yet another annoying topic of our more recent conversations. He got up, pulled the blanket off the bed, and wrapped it around his shoulders. The room was cold, but I thrived in the temperature. Vampires are cold-blooded creatures though we feel only slightly cool to the touch.

"I'm a quarter of the way through. It's all shit. 'Your wounds heal us, O Christ. Your torn, bleeding flesh makes us whole. We suck your bleeding dick...'"

"That's blasphemy!"

I laughed. His conscience was remarkably selective. "Has Rossi said anything about the work?"

"He asked me where you learned Italian. Where *did* you learn it?"

"I told you," I said, scratching my chest. "I've spent the last four years drifting though Italy."

"Being kept, you mean."

"It's an exciting life."

"Not like being a monk."

I thought of Paul's question and posed it to Andrea. "Why did you become a monk?"

"To give my life to God."

"And what's that like?"

"Perfect fulfillment," he answered.

Later, as Paul and I worked quietly in the scriptorium, I couldn't help comparing him to Andrea. He bent his head over the page, brushing his long hair back from his face, quietly burnishing gold leaf, content to have me near. The sensuality of his big hands, his eyes, even his large, aquiline nose—which I imagined nudging my crotch—made me want his mouth all over me. I imagined plunging into him, then holding him tenderly while he slept. Compared to Paul, Andrea was nothing more than a whiny, quick screw.

Paul glanced up and saw me staring at him.

"What?" he said.

"Just thinking."

"How's the translating going?" He deposited his burnisher on the drafting table and sat back in the chair. His green turtleneck—the sleeves, as usual, pushed up to his elbows—emitted the strong scent of our monastery's laundry soap.

"You don't want to know." I had no desire to rehash my conversation with Andrea.

Paul studied me. "Explain it to me, Victor. What in the hell are you doing in a monastery? You can't stand translating a religious tract. You avoid the other monks. You don't think much of your vows. Except when they're convenient." His resentment was clear.

"You think it's easy keeping my hands off you?" I said.

"Don't talk to me about your vow of chastity Tell me how you feel. *You* know how I feel about you."

"It wouldn't work, Paul. Look where we are."

Paul shook his head in disgust.

Tell me what disease you're carrying, I wanted to say.

"I can't take this," he said. "Not touching you, not kissing you. I'd almost rather never see you. If I didn't think..." He broke off, reluctant to finish, but I knew he wanted to say, *If I didn't think there was a chance you'd respond...*

I almost gave in to him. My impulse was to take him in my arms and tell him I loved him. Instead I stood, pushed my chair back, and said, "Maybe we'd better quit spending so much time together." I left the scriptorium without looking back.

The next evening at supper, I avoided looking over at the next table, where he occupied his usual seat. I thought about probing Rossi to see if he might have any information about Paul that could explain my apprehension. But I could hardly stand the thought of a conversation with him. I hadn't liked that priest from the first night of his arrival, when Abbot Anselmo sang his praises after dinner. Nosy little pious prick.

But after dinner when Paul disappeared, I decided to pursue Rossi anyway. I followed him to the large salon near the abbot's office, where the monks gathered for social hour on Sundays. A medieval triptych in tempera dominated the spacious room. The three panels of the triptych showed an angel announcing Christ's birth to Mary, a manger nativity scene, and adoration by the magi—all a fantasy of some first-century theologian. It hung over the fireplace on the largest wall, and faded tapestries of biblical scenes hung on the others. Threadbare oriental carpets were scattered here and there on the stone floor. Massive oak beams, darkened with age, supported the ceiling.

Rossi stood with a glass of wine, listening dutifully to the two hefty scribes, Ricardo and Roberto, as they ranted about the treasures of the scriptorium and fawned over him. I stayed away from them all, pretending to drink wine that I hadn't swallowed in 2,000 years. To pretend was a great deal easier—and more pleasant—than to vomit the indigestible fluid up later.

When the bell tolled for night prayer, the monks trailed away to their choir stalls. I wandered out into the courtyard until they'd all gone, then returned to the salon. Rossi was still there, inspecting the triptych.

"Giotto, isn't it?" I said in English, still holding the glass of wine.

He shook his head. "A contemporary of his. Little known. Fra Vanni." He didn't look at me.

"Vanni? You're right. I've never heard of him."

He turned and surveyed me with condescension. "How's work going on the Ferravi manuscript? You know Ferravi's canonization case comes up next month."

I told him the work was going fine, that I had never been so inspired by a religious treatise, that contemplating the wounds of Christ had awakened me in some kind of profound way, a way I couldn't put into words exactly I spoke with great sincerity, while he nodded, wanting to believe me but full of reservation. It was nice to see him forcing himself to affirm what must be affirmed in his book, no matter how doubtful the source. Having paid the obligatory price, I went on to ask him about Paul.

"Paul?" Rossi's face clouded with suspicion, but I didn't care.

"Yes, the illuminator. I noticed at dinner that he isn't looking well. I wondered if he's all right."

Rossi's thick eyebrows arched. "I haven't noticed anything."

"Well, I might be wrong. He's probably just tired."

I decided talking to Rossi was a waste of time. He probably guarded any personal information about Paul as zealously as he did matters of the confessional.

The bell for compline tolled, and we started for the door.

"You haven't finished your wine." Rossi nodded toward my glass.

"I don't care for it." I deposited the glass on a table near the fireplace.

We walked to the church together, Rossi continuing to chatter until we entered the vestibule. Then his pleasant expression changed to one of seriousness. He dipped his fingers in the holy water font near the door and crossed himself conscientiously. I crossed myself too, pretending to touch the repellent water that was blessed in the name of Joshu's god. Barely discernible in the faint lamplight, the monks sang a solemn hymn by Palestrina. The vault echoed with their bass voices. We traveled down the long aisle to the altar, genuflected, and moved into the choir stalls. I went to my usual seat and Rossi to an empty seat near the abbot.

*   *   *

Restless as hell that night, I walked through Rome an hour before I came upon a priest, apparently on a sick call. When I finished draining his blood, I pried his fingers from the satchel he'd guarded as he struggled with me. It contained a vial of oil used for anointing the sick, a prayer book with colored ribbons to mark pages, and a gold object that looked like a pocket watch. I knew it was a pyx, a container for transporting a consecrated host to the sick. I opened it, dropped the wafer into a puddle of urine released by the old man with his last breath, and went on my way, belching warm blood.

The center of Rome felt close and dank in the autumn chill. I directed my thoughts to the open countryside and lifted into the night. My jacket rippled as I flew, the cold wind stinging my face. I lighted on the moonlit Via Appia. The pines and cypresses along the ancient avenue spread their dark limbs above the paving stones brought there by the Caesars. As I passed the ruins of tombs, robbed of their marble by the Visigoths, I remembered the grand mausoleums of my day and the festival parades that used to march by them. When I came to the brick hovel I knew to be my father's tomb, I saluted it, waiting to feel the presence of his spirit. But I felt nothing. Then, at the church erected over the Catacombs of Domitilla, I did feel a presence.

For a moment I thought my father had come after all. My heart pounded with expectation. Then I laughed at my own stupidity. Why would a Roman aristocrat visit a temple of the Christians he held in contempt? I snapped open the locked door of the church and wandered along the dark passage that led to the catacombs of the Christian dead. Next, I descended the narrow stairway and followed the presence. By now, I recognized it as Joshu.

The last time I had seen him was on Tiberias Lake. The Sea of Galilee, where he told me to meet him when he appeared in New Orleans. I'd arranged my flight to Israel. My crated coffin rested near another among the plane's cargo, sealed in darkness. The decaying flesh of the new corpse made me feel at home. Over the centuries, my resting places always contained the scent of decay, both old and new, reassuring me of my own immortality. As planned, a mortician picked up the crate and delivered it to a mausoleum, which I left after sunset.

Through force of will, I flew above the clutter of stone structures, the palms, and the rugged hills to the Sea of Galilee, where I snapped the chain tethering one of the boats at a pier near a closed rental shop. I rowed for nearly an hour before pulling in my oars and waited another two hours, my impatience building along with my hunger. It had been 48 hours since I'd fed. But my appetite for Joshu was even keener than my appetite for blood. I was fixed to the spot.

It was midnight. My rowboat drifted in the middle of the lake. The full moon, white as a skull, hovered over Nazareth to the east. Cool desert air gusted in my face. It carried the scent of pine. And the scent of blood—the blood of jackals in the rocky hills, the blood of nubile Israeli girls slumbering, the blood of restless boys roving village streets, eager to prove their manhood. Boys like *he* had been.

While I waited I remembered how it had been before Joshu grew serious about his mission, how he'd laughed at my jokes, how he'd shown off the animals he carved from olivewood. I thought of all the times we'd paddled across that very lake, singing, splashing each other, plunging into the cool water on a hot summer day.

When a vessel approached, I figured the rental shop owner or his security guard had discovered the missing boat and decided to look for it. Good, I thought, my meal was coming to me. I leaned back and waited. Then, a flood of white light fell on the approaching boat. It spilled from the moon, which had suddenly moved from its eastern position. I sat up, my heart racing.

Joshu rose, straight and lean, like the boat's mast. The gentle breeze that had been stirring over the water gathered force. Joshu's white robe spread like a sail. Would he walk across the water to me, I wondered, as he had walked to his inept followers in their fishing boat two millennia ago?

"I'm here, Joshu," I shouted into the wind. I stood, spreading my legs to balance myself. The boat rocked violently, but my will was stronger than any storm Joshu could muster. I called to him again.

As his boat grew nearer, I saw another man seated in the stern. His head of dark hair, pulled back into a ponytail, cut a silhouette into Joshu's robe. He stood in the powerful light, naked, his chest heaving. I recognized the athletic frame, now white and smooth as marble. I recognized the intense gaze I had last seen as he lay dying in my arms, refusing to drink my blood and share eternity with me.

"No!" I shouted. "Damn it, Michael." I couldn't stand to see them together.

Michael stretched his muscular arms toward me and stepped forward. But Joshu grasped him by the shoulders and he stopped.

"You can join him, Victor," Joshu called. "You can finally find peace."

Their boat bumped mine now. I reached forward to touch Michael, but I nearly tumbled into the waves and braced myself.

"Are you happy now?" I yelled to Michael. "Did you get what you bargained for?"

Michael's mouth opened, but the wind swallowed his words.

In that moment the pain of losing him returned in all its strength. A vise gripped my chest, and I could hardly breathe. Scenes from the Monastery of St. Thomas flashed before my eyes: Michael and I trekking through the woods surrounding the monastery, laughing together in the greenhouse he tended, lying in each other's arms. Then the night he finally slept in the crypt with me, his devastating announcement the next morning after his nightmare about the murdered Luke. Young, green Luke. "I can't, Victor. I can't give up heaven. Not even for you."

Then the final bloody massacre, with Michael fighting my grip as I forced him to watch me rip open throats. Michael grimacing when the police officer's bullet tore into his flesh. Then, once again, his refusal to accept my kind of healing, my kind of life, before going limp in my arms.

And here he was, so close I could touch him, his jaw fixed, his dark eyes still full of determination but now also tinged with pity.

I bristled. "I'm the one who should feel pity," I shouted. "You're stuck. You're frozen. That's not love." I jerked my head toward Joshu. "You need blood to love. He's drained you. I would never do that."

"Not to *me*," he called. His dark eyes saddened.

"You're not my judge," I shouted. "Neither are you, Joshu! You deserve each other."

Their boat began drifting away, then, picking up speed, it sailed toward the shore, the strange flood of moonlight accompanying it. Panicked at the thought of losing sight of them, I sat down and rowed with all my might against the rolling waves. But the boat stayed anchored to the spot. The light vanished, the wind died, and the moon floated back to its original position.

I snapped the oar over my knee—an easy feat. No longer mastered by Joshu's forces, I willed myself to shore. The area was popular with tourists. Outside a nearby hotel, I came upon a burly doorman dozing on a bench. My footsteps woke him up. He stood and adjusted his cap as though he thought I was a guest.

"No tip tonight," I said, flashing my fangs.

He gawked at me.

I clutched the back of his neck and pulled his fat throat to my mouth. His heavy stubble scraped my lips. His eyes wide, he fought me. A cry started up in his throat, becoming a gurgle as my fangs punctured his jugular. I sucked his blood until I felt full and calm.

Then and there I had set out for Rome. My home, the place I belonged, where the familiar could heal me.

I traveled now through a maze of passageways hewn from volcanic tufa. The walls were lined with niches for the burial of Christian bodies destined for resurrection, according to the early believers, who protected their dead from the contamination of pagan Roman tombs. Resurrection or not, some pope removed the remains—"relics," he called them—when Christianity became the state religion.

Rays from my eyes fell upon faded, peeling frescos of arcane Christian symbols and pious portraits of Joshu grasping a shepherd's crook or casting a net from a boat.

"Joshu!" I shouted. "Where are you?"

My voice reverberated through the clammy caverns. I trudged on through several chambers that served as chapels. One of them glowed with the light of a hundred candles burning on an altar. In a fresco behind the altar, a crucified Joshu, white as chalk, gazed heavenward.

"What do you want, Joshu?" I called.

From a dark passageway, a robed figure glided into the room and stood before the altar. The hood fell, revealing the innocent face of a girl in her early teens. Her black hair curled around her smooth cheeks.

She unfastened her robe and spread it. Her left breast dangled, partially detached but not bleeding—as though her flesh was that of an embalmed corpse.

"The Circus Maximus," she said. Her mouth moved as she spoke, but her voice seemed to issue from a distant source. "I gave my life for him there."

"The lions," I said, unimpressed. "So you were a martyr. Did you get the reward you wanted?"

"Paradise," she said. Her disembodied voice echoed in the chamber.

"Is that what you call paradise? Paradise would be to have him between your legs."

Calmly she drew her hood back over her head, closed her robe, and floated into the dark passageway.

"Why an emissary?" I shouted. "You think the little bitch will convert me? So she gave her life for you. And what good did it do her? I'm not a virgin girl. It'll take more than sainthood to win my soul."

I waited in silence. The flames on the altar danced in the draft winding through the catacombs.

A choir of women in some remote chamber began chanting the *Dies Irae* from a requiem Mass. *O Day of Wrath, O Day of Judgment.* I followed the sound, wandering through the dark maze with my eyes as my lantern. In another chapel deep within the catacombs, candles flickered in burial niches flanking the altar. One niche contained a youth's naked, athletic body.

Crouching at the low niche, I raised a candle to Joshu's face and found the same handsome features I'd first beheld on the cliffs over Jerusalem. But the body before me belonged to a corpse, jagged holes in the hands and feet, the left side of the rib cage gashed beneath the chest.

A knife twisted in my belly.

I touched his cool arm and remembered the day a wasp had stung him there. We'd hiked up the rocky hills above the city and had sat down on a blanket to eat. Joshu had pitched a grape into my mouth, and I'd started to choke on it. He'd fallen back laughing, and his arm had dislodged a wasp nest in the rocks. His arm had swelled up like a wineskin.

"Why are you doing this to me?" I asked his lifeless form.

His eyes opened. Relieved, I started to kiss him, but couldn't. He was resisting me.

"You're in danger, Victor," he said. "Come with me."

"Don't you think I want to?" I shouted. "What in the hell happened to you, Joshu? The boy with the mission. The boy who didn't take shit from anybody Temple priests, thugs—hell, not even the governor! What a mission! Cleansing the lepers. Feeding the hungry. Forgiving the whores. Well, just look at this damned world now. Has anything changed? You're in the wrong place. Safe and pure and worshiped up in your heaven. Is that what it was all about? Are you happy with all your pious followers who mouth the right words?"

He closed his eyes and faded away. My hand rested on stone now.

You and your mutilated martyrs deserve each other, I thought. I got up and exited the maze, the *Dies Irae* ringing in my ears.

Dawn was still an hour away when I got back to San Benedetto. I entered the side dormitory and walked to Paul's cell. Outside his door, I closed my eyes and concentrated until I could hear his even breathing through the oak barrier. My prick hardened for him. When I opened the door, he moved in the bed. My vision adjusted quickly in the darkness, and I saw him clearly, facing the door, propped on his elbow.

"Victor?" he said.

I thought that if I took him then, I could shake off my affection. I could have him the way I had Andrea. And everything would stay simple.

I took off my jacket, slipped out of my clothes, and climbed into the narrow bed with him. I stripped off his briefs and kissed his mouth and ears and neck. I sucked his stiff nipples and snatched at his balls with my teeth. His body was warm from the woolen blankets. I lay with my head on his thighs, breathing in the scent of his crotch. Then I turned him onto his stomach. His buttocks rose to meet my prick. Even unlubricated, his sphincter opened like a hungry mouth as I pushed myself in. He groaned.

As I stretched my body over his and began to pump, I suddenly felt the same strange sense of apprehension I'd noticed the last time I stood in his cell. I pulled myself out and rolled over.

"What's wrong?" Paul said.

I shook my head.

"Don't worry about protection. You're a monk." He rolled onto his side and caressed my chest. "Or are you worried I'm infected?"

"Are you positive?"

"Don't you think I'd tell you?"

"We have to be safe," I said. "It's almost dawn, anyway." I got up and dressed.

Paul lay with his hands clasped behind his head, watching me. "I can come to your room," he said.

"No. Not now."

He stared at me, confused.

I scanned his lean body, searching for some sign of ill health, some reason for the warning signals, but I found none. Without another word, I left and went to the crypt.

For the rest of the week, I avoided Paul. If I couldn't explain my nagging misgivings to myself, how could I explain them to him? And why pursue him anyway? Why create grief?

The night after our failed encounter I found a note from him under my door. I crumpled it up without reading it. During evening meals I sensed him looking my way and finally stared coldly at him. He kept his head down after that. I stayed away from the scriptorium and the weight room. I tried to keep my mind off him. I told myself my infatuation would dwindle, that I could take whatever boy I wanted anyway.

But the more I dismissed my feelings, the more they stirred.

When I returned from feeding on the third night of our separation, I climbed to the dark scriptorium, knowing he would be in bed. I opened the notebook containing my translations and, for the first time in decades, poured out my soul in writing. In Latin, my mother tongue, I filled 30 pages with my maddening desire for Paul, my willingness to give anything to have him, and the sense of apprehension that stood like a steel door between us. Then I ripped out the pages and tore them up.

CHAPTER SEVEN

PAUL

It was hell trying to work the day after Victor's visit to my room. The hot scene on my bed wouldn't stop replaying in my mind. I'd never been so turned on. And the same questions kept surfacing: Did Victor think I was lying to him about HIV? Did he think I'd put my pleasure before his safety? Or was his abrupt exit about something else? Was he fighting his conscience? One fear in particular nagged me: Maybe I didn't get him off.

And if concentrating wasn't hard enough, Brother Roberto and Father Rossi were making it even harder. Roberto sniffed and blew his nose every five minutes at his desk, and some wild hair made Rossi pace between Roberto's, Ricardo's, and Giorgio's desks, pointing out the flaws in their respective scripts. Then he'd turn around and praise my bland revision of the baptism scene: a pale Jesus kneeling in the river, hands crossed on his chest, head piously lowered—the usual dove hovering nearby. Robed in an animal skin, an even paler John the Baptist poured water from a shell over Jesus' head.

"Yes," Rossi said, adjusting his new horn-rimmed bifocals. "Perfect. This is my beloved Son, in whom I am well pleased.' Those are the words our Lord hears during his baptism."

I was tempted to write the words in a cartoon bubble coming from a cloud.

That night, as I waited for Victor in the scriptorium, I wadded up sketch after sketch, unable to get a single line right. He never came. Finally I went to look for him, fumbling through the dark crypt—where I'd never before gone—until I found the door with his name taped over the storage closet sign. But he wasn't in the little room. His habit lay on the bed, so I knew he'd probably walked down the Gianicolo into the city. I left a note, asking him to come talk about what happened. He never showed up.

At supper the next night he sat at his usual place, one table over from mine. During the reading, I hoped he'd look my way. When he did, his cool stare made me want to yell *Fuck these monks and their icy silence!* I thought about running over to his table and pulling him away with me. He didn't show up in the recreation hall afterward, nor the scriptorium that night. I was as fidgety and desperate as an addict in withdrawal, but I didn't pursue him again. What was the use?

The dark coldness of the monastery closed around me like the ocean around a sunken ship. I'd never felt so alone.

My sister Becky called one night. Brother Giorgio, who lived on my floor, left a message—scribbled in weird Italian cursive—on my door.

The night before my flight, Becky had the family over to her prefab house in a scuzzy section of town. My brother Al watched a baseball game on Becky's big-screen TV. Alice and Al's wife, Peggy, fussed over Al's blond girls while Becky's kids, Danny and Jolinda, showed me their new toys. They had both inherited the kinky hair and long eyelashes of their father but had Becky's crooked smile and pointed chin.

Becky seemed on edge all night, yelling at Jolinda for dragging toys out of her room or running in the house. At first I thought she was upset because her new boyfriend, Dean, hadn't shown up for the party. But she didn't really need a reason. It was hard enough being a single parent trying to raise two kids on a minimum-wage salary.

While Alice and Peggy washed dishes, Becky motioned for me to follow her to the bedroom. A king-size waterbed filled up most of the space. Photos of the kids covered the dresser and the walls. Becky shut the door and threw her tattooed arms around me.

"I don't want you to go," she sobbed.

"Oh, Becky," I said, trying not to cry myself. We hadn't been close as children. In fact, Becky used to think I faked my seizures for attention. But when she started dating a black guy I was the only one in the family who supported her. Dad had taught me early on what it was like to be shamed. Now we understood each other.

"It's a whole year," she said.

"It'll go fast."

"What if something happens to you? What if you have a bad seizure?"

"I won't," I said, though I'd worried about the same thing, spazzing out while a bunch of monks scratched their heads around me.

"But what if you do?"

"I don't know, Beck. I won't."

"I'm scared, Paul. I have a bad feeling." She drew back and looked at me with red eyes. Her short, bleached hair stuck out in spikes. Two new rings in each ear matched the one in her nose. That was Becky. She'd adopted the look long before it was cool. "Please don't go."

"Don't be silly," I said.

I wished I'd listened to her, and I didn't want to be reminded of her warning. But I picked up the phone and dialed all the same.

Three minutes into our conversation she confronted me. "What's going on, Paul? Are you OK?"

"Just a cold or something," I said. (Why tell her I'd fallen in love with a monk who didn't love me back?)

"Are you sure?"

If I'd known how much everything would change, how she and little Danny and Jolinda would drift into a hazy distance, I might have told her the truth. I might have broken down and let her call me an idiot and tell me I was asking for it, just so she could say she loved me and wished she could hug me. But I asked about the kids instead, and Mom, and Al and his family.

Before I hung up I told her I loved her (which I rarely did) and I'd talk to her on Christmas. Then I went to bed and dreamed—or seemed to dream—of being imprisoned in a tight, dark chamber. I pounded a wall that was hard and cold as steel. My lips moved as I called for help, but no sound came out. Then, suddenly, it was Victor who was trapped. He pounded and screamed silently He was trying to call my name. *Paul. Paul. Paul.*

My eyes snapped open, but the moment they did I felt they'd been open through the whole dream. And the dream seemed like one of the visions connected to my seizures. Was it a seizure? Considering how run-down I'd been, I knew it was possible.

But whether a dream or a seizure, the sense of panic stayed with me. Less for me than for Victor. He needed my help. I was sure.

The next morning I climbed down to the cold crypt and knocked on his door. There was no danger of letting sunlight into his room since not a single ray penetrated the underground chamber. So I turned the handle to go in, but the door was locked. I knocked and called his name. He didn't answer.

On Saturday night my loneliness drove me to the church, where I listened to the monks chanting compline. Their voices echoed back and forth across the aisle in a gentle rhythm that might have soothed me if Victor hadn't been sitting among them. As much as I tried, I couldn't keep from watching his profile—the sloping brow, the full lips, the angular jaw and chin. I desired him so much it hurt. Thunder shook the windows, dark except for the choir stalls, lit from above. Torrential rain drummed the tile roof. As refrain echoed refrain across the aisle, the storm echoed the tempest in me.

"Now Master, let me go in peace," the frail, big-eared Abbott Anselmo read in his weak voice. "My eyes have seen Your salvation, which You have prepared in the presence of all peoples, a light of revelation to the Gentiles and... a light to... a light." He seemed to forget the words.

Brother Andrea, who was seated next to him, whispered in his ear. The abbot took a deep breath, clutched his chest, and fell forward, his breviary dropping to the floor. Andrea shook him by the shoulder and—as though the abbot just needed warming up—rubbed his hand. Several monks clustered around the abbot's choir stall, looking helpless as toddlers. I approached the group, unsure of what to do. Then Victor crossed the aisle and pushed everyone out of the way.

"Give me some room," he said to Andrea.

Andrea stepped aside to give Victor access to Anselmo. Victor hoisted the old man over his shoulder and carried him to the aisle, gently laying him out. He administered CPR, breathing into the abbot's mouth, pressing his chest, and listening to his heart until the old man moaned, coughed, and pushed him away.

Father Rossi had gone to call an ambulance. He hurried back down the aisle now. "It's on its way," he said. A siren wailed in the distance.

"He'll be all right," Victor said. He glanced at me and looked away.

Rossi nodded, stooping down and tracing the sign of the cross over the abbot's pale forehead.

That week when the scribes chatted about the incident, Father Rossi threw out a perfunctory word of praise for Victor, who had clearly gotten under his skin. But in Anselmo's book, Victor was a saint. When the hospital released him, he threw a reception for Victor in the big, formal hall adjacent to the office. Rossi extended the abbot's invitation to me. Trying my best to get Victor out of my mind, I contemplated skipping the event. But I went.

When the monks had all filed in from the dining room, Anselmo raised his hand to get their attention. He stood next to Victor by the huge fireplace, his head level with the mantle.

"*Benvenuti, fratelli!*" he said. His voice was stronger than ever. He looked 10 years younger, his eyes keen and bright, his short body erect. You'd never know he'd been laid up for a week after a brush with death.

He continued his speech in a loud voice. I couldn't make out much of the Italian, but he frequently used the word *grazie*, beamed at Victor, and squeezed his arm.

Victor looked hotter than ever. Tall, broad-chested, rugged. And unattainable. His gaze met mine while the abbot spoke. I thought I saw regret in his dark eyes before he turned them away.

While the monks drank wine and mingled after the abbot's speech, I noticed Victor slip away. Despite my resolve, I might have followed him, but Father Andrea approached me with a bottle of wine.

"Please," he said, flashing his even, white teeth, "have more." He filled my glass. "Brother Victor is wonderful, no? He made a—how do you say it—a *miraculo.*"

"A miracle?" I offered.

Andrea nodded. "Of course. The same word. A miracle. Your American brother made a miracle."

The last thing I wanted to do was talk about Victor, but Andrea seemed determined to pursue the topic.

"It is good to have someone who speaks your language. A good friend."

I nodded and managed a smile.

Andrea seemed to gloat. "A good friend," he repeated, sipping his wine. "Too bad, he will leave."

"Victor's leaving?" I said, panic welling up in me.

"Oh, yes. Soon, I believe."

Andrea went on chattering in bad English, but I hardly heard what he said. I had to find Victor. I couldn't stand the idea that he was going away. I finally excused myself, deposited my glass on a table, and left the room.

Victor wasn't in the scriptorium or his room, but his habit lay crumpled on the bed, so I knew he was in the city. I stupidly decided to look for him. It was 9 o'clock, and even the narrow back streets buzzed with activity. Kids whizzed by on scooters, dishes clanked in neighborhood trattorias, and laughter and animated conversation penetrated the bright windows of old, crumbling apartment buildings. I crossed the noisy piazza near the Pantheon and turned into a more secluded, run-down area, where diapers and towels dangled on clotheslines in the cold, damp air. A beefy boy smoking on the steps of a church gave me the eye, and for a second I thought, *Fuck Victor. I could have this kid.* But I only wanted Victor. If I didn't have him, I'd be lost, I'd be nothing. Nothing in the world would matter.

Where I went after that, I don't know. I gravitated to the dark—to alleys I'd never entered, to shadowy courtyards that reeked of urine, to shuttered old palazzos near the river. I wandered for three hours; a church bell tolled as I headed back up the Gianicolo. The light drizzle that had been falling turned to rain. I pulled the collar of my jacket up around my face. I was exhausted, but wired.

Trying to get a grip on myself, I trudged through the wet, dark cloister between the church and the dormitories. *Help me. Help me.* The words formed automatically in my head, like a prayer. Even though I hadn't prayed since I'd tried out the night prayer I'd heard in a movie when I was a kid: *Now I lay me down to sleep.* This time the prayer seemed directed to the flesh-and-blood Jesus of my illuminations. The real illuminations I'd been secretly painting. *What the hell's going on?* I thought. *Fuck, I really am delirious!* Shivering, my hair drenched, I finally entered the dark library and ran up the stone steps to the scriptorium. The monks cut off the heat in the library at 9 o'clock, and the scriptorium was freezing. Panting, I stared into the darkness, as though Victor would materialize before my eyes if I concentrated hard enough.

Without waiting to catch my breath, I left the library and went to Victor's room in the crypt. He didn't respond when I pounded on the door. I turned the latch and went in. His habit wasn't on the bed. The room was so neat it seemed unlikely that anyone occupied it. The wool blanket on the mattress lay smooth as a sheet of vellum. The wastebasket was empty. So were the desk drawers. Desperate, I opened all of them, the dresser drawers too, finding most of them empty. I didn't feel reassured when I found some clothes in the bottom drawer. He could have left these behind. I checked under the bed for a suitcase. There was none.

I couldn't shake the idea that Victor had run away, no matter how irrational I knew it was. *Why would he leave his order?* I told myself. *Just because of me? That makes no sense. Where would he go? Back to the States? How? Where would he get the money?* I knew the fear was irrational, but I was cold and exhausted. I hadn't slept for days. Dizzily, I paced the tiny. room, touching the pillow where his head had rested, touching the bed, the dresser. It was like he'd died and the room contained his spirit.

I wandered out into the chilly crypt. Votive candles glowed in each little alcove on both sides of the chamber. I stood at one altar after the other, warming my hands over the flames, scanning the names engraved on the six stone tablets in each niche. Foreign names and dates two and three hundred years old. Suddenly the graves seemed to move. I felt them closing in on me, like the walls in a horror movie, and I escaped to the large open area of the crypt. As a distant bell rang down in the city, I thought I heard someone calling my name. The sound seemed to come from the stairs leading to the church. It wasn't Victor's voice. It belonged to a woman. *"Paul, Paul, Paul…"* she sobbed. Weirdly, I thought of Alice, remembering how like an angel in white she appeared in the grocery store the day of my first seizure.

What's Alice doing here? I wondered. I went to the stairs and peered up into the shadows. The sound stopped. I told myself I was crazy, that I needed to go to bed. But I couldn't. I couldn't leave the crypt. Victor was near me there. Maybe he *would* come back. I had to wait for him.

Who knows how long I paced that dank place? Time stopped for me. Images of Victor ran through my head. I remembered him kissing me, stroking me, entering me... and I thought I'd die if I couldn't have him again. Some time during the night, the voice returned, but by then I paid no attention. I was hearing things. And I didn't care. Nothing could distract me from my thoughts of Victor.

When I was so exhausted I could have dropped to the stone floor and slept like a baby, the smell came. Garlic. A breeze seemed to carry the aroma down the stairs. Then came the sound of a spoon clinking against glass. The sensations scared me like never before. My legs trembled. I tugged on my collar to keep from choking. I tried to concentrate, to hold on to consciousness, but it was no use. The last thing I remember was shouting Victor's name.

CHAPTER EIGHT

VICTOR

Andrea found me one night when I got back from feeding.

He was keyed up after the abbot's reception and hot for me because I was such a valued commodity after resuscitating the old man.

Of course the monks all believed I'd used CPR, but I had only pretended to breathe into Anselmo's mouth—as I'd seen done in movies—pumping his chest with my palms periodically. As I pressed my ear against his chest, I quickly pierced my wrist with a fang, sucked up the red drop that beaded on my skin, and dribbled it into his mouth. The tiny amount could not bestow immortality, but it could revive a dying human.

I came close to knocking Andrea in the head when he described Paul's sorry state since I'd given him up. I took my anger out on his ass instead—which is what he'd wanted all along.

Afterward, on the stairs to the crypt, I heard someone moan in pain and hurried down to investigate.

In the middle of the crypt, Paul lay on the cold floor, his arms and legs twitching as though an electric current charged through them, his head thrashing from side to side on the stones. I ran to him, straddled his torso, and pinned his arms down. His clothes were soaked.

"It's OK, Paul," I said. "It's OK. I'm here."

He clenched his teeth, but foam oozed through his lips. His face was contorted. He moaned.

I bent down until my lips pressed against his ear. "It's OK," I said.

His body relaxed. All movement stopped. For a second I thought he was dead. But then he breathed, deep and steady, as if in a sound sleep. I wiped his mouth with my sleeve and scooped him up in my arms. With a vampire's strength I could bear five men of his weight, so the trip to his cell was an easy one.

I gently laid him on his bed, stripped off his wet clothes, and dried his hair with a towel. He opened his eyes, straining to see me in the dark room.

"Victor?" he whispered in a raspy voice.

I got him a glass of water and raised his head so he could drink.

"It was a bad one," he said.

"Why didn't you tell me you have epilepsy?"

"I don't know," he said drowsily, clasping my hand on his chest.

"Go to sleep."

By the time I climbed into my niche, my skin stung with the coming dawn. But I was relieved to finally understand the reason for my misgivings about Paul.

I'd seen epileptics in medieval monasteries. The monks took their epileptic brothers for mystics, as they had done with St. Francis. Some of these mystics had visions of divine chariots racing across the sky or beautiful women in dazzling white robes. Some even levitated during their visions. St. Theresa of Avila is said to have lifted several feet from the ground as she knelt in ecstasy.

An epileptic in a French monastery where I lived during the 13th century ranted in a language that sounded like a mixture of Arabic and Cyrillic. At first the monks thought he was possessed. They tied his hands and feet to the frame of his bed and prayed over him, swirling incense and sprinkling him with holy water. He thrashed like a fish reeled into a boat and foamed at the mouth. The monks swore he muttered obscenities and finally castrated him. He wept like a girl afterward, then—though he was half-literate—eloquently read passages from the Bible condemning the mistreatment of a brother. The community repented. They even made him abbot.

My senses evidently mistook Paul's epilepsy for a condition that could somehow endanger me. Maybe in his seizures he could expose my identity or draw me into some kind of trap. Who knew? Warning bells rang with some frequency in my life, and many amounted to nothing. Admittedly, the apprehension I'd felt was more persistent than any I'd ever known—but maybe this corresponded to my level of attraction to him. Whatever the reason, I chose to be satisfied by what I'd seen in the crypt.

The next night we walked for hours through the darkest, quietest spots in the city—the deserted Forum and Circus Maximus, the unlit cobbled alleys around the Piazza Navona. The smell of charred chestnuts drifted into the chilly November air from the Piazza, along with the jaunty strains of an accordion. Bundled in a wool jacket, his hand in mine, Paul described his first seizure, his regimen of phenobarbital, his hopes for avoiding seizures, at least severe ones, in Rome. He explained why he'd kept his epilepsy a secret. He didn't want me to think he was a freak. He was sure I'd imagine him foaming at the mouth, spasms jerking his body, and find myself overcome with repulsion—or worse, pity. He said he'd rather never see me again than receive my pity. I assured him that pity wasn't in my nature. We stopped and ordered hot chocolate in a café at the bottom of the Gianicolo. The cold had reddened Paul's cheeks. He held his cup with both hands to warm them. As he swallowed the steaming chocolate, his hazel eyes peering at me over the rim, I thought, *I have never loved before this moment.*

Back in Paul's cell, I lay on the bed and watched him take off his red pullover, then his jeans, then his briefs. His cock curved up beautifully, like a bird arching its neck. He stripped off my briefs and placed them carefully on the night table. Then he climbed onto me, his knees bracing my hips, his thighs forming an arch, and his cock hovering over my belly My prick stiffened toward his cool buttocks.

He lubricated me with a few squirts of the lotion he kept on his nightstand. When he reached back to guide me in, lamplight glinted over his rosy brown nipples.

His torso lifted and fell as he flexed his thighs, his long fingers spreading like petals. He raised his face—stretching his graceful throat—then lowered his forehead, staring into my eyes. His cheeks reddened. His mouth opened and he gulped air.

Determined to give him what he needed, I drilled the boy. I clasped his hands, raised up my head, and strained toward his throat. But my fangs started to descend, so I quickly lay back, turning my face away from the lamp until they receded.

Paul rocked up and down, his belly quivering, his palms pressing my chest as I worked him with my hand. I pumped harder, impaling him deeper until he moaned and shuddered, showering me with his warm seed. Then waves of orgasm exploded in my belly.

I pushed him off and stretched myself over him. His damp chest heaved. I kissed his temples, his eyelids, his lips.

"I love you," I whispered.

With his eyes closed, he smiled as though his dreams had all come true.

Christmas brought snow to the mountains east of the city. I caught its clean scent in the breeze and remembered how my father's ancient villa had looked nestled in the hills under a fine white mantle after a robust winter storm.

Like blocks of ice, the stones of San Benedetto retained the cold. In the unheated church, the breath of the monks turned to smoke as they recited the psalms of the season. Wind rushed up the Gianicolo, scattering the scent of pine and the fishy odor of the Tiber.

Strong and full of energy, the abbot Anselmo had resumed his duties. He sat erect in his choir stall and led the prayers in a firm, clear voice. Andrea hated to relinquish the power he'd acquired when the abbot's health had declined. He clung to me like a schoolgirl with a crush. Screwing him had long since lost its appeal, but I had no choice other than to appease him until I could figure out what I wanted from Paul. After Michael, I couldn't bear another painful ending. It would be foolish to pressure Paul into accepting a predator's life, to expect more than he could give me.

Andrea stole up to the scriptorium from time to time when Paul and I worked in the evenings. He never caught us doing anything incriminating, but several times he dragged me down to his cell. It was like he wanted to show me that no matter what was going on, he was still in charge. When he'd accuse me of having Paul, I'd tell him Paul liked women—then give him something to take his mind off his jealousy.

Games like these have always worn upon my nerves.

On January 6, the Feast of the Epiphany, the monks celebrated a special mass in honor of the wise men who'd come from the east to venerate the so-called divine infant. The spicy smell of incense rolling down from the sanctuary woke me in my dark chamber. The stone shelf under me buzzed as the bass organ pipes sounded. Anselmo dispensed with the usual silence during the evening meal and the monks chattered like kids on a playground, their tongues loosened by Asti Spumanti. That night Andrea played the familiar game. We ended up in his cell. He fumbled out of his habit and stretched his meaty, compact body on the bed, waiting for me. He was so drunk he took me with no lubrication, not even spit. He moaned as I rode him, saliva dripping down his chin.

"I love you, Victor," he said, when in a state of profound boredom I rolled off him. He was too far gone to notice that neither of us had climaxed.

"Go to bed now, Andrea. You're drunk," I said.

"Do you love me?" he whined.

"Of course. Now go to sleep."

He crossed his arms and pouted. "If you loved me, you'd stay."

"You know I can't."

"Just until dawn," he said.

And so I wrapped my arms around the thick-bodied incubus and let him snuggle against my chest. When he started to snore I slipped out of bed, dressed, and returned to the scriptorium. It was nearly midnight. There was little time to spend with Paul before he went to bed.

"What was that all about?" Paul said, looking up from his painting of a wild-eyed, half-naked boy—the possessed man described in one of the Gospels.

I squeezed his shoulders, kissed his head, and plopped into the same chair I'd been sitting in when Andrea had shown up.

"The usual," I said, matter-of-factly.

"The usual?" Paul dipped his brush into a jar of vermilion paint and dabbed his illustration.

"Don't tell me you're jealous," I said. "Andrea's as sexless as the rest of the monks. He's just possessive. I'm his personal counselor about monastery business."

"I thought Anselmo ran the monastery."

"He's been too sick until now. Andrea really has managed the community's affairs. I just want to keep him out of our way. It's a small price."

Paul looked up at me with curiosity.

"What?" I said.

"Why did you rescue Anselmo?"

I laughed. "What a question. Why do you think?"

Paul stared at me without answering.

"He was having a heart attack. He needed help. What more is there to say?"

"I don't know," Paul said, shrugging. "I don't know why I asked." He went back to his painting.

An uneasy feeling overcame me as I watched him. Maybe he detected something about my nature.

Yet I'd seen his trust. In our lovemaking he bared his throat to let me playfully bite him. When I mounted him, he opened for me, free and easy as a kitten. I had taken him on the scriptorium's cold floor, in the weight room while monks chortled in the adjacent recreation hall, and even once in the church. I had mounted him from behind as we lay in bed, and from above with his ankles on my shoulders. I had bounced him on my lap, licking his sweaty pecs, gazing at his sensuous throat as it stretched vulnerably.

And he'd depended on me during his seizures. He'd had two others since the first one, the most recent in the crypt again—not far from my niche. I'd found him naked and unconscious on the stone floor, his arms and legs bruised from thrashing.

I stayed with him during the attacks. In accordance with his instructions, I never interfered, except to push furniture away from him when necessary. And I took him to bed after each attack ran its course.

I began to avoid Andrea and to make excuses for not going to bed with him. He threw me hurt looks during supper and compline and wrote me a couple of whiny notes. Finally one night he pranced into my cell, fishing for reassurance. "A trip would be nice this summer, wouldn't it?" he said, fingering the rosary I'd left on my nightstand. (I'd already thrown off my habit in favor of going shirtless with a pair of jeans.) "We could go to Capri. Or Greece. Would you like that?"

I stretched on the bed, closed my eyes, and wished him away. He jiggled the rosary. Then I felt the cool beads pouring on my bare chest.

"You need to go to bed," I snapped, without opening my eyes.

"I think I need something else." He dangled the rosary beads on my nipples, running them down to my navel. "What's the matter, Victor? Did I do something wrong?" He paused and tried joking. "Don't you like my ass anymore?"

"I like it fine," I said, patting his rump.

He'd obviously primped for me. His dark, curly hair shined. His olive face, closely shaven, gleamed with lotion. He beamed with pleasure at my attention, worked out of his habit, and crawled into the narrow bed, lying on his side, his arm over my chest.

"Do you love me, Victor?" He slipped his stubby fingers into my shorts, feeling my cock and balls.

I pulled his hand up and pushed it away. "I'm not in the mood," I said.

"Because of him?" Andrea sat up on the mattress.

"Go to bed, Andrea," I said. "You're getting worked up over nothing."

He folded his arms and blinked back his tears. "He doesn't know about me, does he? *Bene,* I'm telling him."

He climbed out of bed and fumbled into his habit. I got up and grabbed his arm as he headed for the door. He dragged the nails of his free hand down my chest. I slapped his face, knocking him to the floor.

"Goddamn you," he said, blinking back tears. He winced as he climbed to his feet, clasping his right arm as though he'd injured it.

I couldn't let him go to Paul. As he pushed past me, I gripped his throat and lifted him from the ground. He tugged desperately at my hand, his face red and his gray eyes wide.

A deep hunger welled up in me, as though I hadn't fed in weeks. I threw him on the bed. He gasped for breath, eyeing me fearfully I bent over him, as if to kiss him. My fangs descended. Avoiding his gaze, I pierced his solid throat. He froze, stunned momentarily, then tried to push me off. Within moments he went limp. I gulped his blood. When I was full, regret rushed through me. But now I had no choice. He was still breathing, his open eyes glazed. I cradled his head, then gave it a sharp twist.

I've done it again, I thought, pummeling his motionless chest with my fist. *Again, again, again.*

I snatched the rosary from the bed table and yanked it apart. Beads flew and clattered everywhere. I got up and slammed the desk chair against the floor, breaking off one of the legs. Nausea suddenly choked me. I vomited Andrea's blood into the sink in the corner of the cell and collapsed on the cold floor, facedown.

When the door creaked, I was too sick to raise my head.

"My God," Paul whispered. He took a step toward the bed.

I managed to look over at the bed, where he clasped Andrea's wrist, his dark shirt and pants like a wound against the white wall.

"Believe me," I said, "he's dead."

Paul drew back and stared at the corpse. He glanced at me as though struggling to link me to the murder. Then very calmly he walked to the sink, rinsed the blood from the basin, dampened a cloth, and mopped my neck. He rolled me over and bathed my forehead and cheeks. His expression was strangely serene, as though he was in a state of shock. I was feverish; the cool cloth felt good on my face and the cold stones felt good on my back.

Options flashed through my mind. Explanation. Flight. More blood. And then another solution burst forth from my deepest desires, like a prisoner who'd finally rammed through the bars. Without another thought, I gripped Paul's throat, pushed him to the floor, and sank my fangs into his jugular. Like all my victims, he struggled at first, then relaxed, breathing hard and caressing my chest. When I'd taken in the right amount of blood, I pierced my wrist, as I had during the abbot's heart attack, and pressed it to Paul's lips. With both hands, Paul pulled it to his mouth and sucked, his chest heaving. I threw back my head to relish the almost unbearable heat rushing through me. Every nerve in me burned. I pulled away from Paul, stripped off our jeans, gave him my wrist again, and entered him as he swallowed. Light-headed and crazed, I plunged into him until we both shuddered as though injected with a fiery chemical.

Paul went limp, his eyes glazed, his face drained of color. I waited until his breathing became regular and he fell asleep. The transfusion had worked. I dressed us both, placed a pillow under his head, and confronted the task at hand: the disposal of Andrea's body.

The river was the best place; if the body were to be found there, the police might link Andrea's death to drugs or sex, both available in the shadows of the Tiber's bank. But carrying a body even that short distance could attract attention. Burial within the walls would have to do.

Hoisting Andrea's heavy corpse over my shoulder, I entered the dark crypt, moving from niche to niche until I found the tomb of a monk who had died a century ago, Fratello Carlo Genovesi. He was buried in the lowest grave on the wall.

When I deposited Andrea on the floor his blue lips eerily parted to expose his perfect teeth. Kneeling at the grave, I clasped the lip of the marble tablet with my fingertips and yanked it loose. Mortar crumbled to the floor. I removed the tablet and peered into the niche, where a skeleton lay clothed in a dusty habit.

I shoved Andrea's corpse into the niche, cramming Genovesi's brittle old bones against the brick wall. Andrea still smelled of the shaving lotion shining on his skin.

"Goodbye, Andrea," I whispered.

With no further ceremony, I slid the tablet back into place.

The thick marble would seal in the odor, even without mortar. I got a broom from a closet and swept up the remnants of mortar on the floor, disposing them in my own tomb.

Back in my room, Paul continued to sleep soundly as I finished wiping down the sink and checked for splashes of blood on the bed and floor. The blanket was clean and the few drops on the stones came up easily. Tenderly, I lifted Paul and carried him to his cell. In the dark, I stood over his bed a long time, watching him calmly breathe, knowing the life that awaited him now.

Initiation

Put a penny in your mouth
To taste the sap that marked your birth,
Your first scraped knee,
Your first shaved cheek,
Your first sweet wound of love—or lust.

CHAPTER NINE

PAUL

At first, sharp pains shot through my belly when the sun came up. My head pounded too—so bad I got sick to my stomach and thought I'd never get out of bed.

Food had changed. Garlic tasted strangely sweet. Fruits were so acidic they left ulcers in my mouth. I couldn't stand the taste of milk or cream anymore, and wine made me gag. But I still needed to eat, despite wanting only blood.

My eyes couldn't take sunlight, so my pupils practically disappeared. I avoided windows during the day, and if I had to go outside I wore sunglasses. My skin, and especially my face, turned marble-white, like the complexion of a fiery-haired redhead. Father Rossi and a couple other monks asked me if I was sick. But Brother Andrea's disappearance was too distracting for them to take much notice of me. The abbot announced that he'd contacted Andrea's family and the last monastery Andrea had lived in, but they'd heard nothing. The police were investigating. I noticed a couple of detectives poking around the dormitory. My impulse was to chase them away. To guard Victor. I thought of Alice. She would have died to stop my father from beating me. Like a cat ready to pounce, I watched the detectives from the enclosure behind the church, my heart pounding.

Even the air seemed different, sharper somehow. Breathing almost hurt, as if it was an unnatural act for my new body. Colors and sounds were incredibly intense. The yellow and red and purple pigments on my desk leaped out at me. The bright gold leaf made me squint. The monastery's mellow bell exploded in my ears like a siren. Even the monks' padded footsteps became an irritating drumbeat. And their chants affected me like a sad movie: I got choked up and weepy when I heard their voices drift in the air like birds who'd lost their mates.

Then there was Rossi. Before the transfusion I shrugged off his proselytizing. Now I told him to quit. One day when he waxed on about the apostolic succession of the popes—all directly in the line of St. Peter—I looked up at him from my desk and said, "I'm not a Catholic, Father. And I never will be." That floored him. He shut up, and probably prayed for my soul all day. The formulaic illuminations he wanted nearly killed me now. More than ever, I wanted to paint by day what I painted by night: vibrant scenes swirled with black and red and purple that captured the sensuality and strength of my Jesus. It was as if I knew this Christ personally and had an enormous investment in showing him to the world. But Victor warned me to make no waves. We needed the monastery for now, until I adjusted, until we had plans. Whenever I was tempted to rebel, I felt his beautiful will penetrate me the way his body did, until every last cell of me conformed to him.

Even before he explained what I was, I knew. Understanding came with the transfusion itself, coded like DNA. I knew what he was too. I knew he had given me an existence like his, but with a difference: His transformation was complete. Victor belonged to the night, while I belonged to a realm of shadows. Although I'd never felt so alive, every sense jumping with the least stimulation, my existence was a half-existence. I was like a human brain kept alive, prodded by electrodes as it waited for a new body.

Vaguely, I knew everything had changed between me and my family; I had no real idea how much. No idea at all. Not then.

I could think only of Victor. We were more than married. He was my lover and spouse and creator. And I now recognized him from the visions. I assumed he had somehow caused them as preparation for my new state. But when I described details of scene after scene, he looked surprised.

"When did the visions start?" he said. It was a frosty night in February. We stood on the bridge that led to Castel Sant'Angelo, gazing at the black river. Before leaving San Benedetto, Victor had fed me from his throat, and his blood still buzzed in my nipples and testicles.

"About a year ago, I guess." As I told him about that first vision of him, I could see it all unfold again on the water beneath us: Victor in the boat. Waiting. Then on land. Attacking the burly man.

"I was in a boat?" he asked.

I nodded. "Waiting for someone. I never saw who. And then you fed on a stocky man in a uniform."

Looking troubled, Victor spat over the rail.

"The visions aren't normal?" I said.

"Normal?" he said, piqued. "You think I take on a consort every year or two?"

I was afraid to ask what I wanted to ask. *How many like me have there been? What happened to them?*

"I've never heard of such a thing," he said. "I didn't summon you. I didn't relay images to your mind. You're probably still adjusting. You're projecting the present onto the past."

"I saw you," I said. "How would I even know about your past?"

"I've told you things."

"Not many. You like to guard your secrets."

Victor composed himself. His expression softened and he put his hand on my shoulder. The smell of his leather jacket worked on me like an aphrodisiac.

"You must trust me, Paul. I'll tell you everything. But little by little. Who knows what wires get crossed during the transfusion. Maybe you picked up images from my memories. Maybe your epilepsy makes you especially attuned. I don't know"

"I'll never have another seizure, will I?"

Victor looked away. "I honestly don't know."

Is he uncertain of more than my disease? I wondered. *Is he uncertain of his plans for us? He's hinted that my state is reversible. Maybe he's just testing me. And if I fail, he'll send me back to my old existence. Without him...*

Victor seemed to hear my thoughts. "Don't worry," he whispered.

A breeze suddenly rushed up the river as though the night echoed his words.

*   *   *

Vampire. I said the word to myself while I painted, while I showered, while I ate—trying to register its full meaning. Scenes from old vampire movies flashed through my mind, but they seemed silly. Even contemporary movies with realistic, sympathetic vampires seemed fake. The transfusion gave me an innate sense of a whole alternative history, a history of a race—a misunderstood race—that included me. I wanted to know more about it, so Victor dug up some medieval manuscripts on vampires in the library. They were stored in a room devoted to occult volumes, censored before the modernization of the Catholic Church in the 1960s.

He laughed at some of the accounts. One described a Danish vampire who quaked at the name of a powerful bishop, cowering at his feet as the holy prelate waved a consecrated host at him. Victor said that in monasteries over the centuries, he'd desecrated many a communion wafer, consuming it and letting it mingle with a victim's blood in his belly before retching it up.

Other accounts hit the mark, according to Victor. In one, a monk described a vampire named Sebastian, an aristocrat who terrified a village in France. When the village men finally mustered the courage to storm his castle, they were trapped inside—doors mysteriously bolted—until sunset, when Sebastian rose from his subterranean tomb and massacred them.

We sat at my desk in the scriptorium, examining the illumination in the margin of the manuscript. It was a vampire in a bishop's pointed miter and golden cope. His fangs reached his chin. Blood dripped from a heart he clutched in his delicate white fingers.

"I knew of him," Victor said, tapping the page.

"You never met him?"

"No."

"What about other vampires?"

Victor turned his attention to the book without responding.

"In 2,000 years, you never met another vampire?"

"We don't share territory," Victor said, calmly turning the page. "We may run across one of our own in our travels. But we keep our distance."

My heart skipped a beat as I suddenly imagined myself fully transformed, trying to touch Victor through a wall of glass. "What about us?" I said.

"There are ways to be together. Trust me."

His tone reassured me. I quit worrying about the rules of this new world.

When a violent headache woke me one morning, I concentrated on the chant floating into my cell from the church. The music soothed me. I got dressed and crossed the still, dark cloister to the church. In their stalls near the sanctuary, the monks faced Abbot Anselmo, who stood behind the altar in a purple vestment, his hands extended over a chalice. Candles flickered on both sides of the altar and high above it, the crucifix dangled in shadow.

The monks recited something in response to the abbot's invocation, and their hypnotic voices drew me to them. I entered a pew near the choir. The monks mournfully chanted the word *Sanctus* over and over, dropping to their knees. I knelt too, my eyes glued to the bright chalice as the abbot recited a prayer, raised the host, raised the chalice, and genuflected.

The monks sang as they filed to the sanctuary for communion. Their voices swirled through my head. I salivated as I thought of the communion wafer in my mouth. My hands felt sweaty. I looked at them. My fingernails had instantly grown an inch after the transfusion, and no matter how often I trimmed them, they grew back. They were long and sharp now. The sight gave me a strange thrill. My breathing quickened, my nipples and testicles tingling as they did after feeding on Victor. I left the pew and joined the line of monks. It took everything in me not to push past them and grab a wafer from Anselmo's gold plate.

The monks returning from communion passed me, but I was too fix-ated on the wafers to notice any faces. Suddenly someone stopped next to me and whispered.

"What are you doing, Paul?"

I turned and saw Rossi's dark face, his eyes puffy behind his horn-rimmed glasses. He grabbed my arm and pulled me out of line.

I glared at him. My canines suddenly jabbed my bottom lip. My impulse was to rip into his thick, stubbly throat with my teeth. I looked away and took a deep breath.

"Come on, Paul," Rossi said. "You can't receive communion."

Yanking my arm away from him, I turned around and left the church, hurrying down to the crypt. I knelt at Victor's niche and pressed my hands against the tablet, laboring to get my breath. Through the marble, I felt his hand against mine.

In my mind I heard his voice: *Don't worry. It will pass.*

I didn't want to listen. I wanted to crawl in next to him and press my lips against his throat. I thought I'd scream if I didn't. But he was right. I had to calm down and wait for nightfall. Then everything would be OK.

I kissed the cold stone tablet and left the crypt.

Rossi was waiting for me at the top of the stairs.

"What's wrong, Paul?" he said. "You're as white as a sheet." He felt my forehead.

My body temperature had lowered five degrees since the transfusion, and his hand felt hot on my skin. I pulled away. "I don't feel well."

"You're chilled. We should take you to the doctor."

I shook my head. "I'll be fine. I just have to rest."

He glanced down the stairs as if the reason for my agitation lay there. I had to get him away from Victor.

"I was just blowing off steam," I said, nodding toward the crypt. "Sorry about communion."

He gave me his full attention. "I never knew you wanted to receive. You told me you had no interest in becoming Catholic."

"I didn't know you had to be Catholic to go to communion."

He smiled and patted my shoulder. "You should lie down. We'll talk later."

He walked me all the way to my cell. When I crawled under the covers, he traced the sign of the cross on my forehead. I fought the urge to laugh.

I didn't tell Victor about my experience during Mass. For some strange reason, I felt like I'd betrayed him, and he knew it. He never brought up my trip to his niche, and when Rossi invited me to talk about communion one night after dinner, Victor ignored the remark.

But I think it was no coincidence that Victor invited me to feed with him that night. He wanted to test my mettle, to see if religious impulses stopped me from living his kind of life.

At 2 in the morning we walked the short distance to Trastevere and turned down a rank-smelling back street. In a little piazza wedged between stucco tenements, a group of teenage boys sat around a fountain, smoking and teasing one another in loud voices. I eyed them and looked nervously at Victor. He shook his head.

In a dark courtyard, towels and shirts flapped on a web of clotheslines strung across four run-down, shuttered buildings. Victor motioned to me and I followed him to a pair of double wooden doors. He listened a moment and, hearing no noise, actually pushed the bolt through the doorframe. This was the first time I'd seen him exercise a vampire's strength. A chill went down my spine.

Victor led me up a flight of stairs and down a dirty corridor lit by bare bulbs along the ceiling. He sniffed at several doors, then finally stopped at one near the end of the corridor. He nodded at me, then broke open the door with a quick push. We entered and I softly shut the door behind us.

Victor raised his head in the little foyer as if trying to pick up a scent. I suddenly hoped no children slept in the apartment: I might panic at the sight of a baby in his grasp. We stepped into a large sitting room, where a lamp glowed. Lace doilies were scattered on the worn upholstered chairs and sofa. A painted plaster statue of Christ sat on the television, a big red heart prominently bulging on his chest. The room smelled of garlic, very sweet to my new senses.

Victor motioned for me to follow him down a hallway. The first door was open. A night-light shaped like the Madonna glinted from a wall outlet. Nearby a boy of 5 or 6 slept in a cot. We crept on to the next door, which was slightly ajar. With my keen vision, I could make out the faces of a man and woman in their 40s. Taking one meant taking both, and I hoped Victor would choose another victim. A third door was closed, but Victor inhaled deeply and turned the latch. A teenage girl wearing headphones slept in the lamplight. Faint music wisped from a CD player on the nightstand. Male teen stars gazed down from posters on the wall, and an assortment of stuffed animals filled a shelf. Nodding to me, Victor started in. I grabbed his arm and shook my head. I wasn't ready for this.

Victor stared at me. *You have to,* his eyes said. *Don't balk now.*

I nodded and followed him in, freezing near the door.

He bent over the girl. Her sweet face was scattered with freckles. The blanket came up to her waist. She wore a pink T-shirt silk-screened with the Coca-Cola logo. She turned her head and sighed, still asleep. Victor clapped his hand over her mouth and her eyes flashed open. She tried to push him away, her feet kicking. He pierced her throat and drank until she went limp.

"Stop, Victor!" I whispered, tugging his arm. "Look at her, for God's sake."

Victor straightened and forced my lips to her neck. When I tasted the blood oozing from her wounds, my reluctance disappeared. Heat shot from my crotch to my chest. I licked every red drop from her neck and sucked her pulsing jugular until Victor pulled me away.

"That's enough," he said, bending over to feed again.

High on the blood, I stood by goofily, wishing I could have more.

When he finished he looked up to see how I was doing. "She'll never survive," he said. "I have to take care of her."

Confused, I stared at him.

Victor took the girl's head in his hands and in one quick motion, he broke her neck.

A wave of nausea rose up in my throat when I heard the bones crack. I took a deep breath to keep from retching and followed Victor out of the building, where I puked the girl's red blood onto the sidewalk.

Victor wiped my mouth with a handkerchief. "You can only feed on me," he explained.

CHAPTER TEN

VICTOR

The danger of creating a thrall involves his weakness. I avoided the word *thrall* with Paul, but that's what he was. Not a consort. Vampires have consorts only in the Dark Kingdom. In the world of flesh and blood we go it alone, unless we accept the risks of creating a thrall. A thrall is dependent, unable to draw completely on his previous human strength and unable to draw completely on the superhuman strength of a vampire. The person who used to exist survives, with all his memories, hopes, and personality traits, but without the ability to be satisfied with a mortal life. I knew Paul would gradually discover he could never return to his family, not in the way he had once belonged to them. I knew he would gradually understand the limits of his existence as a thrall, as much as he delighted in his bond to me.

But he still found his condition mysterious and exciting. He saw his new bond to me as a gift. He didn't register my immediate motive for his transfusion: keeping him silent and loyal after he'd found Andrea's corpse. He also didn't know there was no going back to a mortal existence.

He could become a vampire. But the price was his life with me. If we entered a pact like the one I had entered so long ago with Tiresia, he would be completely transformed, and I would fly to the Dark Kingdom to wait for him while he served the required time on Earth. But a thrall depends upon his host, emotionally and physically, feeding only upon his undead creator, no matter how much the blood of mortals entices him. Would Paul have the strength to let me go? A separation would be temporary, lasting as little as the prescribed two centuries, but two centuries might as well be an eternity for someone not yet undead.

The transfusion was a selfish act. Paul belonged to me for as long I chose. But I paid a price. As long as he remained my thrall, I remained chained to a nocturnal existence. And if I offered him independence, I might lose him forever, since he might never choose the Dark Kingdom; or if he did, he might not choose me as his consort there.

Thralls are usually more trouble than they're worth. I'd never been lucky with mine. Of the five others I'd created over two millennia, I'd destroyed four. Two had stopped serving my need for someone to guard my tomb during wartime, and the other two were so inept that they threatened to expose me. The fifth thrall, Tertius, was a beautiful African slave during the final years of the Roman Empire. He spoke perfect Latin and Greek, and could even decipher Germanic dialects. I might have grown to love him, but when he rejected the advances of a slimy bishop, he was burned at the stake for heresy. Fire destroys thralls.

Paul's case was unique. I loved him before the transfusion. He was not a lackey or even a protégé. He was my lover.

One night after lovemaking, Paul talked about his mother's heart attack and his worries about her. He was homesick. He lay on my bed, and I stroked his bare chest. He smelled of my blood, which he'd sucked from my throat as he sat on my lap with my prick inside him.

"Why don't you invite her to Rome?" I said.

"Can I? I mean, will she see the change in me?"

I knew that any mother would recognize a transformation like Paul's, but he needed to see for himself. I shrugged and said, "Invite her and find out."

Paul reflected for a moment and squeezed my hand gratefully. "What about your mother?" he said. "What was she like?"

I'd told him a few things about my life before I met Tiresia: my family's villa above Rome, my father's career as a senator and then an important consul under Augustine, my own assignments in provincial legions, my brother Justin. But I'd never said a word about my sisters—all directed into politically successful marriages—or my mother. The women in patrician families were respected but largely forgotten.

"She was mistress of the loom," I said. "Women in our circle tried to imitate her work."

"Do you miss her?"

"I try not to miss what I can't have." I smoothed his disheveled hair and kissed his head. "I was her favorite. She used to lie to my father for me."

"About what?"

I shrugged. "About my lessons when I was a boy. About observing the ins and outs of Roman protocol, kissing the ass of this commissioner and that. All kinds of things."

"You loved her?"

"Of course."

"How did she die?

"Infection of the womb, the physician called it. I suppose it was cancer." My gaze wandered as I remembered her on her deathbed, servants mopping her face while she hacked and moaned. "She asked me to put a coin in her mouth after she died."

"A coin?"

"For the ferryman. He takes souls across the River Styx, into the Underworld. I paid the fare. And now she rests in peace."

Paul stared pensively at the ceiling.

"Don't worry," I said, patting his chest. "Your mother will be around for a long time."

He caressed my face. "What's it like seeing generation after generation come and go, while you stay the same?"

I laughed. "You make it sound like I'm just a spectator and the world's a stage. I'm in the action, just like you. Babies are born and people die around you every day, don't they? Do you notice a generation slipping away?"

"But what about clothing styles, architecture, technology, language—2,000 years worth of changes?"

"For you it's history," I said. "For me it's memory. I don't philosophize about it. Change is change. It's inevitable."

"But not for you."

"That's not true," I said. I got up and leaned against the desk, my arms folded. "I've moved across the world, from Rome to Palestine, to the far East, to European monasteries, to America. I've had to adapt, learn new skills, new languages. I've had to take risks, flee for my life. And I've felt every possible emotion, at every level of intensity."

"And the emotions have changed you?" Paul sat with his knees up, his arms around his legs, gazing earnestly at me.

"No," I said, grinning at his sincerity, "I never learn a damn thing. I travel from crypt to crypt the same thickheaded bastard."

We both laughed. Then Paul became serious again. "Would you show me your niche?" he said.

"You've seen it."

"I mean the inside. I want to see what it's like for you."

"It's not a good idea," I said, picking up my briefs from the floor and slipping them on.

"Please. I want to see it."

His request was reasonable enough, and I finally agreed despite my misgivings. He would have to see it sooner or later. Why sugarcoat the facts? We dressed and crossed the dark, drafty crypt to my alcove. The monk who tended to such things had replaced the votive candles on the little altar and they glowed bright, emitting a surprising amount of heat in the small space.

Paul squatted in front of my tomb. His turquoise sweater stretched across his broad back. "Frater Anastasius," he said, tracing the engraved "F" with his finger. "1648."

"A lot of the graves are even older," I said.

"Why did you pick his?"

"No reason in particular."

Paul stood and moved out of my way. I pried the memorial tablet loose and deposited it on the floor. He peered into the dark niche, then recoiled.

"He's still in there!"

I laughed. "It's a dusty skeleton in a habit."

Paul reached into the shelf and touched the rotted wool pressed against the back wall.

"It must make you claustrophobic," he said, turning to me.

I shrugged. "I'm asleep. What does it matter? And I need the security. No one will disturb me here."

I replaced the tablet.

As we walked back to my room, Paul asked, "Why monasteries, Victor? How did you get from the Roman legion to a cloister?"

I had already told him about my wild days in Jerusalem as a Roman officer, my need to escape from the law, Tiresia's offer, the long line of mon-asteries. But I had never mentioned Joshu. And I wasn't ready to pour out my soul now, no matter how much I loved Paul.

"Monasteries offer seclusion and lots of convenient tombs," I said. "Not to mention an odor of sanctity—the perfect cover."

"You don't feel anything here?"

"Like what?"

Paul looked around the crypt as if searching for an answer. "God, I guess."

"You've been with Rossi too long," I said.

"I can't help feeling something is here. Maybe because the monks believe in it."

"People believe in all kinds of things. It doesn't mean they exist."

"I never believed that vampires existed," he said stubbornly.

"Fine," I said. "Believe whatever you want. Just be careful."

"Of what?"

"Of anything that can put us in danger."

The abbot had become very chummy since his heart attack. He frequently made it a point to chat with me after dinner about the Ferravi tract or the United States or whatever administrative problem he happened to be stewing over at the moment. One night he asked me to drape the crucifix above the altar with a purple cloth for the Lenten season. The sacristan had an inner ear infection and couldn't climb the tall ladder. When I climbed up to the cross and drew the cloth around the shoulders of the corpus, I felt Joshu's presence. I looked into the sorrowful eyes of the plaster face, half-expecting to meet his real gaze. I was disappointed.

Nagged by thoughts of Joshu, I went back to the catacombs of Domitilla that night. I wound through the stark black tunnels, my laser-sight lighting the way, until I came to the chamber with the crucifix in fresco. I stared into the niche where Joshu had lain. Of course, it was empty.

"Where are you?" I shouted, my voice reverberating through the subterranean maze.

Frigid wind suddenly blasted through the chamber. The cold penetrated my leather jacket and gloves. My lips quivered. I trudged back to the entrance and hiked the five miles back to Rome.

My sense of the spirits inhabiting the city was strangely heightened by the piercing cold. Spirits haunted the dark alleyways, the ancient ruins of Caracalla and the Forum. I had often been aware of their presence as I turned corners where markets used to stand or gazed into Renaissance fountains built over wells of my day. Sometimes I had felt spirits gazing at me from the midst of crowded piazzas.

Now the spirits seemed to draw me to the Colosseum, and I walked to the gloomy structure. Snapping the chains at the gate, I wandered along the dark passages of the broken arena whose construction I had observed during my first century as a vampire. An occasional rat scurried at my steps, but more often it was one of the feral cats that had taken over the place. The chambers where gladiators had once awaited entrance to the arena released their musky odor to my vampire nose as adjacent cells emitted a rank animal stench. Several times as a Roman officer, I'd accompanied a superior to inspect men and beasts before a spectacle. A brutal, broken-toothed captain once gave me the honor of signaling for the floodgates to be opened to a pipeline of water that filled the arena for a mock sea battle.

Above, a breeze rushed through the crumbled stands. The spot where the emperor's box once stood took its original shape in my mind, draped with purple bunting, guarded by soldiers in plumes and gleaming armor, filled with the emperor's family dressed in togas and flowing gowns. The sounds of cheering crowds returned to me when I closed my eyes. When I opened them again my patrician father stood before me, his embroidered tunic, his scant, feathery hair visible in the glow of the city lights. He pressed his fist to his chest to acknowledge an emperor who remained invisible to me. At his side stood my brother Justin, who had been poisoned at my father's orders when his recovery from disease was deemed impossible. Now well and whole, his athletic form stood at attention in a military uniform. His high cheekbones and serene gaze recalled my mother to me.

They showed no awareness of my presence, and for a long time I watched them before attempting to speak, to touch them—even though I knew they were mere shadows. The shouts of a crowd now visible, though hazy, called my attention to the arena, where a pair of gladiators appeared under the moonlight. Their bare chests and arms gleamed with oil. Spikes protruded from leather bands on their wrists. When they raised their swords and shields, the crowd cheered. A gate snapped open and two lions bounded into the arena, jerking to a halt when their chains tautened. They growled at the gladiators and reared their heads toward the stands, roaring at the excited crowd.

The gladiators crossed swords and began to fight, steel clanging, dust rising as they swung and parried. One, an Ethiopian by the looks of him, was clearly superior. His massive body moved like that of a gymnast, pivoting, gliding, thrusting the heavy steel as though it were light as a table knife. Gradually he edged his younger, curly-headed opponent toward the lions, who snarled and swiped at the fighters. The weaker gladiator rallied, swinging his sword wildly but then stumbling. The Ethiopian plunged his sword, and the other crumpled to the ground. The cheers of the crowd swelled as the Ethiopian dragged his wounded opponent to the lions, who lurched forward, ripping into the victim's legs. But before they could advance on the body, the Ethiopian raised his sword high and lopped off his opponent's head, holding it up by the curly locks for the crowd to admire. A brutal scene. And bloody. The sweet red liquid burst from the decapitated torso and dripped from the head. My hunger stirred. Once again reaching out futilely to touch my father's vaporous arm, gazing long and hard at Justin, I hurried from the arena and into the streets.

After flagging down a taxi on the Via del Corso, I climbed into the backseat and told the thick-necked driver to take me to St. Peter's. I didn't want to feed too close to the monastery. He whizzed through the quiet streets, stopping at the colonnades of St. Peter's Square. There was no one in sight.

When he turned to take my money, I gripped his wrist, wrenched his arm behind him, and pounced on his throat.

The monks had begun assembling in the church for matins when I returned. Soft light glowed in the choir. The sun would soon rise, and I was exhausted. Crossing through the dark nave, I descended to the crypt and immediately felt someone's presence. I gazed down the length of the chamber.

Sandal leather squeaked and then Rossi's voice came from the direction of my cell.

"Brother Victor," he said. "I was looking for you." His eyes were puffy. His wet black hair was slicked back and a scrap of toilet paper stuck to a shaving nick on his throat.

"What's wrong?" I said.

"I need to talk to you. Could we go to your cell?"

When I flicked on the overhead light in my room, I concluded that Rossi had already been nosing around. A notepad on the desk had been moved from one side to the other, and the blanket showed signs of someone sitting on it.

"I'll not keep you long," Rossi said. "I know you have to sleep." He motioned to the desk chair as though he was asking permission to use it, turned the chair to face the bed, and sat.

I sat on the bed.

"Brother Roberto told me about your deepening friendship with Paul Lewis," he said. "You must have been lonely before he came—I mean, without another American."

What else have Roberto and Ricardo gossiped about? I wondered. Paul had told me the two monks frequently whispered across their drafting tables.

"I'm concerned about Paul," he continued, looking me square in the eye. "And I know you two are... close."

"Then why don't you talk to him?" I said, irritated by his self-righteous meddling.

"It's a monastic matter. I wanted to speak to you as a member of the community." He hesitated but didn't shift his gaze. "It's not a pleasant topic. I intended to talk to you in the recreation hall last night before the Grand Silence began, but you disappeared. So I'm bending the rule a bit this morning."

The Grand Silence lasted at San Benedetto until after the morning Mass.

"I won't turn you in," I said, determined to stay cool.

He smiled and folded his hands on his lap. "Brother Victor," he said, "are you and Paul involved in a homosexual relationship?"

"No."

"Because if anything like this is going on, it is a serious matter. It would be my fraternal duty to take it to the abbot."

I nodded as though his point was perfectly reasonable.

"Paul is interested in our faith," he continued. "I would love to see him take instructions. But if he's confused by the behavior of a monk... If he doesn't have a clear sense of Church teaching on sexuality... You can see the problem."

My skin ached from the radiation of the rising sun. Needing my niche, I stood to usher Rossi out. "I see what you're saying, Father. If the subject comes up, I'll make the Church's position clear to him."

Apparently my words left Rossi unconvinced. Looking disgusted, he got up to leave. At the door he turned and said, "I believe I need to go to the abbot after all, Brother Victor." Then he walked out.

The monks' chant drifted down the crypt stairs as I went to my alcove. Paul was waiting for me there. I had sensed his arrival during the interview with Rossi.

He was pale and agitated, rubbing his arms as though his thick sweater could not keep him warm.

"I wasn't in danger," I said, clasping his arm. "Rossi can't hurt me."

"What if he pokes around here?" Paul said. His eyes had taken on the strange cast I'd seen in the eyes of my other thralls—the pupils seemed to expand and contract in the gleaming irises. His face was calcimine-white.

"Why should he? You think he's plagued by thoughts of vampires? Come on, Paul."

"But he might be watching you. If he sees you dressed like that, disappearing into the city at night..."

I put my hand on his shoulder to steady him. "He suspects that we're lovers, that's all. He'll go to Anselmo, and Anselmo will tell him to mind his own business. Anselmo is devoted to me. And Rossi is only a visitor here."

"I knew he was down here, Victor. I saw him in a dream, prowling around the crypt. That's why I came."

"It's normal to feel protective. You'll get these signals. Sometimes there really is no danger."

"How will I know when there is?"

I put my arms around him and whispered into his ear, "Give it time."

My skin burned. I couldn't stay outside the niche another minute. Quickly, I removed the tablet, crawled onto the shelf, and pulled the stone to the opening. The last thing I saw before the light vanished was my lover's beautiful face.

CHAPTER ELEVEN

PAUL

On the nights I'd watch Victor feed, I'd feel repulsion and pity in the moments just after his attacks. But as the inevitability of the feeding sank in and Victor clung to the quiet body and sucked contentedly, my horror would dissipate, as if someone had injected me with a drug that numbed my fears while making my other senses strangely keen. I'd watch Victor with the same clinical detachment a surgeon must feel as he breaks open a chest cavity or cuts into an intestine. Then, as Victor drew me to the victim's throat once he had satisfied himself, I'd salivate, ready to lap at the throat myself. And I would have—even though I'd known I would get sick—if Victor hadn't always stopped me. He wanted me to get used to the sight of the two puncture wounds, the smell of warm blood.

When dawn came and Victor was safely in his niche, I'd try to sleep for a couple of hours before work. But a restless kind of loneliness wouldn't let me relax. Bits and pieces of the scenes from that night would flash before my eyes when I closed them. A little boy's startled look. An old woman's veiny hands trying to push Victor away. A bearded man's lips invoking God before sinking into unconsciousness. Details from dark rooms and alleys came too. A holy water font near a bedroom doorway. A studio photo of a toothless infant grinning next to that of a young couple on their wedding day. A scuffed motor scooter chained to a lamppost.

When the weird mixture of loneliness and restlessness made it impossible to sleep, I'd slip on my sunglasses and walk through Rome until the sun climbed too high in the sky for me to stand it.

March rains cleaned the cobbled alleys and Renaissance facades. Barges drifted on the muddy Tiber and palms fluttered in the balmy Mediterranean breeze. In the Campo di Fiori merchants wiped down their booths and unloaded flowers, meat, and fruit from rusty trucks. The city seemed to breathe the warm breath of life. But I smelled dried blood and decay wafting from the tombs in a hundred churches and from the streets and piazzas and the clutter of ruins around the Forum. The eternal city was a giant mausoleum of patricians, slaves, martyrs, barbarians, popes, and poor friars. But the living were oblivious to the rich, earthy scent of those who were buried around them. They carried on laughing, working, and eating as if they'd never join the dead.

Work helped me keep my mind off Victor. I churned out illuminations, and Rossi liked them, especially my Good Samaritan and Woman at the Well. The expressions and poses were conventional—*lame* is a better word for them—but I invented interesting hues tinged with black or violet. Rossi focused so much on the obvious things—faces, postures, settings—that he overlooked my subversive little brush strokes.

Giorgio noticed the color though. He told me the hues reminded him of El Greco's. I told him not to tell Rossi that. He seemed to understand. I felt a little sorry for him. He was young and attractive and wasting away his life among all the geezers at San Benedetto. He was straight. His English had gotten pretty good since I started working, and he told me he'd joined the monastery after his fiancée was killed in a car wreck. I thought maybe the order had taken advantage of his loss to nab him, but Giorgio assured me that he'd planned to enter the Benedictines until he met Cristina. He believed God had taken her just so he would accept his vocation.

Some God, I wanted to say.

By late March the Bible project ran ahead of schedule. The scribes had completed the entire Gospel of Mark and half of all the other Gospels. Rossi had created dummy pages of the whole manuscript on a computer, using a font the same size as the script he created especially for the project. Space was left for each of the illuminations. Rossi, Ricardo, and Roberto copied the printed pages on the vellum. After a six-month apprenticeship, Giorgio contributed to the work as well. Rossi assured us the manuscript would be finished by the end of the summer.

A package from Alice came just before my birthday. I opened it in my cell while the monks took their afternoon siesta. It contained a tin of fudge and six pairs of white socks. There was a letter too, stuck inside a hokey Hallmark card about the joy of a special son. The little pat verse choked me up. It was signed "Love, Mom" with a little heart drawn around the word *love*.

Alice had scribbled on wide-ruled notebook paper, probably from a binder of mine left over from high school. Her sloppy cursive followed the traditional Palmer method. Since the sun had disappeared behind a bank of slate-gray clouds, I raised the shade and read these words:

Dear Paul,

> I've missed you so much this week as I thought about your birthday. I was going through some of your old clothes for Goodwill and found the orange turtleneck you wore for your senior photo that I hated and wanted you to wear a tie. But you always had to be different. That's OK.
>
> I got to thinking about if I died I'd want you to know a few things. Don't worry, I haven't been sick. Doctor says I'm A-OK. Though he wants me to quit smoking of course. I've cut down to a pack a day. Don't yell at me, now, I'm trying. Anyway, I was thinking if anything ever happened to me I'd want you to know that your Grandma Lardner's jewelry is in the bottom drawer of my dresser. I told Becky she could have it, but of course she don't care about that kind of stuff. (Of course she is talking about piercing her tongue, which I just hate the thought of because of infection.) I just thought you might want to keep it as a souvenir of Grandma, and me too since I loved to see Mama in the necklace with little

silver shells. And she's wearing it the photo in my bedroom.

Also in the little desk in your old room are the newspaper birth announcements of all of you kids and one article about Al when he made quarterback for Topeka High. Al would probably like it, but he wouldn't dig through stuff to find it.

The most important thing I always wanted you to know is that your dad was so proud of you and your artwork. He wasn't the artsy type but he thought you could draw really good. Sometimes when we had coffee early in the morning, he saw your drawings on the kitchen table and said he thought you were so talented. I know I told you this before, but I really wanted to you appreciate it. He never told you he was proud to your face because he had a hard time expressing his feelings. Even with me. Don't think he didn't love you. He loved all you kids, just had a hard time showing it.

Anyway that's all I had on my mind. I hope you like the fudge. Becky's kids helped me make it Friday night when Becky went to a rock concert in Kansas City. They are sure cute. I just hate to see the problems they'll have later in life because they're mixed. Everything else is the same old, same old. They've got me working some overtime at the cafeteria because the new addition is open now and we've got a bigger lunch crowd. The roof started leaking above the kitchen and Sam next door told me he'd look at the flashing. Emilio's getting arthritis. Who knows what's next?

I love you, honey. I keep hoping you're OK over there with all the terrorist stuff going on in the world. Stay away from crowds.

I sure love the postcards you've sent. I took them to work to show the girls. Hope you have a happy birthday.

Love,
Mom

I read the letter several times and looked at my watch. It was 9 P.M. in

Kansas. Alice should be watching TV before bed. I really wanted to talk to her. She'd never raised the topic of death before. In fact, she hated talking about dying. I didn't think she'd had another attack and was lying about her health since Becky would have told me if something major was wrong. But maybe she wasn't feeling well or maybe she was depressed. I'd taken up Victor on his suggestion and invited her to Rome. She'd bought a ticket to come, but she mentioned nothing about the trip in the letter. Was she having second thoughts?

When I called her, the answering machine picked up.

"Mom," I said, "Are you there? It's Paul. Pick up."

But she didn't pick up. When I called Becky, her answering machine picked up too. Scenes from the hospital flashed through my mind and I started to panic. As a last resort, I called Al.

"Don't know," he said, clueless as usual. I could see him in my mind: the scraggly beard, the paunch hanging over his pants, the pack of Winston's showing through his shirt pocket. "I ain't heard nothing. Stop it, girls."

Madison and Heather giggled in the background.

It was little comfort, since Al was usually out of the loop when it came to family matters. His wife, Peggy, was better at staying in touch, but she told Al she didn't know where Alice was.

"Maybe she just went to bed early," Al said. "Call her tomorrow."

All day I felt jittery and strangely guilty, as if my transfusion had infected Alice, as though an invisible umbilical cord still linked us and Victor's blood had tainted hers.

What had I become? What price had I paid for this life with Victor? If Alice or Becky or Al could see me standing over Victor while he fastened himself to a little girl's throat, if they could see me fighting my impulse to join him, would they think their Paul no longer existed? That some disease or drug had turned him into a monster? I was a kind of monster to normal people. They could never understand the requirements of a different sphere, as I had begun to. They could never understand how Victor was as much a part of me as my breath. And this distance between my understanding and theirs tore at me. I felt them drifting away. I imagined their shock and disgust. If Alice knew about me, her heart would give out—if only to save herself from the truth.

I finally reached her at 11 that night, 5 A.M. her time. She was dressing for work.

"No, honey," she said. "I'm fine. But you just never know. I better get to work."

"OK," I said.

"How's the other American boy doing?" she said.

"Fine," I said. "You'll get to meet him soon. You're still planning to come, aren't you? You got your passport?"

"I'm all set. I'll talk to you later."

That night I dreamed that I woke up in the dark basement of Alice's house. I lay on a cot near the washer and dryer. The washer hummed away. I got up, switched on the light, and opened the lid. Blood churned red as punch inside. I ran up the stairs, crossed the dark kitchen, which smelled like garlic, and hurried down the hall to Alice's room. The door stood ajar, and I could see the glowing numbers of her clock radio on the nightstand. It was 2:22. More than anything, I wanted to turn around and return to the basement, but my body moved under the direction of some invisible force. The sensation was strangely like the feeling you get in a dream when you're struggling to run with lead feet. But instead of trying to run, I was trying to resist whatever it was that pushed me forward.

I leaned over my mother. The scent of her body lotion mixed with nicotine made me gag. I clamped my hand over her mouth and sank my teeth into her throat. Alice struggled, letting out a high-pitched moan that would've been a scream if she'd had the chance to get her mouth open. As I drank her blood, her tears trickled over my fingers. Then she went slack.

My eyes snapped open as though someone had stuck me with a pin. My heart raced and my back dripped with sweat. Touching my canines, I felt two long, sharp points. I jumped out of bed, turned on the light, and looked in the mirror. Like two miniature tusks, my canines extended almost an inch below my upper lip.

That night, during a walk to the Trevi Fountain, I told Victor about the dream. A warm breeze gusted through the moon-washed labyrinth of narrow streets that took us to Via di Trevi in the center of old Rome. The current drove away the traffic fumes of the city and left the air smelling fresh and sweet.

We turned a corner and came upon the illuminated fountain, which was gushing like a mountain stream. Tourists gathered around, taking pictures and tossing coins over their shoulders for a lucky return to Rome.

"What does it mean?" I asked. "Is my mother in danger?"

"It was a dream," Victor said. "It doesn't mean anything."

"But would I ever..."

"Hurt your own family? Why should you?" Victor sat on the steps of the Baroque church facing the fountain. He wore a dark jersey and jeans.

"I'm not always in control," I said, sitting next to him. "When I watch you feed, I turn into some kind of animal. You've seen me."

"You'll get stronger. You'll have to."

"And the fangs?"

"They'll be under your control soon enough. You need them to feed."

"When will that be?"

"When your project is done." He patted my leg. "It takes time."

A young American couple, both blond and lugging backpacks, heard us talking and asked us to take a Polaroid of them in front of the fountain. After I snapped the picture, they offered to take ours. Victor seemed very amused by the idea and had me pose with him in front of the fountain. The guy watched both pictures develop in his hand.

"Damn," he said. "We show up, but not the fountain." He gave the photo to the girl, who looked disappointed, and then watched the second photo. "Nothing shows up on this one."

"Really?" I said, taking it from him. I was looking forward to having a photo of Victor and me. A piece of the fountain appeared where we'd been standing. A shiver ran up my spine.

When the couple walked away, Victor laughed. "You should see your face."

Dazed, I sat back down on the step.

"Don't worry," Victor said. "We can have our portrait painted at the Piazza Navona. Just no photographs. We can't be photographed. You'll appreciate it, eventually"

I thought about a hallway in Alice's house that was plastered with pictures of us as kids. There were school photos, and studio photos taken at Sears every year, and photos with Santa Claus, and photos with neighborhood friends. In one photo of me as a 6-year-old in our backyard plastic pool, I mugged at the camera in a scuba diving mask. It occurred to me that Victor had never seen a photo of himself and I felt sad.

*   *   *

Giorgio and I started working out in the weight room together during the afternoon siesta. Victor had told me exercise would no longer affect my body—at least not its strength or appearance—but it helped shake the restlessness that plagued me. And, since the room had no windows and just two overhead fluorescent bulbs, the light was bearable.

One afternoon I found Giorgio doing sit-ups on a mat, his hands crossed over his chest like an angel in a sentimental painting. He wore a blue tank top, baggy shorts, and gym shoes. Sweat glued his short hair to his forehead. He beamed when I came in.

"Hey, man," he said, a phrase he got from American movies he'd watched during his high school English classes.

"Hey," I answered. I shut the door and sat on the stationary bike. It took a few minutes to adjust to the strong smell of bleach pouring out of the towel closet. Then I pedaled in earnest, while Giorgio lifted a barbell. He gritted his teeth and frowned as he raised the weights to his chest, which made me laugh.

"*Cosa?*" he said, straining.

"You look like you're constipated," I explained, making a face and holding my stomach.

He puzzled for a second and then smiled when he figured out what I was saying. He proceeded to lift again, screwing up his face even more and groaning, which sent me into hysterics. Loving the attention, he deposited the barbell on the floor, dropped his shorts, and crouched as if to take a dump, moaning even louder than before and pretending to strain. His goofy face tickled me, and I laughed till my stomach hurt.

Suddenly the door opened and Father Rossi walked in. He eyed Giorgio, who blushed and pulled up his shorts. Then he looked gravely at me.

"I'd like to talk to you, Paul."

Reassuring Giorgio with a glance, I followed Rossi out to the cloister behind the church, which, luckily for me, was in the shade. We sat on a stone bench under a pine, facing the fountain presided over by the Virgin Mary. The air was cool in the shade, but I baked in my sweatpants and sweatshirt. I inspected my nails to make sure they hadn't grown back to their usual long points since I last trimmed them. Satisfied that they looked normal, I rested my hands on my legs.

Rossi made the sign of the cross and bowed his head for a moment. Then he took in a deep breath, exhaled, and turned to face me. "I'm worried about you, Paul," he said quietly. "And I'm not sure what to do."

"We were just playing, Father," I said.

He shook his head, his brown eyes steadily gazing at me. "You don't realize how easily the devil enters our lives. We let down our guard a bit here, a bit there, and before you know it we're in over our heads. And then, when our culture tells us something is normal, temptations don't even seem like temptations."

"Are you talking about being gay?" I said, irked that he wouldn't even say the word.

"Homosexuality is a perversion of the moral order. This is what the Catholic Church teaches."

Fuck the Catholic Church, I wanted to shout, but instead I said, "Well, I'm not Catholic. And I'm gay, and that's just the way it is. I'm not asking for your approval."

He looked sad and disgusted. "This is a monastery. The monks have taken a vow of celibacy."

"Good for them," I said.

"Including Brother Victor," he added. "If you and he are sinning in this place, I have an obligation to stop you. Project or no project. Living by the teachings of the Bible is more important than illuminating it. But your work is beautiful, Paul. Why jeopardize it? You read the words you illustrate. I know you do. Open yourself to them."

"I do, Father. And I don't hear them saying what you're saying."

"If Brother Victor is putting ideas in your head—"

I held up my hand to stop him. "No, I think for myself. And Victor's already told you there's nothing going on between us." I hated lying, but I owed him nothing and wanted security. I couldn't wait to get out of this place.

Rossi took off his glasses and rubbed his eyes. He gazed at the fountain. "Would you pray with me, Paul?"

"No." I stood and walked to the dormitory. Once inside, I looked out the hallway window. Rossi still sat on the bench, hands folded and head bowed. That's the last thing I remember seeing before waking up on the floor in the corridor, my chin wet with saliva, my head sore from hitting the hard tiles.

An old monk with hairy white eyebrows bent over me.

CHAPTER TWELVE

VICTOR

Since coming to Rome, I'd kept tabs on the news coverage of my feedings. The same headlines that had always appeared—wherever I made my home—showed up in *Corriere della Serra*:

MURDER VICTIM DRAINED OF BLOOD
VAMPIRE-STYLE KILLING
POLICE TRACKING VAMPIRE-LIKE KILLER

I didn't read the details about my victims' lives. Why regret what I couldn't change? But I did pay attention to police leads. For all the bombastic promises of Rome's chief of police, I could see he had traced nothing to San Benedetto. Compared to statistics in big American cities, the number of Rome's violent crimes was amazingly low. But the police managed to round up several suspects, mostly prisoners on parole, and also investigated foreigners with violent records.

Chances of linking the monastery to the crimes were slim. I'd never visited the city in my habit. And no police inspector would look for a murderer among a bunch of wizened monks in a monastery that predated

St. Peter's Basilica. Unless a monk in the monastery tipped him off. And I trailed nothing from my feedings to San Benedetto.

That's why I knew the police inspectors poking around the monastery focused only on Andrea's disappearance and not on the killings in the city. Of course, their probing in that direction concerned me, especially when they began interviewing all the monks. Because of my nocturnal schedule Abbot Anselmo arranged a special appointment for me during the evening recreation hour. I met the pair, a woman and a man, in the antechamber outside the abbot's office.

"This is Inspector Ramadori," Anselmo said, gesturing to the woman, "and this is Signor Morello, Assistant Inspector."

"We'd like to ask you some questions about Father Andrea," Ramadori said, in a clipped, abrasive voice. "We're investigating his case."

She was a plain woman in her 30s, with thick eyebrows and short, dark hair. She wore a navy suit.

Her tall, thin assistant was younger, boyish-looking, with long sandy-brown sideburns. His own black suit hung on him, a size too large. He carried a leather briefcase.

Ramadori turned to Anselmo. "Do you mind, Father?"

With a nod, Anselmo gestured toward his office.

We sat in armchairs arranged around a low mahogany table in a corner of the spacious room that also contained the abbot's uncluttered desk and tall bookcases loaded with volumes.

"The abbot tells us you are new here, Brother Victor," Ramadori said, nodding to Morello, who pulled a pad from his briefcase and a pen from his breast pocket.

"Yes."

"He says you were friendly with Father Andrea. Did he ever talk of leaving the monastery?"

"Not that I recall. Do you have any leads yet?"

"We've just started the investigation in earnest," she explained. "We've had a backlog of cases. Can you tell us about Father Andrea? What was he like? What did he talk about?"

"Just the usual monastery stuff," I said. "Administrative matters he was handling for the abbot—furnace repairs, some medical problems."

"His own?" Morello said.

I shook my head. "A couple of the older monks."

"Think for a moment, Brother," Ramadori said. "Did he ever seem frightened or agitated? Did he ever seem secretive?"

I studied a smoke-darkened medieval painting on the wall behind the detectives. It depicted a bejeweled Herodias holding the gruesome head of John the Baptist on a platter. "He could be moody," I finally said. "But so can half the monks in the monastery. Including myself, I suppose."

Morello scribbled away.

"Tell me, Brother," Ramadori said. "Did the two of you leave the monastery at night? I know you go out into the city"

I figured Rossi had told her this. "It gets a little dull spending the whole night alone."

"I understand," Ramadori said perfunctorily.

I decided she was more than plain. She was ugly. Her features were large and asymmetrical. Checking my mounting impatience, I asked her if she suspected foul play.

'Anything is possible, Brother," Ramadori said. "We're still interviewing the monks and searching the monastery for clues. We're also consulting his family members. Tell me, Brother, did Father Andrea have any enemies at San Benedetto?"

I chuckled. "Monks can be petty sometimes, Inspector, but we're pretty harmless. I don't think anyone at San Benedetto had it in for Father Andrea."

"I see," she said wearily. She stood, and Morello quit scribbling and scrambled to his feet. "Thank you, Brother. Please contact us if you think of anything that could help. No matter how insignificant. Father Anselmo has our number."

I led the detectives back to Anselmo and went to my cell. I was hungry but prepared to delay my departure until they were off monastery grounds. I climbed up to the scriptorium to talk to Paul.

The large room was dark except for the lamp on Paul's drafting table, and even that was too much light for him. He shielded his face with his hand as he painted, glancing up and smiling when I came in. His skin had turned white as alabaster since the transfusion, and in his eyes glimmered the strangely seductive fire that would tell any vampire he was facing a thrall.

"How'd it go?" he asked. He put his brush in a jar of solution and stretched his arms.

"Just fine," I said, kissing him and pulling up a chair. "Rossi must have told them I creep into the city at night. They asked if Andrea ever went with me. Maybe they think he made trips on his own and someone did him in. Did they ask you about me?" I knew Paul had had an interview with them earlier that day.

He shook his head. "They just wanted to know if I ever talked to Andrea. Their English wasn't great. I think they were interested in me because I keep different hours than the monks. They thought maybe I'd seen Andrea coming or going."

"Good. They're looking for someone on the outside."

"What if they search the crypt?"

I shrugged. "They'll examine the whole monastery So what?"

"But the crypt would be a likely place to hide a body."

"*If* there was a body. And *if* the killer was a monk. They have no reason to suspect either."

Paul didn't seem reassured.

"What's on your mind?" I said, stroking his cheek.

"Why did you kill him?"

I'd been waiting for this question. "It couldn't be helped. He planned to expose me."

"As a vampire?"

I shook my head. "As an impostor."

"You were using him." Paul's eyes flashed with anger. "You fucked him, and then you had to shut him up. Are you using me?"

"For what?"

"I don't know."

"You don't know because there is no logical reason. I made you because I wanted you." I touched his thigh. He shuddered. I got up, stood behind him, and slipped my hand under his jersey to caress his smooth pectorals. I brushed his hair from his neck with my face and kissed his cool skin.

His chest rose and fell rapidly under my touch. His heart thumped like a drum.

"Looks like you've recovered since yesterday," I said. He'd told me about the seizure that followed his talk with Rossi.

"I'm back on the phenobarbital," he said. "Why do I still need it?"

"I don't know."

He clasped my arm, pulled up my sleeve, and licked at the flesh.

"You want some?" I whispered, reaching down to caress his crotch.

His fingernails grew longer and sharper, clawing at my forearm.

"Go ahead," I said.

With one quick stroke, his nails slit my skin. He lapped at the beading blood. Then, squeezing my arm, he sucked.

Fire exploded in my testicles and leapt up into my belly and nipples. As my knees weakened, I braced myself against his broad back.

"That's enough," I whispered, drawing my arm away.

I traced a finger over the wound. It vanished, along with every speck of blood. But Paul's lips dripped with it. I pulled him from the chair and lapped his mouth clean.

When I left Paul, I climbed down to the crypt, where the faint scent of intruders lingered. A team of crime inspectors had awakened me that morning as they wandered around the cavernous mausoleum. But there was no sign of disturbance in the little alcove where I'd buried Andrea, nor anywhere else in the crypt for that matter. Even if the police had reason to suspect that his body was hidden in the crypt, they'd have to pry open almost 300 tombs. And in case they compared seals around the marble tablets, I'd loosened the mortar on tombs throughout the crypt so they would match Andrea's grave.

Restless, I roamed the streets of Rome for hours, finally attacking a baker as he fumbled with the lock on his shop door at 3 in the morning. A strong, burly man, he fought me harder than anyone had in a long time. Provoked, I yanked his long hair and slammed his face against the metal shutters covering the shop windows. I dragged him inside, pushed him to the terra-cotta floor, and straddled him, pinning back his bulky arms. A fluorescent light glowed in the glass pastry case, which contained a few small tarts from the day before. His eyes widened as my fangs descended.

"My God," he said. Then he shouted for help, but the street was empty and I knew no one would hear him.

I nuzzled his fat neck, excited by our struggle. I bit him and sucked his jugular for several minutes before he lost consciousness. When I was full, I got up and planted my foot on his throat, depriving him of oxygen until he was completely dead.

Dawn was a couple of hours away, and I was still restless. With a strange longing to see my old home, I rose into the night and fought mountain gusts all the way to a spot 30 miles south.

An 18th-century villa stood where my father's had stood two millennia before. It looked over gardens terraced on the hillside, gardens in the exact location of my father's gardens. From the villa's portico I gazed at rows of boxwood, date palm, and wild-growing shrubbery—all in the shadows of an unclouded moon. I closed my eyes and remembered the aroma of vineyards, of hay from the surrounding fields, of my mother's jasmine wafting from the courtyard. Suddenly a distant song rose up on the current. The voice belonged to a woman.

At the far edge of the gardens strolled a matronly figure draped in white. She stopped and seemed to gaze up at me.

"Victor?" she called, her thin, fragile voice rising on the wind.

My breathing quickened. I leapt from the portico, sailing 50 feet to the nearest terrace. Then I ran down through the descending gardens until I came to her. She sat on a stone bench.

"Mother," I said, dropping to my knees before her on the damp earth. She looked at me blankly. A hood enclosed her sad face.

"Mother! It's Victor." I foolishly reached for her hands, which were folded meekly on her lap. But my hand passed through the apparition. "What are you trying to tell me?"

Her eyes scanned something in the distance, then finally came to rest upon my face. She raised the back of her hand to her mouth and contemplated me—with regret and pity, it seemed—as though she grieved for what she had produced.

"Blood," she whispered. "Blood."

"Whose blood?" My impulse was to shake her narrow shoulders.

She sat stonily, like a weathered cemetery statue. I gave up trying to learn her meaning. "Do you see Father? Justin? What kind of existence do you have?" Although the spirits of Justin and my father had appeared to me throughout the centuries, they had never communicated with me. In fact, they had never acknowledged my presence. For the first time, my eyes rested on the spirit of my mother, and she was determined to speak. But only one word fell from her lips.

"Blood," she whispered again. Then she stood and slowly walked away—her robe dragging on the ground—until she faded into the night.

I paced the grounds to calm myself. My desires had produced her, I decided, and I upbraided myself for succumbing to illusions. If allowed to perceive me, the ghost of my real mother would have wept for joy. She'd have reassured me that she prospered in the Underworld with Father and Justin.

But what I saw when I returned to San Benedetto made me doubt my assessment. In the church, Paul knelt before the altar. Hundreds of candles glowed in the sanctuary. They covered the altar, the floor, and the beam above. Stripped to his waist, Paul recited an indecipherable mantra, whipping his back with a scourge over one shoulder, then the other. This so-called self-discipline had been a routine practice in monasteries until recent, more enlightened times, when it fell into disfavor. But it persisted among fanatical monks. The scourge was made of leather cords attached to metal spurs that tore the flesh.

In the flood of yellow light, brutal incisions gleamed on Paul's back, crisscrossing haphazardly like the paint strokes of an angry child. My mother's sad voice echoed in my head. *Blood... blood... blood...*

I ran to Paul to make him stop. But when I got to the sanctuary the light vanished. *He* had vanished. The air hung still and cool, without a trace of smoke or blood.

Hurrying to Paul's cell, I found him in his bed.

"Victor?" he said.

"You're all right," I whispered. I stripped and got into bed with him. Kissing him deeply, I worked off his briefs and caressed his chest, arms, and belly. I kissed his lips and throat and nipples. I kissed the beautiful arch of each foot as I raised one after the other over my shoulder. He moaned for me, clung to my chest, and climaxed with the motion of me inside him. I climaxed and collapsed, flush with tenderness.

CHAPTER THIRTEEN

PAUL

How can I get Rossi today? Figuring out an answer to this question gave me a perverse thrill. I'd never been malicious and wondered if this mean delight came with my transformation. Maybe I needed toughening before I could enter Victor's life completely, which is what I wanted more than anything in the world. Maybe I was becoming truly demonic. At times the thought scared me, but mostly it didn't faze me at all. And it wasn't like Rossi was such a kind, gentle soul that I should have felt remorse. He thrived on control. Maybe he needed cutting down to size.

I liked to push his buttons by contradicting his beliefs. That's what I did on Monday of Holy Week. The whole manuscript team had gone down to the refectory for the usual morning break. The cloudy day made the light in the large hall bearable. Rossi looked pale and tired as he stood at the window, quietly sipping his coffee. He had refused his favorite pastry when Ricardo offered it to him, and I figured he was fasting during the last week of Lent, something encouraged but not required of the monks, according to Giorgio. I carried him a plate of pastries.

"Would you like one, Father?" I took a bite of my own.

He shook his head and looked back out the window.

"Come on, they're great."

"I'm fasting," he said quietly.

"Why?"

"It's a Lenten custom."

"What's the point of going without food?" I licked fruit filling off my fingers.

Rossi seemed to sense that I was egging him on, but he forged ahead anyway with the inevitable religious mumbo jumbo. "We mortify our flesh to remember our Lord's passion and death. He suffered for us. We join our sufferings to his."

"Seems kind of masochistic," I said.

"It's a free act, Paul. Done out of love." Rossi sighed. "Think what you want. It's part of our tradition."

"Giorgio," I called to the table where Giorgio, Ricardo, and Roberto were sitting. "How come you're not fasting?"

Too chicken to get involved, Giorgio pretended not to understand. So I asked him, "*Perché tu mangi, e Padre Rossi non mangia?*"

He shrugged.

I shook my head. "It's a wonder the church has held up so long." I walked away before Rossi could answer.

On Good Friday I decided to mess with his mind again. He loved it when I showed any kind of interest in his religion, so I attended the midday service to once again encourage his hopes. Spicy incense drifted through the church. The tabernacle door stood open, revealing an empty hollow. Giorgio had told me that the gold ciborium full of consecrated wafers is removed on Holy Thursday night to commemorate the arrest and removal of Jesus from the Garden of Gethsemane. *Poor Jesus,* I thought, *snatched out of the bread box.*

The service started with the stations of the cross. Father Anselmo, accompanied by two monks bearing candles, stopped at each of the 14 medieval paintings of two-dimensional figures depicting Jesus' final walk to Calvary. Anselmo announced the title of the station, the monks genuflected, he read a prayer, then the monks chanted a somber tune as he marched to the next station. I stood alone in the nave, fully visible to Rossi. When he glanced at me every now and then, I tried to look devout, kneeling when the monks did.

Then came a very weird, waxworks kind of ritual. Flanked by monk acolytes, Anselmo marched up the aisle behind Giorgio, who lifted a three-foot-high crucifix wrapped in a purple cloth. Three times the abbot sang out something about the wood of the cross, the procession stopped, Giorgio lowered the crucifix, and the abbot peeled back part of the cloth to reveal a leg, then an arm, until the whole corpus was finally exposed. Then Anselmo stood near the altar and directed the monks to file up to kiss Jesus' feet as the organist played a dirge.

When the last monk left his choir stall, I joined the line, watching Rossi as I advanced to the altar. He knelt, his hands clasped, his head bowed. But as I passed, he glanced up and smiled at me. I smiled back.

Giorgio watched me placidly as I knelt before the crucifix. When I took both feet in my mouth as though they were a Popsicle—or something else—I glanced up and saw a look of horror on his face. The abbot stood with closed eyes, oblivious to the blasphemy.

As I was on my way back to my seat, Rossi eyed me with disgust.

But the little sacrilege came back to bite me in the ass.

That night Victor was in a gloomy mood. A fierce storm kept us off the street, so we sat in the scriptorium, Victor quietly thumbing through a book on the occult while I painted. At midnight, he went to feed. I didn't bother asking him if I could go along. As I sat alone in the big chamber, the crucifix-kissing ritual ran through my mind, and before long I found myself climbing down to the dark church.

Thunder shook the windows and lightning flashed garishly on the altar. The crucifix from the ceremony was mounted on top of it. The meager red light of votive candles cast a shadow on the tabernacle door, which stood open still. Jesus wasn't home. He hung on the cross, his white plaster body glimmering in the storm. From the beam far above the altar dangled another image of him, like a distorted shadow. I felt a presence so concentrated in the sanctuary, so magnetic it pulled me to the altar. I knelt on the flagstones, transfixed. When I reached to touch the feet of the corpus, the feet I had defiled, they turned to flesh. I stood to examine the cross. Thunder rumbled. A sudden flash of white light through the windows revealed a life-size body on a crucifix that towered over me. The body twisted in pain. The flesh smelled of sweat and vomit, mixed with the metallic scent of blood. His tortured, bearded face—with its rugged, dark features—looked down at me, blood streaming from the long thorns pressed into his head.

"Paul," he whispered, then shouted, "Paul!"

"What are you?" I said, my heart beating frantically in my throat.

"He knows."

"Who?" I thought he meant Rossi. I thought he was trying to tell me that Rossi understood spiritual mysteries and that I had to repent.

"Come to me," he said, his voice straining.

It didn't occur to me for a second that his meaning was figurative. I wanted to hold his naked, torn flesh. Desire rushed through me like a fire with the power to propel, and it did. My body lifted into the air until my eyes were level with his clear, beautiful eyes, which peered back at me from under swollen lids. I wrapped my arms around him, inhaling the odor of sweat and blood from his neck and hair. My impulse was to rip into his flesh and drink from his jugular. My fangs descended.

"Victor knows," he suddenly whispered.

I dropped to the floor. When I looked up, only the small, lifeless crucifix stood on the altar.

Like an idiot, I sat on the cold floor, unable to move or even reason. An old Simon and Garfunkel song played through my head, something about a hammer, a nail, and a sad bird flying away. A weird sort of longing filled me, a longing for something I couldn't even define but that was somehow expressed in the song. And the simple, innocent melody made me cry. What had I become? What had I left behind?

I didn't know what to make of the vision. The trancelike state I'd experienced resembled my seizures, but I hadn't lost consciousness. In fact, my senses sharpened during the scene and got confused only after it.

The next night I said nothing about the vision to Victor as we strolled through Rome's famous Protestant cemetery, near the pyramid of Caius Cestius. I was worried that my ecstatic experience would anger him, and I felt I'd somehow betrayed him. Victor had broken the cemetery's gate to let us in, and we wandered through the sinking headstones, locating the graves of Shelley and Keats. On the lonely tombstone of Keats we read the words: *Here lies One Whose Name was writ in Water.* Feral cats darted through the monuments like transformed souls of the dead. Used to being fed by visitors, one sleek gray cat rubbed against our legs. Victor hissed, then laughed when the cat arched its back and hissed back before slinking away.

We'd hiked the three miles to the cemetery in the south part of the old city, so we took the subway back to the Vatican area, the closest Metro stop to the monastery.

"What's the matter with you tonight? You're very quiet," Victor said as we approached the colonnades of St. Peter's.

"Nothing."

"Have you had another seizure?"

"No. Not exactly"

"What then?"

Despite my reluctance, I told him about the vision on the altar. At first he said nothing, but his playfulness disappeared. He glared at me, then seemed to make some kind of resolution.

"Come on," he said, grabbing my arm.

"Where are we going?"

Without answering he led the way across the dark, empty piazza toward St. Peter's.

We climbed the steps of the portico. At the entrance, Victor touched the massive oak door and tilted his head as though waiting for some sensation.

"The alarm's not on," he said. He grabbed the handle and in one quick, powerful move broke the bolt and swung the door open. We stepped into the dark narthex.

"What are we doing?" I was scared by the anger I saw in him.

"You'll see."

Our footsteps echoed in the cavernous basilica that extended as long as two football fields before us. I'd already toured it several times, but it seemed a different place in the dark, like a giant mausoleum full of effigies and statues and deep niches. My vision pierced the shadows. To the right of us Michelangelo's *Pietà* rested tranquilly in a chapel shielded by a glass wall. Ahead, under the dome, loomed Bernini's baldacchino, which formed a canopy above the main altar. The baldacchino's four bronze columns twisted like coiled snakes. In the apse beyond the altar, the shadowy throne of St. Peter, bumpy with ornamentation, was fixed high on the wall beneath a dark window.

"Beautiful, isn't it?" Victor said. "But you know what used to be in this spot."

I nodded. "Nero's circus."

"I remember it," he said. "I remember when they crucified Peter there, in the middle of a wild audience, upside down. A withered old man from the Judean province. With big dreams. A smart investment, huh?" Victor raised his hands and glanced up to the vault. Then he grabbed my arm. "Come on."

We moved to the altar, and Victor sprang onto the massive slab as easily as if it rose only a foot—instead of four feet—off the ground. He extended his arms and yelled, "Here I am, Joshu," pivoting from side to side, like a prize fighter in front of a roaring crowd. "You want me, you've got me! But keep your hands off him."

Then he reached down and—as if I were as light as a mannequin—yanked me up. He peeled off my jersey and pulled my jeans and briefs down to my ankles.

"Get on your hands and knees," he ordered.

I did what he said, scared and excited.

The initial thrust hurt, but I wanted him so much I took him without resistance. He gripped my sides and rammed away.

Then he turned me over, tore his wrist with his teeth, placed the wound to my mouth, and continued to ram me while I sucked the blood. The pleasure was almost unbearably intense. My head felt warm, like it was floating in blood. Every nerve in my body buzzed. I tightened myself around Victor, wanting him deeper and deeper inside me, moaning, and finally exploding as he exploded.

After that night, the mean streak in me intensified. I didn't care what I said, what I did, what I thought. I didn't care if I drove Rossi crazy or if I scandalized Giorgio. I got a kick out of making the manuscript team squirm. "*You* think Jesus was gay?" I said one day as I dabbed away at a painting for the Gospel of John. And one day I brought up the whole "pedophile priest" business going on in the States. Rossi bristled and preached at me. Ricardo and Roberto sanctimoniously ignored me. Giorgio didn't know what to think. Despite his confusion, he stayed loyal—though I couldn't have cared less.

As for my family—I felt myself breaking away, as if I had boarded a big, powerful ocean liner, gliding out to sea as they waved to me on the docks.

Easter night, after Victor went out to feed, I climbed to the scriptorium. The work I did every night—my real work—absorbed me. The images became more severe, more violent. My strokes grew heavy and asymmetrical. Colors clashed on the vellum sheets. In the most recent painting, inspired by the Good Friday vision, I created a stylized crucifixion scene with jagged lines of red and black. But the painting wasn't on my desk where I'd left it. Thinking the prudish Rossi had stuck it in the cabinet where I kept my other paintings, I opened one thin drawer after another. They were all empty.

I ran down the stairs and crossed the dark cloister to Rossi's cell on the first floor of the lateral dormitory. I opened his door without knocking and flicked on the light.

In his bed, Rossi squinted and shaded his eyes with his hand.

"Where are my paintings?" I said.

"Sit down, Paul." Rossi felt for his robe at the bottom of his bed.

"What did you do with them?" I glanced around the room. A Bible and a notebook sat on the desk. None of the drawers were big enough to hold the vellum sheets. No table stood in the room.

Rossi got up and slipped his robe over his gray pajamas. He picked up his glasses from the night table and put them on, brushing his oily hair back from his face.

"I'm sorry Paul," he said, clasping his hands in front of him. "We can't have them here."

"What do you mean? Where are they?"

Rossi shook his head.

"Did you throw them away?" My face burned in anger.

"I destroyed them. If you'll sit down, we can talk."

"Who in the hell do you think you are?"

"Please, Paul," he said, eyeing me in his patronizing way. "When you calm down and think this over, you'll realize I did it for your own good. You're a nice young man. But something is happening to you."

In that second, I snapped. Rossi's lips kept moving, but I didn't hear a word. Adrenaline rushed through me, and I grabbed him by the throat and squeezed. My fangs descended. Rossi's eyes bugged out, almost ready to pop from their sockets. Then he winced. His hands, which had been trying to pull mine away from his throat, suddenly clutched at his chest. I released him, and he crumpled to the floor, dragging down with him the blanket on his bed. He lay still, his brown eyes wide open, like two drops of chocolate.

CHAPTER FOURTEEN

VICTOR

A mechanism in the brain of a vampire keeps track of his thrall, and the moment I entered the church I knew Paul waited for me at my niche. Bloated from feeding and weak with the coming dawn, I would have to send him away, as much as I wanted him to crawl onto my shelf and rest in my arms until the next nightfall.

He sat on the floor of the alcove, his knees drawn up to his chest, his hands clasped around them, and his head bowed. He didn't look up when I appeared in the archway.

"What's wrong?" I said.

He looked up. He was pale as the memorial tablet behind him, his face a stark contrast with his black T-shirt. Like a drug addict coming down from a high, he had bloodshot eyes, blue lips, and tangled hair. "Rossi's dead," he said. "I killed him." He described the scene in Rossi's cell.

"So you didn't try to feed?" I said.

He shook his head.

"Then there's no evidence against you." Wounds on Rossi's throat could cause a problem. So could vomit containing Rossi's blood—which would definitely exist had Paul tried to feed. "Let's go look at him."

"Why?" Paul said irritably.

"We have to make sure everything's clean."

Paul's stunt didn't surprise me. I'd watched him growing restless and provocative, taunting Rossi, asserting himself in front of the manuscript team, rebelling against Rossi's little scriptorium rules. I saw the glint of cruel pleasure in his eyes when he watched me feed, his growing appetite for blood, his need for pain when we made love. He acted like a full-blown thrall. And he excited me.

Rossi lay on the floor of his cell, one leg tucked beneath the other, his head crooked to one side, his eyes open. His face and hands and feet had turned yellow and waxy. I squatted down to inspect him.

"Direct the desk lamp this way," I said.

Paul twisted the gooseneck light toward Rossi's face.

I moved aside the collar of Rossi's robe and examined his throat. Then I lifted his greasy head to check the back of his neck. "No marks," I said. "How long did you hold his throat?"

"Not long," Paul said, crouching down to look at Rossi. "Maybe 10 seconds."

"Then it must have been a heart attack. You scared him to death. Congratulations."

"I didn't come here to kill him. Something came over me. I was out of control."

I patted Paul's cheek—rough with a morning beard—and kissed his lips. "Everything will be OK," I whispered. "One of the monks will find him here, cold as ice, and call for an ambulance as a formality. Medics will come and see that he died of heart failure. The coroner will confirm it. Nothing's out of place here."

Birds chirped frenetically in the cloister when I passed through it on my way to the crypt. Exhausted, I crawled onto the dark shelf and strained to pull the marble tablet into place. Rossi's frozen eyes stared at me in the darkness, but I quickly fell asleep.

What I expected to happen did. Rossi apparently had already suffered one heart attack in the States and was supposed to be on some medication, which he hadn't bothered with. No inspectors showed up to examine the room. None of the monks seemed alarmed. Paul relaxed. A funeral was planned for Friday of that week, to give some of Rossi's relatives time to travel up from Brindisi, the port town in the heel of Italy where you could board a ferry for Greece.

A couple of nights after Rossi's death, Anselmo asked me to come to his office during the evening recreation period. I figured he wanted my advice about something, and I was right.

When I sat down in his office, he came around the desk and sat across from me. "I'm a little concerned about the manuscript project," he said. "A few months of work remain." His bright eyes and animated manner belied the deep creases lining his forehead and running from his large nose to his lips.

"Can't Roberto and Ricardo take charge? And Paul can just finish the paintings he's agreed to do."

Anselmo frowned and interlaced his knobby fingers on his lap. "That's what I'm worried about. Father Rossi told me that Paul needs direction. He's not Catholic, and apparently he has some strange ideas about depicting biblical scenes."

"You could look over the paintings yourself," I said.

"I'm no good at that kind of thing." Anselmo sighed. "Oh, well, I guess we can just put ourselves in God's hands."

I nodded.

"You know, Victor," Anselmo said, hesitating, "Father Rossi had some strange ideas about you and Paul."

"Yes. He told me."

"It's just ridiculous. I told him it's natural for two young Americans to strike up a friendship. Anyway, would you keep an eye on his work?"

Rossi's relatives arrived on Thursday: three brothers, two sisters, and their spouses and children. They stayed in guest rooms adjacent to the large reception hall in the front building. It was strange to see women and children in the monastery and to hear their voices echo through the cloister. Their presence bothered Paul. He retreated to the scriptorium and didn't come to dinner. It was just as well. Rossi's family ate with the monks. The olive-skinned brothers resembled Rossi and even gestured like him. One of his sisters, a heavy woman with big features, had clearly been crying all day. The sight of them would have overwhelmed Paul.

I left him alone that evening, strolling through the well-lit, manicured grounds of the Villa Borghese until after midnight. Then I followed the path down to the empty Piazza del Popolo, where the twin domes of Santa Maria dei Miracoli and Santa Maria di Montesanto flank the Via del Corso. I headed down a dark side street and approached a shaggy-haired college boy who was reading a textbook at a bus stop. "*Scusa*," I told him. "Do you have the time?" His blood tasted of curry and peppers, so I drank little and left him alive.

Paul wasn't in the scriptorium when I returned, so I figured he'd gone to bed. I sat there alone, reading and mulling over the best course to take with him. We couldn't stay in the monastery forever—the manuscript project would be done by summer's end. We would have to return to New Orleans and live off my accounts in Swiss banks until Paul agreed to the next step in his transformation.

And what if he didn't agree? Could we remain content as host and thrall? Accepting a subordinate position might get more and more difficult for him even as his fear of losing me made him resist the life I could offer.

When I passed through the nave of the church on my way to the crypt, candles burned around Rossi's coffin, which rested on a trestle between the choir stalls. An old monk, taking his turn keeping vigil dozed with his chin on his chest. In a nearby pew, Paul sat erect, his eyes fixed on the coffin.

I walked up the aisle and touched his shoulder. He didn't turn. He didn't speak. I approached the unfinished pine coffin. Rossi lay with his hands folded on his chest, a rosary laced between his stubby fingers. The hood of his habit framed his waxy face, his jaw dotted with gray beard. The chemical scent of embalming fluid reeked in my nostrils, and I drew back.

Eyeing the sleeping monk, I took a seat next to Paul. He looked frazzled and in need of a shave. His hair was oily, his shirt wrinkled.

"What are you doing?" I whispered. "This will just make you feel worse." He stared ahead without answering.

"He would have died of heart failure sooner or later," I said. "Don't blame yourself."

We sat in silence, the candles flickering in the dark, drafty church, the dark crucifix hanging like a grim exclamation point above the coffin. As dawn advanced, I kissed Paul's cheek and left him sitting there, his body still as a statue.

They buried Rossi in the niche across the crypt from my niche. The chanting of the *Dies Irae* woke me from a deep sleep. *Day of Judgment... Day of Wrath.* I sensed Paul's presence among the invisible crowd and knew that he had to come, if not to watch Rossi's coffin slip into its tomb, then to protect me from stragglers who might wander into my alcove. In that hazy moment, I resolved to tell him everything, to set before him the terms of a life like mine.

A week later the balmy air smelled sweet with spring blossoms as Paul and I picked our way through the ruins of the Forum, the traffic on the Corso humming in the distance. The white moon had risen to its zenith.

"This place was the heart of the city," I said, gazing around at the rubble that jutted from the ground like tombstones. "Magnificent buildings, crowded squares, paved avenues, chariots, monuments to the gods. Eternal Rome. Who knew?"

Paul listened quietly—and keenly. His despondence had lifted. The glimmer of cruelty had returned to his eyes, and he was eager to hear whatever I had to tell him about my life.

We sat on the stone steps that once led into the Basilica Julia and now stretched before nothing—like a limb severed from a body.

"It started in Jerusalem," I said. "I was an officer under the Governor of Judea, Pontius Pilate. I was assigned to his own quarters. My life started in my father's villa, not 30 miles from this spot. My father was a statesman. My brothers were officers in the provinces. I hated Judea. I hated Pilate. He was a slimy, ineffective guardian of Rome's interests. But I found a jewel in Jerusalem. Hardly more than a boy Beautiful, passionate. I discovered him in the cliffs outside the city, dancing naked."

"You fell in love with him?" Paul said.

I smiled, seeing Joshu in my mind, dark, lean, sinewy, his arms beating the air as he swirled among the rocks. "I'd never seen a cut penis. It whipped his thighs as he danced. Made me hard."

"He was a Jew?"

"I thought his sect was insane, mutilating their boys like that," I said, laying my hand on Paul's thigh. "I could never understand his people. One possessive god. Purifications... rituals. Laws against images. Even the emperor's image on banners and medallions. The very emperor they owed their lives to! But Joshu was different from the other Jews. He preached love. He was obsessed with his god. He called him 'Father.' You know who I'm talking about—Jesus."

"*The* Jesus?" Paul struggled to comprehend.

"The one in your illuminations. The Lamb. The Christ. The Son of God, crowned in the heavens. That's what centuries of followers have made him. He had a mission—that's the truth about him. And he chose *it* over me."

I told him all the rest. My spree of violence in Jerusalem when Joshu rejected me—the rapes, the beatings. Pilate's pursuit of me. The sorceress, Tiresia, who offered me an escape—into darkness. My vow against the Christian god. My encounters with Joshu through the centuries. Then, the Dark Kingdom and Michael. He listened, mesmerized, absorbing everything without speaking. When I finished, we sat in silence, our jeans damp with dew. I waited for the question that Paul finally quietly asked.

"So, where do I fit into your story? Am I a distraction from Joshu? Some kind of substitute?"

"Don't tell me you've never loved someone," I said.

He shrugged. "I guess you could call it love. A guy named Rick Perez."

"A hot Latin boy?"

Paul smiled. "A guilt-ridden Catholic boy. He joined the Benedictines. He's the one who got me the job with Derek."

Paul went on to describe the frustrations of loving someone so guilt-ridden.

Jealousy suddenly stirred in me, surprising since this cloistered coward posed no threat. I dismissed the ridiculous feeling.

"You still haven't answered my question," Paul said.

I took his hand in both of mine. "I love *you*. The past is the past."

"What about this place, the Dark Kingdom? You still want to go there?"

I told him the truth. And I explained the rule about replacing yourself before entering the Kingdom and the rule against two vampires living side by side on earth.

"So Michael would have had to live without you?"

"For a brief period."

"How brief?" he said, the wheels clearly turning in his mind.

"Two hundred years. What's that compared to eternity?"

"Who makes these rules?"

"Doesn't matter," I said. "They exist."

Paul got up and, facing away from me, leaned against the lone column remaining in the Basilica ruins. His broad shoulders tapering to his waist formed a perfect triangle. "What happens if I can't do it?" he said, turning toward me.

"You stay the way you are," I said.

"And I can't go back, can I?" he asked fearfully.

I didn't need to answer. He turned away again and gazed toward the jagged remains of the Temple of Saturn.

That night, tight within my tomb, I slept fitfully. My senses wouldn't shut down. The odor of Rossi's slowly decaying corpse—detectable only to me—hung in the air. I heard rats scampering through the drains beneath the monastery I heard monks moan in their sleep and strange whispers in the cloisters.

Haunting scenes flashed before my eyes: Andrea's rotting corpse, my mother's frightened face the night I returned to the villa, Joshu grimacing on his cross. Joshu lying pale and stiff in the catacombs.

Joshu.

I calmed myself by remembering the morning Joshu and I had boarded a fishing boat on Tiberias lake and the tanned old owner had shared his dry bread and passed around his flask of wine. After a few long swallows, the crusty fisherman had broken into sobs, suddenly confessing he'd secretly poisoned his neighbor's donkey after some small argument. I had merely laughed; but Joshu had laid his hand on the old man's shoulder and whispered something. The stooped body had quit trembling instantly. The man had curled up on the bottom of the boat, closing his eyes like a baby in a crib.

"What did you tell him?" I'd asked Joshu.

"That I forgive him." Joshu's brown eyes had been serious.

"You?" I'd said. "What did he do to you?"

Joshu had stared at me without answering.

I'd kissed him on the lips, then wrestled him to the edge of the boat and shoved him headfirst into the water.

Savoring the feeling of contentment I'd experienced so long ago, I began to relax and drift off. When I finally fell asleep a nightmare came. In it, Paul, stripped to the waist, rode behind a white-robed Joshu on a black horse. The day was bright. The horse galloped down a rocky hillside but then lost its footing and fell, throwing Joshu and Paul. They landed on a flat boulder. Paul lay on his back, unconscious, a bloody gash on his forehead. Joshu lay near him, also unconscious. But then Joshu opened his eyes. And Joshu crawled to Paul, who was my thrall and my lover, and he stretched his body over him in the form of a cross. And he covered my lover's mouth with his own. And Paul suddenly revived and struggled to breathe. As Paul tried to heave Joshu off, Joshu's white robe turned blood-red.

A woman's voice wafted from the mountaintop. "The Blood of the Lamb," she called over and over. "The Blood of the Lamb. The Blood of the Lamb."

I stood on the rocks near them, frozen in place, trying to shut out the chanting. The sky darkened. Lightning ripped through slate-colored clouds. The chanting swelled.

I woke up in a sweat. The tomb seemed to be closing in on me. The voice from the dream sounded just beyond the marble tablet, resonating in the crypt.

"The Blood of the Lamb. The Blood of the Lamb."

In a flash of recognition, I knew who called. Her presence was as tangible as the cold tablet against my hand. It was Michael's grandmother.

Jana.

The powerful presence I'd felt as I walked through the streets of Rome had invaded my place of refuge.

It must have been noon when the sun exerted its greatest power over me. I could hardly turn my head at this time of day. My will, recharged in sleep, idled futilely. Could Jana move matter without a human instrument? Could she remove the marble shielding me from the day? Could she position a stake over my heart and force it through my ribs? I doubted it. *If so,* I thought, *she would have destroyed me by now.* Still, in my groggy, drained state, the possibility worked on me like an insistent pain breaking into sleep.

A confused realization heightened the torture: She knew of Joshu. She had access to my feelings for him. She liked reminding me of his rejection. Her voice came closer. "The Blood of the Lamb. The Blood of the Lamb." Her lips moved just inches from my ear.

I strained to say the word hovering in my brain like a balloon on a string just beyond my grasp. *Joshu.* Why invoke him? What could I expect from him? My head was too fuzzy to answer such questions.

The tablet shifted. A crack of light appeared. But no—in my panic I must have imagined it. Then the chanting ceased. The tablet rested secure. All traces of sound and motion evaporated. And I fell into a profound sleep.

NIGHTFALL

It's night, the moon a sliver pale.
Like a cat, my robe crouches in its meager light
I could cry at such a sight,
—at any sight—
and bless him for my tears,
the man who chased the night away
and brought a better night.

CHAPTER FIFTEEN

PAUL

The black script swirled before my eyes. Words from John's Gospel about the blind man rang in my head: *Go wash in the pool of Siloam.* But I couldn't focus on the illustration for the story: a man covering his eyes with his hands in shame. A vise seemed to tighten on my throat. Acrid-smelling, nervous perspiration dripped down my sides. It was no use. I pushed away from the drafting table and stood.

"I'm done for the day," I said.

Giorgio, Roberto, and Ricardo looked up from their drafting tables; they were not surprised by anything I did or said lately.

"Just leave the finished pages on the table and I'll do the illuminations after my mother leaves."

"She's staying a week?" Giorgio asked. His soft puppy eyes gazed warmly at me. Since Rossi's death, he'd become even more intent than usual on showing his affection and support. Maybe he thought I regretted the way I'd treated Rossi before he died.

"Yes," I said. "She gets in this afternoon."

"She won't be staying in the monastery, will she?" Roberto blurted. He'd trimmed his gray beard close, which accentuated his jowls and fleshy face. "Female guests should not be allowed in the cloister." He eyed me resentfully, as usual, like someone who'd been given orders to tolerate me.

Anselmo had probably issued such orders when Roberto complained to him about my work.

"Yes, she will, as a matter of fact. Father Anselmo insisted on it." Making the dig felt good.

Roberto snorted and turned his attention back to the vellum.

The fact is I had struggled over where to board Alice. My first impulse was to reserve a room in a pension, far from Victor's grave, far from our trysts, and far from monks like Roberto and Ricardo, whose hostility for me would raise questions in her mind. She'd have enough of her own questions. Just one look at my milky complexion, my long nails, my fierce eyes, and she'd know something was up. How would I explain, reassure her? I didn't know the answer.

But my feelings for her had not changed. If anything I felt more protective, more determined to hold on to her despite my new kind of existence. I wanted her inside the cloister where I could watch over her, not in the middle of a foreign city where she couldn't communicate. With no family outside of Topeka and no money, she'd never traveled far from Kansas; I'd paid for her entire trip. I made plenty of money on this project, almost $8,000 a month—most of which I saved, since room and board were free. When I underwent the final transformation, I could give her my savings. I probably wouldn't need them as a vampire. Victor gave me the impression he had lots of money somewhere. Anyway, for the duration of her visit my money would keep her safe and comfortable in Rome.

As hard as it was to admit, I wanted to protect Alice from something much more frightening than a foreign city. I wanted to protect her from Victor. In his eyes I now saw centuries of rape and murder. I saw ruthless feedings on innocent children, weak old men, and defenseless widows like Alice. I knew when he tore into throats he hardened with excitement. I knew it because I'd seen it. Worse, I'd experienced it myself as I watched him, and I knew *I* would be the same. Along with his searing gaze, blood, and hard flesh, his soul had penetrated me. Victor was in me. More unspeakable than my fear that Victor would hurt my mother was my fear that I might do it myself.

Maybe I'd invited her to Rome just to prove I wouldn't hurt the person I loved more than anyone on earth. Maybe I believed this was the last visit we would ever have, that after a complete transformation I wouldn't be able to bear letting her see me again.

It was sunny as hell at 3 o'clock when I arrived at the airport. If only Alice could have flown in at night, she wouldn't have been able to notice my coloring, or my discomfort in the sun, which still came and went. My sunglasses could hide only so much.

Standing with the crowd near Customs, I spotted her—in a turquoise pantsuit with three-quarter-length sleeves and a white mock-turtleneck top—and waved as the uniformed officer checked her passport. She smiled and waved back. Her short hair was grayer than it had been when I left Kansas. And she looked thinner.

The parade of people through the customs line moved at a crawl. Two chatty college girls with ponytails blocked my view of Alice, and they kept stopping in front of her to whisper. I wanted to break through the ropes and push them out of her way.

Finally she cleared the line of passengers, rolling a suitcase behind her, and I hugged her. She smelled of nicotine, but I didn't care. I didn't want to let go.

She drew back, adjusted her purse strap, and looked at me. "Let me see your face, silly."

I held my breath as she took off my glasses. She frowned and stared for a moment, touching my cheek as if she wanted to say something but held back. Finally she managed to say, "You need some sun. You're spending too much time stuck away in that library."

Relieved at not having to explain anything, I kissed her cheek. "You look great," I said. And she did, despite being thin. She looked rested, her greenish eyes clear, their usual dark circles barely noticeable. Her high cheekbones, square jaw, and broad forehead had always given her an air of strength and intelligence, even in her white cafeteria uniform. She was tall, just a few inches shorter than I was, and statuesque. With more sophisticated clothes, more polished speech, and more graceful carriage, she might have passed for a CEO.

Our wiry, mustachioed taxi driver quit trying to talk to us when he ran out of English phrases. Holding my hand, Alice looked out the window quietly for a few minutes before turning to me with concern on her face.

"What's the matter with you, honey?"

"Nothing, Mom." I squeezed her hand.

"Are you sick? Is it AIDS?"

"Oh, come on."

"Then what is it? You're as white as a ghost. You don't look good. Your eyes... I don't know..." She shook her head as if she couldn't quite put her finger on the change.

"It's like you said. I'm cooped up in the library all day. And I did just get over the flu or something."

"Have you been to the doctor?"

"Yes. One of the monks is a doctor. He runs the infirmary at the monastery." I figured Alice wouldn't be able to check the story out with Brother Claudio, who spoke very little English.

"And he knows about the epilepsy? Have you been having seizures? Are you forgetting to take the pheno?"

"No, I just had the flu. There's nothing to worry about."

She nodded and patted my leg, as though resigning herself to my answer.

We talked about her recent visit with the doctor and her meds, and then she seemed to relax. As we entered the city, her eyes lit up. She looked out at the Victor Emmanuel Monument and said, "I can't believe I'm in Rome!"

The taxi let us out in front of the monastery Alice seemed nervous when we crossed the entrance cloister and encountered the church.

"Don't worry," I said. "You'll get used to the Catholic stuff."

"Are you sure it's OK for me to stay here?"

"Of course. The abbot is thrilled to have you. Come on." I took her to Anselmo's office.

Anselmo beamed when I introduced him to Alice. "*Molto piacere!*" he said, taking her hand in both of his and rising on the balls of his feet like an excited kid. With his big ears and bright brown eyes, he reminded me of Snow White's dwarf Dopey. "We are very happy to have you here, Signora Lewis. Your son is a magnificent artist." His English was labored, but he was determined to welcome her in style.

Alice smiled appreciatively. "Thank you, Father. I'm very proud of him."

I took her to her room, which was in the same building as the abbot's office, on the other side of the big reception salon. Apparently a couple of sitting rooms had been converted into guest rooms in the last 10 years or so, to accommodate female guests, which the monastery had begun to allow. The room was about as sparse as the monks' cells, with just a single bed and nightstand, an armchair with a reading lamp, and a dresser. But the lone window looked out at St. Peter's, and there was a bathroom, complete with a shower and bidet.

"What is it?" Alice asked. "It's too low for a sink."

"It's for soaking," I said.

"Soaking?"

"Your bottom," I whispered, patting her rump.

"Good grief!" she said, laughing.

She left her jacket on the bed, and I gave her a tour of the lush grounds and the church—except for the crypt, of course. Since the scribes were still taking their siesta, and we'd be spared Roberto and Ricardo's smug glances, I led her up to the scriptorium to show her some of the finished manuscript pages. She loved my Nativity illumination in the Gospel of Luke. To me, it was a pretty standard rendition—as specified by Rossi: baby Jesus in Mary's arms, Joseph looking over her shoulder, the head of a cow, two adoring shepherds. But I had handled the colors and shading well. They lent a somber quality to the happy scene.

"It's just beautiful, honey," Alice said, bending over the page. "Look at the blues. And just think, it will last hundreds of years." She straightened up and kissed my cheek. "I'm so proud of you."

We strolled down the Gianicolo, spent an hour in St. Peter's Basilica, whose incredible dimensions impressed Alice, and then had cappuccino in a little outdoor café near the basilica. The tables were filled, mostly with a group of German tourists taking one another's picture.

I tried to sit without my sunglasses, but my eyes were too sensitive that day to dispense with protection. Alice didn't comment on the sunglasses again. She knew it would do no good to probe anymore. I enjoyed sitting quietly with her, watching the crazy traffic on the street and the passengers loading into packed buses that pulled up to the curb not far from us. It struck me that I might never sit with my mother in the sunshine again.

As we walked back, I realized she hadn't brought up Victor's name. He and I had plans to take her to dinner that evening, and I mentioned it, still apprehensive at the thought of their meeting.

"And he's a monk?" Her concern was apparent.

"Yes."

"You and Victor are... together?"

I nodded.

"But if he's a monk, isn't he breaking his vows? Won't he get into trouble? You might lose your job."

"The project's almost over. Want to stop and rest a minute?" We'd started climbing the Gianicolo, and Alice's pace had slowed, her breathing becoming labored.

We sat on the low wall near the sidewalk, shaded by a big pine. Cars whizzed up and down the hill.

"What are you going to do after the work's done?" she said. "Is he going to leave the monastery? I just don't understand why you got involved with him, Paul."

The irony of the moment almost made me laugh. Alice worried that I was stealing a monk away from a monastery. I'd gotten myself into a little pickle.

"I love him," I said.

"But this is Rick all over again. He'll play you along and then run back to the monastery. You'll get hurt again. Why not find someone who's free of all this baggage?"

"Trust me, Mom. He's going to leave the order. He planned to before he ever met me."

She sighed and took a cigarette from her purse. "Don't say a word," she said as I eyed her. She was clearly declaring her own independence since I was insisting on mine.

When we got back, I made her rest. She'd slept little on the flight and looked exhausted. I wondered if I'd done the right thing in bringing her to Rome. Now she was worried about my health and my relationship with Victor. What did I expect? Maybe deep down I wanted her to know everything. The intensity of my love for Victor. The unimaginable bond between us. The future ahead. But how could I expect her to understand the nature of our relationship or our future when I didn't understand them myself?

* * *

A plaintive chant wafted from the church as I waited in the rear cloister for Victor to emerge from his niche. The dark campanile loomed like a giant hooded monk guarding the cloister from worldly intruders. Victor found me seated on a bench in the rose garden, inhaling the heavy perfume of the flowers—so intense to my new senses that my head spun.

I got up and kissed him long and hard till his icy lips turned warm as bathwater.

"She's resting," I said.

"How's it going?" He kissed my ear and then my throat, his mouth lingering there. He smelled like the crypt, the wool of his habit damp and hinting of mold.

"She notices something. She's afraid I'm sick."

"Not surprising."

"And she's worried I'm involved with a monk."

Victor laughed hard, then uncontrollably, the scent of blood rushing from his mouth. Suddenly he stopped and turned his head. Alice appeared on the stone path that wound around the church. She timidly approached us.

"Alice, this is Victor."

"Nice to meet you," she mumbled mechanically.

"Did you sleep OK?" I said.

She nodded. "The singing woke me up." She stared apprehensively at Victor.

"You get used to it," he said, clearly amused at her discomfort.

Alice walked quietly during the 15-minute stroll to Trastevere. She took in the earthy, picturesque neighborhood where stucco crumbled and shutters hung askew. At the Piazza di Santa Maria several young mothers sat with baby carriages on the bottom step of the octagonal fountain's pedestal. A group of teenagers sat closer to the water, joking and laughing. Plates clinked and conversation buzzed in the bars and restaurants around the square. Even at this hour tourists strolled through the dimly lit arches on the facade of the medieval basilica. We found a table in a family-run trattoria around the corner from the piazza and ordered the pasta special, tortellini with red sauce. By the time the bearded proprietor brought it out in huge bowls, Alice had already finished a glass of Chianti and seemed more relaxed. Victor pretended to sip his wine, occasionally going through the motions of pouring out more from the carafe.

"So, are you a priest?" Alice suddenly blurted at Victor, interrupting the small talk I was making about Trastevere's atmosphere.

"No. A brother," Victor said.

"Well, what's the difference?" Alice poured herself another glass of wine. "Can I smoke in here?"

"It's Italy," Victor said. "You can smoke anywhere."

"You haven't touched your pasta," I said.

Alice dismissed the comment with a wave of her hand, dug a cigarette out of her purse, and lit it. "What do you plan to do if you leave the monastery?" she said.

Victor shrugged, staring over his glass with a glimmer of malice in his eyes that alarmed me.

"I mean, will you get a job back in the States? Teach or something?"

"Or something," Victor said.

The grip on my glass tightened. My temples pounded.

"You know, Paul doesn't have much to live on himself. He gave up his teaching job to do this Bible work. Even if he gets back on at the public schools, they pay peanuts."

"Oh, I've got a fortune," Victor said glibly. "Family inheritance."

Alice glared at him. She assumed he was joking. She waved to the waiter and gestured to her cigarette to indicate she wanted an ashtray. Then she launched into a diatribe about responsibility and finances, but I heard only garble and watched her face blur and inhaled an aroma of garlic that rushed at me, accompanied by the clinking of a spoon against a glass.

The scene before my eyes was Alice's front yard, white with sunlight. Alice wore shorts that exposed her pale legs, squiggled with blue, as though a tattoo artist hadn't been able to get a purchase on the skin. She walked down the gravel drive to the mailbox, removed a bunch of mail, thumbed through it, and started back toward the house. On the drive, near her green Saturn, she winced, dropped the mail, and tried to brace herself against the car's trunk before slipping down to the gravel. Grimacing, she clutched her chest. Then her entire body relaxed, her blank eyes staring at the summer sky.

When I regained consciousness, I was on the floor of the trattoria. Alice and Victor were crouched over me. The proprietor was yelling something about calling an ambulance to one of the waiters. The dozen or so patrons chattered excitedly.

"You're all right, Paul." Alice wiped my face with a damp linen napkin.

I tried to sit up, but Victor made me lie still. *"Lui sta bene,"* he said, reassuring the excited proprietor, who leaned over me now, nervously rubbing his beard. *"Non bisogna una ambulanza,"* he added, translating for Alice, "No ambulance."

"Lift up his head up," Alice said to Victor.

When he did, she held a glass of water to my lips and I drank.

Victor called a cab. By the time it arrived, I was strong enough to stand and walk to it. Alice and Victor sat quietly on either side of me in the backseat.

At San Benedetto, Alice confidently barked orders at Victor to get water and help me into bed. Then she arranged the blankets, opened my window, and pulled out the desk chair, determined to sit by me until I slept, dismissing Victor.

"Thanks, Mom," I said wearily, before falling asleep.

The next morning, even though my strength had returned, Alice continued in caretaker mode. She watched me take my pheno and arranged with the abbot to have breakfast brought to my room. When I finally convinced her I was fine, she lectured me about taking my meds, then strolled with me down to the Piazza Navona. There we had lunch under a café umbrella and watched the crowds buying from vendors, gathering at the Bernini fountains, and coming and going from restaurants around the square.

We continued on to the Spanish Steps, which cascaded brightly into the lively piazza, and sat a long time on the stairs, taking in the sun and the activity below. We strolled along the chic Via Veneto, where Alice bought a purse in a boutique, and we took a taxi to the Colosseum and Forum. All day, my premonition lurked in the back of my mind and I kept thinking I might never see her again once she left Rome.

By evening we were both exhausted. After buying slices of pizza from a vendor on the Gianicolo, we returned to San Benedetto, and Alice went to bed.

At 9 o'clock Victor showed up at my cell. I was stretched out on my mattress.

"How are you feeling?" he said, sitting next to me.

I propped myself on my elbow. "During my seizure I had a vision. It was a premonition, just like the other ones I've had." I described the scene that had unfolded before my eyes. "I want you to save her. The same way you saved Anselmo."

Victor seemed less than happy at the suggestion.

"Can you?" I said.

"If you want."

"Will you do it?" I gripped his arm.

He leaned in for a kiss. The familiar chill in his lips reassured me.

Chapter Sixteen

Victor

In this obsession with his mother, Paul had to be humored. His old life was over, but his new life hadn't begun. And before he ever agreed to the final transfusion, he needed to say goodbye to his family. A nocturnal existence limits contact, and wherever intimacy exists, the limitations strain. Besides, the mortal family feels the new, frightening distance between them and the vampire so deeply that he can't bear to see their pain and he's tempted to confess what he is, though he knows the futility of such a confession. How could they believe him, or if they did, how could they live with the knowledge?

Faced with such a predicament, I'd never returned to my family as a vampire. I had to wait until my mother and father died to lay eyes on them again, and then only across an invisible chasm separating our spheres of existence. We were ghosts to one another.

So I couldn't begrudge him the kind of visit I never got the chance to have when Tiresia yanked me out of the world of daylight. But Paul's mother didn't deserve his devotion. So she'd protected him from his drunk of a father and worked overtime in a cafeteria to put food on the table for him? These were her duties as a mother. So she loved him? What mother wouldn't? He was beautiful and talented—far more than anything a white trash Kansas family deserved. She didn't possess a modicum of the grace and nobility of my mother, the stately wife of a paterfamilias.

Paul should have said goodbye and left it at that. But if as a vampire he might be able to see his mother's true worth, he couldn't now I saw prolonging her life as a mistake. Paul might put off taking the next step indefinitely as long as she was around. I was tempted to let her die as fate dictated—within the year, judging from the weakness I felt when my hand brushed hers as we knelt over Paul. But if she died before he took the final step, he might hate me for allowing it and resist my plans for him.

On her final night in Rome, I stopped by her room after I returned from feeding. (I'd decided to follow the same procedure I had used with the abbot.) But her bed was empty. I found her waiting outside my cell in a pink terry-cloth bathrobe and slippers, her face greased with lotion.

"I've been waiting for you," she said impatiently, inspecting with disapproval my jeans and jersey "It's 3 in the morning."

"Is it? I lost track of the time." Obviously Paul hadn't told her about my nocturnal schedule, not that she'd see it as an excuse to prowl the streets of Rome.

"Where have you been?"

"Walking. I couldn't sleep."

My face was still flushed from feeding, and she eyed me with disbelief.

I said, "If there's something you want to talk about, let's get it over with. I'm tired." I unlocked my door and led the way in, clicking on the desk lamp.

She stood near the desk, tightening the belt of her bathrobe. I sprawled on the mattress and kicked off my hiking boots.

"What do you want from Paul?" she said.

"Paul and I are planning a life together," I said. "You might as well accept it. I don't want anything he doesn't want." I closed my eyes and stifled a belch produced by the blood of two vagrants I'd found asleep in a doorway of a dilapidated apartment building near the train station.

"I don't believe you."

I opened my eyes. Alice stood with her arms crossed, a fierce, defiant look in her eyes. Her jugular was prominent, throbbing—I knew—in her excitement.

"I think you don't have a penny to your name," she continued. "You want to leave the monastery and mooch off Paul. You've got him wrapped around your finger."

"You don't have much faith in your son," I said, yawning.

"You don't know me," she said, "and you don't love Paul. If you did, you'd leave him alone. I'm going to speak to the abbot tomorrow. I just wanted you to know."

She turned and left the room, her slippers softly scuffing the stone floor.

I got up and followed her into the crypt. When she turned to confront me, I grabbed her by her scrawny throat. She yelped in pain, her pupils dilating. Staring into them, I willed her to submit. Her body went limp, and I lowered her to the floor. For a moment the sound of blood pulsating in her jugular became like a hypnotic war drum in my ears, awakening all my senses. I bent and inhaled its aroma, grazing her throat with my teeth. I struggled a moment but managed to withdraw from the overwhelming urge to feed. Using my fangs, I pierced my wrist then held it forth to her mouth and willed her to drink. She obediently lapped the blood, continuing to suck at nothing when I pulled my wrist away Hoisting her over my shoulder, I climbed the stairs and crossed the dark cloister to her room, depositing her on the bed. Pressing my fingertips against her forehead, I erased her intention to speak to the abbot. With my blood in her, she easily relinquished the thought.

That night Paul lay under my arm, both of us naked on the bed, the rich smell of his semen lingering in the air. He sadly described how hard it had been to part from his mother at the airport, how he'd clung to her when they embraced as though he would never see her again. He waited for me to reassure him that I'd kept my promise, and I did. Of course I said nothing about the confrontation in my cell, information that would only have brought him pain.

"How long can she live now?" he asked.

"To a ripe old age," I said with regret, knowing he might be unwilling to leave her behind when the moment came.

"It's strange," he said dreamily, "to think that Alice and I both have your blood in us. Was she afraid when you did it? Will she remember anything?"

"It happened quickly. She won't remember."

He sighed and kissed my hand.

*   *   *

For the next few days, he was quiet, eager for my blood, his comfort after saying goodbye to his mother. I hardened with pleasure as he sucked my throat, tempted to keep him a thrall forever.

One night he seemed to read my mind.

"What's it like having a thrall?" he said, pulling up his gym trunks. Wet hair clung to his forehead and temples. "That's the correct word, isn't it?"

I nodded. I'd let the word slip once or twice, instead of using the more flattering "consort." Anyway, why deceive him about something as petty as a word? We'd been lifting weights when his urge for blood brought us to the floor, where we'd spread towels over the cold stones to let him feed with me inside him under the bluish fluorescent lights.

"Is it some kind of high—having that much power?"

"You're the one with power." I kissed his cheek, which was salty with perspiration.

His gaze challenged me for evading the question. "Why didn't you make Michael a thrall?"

"Why does it matter?" I wiped his semen from my chest with a towel and pulled on my T-shirt, my body cool as a statue despite the vigorous exercise.

"I want to know."

I'd been waiting for this dangerous question, but I shrugged, answering nonchalantly in order to reassure him. "Michael was different. Very religious. And indoctrinated by his Vodun grandmother. She had power over him. He resisted my kind of life from the start."

As I spoke, Paul seemed to half-listen while the wheels turned in his head. "You had to make me a thrall," he finally said. "I saw what you did to Andrea, and I could've exposed you. You had to make me a thrall—or kill me."

"I was in love with you. I never would have hurt you."

As despondent as a soccer player who'd just lost a game, he sat on the weight bench and mopped his face with a towel.

I sat down next to him. "Do you believe me?" I squeezed his bare thigh, which was covered with light-brown hair. "Don't compare yourself to Michael. You're nothing alike."

"Except for your power over both of us."

"What does it matter, Paul? Think of what I'm offering you. So what if you're dependent on me for a while? It's nothing in the long run."

I got up, pulled him to his feet, and kissed him hard. He raked his fingers through my hair and pressed himself against me as though he wanted to enter me for once. When we sank to the floor, I let him.

CHAPTER SEVENTEEN

PAUL

Victor kneels over a guy with dark hair in a ponytail The guy is striking but his face twists in pain as he clutches his stomach. Victor strips off the guy's shirt to inspect him. Blood spurts from his stomach. Victor wads the shirt into a tourniquet and, cradling the guy's head, presses the shirt against the wound. Blood oozes through the fabric. The guy gasps for breath. Victor begs him to fight for his life. Stripping off his own shirt, he guides the guy's mouth to his nipple. "Drink," Victor says. But he won't. So Victor snaps his neck...

This was the dream I had the night of my conversation with Victor about Michael. I knew the wounded guy in the dream was Michael, and that Victor had offered him a vampire's life. But Victor never told me that he killed Michael. Why would he have done that? And why wouldn't he have told me about it?

I tried to shake off the weird fear that crept over me. *It's just a dream,* I told myself, *not reality.* Maybe my subconscious had transformed Victor's animosity toward Alice into this nightmare. Maybe the stressful visit had caused it, my fears for Alice, the guilt of abandoning her kind of existence. Maybe in my subconscious Victor took the role of deceitful murderer who only pretended to love. Doubts had plagued me about Victor's truthfulness. What if he hadn't really saved Alice? What if he was only humoring me?

Or maybe my difficult metamorphosis was to blame for the dream.

Maybe my tired mind had created a different scenario from the one Victor reported. Who knows why a mind distorts things in a dream? But the question wouldn't stop echoing in my head: *Why did Victor kill him? Why? Why?* And lodged deep inside of me, a more frightening, unformulated question about my future with Victor tried to take shape.

Maybe sheer panic explained my fears. Victor would turn me into a vampire and abandon me for this Vampire Utopia, the Dark Kingdom. I would prowl around in the night, strewing corpses as I fed. Even worse, I would prowl alone, waiting for the day I could join Victor—unless someone with a wooden stake and a lot of nerve found me first.

Did he think I could live a year without him—let alone 200 years? I pondered the two centuries that had elapsed since the American Revolution, the advances of technology, the evolution of social rules. How different life must have been for homosexuals in the days of George Washington, homosexuals so invisible that history books never mention them. They depended on invisibility for the sake of survival, just as vampires continue to in the modern world. So much time, so much history would pass again, 200 years of forced invisibility before we could take up life together.

But my fear included another weird element: In spite of my obsession with Victor—or maybe because of it—I wanted to hurt him. How could he turn me into a thrall who couldn't bear sunlight or the tolling of a bell? Why did he get to call all the shots? I had moments of intense rage. At one point I cut so deeply into the vellum trying to correct a painting mistake with a razor blade that I ruined the page. Old bald Ricardo lashed out at me.

"*Madonna!*" he said, picking up the page. "*Che fai?*"

I really was sorry, but secretly I blamed Victor. He was using me. And if I refused to suck his nipple, I'd meet the same end Michael had.

But just a few hours after I'd ruined the page, when I was finally alone in the scriptorium, Victor sneaked up on me. He buried his face in my neck and wrapped his arms around my chest, and my whole body opened to him like a flower in the rain.

That's how it went for me over the next few weeks. Images of Michael flashed and resentment followed, then fear of Victor, then fear of losing Victor, then exhilarating moments of sucking his tongue, his penis, his blood. And exhilarating visions of myself as "Lord of the Night."

Sometimes I thought I was going crazy. Some force took over my body, the way it had when I choked Rossi.

One night in late June, as I painted Jesus riding into Jerusalem while his followers raised palm branches in homage, an image of Victor's Joshu dancing naked wouldn't leave my head. I imagined Victor leering at him from behind a rock. And then Joshu became Michael—his beautiful, chiseled body moving with the sensuousness and power of an Olympic figure skater. And then Victor pounced like a cat, tearing into Michael's throat with his fangs as Michael's arms and legs flailed at the desert ground.

My hands shook. My heart pounded. The light in the scriptorium intensified, blurring my vision. When I closed my eyes the light flashed, the way it does after someone pokes you in the eye. Like an automaton, I picked up a jar of vermilion paint and a brush, then walked down the stairs, through the cloister, into the church. As I stood in the dark nave, a woman's voice echoed against the walls. It was the voice I'd heard before my first seizure as a thrall. At first I thought she was speaking in Italian, the big, empty church distorting her words. Then the sound crystallized into a name: Michael. *Michael. Michael. Michael.* To the rhythm of her chant I moved across the nave and down the steps to the crypt.

At Victor's tomb, I dipped my brush into the vermilion and began to paint. My heart seemed to throb inside my head. An invisible hand forced my hand. The word *Killer* formed on the marble tablet above the engraved name of Frater Anastasius. The red paint marked the white tablet like blood on the sheets of Victor's prey. I stared at my work, unable to move, struggling to get my breath. It was as if a powerful pump sucked the oxygen from the air.

Footsteps reverberated in the crypt. They stopped at the alcove. I couldn't turn to see who stood under the arch, but I knew it was Victor.

"What are you doing?" he said. "Paul? What are you doing?"

He grabbed my arm and turned me so that I faced him. The jar of paint fell to the floor. It didn't break, but the paint splashed over my shoes.

"I'm sorry," I said. My head was splitting. My face burned with fever. The smell of Victor's leather jacket made me queasy.

Victor felt my face. "You're sick."

My legs weakened, then finally gave way. My head swirled with brutal light before I lost consciousness.

The monastery's infirmarian, Brother Claudio, a bearded, snowy-haired monk, had nursed San Benedetto's sick and dying members for three decades. He'd abandoned a successful medical practice to enter the monastery, leaving all his money to a public hospital in Rome. Every day he took my temperature and pulse, gave me the meds he'd prescribed, and scribbled on a chart with a fountain pen.

On my third night in the infirmary, as I lay on my bed in the long, narrow room, aching with fever, I heard him talking to Victor in his office around the corner. He spoke slowly in clear Italian. I could make out most of his words.

"It's just a virus," he said. "He's running a low fever. He's got some intestinal problems. But the vital signs are fine. His blood work came back fine too. I just got it back today from the hospital."

"Why isn't he getting better?" Victor said.

I imagined Claudio at his desk, removing his glasses and placing them on his worn breviary—the way he had the day I came to see Giorgio when he'd come down with the flu.

"Some of these bugs can be stubborn," he said. "The fever is low-grade. No reason for concern. Brother Luca had the same thing. He was in bed two weeks. Strong as a horse now. I'm more worried about old Angelo. Third time he's fallen this month. If he breaks a hip, we'll have to send him to a convalescent home. Anyway, I'm off to bed."

"I'll just look in on him," Victor said.

"Be sure to turn out the lights when you leave."

A reading lamp glowed by a wooden chair in the infirmary, casting soft light on Victor as he approached me in his habit and sandals. He leaned over and kissed my hot forehead.

"How do you feel?" He brushed my hair from my face. "Any better?"

I nodded and reached for the glass of water on the nightstand. Victor handed it to me, holding up my head while I drank. I'd kicked off my sheet and wore only a pair of briefs, but my skin still baked.

"Claudio says the bug will run its course," he said, taking the glass from me. "Just be patient."

"What is happening to me?" I said. I'd asked the question before, but Victor never answered to my satisfaction. "This low-grade fever is pretty damned high for someone with a body temperature of 93. I should be dead."

"You won't die."

"How do you know?"

"I just do."

"What about these dreams?" I'd had the dream about Victor and Michael several times now, and I didn't know which was worse: watching Victor hold another man or watching Victor break his own lover's neck.

"I told you. I didn't kill him." Victor sat on the bed.

Exhausted and exasperated, I closed my eyes and sighed.

"Are you still hearing her voice?" Victor asked.

I shook my head.

Victor had told me all about Jana. But the facts were jumbled in my feverish head. Something about voodoo. Something about avenging Michael's death. It was all too much to take in. And why in the hell did she want to prey on me?

"Keep resisting," Victor said, kissing my forehead.

"Sure," I whispered, just wanting to sleep peacefully—if only that were possible.

Victor got up.

"What if I actually did hurt you?" I said.

"You won't."

"Because you'll stop me?" I looked up at him. He'd grown a goatee, which made him sexier than ever. If only all this chaos would end and I could spend my life with him. But what exactly was my life? What would it be after a final transfusion?

"Because you'll stop yourself," he said. Then he kissed me and left the infirmary.

An hour later, when I finally started to doze, the familiar sound of a spoon against glass rang in my head and the aroma of garlic rushed over me. Then came the vision. It was like the other visions, which I now understood as Jana's method of connecting me to Victor, at first to love him, now to hate him: *Light from inside an apartment building falls on the dark street. Victor grabs a buxom, middle-aged woman who's brought a bag of garbage out to the curb. She screams as he drags her to the side of the building. He knocks her head against the wall to shut her up, rips into her throat, and guzzles her blood. Blood covers his hands and his white sweatshirt. When he finishes, he removes his sweatshirt and wipes his lips on it. Leaving her corpse in the alley, he hurries into the shadows.*

On restless nights I'd been painting scenes from the Book of Revelation, and a passage about the Antichrist now rushed into my hazy, feverish head: *"The beast opened its mouth to utter blasphemies against God, blaspheming his name and his dwelling. And the sea gave up the dead that were in it. Death and Hades gave up the dead that were in them, and all were judged according to what they had done."*

After six days in the infirmary, the fever broke. My sweat soaked the sheets. I could breathe again. My head stopped pounding. The weird, wired feeling subsided, and I slept like I didn't have a care in the world. Brother Claudio made me stay put for another day, just to make sure. I wolfed down the tortellini soup he brought me, my taste buds back to normal. The sound of the monastery bell lulled me instead of crashing against my eardrums. Even sunlight didn't bother me. I stood at the window and gazed at the bright rays glancing off the dome of St. Peter's.

Was I changing back to what I had been?

Maybe God or whatever power ruled the universe was trying to save me. Or maybe that power was trying to save Victor from what I might I do if Jana got into my head again.

The gentle blue sky called to me. I had to answer. I showered and shaved, crept back to my cell, packed some things, left a note on my bed, and crossed the cloister, which was lush and green from the June rain. The aroma of bread wafted from the monastery kitchen. I glanced at the arched windows of the scriptorium, where Giorgio, Roberto, and Ricardo worked on the final pages of the manuscript. All my illuminations were up there. The pages for the project meant nothing to me, but the scenes I'd painted in the night had come from my soul. It killed me to leave them.

I glanced at the church that sheltered Victor's dark bed. But I couldn't let myself think of him.

I walked down the Gianicolo, crossed the bridge to the Corso, and waved down a cab on the noisy, congested street. Since I'd gone to the bank before I got sick, I had enough cash for fare to the airport. Along the way, I smiled remembering the day Rossi picked me up at the terminal, how he seemed like such a kind, good-natured priest—even though he drove like a maniac. Then I saw his hateful face as I choked him and pushed all thoughts of him from my mind.

Memories of Victor rose up in me like a quiet tide—our first walk through Rome, the first time we kissed, the night he finally came to my bed—but I couldn't surrender to them if I wanted to escape. I distracted myself by imagining Alice's reaction when I walked in the front door. She'd be sitting in her recliner in front of the TV, watching *Survivor* and smoking a cigarette in her pink terry-cloth bathrobe, her hair still wet from a shower. Emilio would be curled on her lap. He'd yap when the door opened, then hop down and scurry over to me.

"Paul!" she'd shout, stubbing out her cigarette and jumping out of the recliner to hug me. "Honey, what you are doing home?"

"I wanted to surprise you," I'd say.

She'd chuckle hoarsely. "Well, you sure did."

I'd search her face—which would be shiny with Mary Kay moisturizer—for a sign that she really was healed and strong, that Victor had kept his promise, that she was bound to live another 30 years.

The cab pulled up to the terminal.

The gaunt woman at the ticket counter eyed me nervously when I said I wanted a one-way ticket to Kansas City on the next flight. She probably thought I was a terrorist.

"You don't already have a ticket?" she said with a strong Italian accent.

"There's an emergency at home," I explained, placing my passport on the counter. "I've been working in Rome. I didn't plan on leaving until September."

She examined the passport carefully and typed something into the computer. "The next flight is in the morning. 5 A.M. There are still some seats available."

"Do any other airlines have an earlier flight?"

She checked the computer. "I'm afraid not."

"OK. I'll take one ticket."

She typed away, watching the monitor. "A one-way, standard fare is about $1,800."

Without blinking an eye, I pulled out my credit card. What did I care about money?

"If you wait a week, the cost is about $600."

"I said it's an emergency," I snapped.

She glanced at a security officer helping a ticket agent with a bag.

"I'm sorry," I said. "My mother's in the hospital." I hoped the lie would assuage her fears.

She nodded and issued me a ticket. But at the metal detector, an attendant seemed to be waiting for me. He must've been warned about a "suspicious passenger." He patted me down thoroughly, made me remove my shoes, actually had me unzip my jeans behind a screen, and emptied everything out of my carry-on, which contained a few toiletries, some underwear, and a fresh shirt. I'd left everything else behind, including the expensive burnisher and brushes I'd brought with me.

When I finally got to the gate, I felt weak with hunger. But the smell of pizza and grilled sausage drifting from the airport eateries turned my stomach. My head pounded, and as dusk descended outside the plate-glass windows the fluorescent bulbs glowing in the gate area burned my eyes. I wanted only one thing: to taste Victor's blood. No, it wasn't a question of wanting, the way you want a candy bar or even something more compelling, like sex. I needed Victor the way you need air after a minute of holding your breath. And then I knew it was futile—trying to go back to my old life as if nothing had happened, as if I could escape from purgatory on my own. As if I could spend even a single night away from him.

I took a cab back to Rome. The monastery bell tolled 9 when I crossed the entrance cloister.

CHAPTER EIGHTEEN

VICTOR

While Paul was sick, I sat in the scriptorium and read a volume on Vodun, commonly called voodoo. It originated in West Africa. Slaves brought it with them to Haiti and mixed it with Catholic rituals. Vodun had a pantheon of spirits, like the Christian saints, who required ritual sacrifices for their blessings and for their protection against evil spirits. A mysterious, remote god named Olorun ruled over them. Vodun priests danced, chanted, and offered animal sacrifices. According to Michael, Jana had been a priestess. Now it seemed she'd joined the pantheon.

Who was I dealing with? How could I save Paul from her? Michael had recounted Jana's history to me, and I reviewed it to determine her points of weakness. She was born in Haiti to a Creole man named Boudreaux and his wife Mara, the descendent of African slaves. Mara gave birth to 10 children, but all the girls died, except for Jana. Mara lavished her with attention, teaching her everything she knew about Vodun—incantations, rituals, and methods for contacting spirits. According to Michael, Jana worshiped her mother. When Mara drowned in a ferry boat accident, the 9-year-old Jana didn't talk for an entire month. The nuns at her convent school punished her—for her own good, naturally. They forced her to kneel with her hands raised for an hour at a time, paddling her when she lowered her tired arms. Jana countered by dressing her dolls up in habits, sticking them with pins, holding them above flames, and other tortures. Two of the nuns had strokes; one died. Another fell and broke her leg. Word got around about Jana's rituals, and the little girl was expelled, to her relief.

She cooked and cleaned house for her father and brothers and spent every evening from sunset to midnight at her mother's grave. Michael had said that Jana and her mother spoke to each other and that Mara continued to teach Jana from the grave. Boudreaux moved his family to New Orleans when he lost his factory job, and Jana continued practicing Vodun in the French Quarter, where her father opened a shoe repair shop. She developed a following of women, who paid her for tarot readings, spells, and midwifery. Michael showed me photographs of Jana as a young woman. She was beautiful. Her heavy-lidded eyes were black as tar, her lips full, her cheekbones high, her complexion very dark in the black-and-white photos. She looked hard-boiled even at that age, like a world-weary hooker who took nothing from no one. She married a Creole boy but left him after giving birth to Michael's mother, Anna. Jana and Anna were inseparable, more like sisters than mother and daughter. Michael's mother married a jobless drunk with charm and the good looks Michael inherited. Michael was born two years later. Jana took a liking to Tony, despite his shiftlessness. Shortly after two loan sharks pressured him for repayment, they both died in a fiery car wreck.

Jana continued to protect Tony and Michael when Anna died of ovarian cancer. The old woman lived and breathed for Michael, teaching him her treasured rituals and methods for contacting spirits—including Anna's. But when Jana died of a stroke, Michael sought spiritual nourishment elsewhere. He became a devout Catholic, and finally a monk. From the grave, Jana tried to lead him back to Vodun. She was still trying when he died. As I told Paul, she must have lost all access to Michael when he entered Joshu's heaven, and blamed me. She thought he'd eventually abandon Catholicism in favor of Vodun, and I'd interfered.

Could I appeal to Jana's love to save Paul? Could I convince her that like Michael, Paul was an intuitive, innocent boy? I doubted it. She hated me too much to care. And Paul offered her the only way she could pay me back.

One night, while brooding over Paul's illness, I sat on the Spanish

Steps, the twin towers of Trinità dei Monti looming behind me. Tall shuttered houses painted tan, cream, and russet clustered around the lively square below. High-priced boutiques lined the fashionable Via Condotti on the other side of the piazza straight ahead. Young couples strolled arm in arm past the fountain at the foot of the steps and along the store windows.

Hungry, I watched for prey Several solitary figures sat on the grand stairway, but none appealed to me. They were either ugly or fat or old, and I craved beautiful flesh. A dark-headed boy on a motor scooter caught my attention. He had stopped near the fountain to drink from a bottle of water. But as I stood to pursue him, two more boys on motor scooters rode over to him and began talking.

Finally I crossed to the Via Condotti and turned down a side street, where I saw a sign for tarot card readings. A strange chill overcame me, like the one I'd felt recently in the Piazza Navona. I felt a presence, someone walking behind me, watching me. But when I turned, I found no one.

"What do you think?" I whispered. "You think you can touch me?"

The aroma of rich, delicious blood drifted from the tarot shop. I salivated at the smell, my heartbeat accelerating. I entered the dark shop. Candles glowed on pedestals draped in velvet.

"Come in, please," a woman called from behind a beaded curtain.

Drawing aside the beads, I stepped into a small candlelit room where a stunning woman in her 40s sat at a round table. She wore a sheer robe over a lacy dress that might have been a negligee. Her full breasts looked lovely through it. Her thick, dark hair fell over her shoulders. Her lips and long nails were painted brilliant red.

"Would you like a reading?" She had a low, provocative voice. Her almond-shaped eyes inspected me with interest.

"How much?" I reached for my wallet but she held up her hand.

"First, see if you like what I say. Then pay for a reading."

I sat in the chair across from her. She shuffled a deck of cards and laid them out in two lines.

"These two cards," she said, "are very interesting. The King of Wands and the High Priestess. You and I." She glanced up at me. Her eyelids were purple with mascara and lined in black. "It means we both have special powers. Do you mind?" She reached for my forearm. "Yes, I feel it. Spiritual power. But you're not religious, are you? Then what is this power?"

"You're the fortune teller," I told her. "You tell me."

She smiled. "I don't tell fortunes," she said. "I just see the truth."

"So what truth do you see?"

She eyed me scornfully and released my arm. "I see someone who hides," she said, perfunctorily examining the cards. "Someone who hides in the night. I can't see the crimes. They're obscure. But I can see they are deadly."

"Then you should be afraid, shouldn't you?" I was tired of her melodrama. "Or do you say the same thing to everyone who comes in off the street?"

She peered up at me and smiled.

I gazed intently back at her. "Tell me the real truth. What do you see in the cards?"

She examined the cards, seriously this time, turning over two from the deck, frowning, shuffling, and turning over two more.

"What is it?" I said.

She raised her hand to my question and continued shuffling and turning cards. "I have never seen this," she said, shaking her head. "I draw the High Priestess every time." She scooped up the cards and handed me the deck. "Here, you shuffle."

Once I'd shuffled the deck, she told me to turn over a card. I did. It was the High Priestess.

"*Madonna!*" She hurried to make the sign of the cross.

Even I was incredulous. "Not trying to frighten me, are you?"

"Check the cards yourself. They are not marked."

I thumbed through them and found she was telling the truth. "What's the significance of the High Priestess?"

She shrugged, gazing thoughtfully at the deck. "There is no single meaning. But here I see a strange power. Maybe I was right. Maybe you are hiding."

"From a woman?" I suggested. Hunger gnawed at me. I had no more patience for games, hers or Jana's. I eyed the fortune teller's heavy breasts as they throbbed with blood beneath the negligee, and my fangs descended.

Her eyes widened. She got up, knocking over her chair, and backed away as I approached her until she stood against an oval mirror on the black wall. I kicked the chair out of the way and grabbed her wrists. She opened her mouth to scream, but I clamped my hand over it and pushed her to the floor. I tore off the negligee and nuzzled her breasts. Hard with desire, I lifted my fangs to her throat. But the woman's face had changed. I squinted, hoping the darkness was playing tricks on me. But the familiar features, the broad cheekbones of my mother did not melt away. Her gray eyes opened and she mouthed my name. Her fine white hair stuck to her face.

I leapt up from her naked body. Her breasts lay like two empty stockings. Her arms and legs were thin and fragile. To distract myself from the indecent sight, I focused on her face.

"Mother," I whispered. "What are you doing here? Who brought you?"

She moaned and stretched her eyelids without speaking. Then she opened her mouth and blood poured out. Despite myself, I longed to lap it up. I ran outside and fought to catch my breath.

A cold breeze rushed from the shop, and again I felt the strange presence.

"Goddamn you," I said. The image of my mother's naked body flashed before my eyes, and I gagged.

When my strength returned, I trekked down the street until I smelled more blood. Inhaling deeply to keep from gagging again, I broke into an apartment building and followed the scent to a corner apartment on the ground floor. Quickly, I forced the bolt and traced the blood to a back bedroom, where an old man snored. I seized his throat and drained him, keeping my eyes closed in case Jana decided to repeat her trick.

Dawn was close when I entered the front cloister of San Benedetto. Unsettled, my head pounding, I sought the safety of my tomb.

Jana's little game continued over the next few nights. During a feeding, I'd suddenly find myself sucking the jugular vein of my mother or my father or Justin. When I squeezed my eyes shut and tried to block out the image of a face I loved, one of their voices would call my name. The scent of blood fused with the scent of my mother's jasmine perfume or the medicinal odor of the ointment Justin used to soothe his muscles.

Some nights I fed so sparingly that I returned to the monastery weak and exhausted. Frequently it took two or three victims before I managed to shut out the painful images and feed. To beat the dawn in my weakened state, I rallied every drop of energy in me.

One morning as I climbed back up the Gianicolo, a rim of light appeared above the tiled rooftops to the east. I braced myself for a cataclysm, futilely shielding my eyes with my arm. I thought I'd miscalculated the hour. I would never be able to find cover in time to escape the sunlight. Two millennia of darkness would soon explode into a dazzling, final inferno. Joshu's name came to mind. But I wouldn't let myself call to him. I didn't want his brand of salvation. Wind rolled up the hillside and I opened my eyes to find the blazing line had vanished. Another trick.

I speculated about the limits of Jana's powers. Could she do more than harass? Could she open my tomb while I slept? Could she prevent me from entering it? I'd sometimes felt her presence hovering in the crypt when I arose. Did she come to torment or to destroy?

I worried even more about her plans for Paul. He told me he'd tried to run away and got as far as the airport before turning around. I wondered if she'd made him go. I hoped that had been her goal all along, ripping him away from me, because that she could never do. He could leave me behind no more than he could separate from his own soul. But she could make him jeopardize my security, as his scribbling on the tomb had already demonstrated. Just how much power she had over him wasn't clear. As a thrall, he remained vulnerable. Once transformed, he could fight her.

Jana finally seemed to leave Paul alone. We relaxed. Paul worked hard all day on the illuminations, eager to finish the project, but in the evening we worked out in the weight room and strolled through the city.

During a summer festival when many churches kept their doors open until n, we spent several evenings inspecting the art in Santa Maria del Popolo, not far from the Spanish Steps. The gilded chapels in the baroque church glittered in the lamplight. Paul studied Pinturicchio's lively frescoes

and Caravaggio's somber, realistic paintings—the one of St. Peter's crucifixion especially caught his attention. He sketched details from it onto a
pad while I sat in a pew, captivated by his beautiful profile and sure, graceful hand moving on the paper.

Afterward, Paul and I were walking near the Pantheon when he suddenly turned to me.

"Do you feel something?" he asked.

I gazed at up at the giant granite columns of the portico under a night
sky washed with light from the city. "No," I said. "I don't feel anything."

He shrugged. "I guess Rome is full of ghosts."

Both of us on the alert, we strolled in silence all the way to the Colosseum.

"Let's go in," I said.

I broke the gate open and led him through the dark stands, my mind
returning to the apparitions I'd last seen there. We gazed down at the deep
shadows of the arena.

"I once saw a gladiator torn apart here," I said with my arm around
Paul. "But not before he killed two other men. One of them was very popular. Marcus the Terrible. The crowds jeered when the gladiator ran a sword
through his belly. They roared when the lions were released and they tore
off the gladiator's limbs."

"Did blood repulse you then?" Paul asked quietly.

"I don't remember," I lied. Blood had never repulsed me, but I didn't
want him to think I'd been a predator from birth.

I pulled him to me and kissed him.

He sucked my tongue, clutching me tight.

"Thirsty?" I said, pulling down the collar of my shirt to expose my
throat.

He moaned and we sank to the floor.

His blood coursed under my nose. It worked on me like an aphrodisiac.
My sinus passages distended. I felt light-headed. My belly glowed with heat.
My nipples buzzed. I stripped off his shirt and jeans, then mine. He lifted
himself to take me.

"Go on," I said, feeling his lips on my throat as I entered him. "Drink."

My blood heated as he swallowed, pulsing through me like an electric
current. Spasms of orgasm rippled through us both.

We lay quiet for some time. Down in the arena feral cats screamed as they mated in the dark. Then I sensed her presence. Getting up on my knees, I gazed at the arena. A white-robed figure stood in the center, extending her arms to the cats around her as though they were her subjects.

"Do you see her?" I said.

"Yes." He clutched my arm.

Jana laughed, her distant voice reverberating against the ancient walls and then fading as her figure vanished.

A week passed before Jana's next trick. It was late one night. Paul and I were in the scriptorium talking about my brother Justin. Paul could see how much Justin had meant to me. He asked a lot of questions about him.

"I can take you to him," I said. "Turn your chair around."

He did. I turned off the lamps on both our desks. The scriptorium was dark as a cellar. The moonless, cloudy sky draped the high windows like a black veil.

I moved my chair forward. "Give me your hands," I said, taking them in mine. "Now close your eyes."

I closed my eyes and summoned the image of my father. "You see a man," I said, "a white-haired man in a toga."

"Yes."

"Next to him is another man. Young, square-jawed. He's looking at you."

"I see him." Paul clutched my hands tightly.

"It's Justin. Before he contracted syphilis in Jerusalem." I hesitated, reluctant to open old wounds. "He died."

"Died?" Paul murmured. He was entering a trance. Through his hands I could feel his heartbeat slowing.

"Yes," I said. "He died. In the year 20. Tiberius was Emperor. Justin was a Roman officer. A junior officer. He contracted the disease in Palestine."

"And he died?"

"Yes," I said. "Can you feel his arm? Touch it. You see how strong he is?

"Yes."

"He's a good rider. A good wrestler. My youngest brother. We grew up 30 miles from here."

The sight of Justin's image choked me up. I watched him standing in the sunny courtyard of my father's villa. Suddenly Paul entered the vision, without my willing him there. He lay down on the stones and Justin knelt over him, pinning back his arms, his mouth on Paul's throat.

"What are you doing?" I said, confused. Entering the vision, I grabbed Justin's shoulders. Perspiration soaked the back of his white tunic. His muscles tightened under my grip. He resisted me, and I was afraid to rip him away from Paul. His teeth could tear Paul's throat. "Justin," I pleaded. "Why are you doing this? Let go of him."

Justin released him. Without changing his position, he twisted his head up and gazed at me, bloody-mouthed, like a vicious dog. I pushed him off Paul.

The wound on Paul's neck wasn't deep. I clamped my hand over it and—fighting my urge to lick the blood—gripped his hand and willed us back to our original positions in the safe scriptorium. I turned on the desk lamp.

Paul sat across from me looking dazed and pale. The marks on his neck beaded with blood.

"What happened?" he strained to say. "What the hell happened?"

I clasped his hands. "I don't know. I can't explain it." This was no lie. Justin had seemed to mock me, as if we'd encountered his spirit, not just a projection of my thoughts.

For days I replayed the bizarre scene in my mind. I saw Justin glaring up at me, his lips bloody, his eyes daring me to hate him for acting like me. A strange shame overcame me at seeing my innocent brother play the predator. I hated Jana for causing it.

CHAPTER NINETEEN

PAUL

So you'll do it?" Giorgio said as he straddled the tension bench, lean and leggy in his blue shorts and T-shirt embossed with a McDonald's decal. He slipped his ankles behind the padded knobs and slowly raised his legs, his thighs and calves bulging under the strain.

"Sure," I said, pedaling away on the stationary bike. "What's 10 miles?"

My energy had surged lately, my body acclimating to its new chemistry. I churned out illuminations by day, traipsed through the city with Victor by night, and still itched for activity. Giorgio and I had begun running during the afternoon break. We jogged along the Tiber, through the beautiful lawns and formal gardens of the Villa Borghese, and in the park higher up on the Gianicolo, where a lake stretched beneath the pines. The sun still annoyed me, but it no longer burned my eyes. With sunglasses I got along just fine.

A few local businesses were sponsoring a mini marathon around the perimeter of the old city to raise money for cancer research. Giorgio had been after me to sign up with him for the race, which was scheduled for the last week of July. Now that I felt like Superman, the idea appealed to me. We paid our entrance fee in an office building near Stazione Termini, the busy modern train station to the northeast of the Colosseum.

The curly-headed woman behind the counter gave us plastic-coated cards with numbers to pin on our T-shirts the day of the race. Mine was 666, the number assigned to the Antichrist in the Book of Revelation. I laughed when Giorgio frowned and tried to exchange it. The woman shook her finger and said, "*Non si può*," as if she was defending a doctrine of the church.

"Don't worry about it," I said to him. "It's my lucky number."

On the morning of the race we hopped a bus to the Villa Borghese and followed signs posted along broad avenues to the lake in the center of the park, where the runners gathered. Luckily for my eyes, the day was gray. A fine mist sifted through the clouds. Runners stretched and sprinted on the lawns to get the juices flowing. They adjusted their numbers, peeled off sweatsuits, stood chattering in groups around the lake, and jogged off to the park rest rooms. Spirits soared. Giorgio mumbled a prayer as he pinned the devil's number to the back of my T-shirt.

A fat guy with a megaphone assembled the participants behind a starting line. The mob of runners stretched back a good 25 yards. Giorgio and I stood in the middle of the crowd. When the whistle blew, it took several minutes before movement rippled back to us, and we started off in a slow trot.

The route followed the river, the runners treading on the wide sidewalk. For the first few miles everyone jogged easily, talking and cutting up. Giorgio and I ran side by side behind a shapely woman in red spandex. I nudged him and laughed when I caught him staring at her ass. As the river curved ahead of us, I noticed a few beautiful men running shirtless.

By the time we reached the Olympic Stadium, four miles away, the file of runners had thinned substantially. The woman in spandex was one of the first to quit. More dropped out as heavy rain fell and thunder boomed. The man with the megaphone drove by in a little red Fiat, directing us to take shelter in a church ahead.

"We better go," Giorgio said.

"Go ahead. I'm OK." The storm invigorated me. And a strange, perverse kind of pride wouldn't let me quit, not even briefly.

Giorgio stuck it out until lightning flashed above the tree-tops, then he waved and headed for the church.

Twenty runners remained on the course, their wet T-shirts and shorts clinging to their bodies, their hair plastered to their heads. A wave of deter-mination pulsed through the whole group. From the looks of the lean fig-ures and their measured, relentless strides, they were serious runners.

As we cut away from the river on the return leg to the Villa Borghese, one guy shot out ahead of everybody. This triggered an urge in me to be top man. My stride widened. My fists punched the air and my feet kicked up high behind me. The front-runner's red bandanna stirred me the way a red cape stirs a bull. After a mile of dogging him, I charged past him, my feet thudding on the sidewalk.

An explosion of lightning fueled my steps as I sprinted through a park. Cypresses and pines sagged in the deluge. A crowd of supporters under a shelter cheered me on as I passed.

"*Dai!*" they shouted. "*Forza!*"

Then they hooted again and I knew my competition wasn't far behind. I turned and saw him grinning beneath his red bandanna.

As he gained on me, I gritted my teeth and picked up speed. The lust for winning consumed me like never before. I believed that if he passed me I might lunge at him. I might rip open his throat with my teeth. I imagined his blood in my mouth, his hot, pulsing throat against my lips. That image propelled me. Trees flashed by, the rain pounded me, and more crowds cheered from the shelter of awnings as I crossed the wide Corso D'Italia.

My opponent ran on my heels, his breathing hard but controlled. *Is he trying to trip me?* I thought, tempted to stop in my tracks and let him crash into me. But he swung around to run at my side, still grinning like an idiot, his short beard dripping.

"*Ciao, bello,*" he said.

My canines descended; my heart beat in my throat. The grin vanished from his face. He fell back, and I charged ahead, daring him in my mind to approach again. A few moments later, he did. His arms and legs moving like pistons, he passed me, without so much as a glance in my direction. He was probably trying to avoid another frightening hallucination induced— as he had likely reassured himself—by the final bursts of adrenaline.

The challenge infuriated me. I bore down on him. Even in the rain, I could smell his sweat. And his blood. An urge to attack muddled my senses. Through the dark lenses of my sunglasses, I kept his neck in sight. I might have pounced on him, but an image of Victor broke through the chaos in my head. Under a furrowed brow, his black eyes bore into me. His will closed on me like a fist. I dropped back, fighting for air. When I came to my senses, the runner was a good quarter-mile ahead.

I picked up speed, and was on his heels as we approached the finish line. A crowd under umbrellas and jackets cheered.

"*Dai*, Paul!" someone shouted. I knew it was Giorgio.

I bolted forward. Still, the runner shot over the finish line ahead of me. The crowd shouted and clapped. A tall man in a yellow poncho yelled through a megaphone, "*Il vincitore*."

People patted my back as I bent over, hands on my knees, struggling to recover my breath. I glanced up to see the winner's red bandanna tossed up above the crowd.

Giorgio and I boarded a packed bus that let us off near the Gianicolo, and we trudged up the hill to the monastery, gulping water from a bottle along the way. The rain had stopped. The muscles in my legs had tightened, and I was spent but exhilarated—and thankful Victor had intervened during the race.

That night I told him so. I felt more content than I ever had. And I was ready to talk about the next step in my transformation.

"The strength I felt today," I said, "is that how it always is for you?"

We lay naked on his bed, his blood in me, my sphincter throbbing still from his hard flesh. I ran my fingers through the soft fur on his chest. Another storm had blown in. The rumble of thunder penetrated the brick and stone of the structure above us.

"Yes," he said, kissing my head. "Except at dawn. Then my skin burns and the energy drains from my body, just like someone pulled a plug."

"So you're vulnerable then?"

"Until I'm safe in the tomb."

"But even then..."

He nodded. "The fables have that much right. Once a vampire is at rest, exposure to the sun will destroy him. So will a stake in the heart."

"Have you ever been in that kind of danger?"

Victor chuckled. "In a Paris monastery back in the 1750s, a plasterer working in the chapel followed me to the crypt one night, along with two of his cohorts. I don't know why my radar never picked him up. He'd been watching me apparently. He knew what I was. He knew what it took to get rid of me. I had just climbed into the tomb, a free-standing grave under a sarcophagus of the monastery's first abbot. I sensed someone outside and waited. After some whispering, the sarcophagus moved. A thread of light appeared. I heard the plasterer count to three and the lid moved again. With one thrust, I slid the marble cover down. The men jumped back. I sprang up, grabbed the stake and mallet from the plasterer, and flung them across the crypt. His buddies grabbed me as I choked him, but I finished him off. Then I killed both of them."

"So your strength was still intact?"

"I'd fed well and gotten to the tomb early, a good hour before dawn. Otherwise they might have succeeded." The levity in his gaze faded. "There's no such thing as perfect security for a vampire," he said. "You can't expect it."

"But the chances of someone finding you in the tomb, let alone knowing what to do..."

"Yes, they're slim. But you can't live 200 years without danger." He stroked my hair. "And it would be 200 years, Paul. Alone."

"I could do it," I said.

"Right now it probably seems like forever. But for a vampire, the years just fly by."

"You don't have to convince me. I'm ready." I propped myself on my elbow and looked him in the eye. "I mean it. What are we waiting for?" Adrenaline rushed through me at the prospect of the final transformation.

Victor smiled and shook his head.

"What?" I said. "Why not do it now?"

"Before you lose your nerve?"

"I won't."

"We'll know when the time is right."

Victor's tone said *end of discussion*. Pissed, I rolled away from him. What more did he want? I was ready and willing. We needed to seize the moment.

"I want you to know what you're getting into before you agree," he said.

"Bullshit. You're still having doubts. This Jana business has you worried." I lay back and sulked. "I know what I'm doing," I said. "My thinking is perfectly clear."

"There's no hurry. Finish the illuminations." He put his hand on my leg. "Let's enjoy the time we have together."

The excuse about his reluctance to leave didn't convince me. He doubted me. Not just because of Jana's influence. He didn't think I had the guts to live like he did. I wondered if he really loved me at all. And then I started thinking again that he was using me the way he used Andrea. I got up and dressed.

"I love you, Paul," Victor called as I walked out of the room.

I tried to paint but couldn't concentrate. The crazed resentment overwhelmed me. He'd robbed me of life and turned me into his slave, and there was no going back. I'd never felt so angry and out of control. I paced the empty scriptorium. *Who in the hell does he think he is?* I kept asking myself. *He makes me a slave and promises me a perfect life with him that'll last forever. And there is no such life. This Dark Kingdom stuff is nothing but a big fucking lie. He's a fucking monster. He's made me one too.*

Driven by an urge to lash out at Victor, I finally headed back to the crypt. But as I crossed the nave of the dark church, I found myself running up to the altar to grab one of the gold candlesticks that rose on either side of the stone slab. I removed the thick candle and carried the heavy holder away, glancing back at the dark crucifix as I left the church.

All along the Via del Gianicolo, cars were parked against the curb. Walking down the sidewalk, I swung the candleholder like a bat against windshield after windshield. With the impact of the heavy base of the holder, glass cracked and fragmented. Car alarms wailed. But I didn't stop bashing. Then suddenly a memory popped up of my father hurling dishes against the wall after my mother said something that pissed him off, something about his drinking. Every last plate ended up broken. Becky and Alice and I sat frozen during the rampage, praying that the plates would satisfy him.

The memory brought me to my senses. I stopped swinging and looked at the candleholder like I'd never seen it before, like someone had stuck it in my hand. I started crying like a baby, feeling sorry for my mom and for myself.

It was 2 in the morning. Lucky for me, the owners of cars with alarms were either sound asleep or so used to alarms going off that they didn't even bother to check. Lugging the candlestick, I hurried back up the hill. All was quiet in the cloister. I replaced the candlestick, noticing the scratched and dented base but not much caring.

Exhausted, I fell on my bed without undressing. Every muscle in my body ached. I'd just dozed off when the door opened. The faint scent of mildew made me open my eyes. But I shut them again and told Victor to leave.

He crawled into bed next to me and laid his hand on my chest.

"Are you all right?" he said.

Of course he knew what I'd done. He knew every move I made. I didn't care. "Go away," I said.

"If you want to do it now, we can," he whispered, nuzzling my ear.

In that moment, transformation was the last thing in the world I wanted. I was scared of myself, and of Victor. I wanted to go back to the way I used to be. I wanted my family and the hometown nestled against the skinny Kansas River.

"Paul?" he said.

I shook my head. "You were right. There's no hurry."

He lay still beside me, caressing my chest until I fell asleep.

When I woke up the next morning, alone and undressed, I wondered if I had only dreamt about Victor. I felt too weary to get up, and the sunlight bleeding through the shutter hurt my eyes.

CHAPTER TWENTY

VICTOR

When the police had finished their inquiries of Andrea's family, they followed several leads without success, then returned to San Benedetto. The crime crew again examined Andrea's cell and office for clues, while Ramadori and Morello questioned Anselmo and the monks. The interrogations lasted the entire day. The pair left before dinner and returned in the evening to interview Paul and me. As the only residents who kept nocturnal schedules, we might have noticed something missed by the others.

This time the detectives interviewed us in the scriptorium. I acted as translator for them and Paul when necessary.

"This is where you spend your evenings, then?" Morello asked.

The woman, Inspector Ramadori, was again dressed in a dark suit. She clicked across the flagstones in her pumps, inspecting the calligraphers' desks along the walls.

"Yes, most nights," Paul said.

He and I sat on desk chairs we'd pulled out for the interview In his baggy, wrinkled suit, Morello sat next to Paul, his long legs crossed, a notepad on his lap.

"From when to when?" asked Ramadori.

"I come up after dinner," Paul said. "I work till late."

"How late?" asked Ramadori.

Paul shrugged. "Sometimes midnight. Sometimes later."

"Any reason for such late hours?" Morello glanced up from his pad.

"I work best at night."

Paul's navy T-shirt accentuated his paleness. His skin was translucent and his eyes as sharp and beautiful as those of an animal in the wild. He sat back in his chair, his legs crossed, looking more rested than I'd seen him in a long while. Still, he clearly hated the interrogation.

His recent moodiness, his fits of rage didn't surprise me. The new body chemistry as a thrall made emotions fluctuate violently. Yet the extreme intensity of the changes in Paul suggested Jana's continuing influence. I watched for signs of her.

"And you, Brother Victor," Ramadori said, standing behind her chair. "You also arrive after dinner?"

'After night prayer," I said.

"Compline, I believe it's called," she said, staring intently at me. "It's at 9 o'clock."

"Yes."

"So you are here from 9 until dawn?"

"No. I take a walk, pray, write letters. The usual sort of routine."

"For a monk." Morello grinned inanely.

I forced a smile.

"Where do you walk, Brother?" Ramadori said.

"Depends. Sometimes I stick to the cloister. Sometimes I walk to Trastevere or to the Villa Borghese."

"The Villa Borghese? That's quite a hike."

"I have a lot of time on my hands."

"Do you walk too, Signor Lewis?" she said to Paul, who understood the question without my translation.

"Yes, sometimes."

"With Brother Victor?"

"What's the difference?" I said, suddenly feeling protective of Paul.

"We're just trying to establish your movements, Brother," Morello said.

"That's right," Ramadori said. "You might have seen something that could help us."

"We've already told you, we didn't see a thing," I said.

She nodded. "And yet, Brother Andrea apparently left at night. After the others had retired."

"The monastery's a big place, Inspector," I said, reassuming a calm tone. Impatience would only arouse suspicion.

"True. Very true." Ramadori sat; she smoothed her skirt. "Please excuse my asking again, but can either of you think of any reason Brother Andrea would want to leave San Benedetto?"

"No," I said.

Paul shook his head.

"I know you were friendly with him, Brother Victor."

I nodded. "That's right. He said nothing."

"And he never mentioned anyone who wanted to harm him?"

"No."

Ramadori reflected a moment while Morello scribbled. "You must miss him?" she finally said.

"Of course," I said matter-of-factly.

"But monks are taught to avoid attachments, right?"

"That's right."

"And you, Signor Lewis. Did you know Brother Andrea very well?"

"No." Paul was noticeably piqued by the subject.

Morello stared hard at him.

"Can you think of anything that might help us, Signor?" Ramadori said. "Any place we might have overlooked?"

"What, you think his body is hidden on the premises?" Paul said flippantly in English.

I glared at him and turned to Ramadori. "He said, how should he know?"

"We've no reason to believe foul play was involved, Signor," Morello said.

"Oh, I don't know," Paul muttered, his eyes full of mischief. "Maybe you should search the place again."

"Nothing," I said dismissively, when the inspectors turned to me for a translation. "We know you're doing your best, Inspector." I got up and stood behind Paul, my hands on his tense shoulders, to calm him. "The disappearance has upset everybody here. We're all frustrated. We've wracked our brains for clues. We've blamed ourselves for not noticing something. It's possible, isn't it, that Andrea just got tired of monastic life and ran off somewhere? Maybe too ashamed to let us know his whereabouts, or afraid he'll be talked into returning? There's no reason to think someone harmed him, is there?"

For the first time, Ramadori's professional demeanor relaxed. Her eyes filled with sympathy. "No, Brother. As I said, there's no evidence of foul play. Just facts without an explanation."

"Like what?" I asked.

She sighed. "Well, Brother Andrea took nothing with him. As far as we know, he contacted no one outside the monastery to pick him up. And there's no evidence that anyone came to get him."

"So there's no evidence of an attack here either—or a kidnapping?" I said.

"That would be true." Ramadori's thick eyebrows arched and she lowered her gaze, as though she wished to avoid alarming us.

"Unless someone here did it," Paul said in English. "Is that what you're saying?"

I translated, squeezing his shoulders hard.

"I'm afraid so," Ramadori said. "It's not a pleasant scenario. And there's no evidence for it. Unfortunately, that very lack is incriminating."

Morello raised his eyes from his notepad and nodded.

When Ramadori finished with us, I walked her and Morello to the monastery entrance and returned to Paul. He sat at his desk, staring at a manuscript page.

"You've got to keep your head," I said, standing over him. "They don't suspect anything. They have no evidence."

"They'll eventually start digging."

"Why should they? There's no evidence someone from outside the monastery harmed him. And no one inside has a motive." I pulled a chair over and sat next to him.

His brow furrowed. "What if one of the monks was on to your relationship with Andrea and said something to Ramadori? Maybe that's the real reason for our exclusive interview."

"Then why include you in it? Come on, Paul, it'll blow over." I sat back in the chair.

"And if not, you can take off, right?"

I reached over and touched his leg. "You think I'd leave you behind?"

"Or maybe just get rid of me," he said.

"I'm not going to listen to this." I got up and headed for the door.

"Victor!" he called.

There's a way out for both of us, I wanted to say. But I kept walking. Why remind him of the option until he was capable of choosing it?

The manuscript team finished writing the text of the Gospels by late August, after spending a chunk of the summer redoing marred pages. And Paul had finished all but two illuminations. Looking hardy as ever, Anselmo congratulated the team at dinner one night. During the recreation hour the monks chattered excitedly. Paul had already climbed to the scriptorium, but I stayed in the recreation hall. I felt sociable, hopeful as I was about the next move in my life with Paul.

He had seemed to grow steadier and more focused. Jana left him alone, getting a better kick out of messing with my mind during feedings or making her presence known as I rambled through the city. She knew she couldn't touch me, and I figured she'd get tired of her games eventually. As long as she kept her hands off Paul, I wasn't worried.

As I chatted with Giorgio near the billiard table, Paul's name caught my ear. Roberto and Ricardo, the two portly head calligraphers, were in a corner gravely conversing with Pietro, a tall, gaunt monk with a grating, nasal voice. I left Giorgio and wandered over to the group. They quit talking when they saw me.

"Congratulations on the progress," I said.

"Thank you," bald Ricardo said, eyeing me suspiciously. His wide-set eyes and wide mouth made him look like a fish.

"You'll be finished before you know it."

They all nodded perfunctorily.

"And you're happy with Paul's illuminations?"

The three monks glanced at one another, as though gauging how far to trust me.

"We're concerned about him," Ricardo finally said.

"Isn't he keeping up?"

"Have you seen the illuminations he works on at night, Brother Victor?"

Roberto asked, his round brown eyes widening. His thick gray beard needed trimming, and his hair was disheveled.

"No," I said. Paul had become increasingly protective of his paintings, rarely showing me his work. I'd chalked it up to his struggles as a thrall. "What's wrong with them?"

"They're inappropriate," Ricardo said.

"They're scandalous," tall Pietro corrected him, the nostrils of his bulbous nose flaring in indignation.

"Scandalous?" I couldn't help grinning at the prudes.

"His pictures are pornographic," Pietro whispered.

"Even Michelangelo painted nudes," I said.

"His figures aren't just nude," Roberto explained, rising up on the balls of his feet to emphasize his moral authority. "They're... indecent."

"And grotesque," Pietro added.

"We've considered telling the abbot," Roberto said, glancing across the room at Anselmo, who sat on a sofa, laughing with Giorgio. "But we don't want to upset him. Not when he's doing so well."

I wanted to tell him he deserved to be offended for snooping, but I thought better of it. "If the illuminations bother you so much, why don't you talk to Paul yourself?"

Ricardo shrugged. "I tried. He seemed to listen. But nothing changed."

"I said something too," Pietro threw in, tugging at the cord around his thin waist. "Paul said it was none of my business. And he continues painting the same coarse subjects."

"Indecent," Roberto blurted, shaking his head.

Curious, I went to the scriptorium that night after I returned from feeding. I began opening the thin drawers of the metal cabinet containing the finished pages of the manuscript. The top two contained familiar pages. But in the third drawer I found a set of pages I'd never seen. I carefully drew them out and deposited them on a long table used for drying pages. There were 10 in all.

One illumination showed a man in a red cape, opened in front to reveal a muscular chest covered with dark hair. The man's build and features were remarkably like mine, although the obtuse calligraphers probably didn't notice the similarity. In front of him, the man clutched a naked youth who was stooped over, grimacing in pain. The calligraphic text, which Paul must have done himself, was from chapter II of the Book of Revelation, recounting the Antichrist's successful attack on the faithful followers of the Lamb. Apparently, Paul envisioned rape as an ingredient of the conquest.

On another page, the same caped man pinned a woman's arms as he pounced on her throat. Desperate terror filled the dark eyes of the woman. Blood dribbled down her naked breasts. The same predator appeared on every page, ripping into jugulars, snapping necks, straddling naked crotches of men and women. No wonder the calligraphers were worried. Despite their reluctance to disturb the abbot, they might eventually approach him. What strange idea had overtaken Paul? What in the hell was he doing?

The next evening I confronted him in the scriptorium.

"You looked at the illuminations?" he said, calmly depositing his brush in a jar of blue paint. He wore a tank top and shorts in the warm room.

"What were you thinking? Painting me. You might as well put a sign on my tomb announcing what I am. But you already tried that, didn't you?" I crossed my arms and leaned against a calligrapher's desk.

"I couldn't help it," he said quietly. He looked down at the page on his desk. "I can't get this idea out of my head about the Antichrist. He's like a perverse twin. Christ conquers. The Antichrist conquers. Christ promises eternal life. The Antichrist promises eternal life. He's the powerful beast. The beast who rides his followers." Paul laughed at the innuendo. "He overwhelms them. Isn't that what Christ does?" He grinned sheepishly at me, his green tank top bringing out the glimmer of green in his eyes.

I went to his desk and caressed his head. He nestled his cheek against my stomach.

"How long has this been going on?" I said softly.

He remained quiet for a moment before lifting his face and staring innocently at me, like a child who has no understanding of danger. "Tell me about the Christ," he said. "Joshu. You loved him?"

"That was a long time ago," I said. "It's not important."

"That's a lie. You love him now. This minute. You've never stopped."

"Love him?" I said scornfully.

"You live to hurt him. Every victim is a blow aimed at him."

"I live for myself. I feed to survive."

Paul pulled away from me. "I think I hate him," he said. He picked up a pencil and sketched a face on a pad. The features that took shape belonged to Joshu, the same playful smile and probing eyes that drew me to him so many centuries ago.

"You've seen him." I stared at the sketch. "Did she show you? Jana?"

Paul crossed out the face. "Leave, Victor," he said softly. "I've got work to do."

Rome that night buzzed with energy. A local soccer team had beaten a competitor from Umbria, and revelers filled the bars and cafés around the bright Piazza Navona. Tourists caught the excitement, noisily chattering at their tables and liberally pouring out wine. In the midst of the commotion, I searched for a sign of Jana, determined to bend her to my will. At the spot where she'd last made her presence known on the piazza, a gypsy boy played an accordion for a crowd of tourists. I waited, silently daring her to appear. But she didn't.

Later, I paced the crypt until my restless body registered the coming dawn. What would I do if I lost Paul? What if he slipped from my hands the way Michael had? I thought of Michael begging me to stop my killing spree that last night in Knoxville, when I made him watch me tear into the throat of a shopkeeper, then a woman stepping out of her bath. I saw him again, dying in my arms, of a bullet wound meant for me.

A realization suddenly came to me.

Clenching my teeth and fists in concentration, I stood in the center of the dark crypt and willed Jana to appear.

A breeze rushed through the chamber. The flames on the altars flickered and then flared. A figure took shape at the altar near my niche. Her aged, striking face was the color of coffee with cream.

Jana.

Steely-eyed, she glared at me. Her slight frame was draped in a long, sleeveless white dress. Her feet wore a pair of thongs. Her hair hid beneath a checked bandanna knotted on her broad forehead.

The flames on the altar expired. Smoke curled up and filled the alcove.

With my eyes fixed on her, I summoned the image of Michael on that last night: prone on the ground, blood oozing from the shirt I pressed against his bare belly. Her lips began to tremble. She grimaced and fought to move her limbs, but she was frozen to the spot.

"Look at him," I said.

She closed her eyes in pain, shaking her head, and finally managed to reach out her broad hands in the gesture of a plea. The image of Michael tore at my gut, but I'd have put up with anything to keep her in check.

I knew the real Michael was not in the image, just as she knew it. But our pain persisted.

When I'd had enough, I released her from my will. She fell to her knees and buried her face in her hands. Spasms rippled through her body as she wept. Still sobbing, she faded into a specter as transparent as gauze, then vanished.

Drained, I climbed onto my shelf, struggling with the tablet until it sealed me in the closed grave. Jana's sobs echoed in my ears. The image of Michael, bare-chested and bloody, lingered before my eyes. I hated her for what she'd brought me to. I would send her to hell if I could.

The invisible dawn burned my throat and eyes. My heart slowed to the dull throb of a pendulum. In my tired mind, Paul's face collapsed into Michael's. Then all my senses merged, shrinking in the center of my brain to a fiery point that flickered and died.

Chapter Twenty-One

They were happening again: the dreams of Victor killing Michael. In one dream, blood dripped from Victor's mouth as he raised his head to check for intruders. He looked like a Rottweiler I'd seen in a news report; someone had caught the dog on video as he tore into a stripped and mangled little girl.

Victor's denials rang in my head, but the horrific scenes continued. In another dream, Victor set upon Michael's throat with so much intensity—caressing Michael's naked chest—he could have been making love to him. Each time my senses reacted as if the sight were real.

And I hated him for making me his slave. Sometimes during the day I found myself in his alcove, my hand on the tablet marking his tomb. I had no memory of leaving the library and climbing down to the crypt. But there I was, probing the engraved *Frater Anastasius* with my finger, tugging at the edges of the tablet like I wanted to pry it off.

I fought Jana's will. When the hallucinations faded, I saw through her lies and loved Victor more than ever. I even felt sorry for him because of his losses, because of his kind of existence. But the strange thing was, I felt sorry for Jana too. I imagined the dark-eyed Creole woman in the white dress that I'd glimpsed at the Colosseum when she appeared to Victor and me. Deep grooves marked her forehead and ran from her nose to her lips, but her eyes were sharp and fierce. She'd lost a grandson who had no chance of defending himself. She'd lost his mother too. Maybe

Jana planted this sympathy in me or maybe I felt it on my own. I don't know.

Victor treaded lightly around me. Even though I tried to keep the obsessive thoughts to myself, he knew they tormented me. In the scriptorium I caught him looking at me as I fought the images and forced the brush to move on the paper. Sometimes he got out of his chair, stood behind me, and wrapped his arms around me.

He felt my presence in his alcove whenever I wandered there, which I did nearly every day. I sensed his hand pressing the stone tablet as he lay on the shelf and wondered if he raised it to guard his tomb or to comfort me. What was I capable of in her hands? He must have asked that question as often as I did. He must have considered the risk he was taking with me. He must have contemplated squeezing the breath out of me as I lay against him in bed, sucking blood from his wrist.

I was caught in a vicious circle. I could get rid of her by taking Victor's place, but under her control the courage to act drained from me. I couldn't let go of Victor, not even to keep him. Besides, Victor wouldn't change me until I was completely free. He'd sworn to that.

Somehow I finished the illuminations. Maybe Joshu watched over me until I put the final touches on a painting that appeared on the last page of the Gospel of John. The perfect calligraphy described the appearance of the risen Jesus to his disciples. He tells them where to lower their fishing nets, and they catch hundreds of fish. Then Jesus commands Peter to feed his sheep. Peter turns and sees the beloved disciple John standing nearby. He gets jealous when Jesus says John might remain on earth until the second coming. I painted Jesus looking into John's eyes, wishing the beloved disciple could go with him to heaven.

On September 20, when I'd been in Rome almost one year, the abbot called me into his office to settle up my fees and congratulate me. He was determined to talk to me without an interpreter. With his bad English and my bad Italian we managed to have a short conversation.

"Your work is beautiful," he said, beaming from an armchair. His black habit was spotless and smooth. His sandals, planted firmly on the tiles, exposed buckled, yellowed nails.

Sunlight flooded through the high arched windows behind his desk.

The rays still bothered me, but I'd gotten used to the discomfort and no longer had to squint.

"Thanks, Father."

"I have added a *supplemento* to your final payment."

It took a second before I realized I was getting a bonus. I smiled. "I appreciate it," I said. I was exhausted after a night of weird dreams about a vicious black dog that kept turning up wherever I went. He snarled at me from behind a glass window, chased me in a cemetery, and blocked the stairs to the crypt. Jana's doing, I figured.

"You will stay for the *festa*?" he said, his kind brown eyes gazing hopefully at me.

I nodded. The monastery was throwing a party in a week to celebrate the completion of the manuscript. Benedictines from other monasteries would attend as well as some bigshot Vatican officials. Something had to give soon. Either Victor had to change me, despite Jana, or we had to go somewhere else and prolong all this uncertainty.

On Sunday afternoon, Alice called. She sounded chipper as ever.

"Did you get the package yet?" she said.

"Yeah. The fudge was great. The monks loved it too." I'd actually given the whole box of fudge to Giorgio, Roberto, and Ricardo. I gagged at the sight of the same rich chocolate I used to beg her to make.

"It was two batches," she said.

"I know," I said appreciatively.

Emilio barked. Water ran. I knew Alice stood at the kitchen sink in her bathrobe, rinsing a dish she'd used for popcorn—her favorite bedtime snack.

"Guess what, honey? I quit smoking."

"Great, Alice."

"No, really. I haven't smoked since May. Ask Becky."

Has this newfound willpower come from Victor? I asked myself.

"And the doctor said my blood pressure has dropped. Oh, Becky and Dean have finally decided to tie the knot. No big wedding, though. They're going to the justice of the peace. So when you see her next she'll be wearing a ring. On her finger for a change."

I smiled. Becky had already told me in a letter, a long one for her, two notebook pages of round characters in blue ballpoint. She was thrilled the kids would soon have a real dad. They'd decided to keep her house. Dean was remodeling the basement.

"I can't wait to see you, honey," Alice said.

I told her I loved her before I hung up.

That evening Victor and I quietly browsed at the bookstalls on the bridge leading to Castel Sant'Angelo. The late September sunsets gave us the entire evening together if he skipped compline, which he did frequently now. With my work finished, I'd have to leave San Benedetto one way or another, and Victor's withdrawal from monastery life meant he was ready to leave too.

It was a warm night with a clear moon, and customers crowded the bookstalls. The old, worn books smelled good. I stopped at a booth with several shelves of English titles and thumbed through the brittle pages of a 1920s Library Edition of Dickens's novels. I admired the reproductions of the original illustrations by Robert Seymour and Halbot Brown, geniuses of caricature. The detailed engravings of pretentious banquets and crowded London streets captured the melodrama and fun of Dickens. Then I remembered that Seymour had killed himself halfway through *Pickwick Papers*, and I suddenly felt a wave of panic.

"Let's go back," I said to Victor. He was paging through a book on ancient Rome.

"Go back already?"

"I want to paint."

He nodded, knowing why I had to paint immediately.

My head pounded as we walked along the river. My hands trembled, as if I needed food. When we turned up Via del Gianicolo, a huge black dog, digging under a bush, bared its teeth at us. He rushed toward me but stopped abruptly at my feet, growling with his ears back. He stepped away, circled us, sniffing, then ran toward the river.

CHAPTER TWENTY-TWO

VICTOR

Every time I fed, I steeled myself for another perverse transformation of the victim into my mother, father, or brother. But my threat to Jana had worked. She left me alone.

But what about Paul? How could I free him from her?

He cowered in the corner of the reception hall during a party thrown by Anselmo to celebrate the finished manuscript. With every toast raised, Paul, white as new plaster, grew more heavy-lidded and despondent. He looked like a drugged-out zombie, squinting in the soft light of the overhead lamps and fumbling with hands extended to him in congratulation. The monks must have thought he was drunk and deserved to be. No one looked concerned. During a final toast—to the memory of Rossi—his senses seemed to sharpen. He stared wide-eyed as the shaggy-bearded, burly Roberto sang Rossi's praises, then he set down his glass without having drunk from it and eyed the door nervously, as though at any moment Rossi himself might walk in.

Later, in the scriptorium, Paul's work absorbed his full attention. I watched him from my chair at a drafting table. He leaned over the page with his brow furrowed, painting as if he'd seized on an idea that would be lost if he didn't transfer it quickly to the vellum. His hand moved deftly, with quick, bold strokes. Without looking at the page, I knew he painted the caped man.

Was the reproduction of my face an indictment or a tribute? I couldn't tell. I only knew that we needed to leave San Benedetto. Jana's influence over Paul flourished in the monastery. The spirits of saints, the holy relics buried beneath the altar, the sacred rites—all somehow empowered her. Perhaps it was because she had always stirred a bit of Catholicism in with her magic.

When it was time to feed, I reluctantly left Paul in the scriptorium. A front had swept down across the Alps. A storm pounded the city. I fed quickly on an old vagrant in a doorway and rushed back to the monastery with the rancid taste of his blood lingering in my mouth.

It was after 2, and my clothes were soaked. Paul should have been in bed. But because of his intensity that evening I checked the scriptorium. His chair was empty. On his desk rested the finished page. In the illumination my own eyes stared back at me. My fangs hung from my mouth like stalactites. Blood dripped down my chin as I knelt over a white corpse. The face belonged to Andrea.

I rolled up the page and carried it downstairs through the dark library and cloister to the dormitory. At Paul's cell, I found the door open. The desk lamp glowed in the empty room. His clothes were on the bed.

Something drew me to the church. In the sanctuary, tongues of fire danced on the communion rail, the altar, and the flagstones. In the midst of the flames, Paul knelt, naked, his face lifted to the crucifix hanging from the crossbeam. The scene reproduced exactly my premonition. Rhythmically, from one side to the other, he beat his back with a little scourge Giorgio had given him as a joke when he found it in the archives room. Stripes of blood fanned Paul's white shoulder blades.

"*Spes nostra*," he sang in a monotone, repeating the phrase with the urgency of the rain striking the roof. *Spes nostra, spes nostra*—our hope, our hope—the same words Michael had sung as he knelt in a trance before the crucifix at the monastery of St. Thomas. I remembered the anger, the jealousy rushing through me as Michael gazed lovingly at the beautiful corpus of Joshu. Now the words stung me even more fiercely. Michael's hope had become my loss. Paul seemed to be going down the same road.

"Paul," I called.

He showed no sign of hearing me.

"I'm here, Paul. You don't need his help. Not against me. You don't need his forgiveness."

I grabbed the scourge and flung it away, but Paul continued the mechanical motions of self-flagellation, one side then the other. When I clutched his hand, he resisted. His strength surprised me, but I held him fast. Suddenly he collapsed on the floor. His body jerked in spasms.

I thought about covering him with my jacket, but it was too wet to help. I knelt down and gathered him in my arms. He writhed in my arms as I carried him to his cell, moaning and muttering the words of the chant. I lay him on his bed and did my best to clean his back while he trembled. Then, spreading the blanket over him, I tried to hold him still.

"It's all right," I whispered. "I'm here. It's all right."

A sweat broke out on his face. His hair was plastered to his forehead. He gasped for air, his body still jerking.

"Your judgment has come, Babylon," he muttered. The words were from Revelation. "Give up the dead."

I glanced around the room. Jana's presence was as palpable as the rain drumming the windows. But she feared me too much to become visible. I summoned the image of Michael again, bleeding on the ground in his final moments. I willed her to see the scene.

"Do what you want," Paul suddenly mumbled. "You can't make me see."

They were her words coming from his mouth. I held his arm firmly.

"You murdered him," Paul said, his eyes still shut. "You took his blood."

"I wanted him to take mine. He could have lived."

"Like you? Preying on innocent people?"

"He loved me. Nothing you do can change it. You'll never see him again. So take a look at me. Here he is." I thumped my chest.

Paul groaned. The seizure subsided. But the fever didn't. I brought two more blankets from a storage closet and piled them on him. It was just a matter of time, I thought, before the fever broke. But when dawn approached, his skin still burned. I had no choice but to get Brother Claudio.

Calm as always, the disheveled monk accompanied me back to Paul's cell, a black medical bag in hand. He felt Paul's forehead, took his pulse, and inspected his eyes with a tiny flashlight.

"Will he be all right?" I said.

"I don't know."

On the way to Paul's cell, I'd reported simply that Paul had collapsed.

"How long ago?"

"A couple of hours."

"Why didn't you come for me right away?" Inserting a thermometer in Paul's mouth, Claudio cast me an angry glance.

"I didn't want to leave him. What's wrong with him?"

Claudio shrugged. "Maybe a relapse. Maybe a reaction to some kind of medication. Do you know if he's taking anything?" He glanced around the room for a sign of drugs.

"No. He's not."

"You're sure of it?"

"Yes."

"Check his closet all the same," he said.

For appearances' sake, I obliged him. When I opened the top drawer in the closet, amid briefs and socks I found a stack of holy cards, a rosary, and a plastic bottle marked HOLY WATER. Paul must have gathered these things as amulets against Jana.

"Find anything?" Claudio said.

"No." I shut the drawer and inspected the others. There was nothing unusual.

When the thermometer beeped, Claudio removed it and looked relieved. "It's only 100," he said. "He feels a hell of a lot warmer than that. What's this?" He examined a spot of blood on the sheet and rolled Paul to one side to find the source. "My God. Did you know about this?" He looked up at me, his eyes wide with alarm.

I had to tell him about the scourging. He shook his head, dug into his bag for some kind of ointment, and sent me for a clean damp cloth to wash the oozing wounds. Paul seemed oblivious to any pain.

"I have to leave," I said. Claudio had finished cleaning and was anointing Paul's back with antiseptic cream. I'd spread a towel beneath him to absorb further bleeding.

Claudio nodded, aware of my skin condition. He pulled the desk chair over to the bed.

"He'll be all right?" I couldn't take my eyes away from his pallid face.

"We'll know in time," he said grimly. "I'll be here with him. Don't worry."

The rain had stopped. Birds sang on wet branches. By the time I descended to the musty crypt, the adrenaline that had coursed through me was depleted. In the niche I drifted off to the awful echo of Paul's voice: *Your judgment has come. Your judgment has come. Your judgment has come.*

When I woke up, for a moment I remembered nothing. But my head felt dull and my limbs useless. And when I asked myself why my body seemed made of lead, everything came back to me.

The monks recited evening prayer as I passed through the church. As though he sensed something wrong, Anselmo stared at me from his choir stall, but I kept walking.

Still in the chair next to Paul's bed, Claudio looked up from his breviary when I entered the cell. His thick glasses magnified his bloodshot eyes.

Paul slept, but he pulled away from my hand and mumbled when I felt his forehead.

"Still not much of a fever?" I glanced at Claudio, who watched me intently.

"No."

"Has he been like this all day?"

"Sometimes. Sometimes he's slept peacefully. That's what Giorgio and the others tell me. They took shifts while I got some rest." Claudio marked his page with a ribbon and lay the breviary on his lap.

"What is it?" I said, wishing the normal question could transform Paul's condition into something normal. "Shouldn't we take him to the hospital?"

"It would do no good. There's nothing physically wrong with him."

"Of course there is," I said. "He's overworked. And he hasn't had enough sleep."

Claudio shook his head. "It's something else. The scourging. The strange illuminations. Roberto and Ricardo told you about them?"

"That's what I mean. He's overworked and obsessed with all the crap in the Book of Revelation. It's brought on a relapse of whatever he had before."

"He's been muttering things," Claudio said gravely. "Words from the Book of Revelation. And blasphemies."

"Blasphemies?"

Claudio nodded. "Cursing Christ. Cursing the Blessed Mother. Cursing the Holy Apostolic Church. When we brought him a sacred host, he spat on it."

"So what are you saying? He's possessed? Not very scientific, Brother." He was moving in the right direction. But could he rescue Paul?

"It's because I am a physician that I can say it. Evil exists, Brother Victor. Don't you believe that? Satan comes to people who invite him. I once saw another soul tortured like that." He nodded toward Paul. "A little boy in Trastevere. He was exorcised and his health returned. You can go down and talk to him yourself. He's a grown man now."

"Satan," I muttered, exasperated.

"Don't underestimate a little boy's potential for evil. Remember your Augustine. Children can be evil incarnate, he said." Claudio removed his glasses and rubbed his eyes, then looked up at me. "Tell me, Victor. What exactly is your relationship with Paul?"

I glared at him.

Unruffled, he repositioned his glasses on his nose and continued. "I only ask you to examine your conscience. This could be the portal that admitted Satan. Pray. For him and yourself."

I turned to Paul. I wanted Claudio to conduct the exorcism. If I couldn't force Jana to leave Paul, maybe the conventional rituals could. Satan or no Satan, she apparently recognized their authority.

That night, after the monks had retired to their cells, Claudio, Anselmo, and Giorgio joined me at Paul's bedside for the exorcism. Claudio had apprised the abbot of everything. Mustering his authority in the grave situation, Anselmo swore us to secrecy.

"There is no need for the others to know," he said, kissing a purple stole and draping it around his neck. "The devil doesn't deserve publicity And the community needs no spectacle."

Giorgio nodded docilely. He'd assisted the abbot in the office since Andrea's death and had evidently proven loyal and competent. Now he acted as acolyte, lighting two candles on the bed table. Between them he propped a crucifix in a stand. Then he spooned incense onto some charcoals in a silver censer. The dark room clouded with smoke.

Paul moaned. His condition hadn't changed. Pale and feverish, he thrashed as if he was in pain.

The abbot removed a bottle of holy water and his prayer book from a bag. Giorgio stared at Paul, crossing himself, then clasping the rosary dangling from his habit.

Anselmo moved to the bottom of the bed. Standing there, prayer book in hand, he seemed to be praying over a corpse. "Christ will rescue you from the grip of Satan's power," he read, and he made the sign of the cross over Paul.

Paul screwed up his white face.

Next to the abbot, Giorgio nervously swung the censer.

"After his crucifixion," Anselmo continued, "Christ descended to hell. But Satan's domain could not hold him. He released the captives. He consigned Satan to hell forever. Christ's power is complete. Christ's salvation is for all who call upon his name."

Paul continued to moan.

The abbot paused to observe Paul's response. "Christ's power is complete," he continued. "He commands you to leave this sinner. In the name of Christ I sprinkle you with the waters of your baptism." He removed the bottle of holy water from his pocket, poured water into his hand, and flung it over Paul.

Spasms shook my beloved. I bent over and grabbed his arms.

"Stand back, Victor," Claudio said. He stood on the other side of the bed. "He's not hurt."

Reluctantly, I released him.

The abbot removed the vial of oil from his pocket and poured some into his palm. I stepped back to allow him access to Paul. On the other side of the bed, Claudio held Paul's head still while Anselmo dabbed his thumb with oil and traced the cross on Paul's forehead.

"May this holy oil summon the power of Christ the King. May he save you from the forces of destruction."

Paul sucked in a breath as though someone had poured cold water on him. He let out a high-pitched moan through his teeth, struggling to move his head.

"You're hurting him," I said, starting to think this hocuspocus was worse than useless.

Ignoring me, Anselmo took the censer from Giorgio and walked around the bed, swinging it over Paul, the chains clinking rhythmically against the silver casing.

More prayers followed. Then Anselmo directed us to kneel on the tile floor. I wanted to send them all away and climb into the bed with Paul. I'd promised to protect him and now I was handing him over to inept monks. But I did kneel, my eyes fixed on Paul, who had stopped thrashing but continued to moan. An image of Jana came to me, her dark, keen eyes, her high cheekbones, the turban she wore the first time I saw her. She was laughing, reeling back her head, pressing her dark, veiny hand to her breast in delight. I pushed over the bed table. The crucifix and candles flew across the floor.

Anselmo and Giorgio stared at me. Claudio stood, righted the table, and returned the crucifix and candles to it. He motioned for me to follow him outside the cell.

"You can't do any good in there," he whispered to me in the dark corridor. "In fact, considering your relationship with Paul..." He stopped, embarrassed.

"Go to hell," I said.

He didn't flinch. "If you want to help him, go pray."

I went outside and paced the cloisters for an hour. The air was brisk after the storms, and the grounds were spongy and smelled of resin because the gardener had just cut down a diseased pine. When the tower bell tolled 12, a light flashed in the scriptorium, as though a bonfire had swelled and then quickly dwindled. I entered the library and climbed the stairs. An overhead light burned, but the desks were empty. A vellum page lay on Paul's desk. The illumination once again featured me as the Antichrist: The sun blazed orange and yellow as I raised the red cape to shield myself from its rays. My cheeks and hands were already charred, and my face twisted in pain as I sank to the ground.

I grabbed the paint knife and sliced the vellum, digging the blade into the desk. Blood oozed up from the paper as though it were flesh. But when I touched it, the vellum was dry. I threw the knife on the floor and walked back to Paul's cell.

Only Giorgio remained with Paul. He raised his head from the desk when I entered the room. The candles near him had burned low.

"He's sleeping," he said.

Paul breathed easily, his face calm. I clasped his hand, now cool as marble. "Where's Claudio? Why isn't he here?"

"He thinks Paul is out of danger for now."

"For now?" I looked at Giorgio's cherubic face, his soft hair curling over his ears. His cheek was red from resting on his arms.

"He said the fever's gone and he's resting, but we still need to watch him."

"Go get some rest," I said. "I'll stay with him."

"Claudio told me not to leave him."

"I said I'll stay with him."

"Well, I guess that's all right." Giorgio rose reluctantly. He stood over Paul and made the sign of the cross before leaving the cell.

I blew out the candles then, checking the hallway to make sure no one was coming, I locked the door. Stripping off my habit, I climbed onto the bed, pulled back the blanket, and stretched myself over Paul's cool body.

"Fight her," I whispered in his ear. "Feel my heart." I pressed my chest against his. I clasped his long hands and stretched them out to his sides until we both formed a cross. "Fight her," I said.

I summoned Jana's image in my mind and willed her out of Paul. Sweat formed on his chest, matting the hair on mine, making me adhere to him. Paul whimpered and struggled as I pinned him to the bed. Then his body relaxed. With my fangs I tore open my wrist and held it to his mouth. He sucked for a moment, grimaced, and vomited into the sheets.

I held up his head to keep him from gagging. When he finished, I wet a towel and wiped his face and the sheets.

Is this it? I thought as I lay by him, watching him breath. If he couldn't take my blood, he couldn't survive. I kissed his soft chest, his vomit-soured lips. I laced my fingers through his and brought his hand to my face. If she took him, I decided, there would be nothing left for me. I'd walk out into the daylight.

Then I thought of her winning and went crazy. I got up, threw on the habit, and left the monastery, hurrying down the Gianicolo and turning in the direction of St. Peter's.

With one fierce tug the bolt of the basilica's massive door snapped. I waited. But like the time Paul and I had come there, no alarm sounded.

My footsteps resounded on the glassy marble surfaces of the palatial chamber as I made my way to the apse. There, Bernini's canopy loomed above the altar, supported by the spiraling bronze columns. Soft light shone within the rotunda, etched with the words *Tu es Petrus*—you are Peter. Peter, the ignorant fisherman commissioned by Joshu to lead his ignorant flock. The golden throne, symbol of Peter's privileged position, rested high on the front wall. Willing myself to the spot, I sprang up, lighting on the seat, and sat down.

"So this is what you wanted, Joshu?" I shouted. "A palace for popes?"

My voice echoed beneath the dome and trailed off down the nave.

"How can you let this happen? You've got Michael. Why begrudge me Paul?"

Leaping down, I ran to the front of the church. Behind the glass in its little side chapel, Michelangelo's *Pietà* glowed white as soap under a spotlight. With one strike of my fist, the glass shattered. An alarm sounded. Kicking through shards with the sole of my sandal, I approached the sculpture of the beautiful dead boy on his mother's lap.

I touched the boy's smooth face. "You were better off dead," I whispered. With one quick movement, I tore the head from the marble figure and dropped it on the floor. It broke into pieces.

A siren blared in the piazza. I waited in the dark vestibule. Two officers entered, waving revolvers. As they passed into the nave I followed them, grabbing them both by the neck. They struggled, one of their guns firing. I dropped one man and twisted the neck of the other. His body collapsed. The surviving officer—a slight, well-proportioned man in his 20s—pointed his gun at me with both trembling hands.

He glanced down at his dead comrade, his close-set eyes full of fear.

I smiled, hands on hips. "Go ahead."

He fired. He was less than 10 feet from me, but he missed. He fired again and the bullet entered my stomach. Wincing, I waited. The wound closed in seconds. Before he could fire again, I sprang at him, snatching the gun and tossing it aside.

I pushed him to the floor, tore off his pants, and rolled him around to enter him from behind. But as I knelt over him, a sense of foreboding rose in my chest. Turning him over, I fell on his throat, stunning him, and quickly drank until I was satisfied. Then I snapped his neck and left the church.

The strange sense of dread grew when I crossed the entrance cloister. The dark eastern sky had faded to gray. Down in the crypt, a shadow moved near my tomb.

"Who's there?" I said, approaching the niche.

Paul turned and faced me. He wore only his briefs. He stood like a life-size cardboard silhouette before the candlelight.

"What are you doing here?" I asked. "Are you all right?" I reached for his arm, but he pulled away. "What's wrong?"

His vacant expression made me wonder if he was sleepwalking.

"I lied, Victor," he said.

"You shouldn't be here, Paul. Let's go back to your cell."

When I moved toward him, he stepped back.

"I never loved you. I've been pretending all along."

"You don't know what the hell you're saying."

I went out into the crypt, looking for her, expecting to see her shadow behind a column or within one of the recessed chambers where flames flickered. But she was nowhere.

"Face me yourself!" I shouted. I was exhausted. My eyes and throat burned with the mounting radiation. I needed my tomb.

"I'm here to finish my work," Paul called from the opening of the niche. He pointed back to my tomb. "This will be the last time you crawl in."

"Paul, look at me," I said. "Look at me, please."

He did look, his gaze blank, lifeless. With no connection to him, I had no chance of overcoming her.

"You don't think I can do it?" he said. "Go see where you put Andrea."

Three niches over, I found a gaping hole in the mausoleum wall. The marble tablet that had sealed Andrea's grave lay on the floor of the alcove. Bits of dried flesh still clung to the skeleton on the shelf. Andrea's dark curls lay in a pile near the skull.

My head pounded. I could last another five minutes and no more. What choice did I have?

Paul stood in the center of the crypt now, his supple body more beautiful than the statue I had disfigured in St. Peter's. I advanced slowly toward him.

"Please wake up, Paul," I said. "Please don't make me do this."

Paul gazed at me like a blind man.

Now, so weak that every breath took an effort, I felt her presence. A shadow moved in an alcove, but she stayed hidden. She knew I had to kill him. And she knew it would torture me for the remainder of my existence.

"Please, Paul."

He let me touch him. His smooth neck, his shoulders, his arms. He stood meekly, waiting for me to take him. I grabbed his throat. Then I stopped and drew back.

"Joshu," I shouted. "Help me!"

I waited in the dark chamber. Nothing broke the silence. I scanned the alcoves, looking for a sign of him. But nothing changed. Then at the entrance to my niche, a vaporous figure appeared, solidifying into Joshu. A white robe flowed on his athletic frame, the robe of the Lamb described in the Book of Revelation. A crown rested on his head. His kinky dark hair fell over his shoulders. His smooth face was translucent and his eyes so clear they could have belonged to a child who had never lost a moment of sleep from fear or worry.

"There's not much time," I said.

"It's still enough, Victor."

"I'm not asking for me." I motioned to Paul, who gazed blankly into the air. "Free him."

"You think my God responds to demands? He's a God of love."

"Then where's his love for him?"

Joshu looked at me as he used to look at me, as if he saw Victor Decimus, not some generic lost soul. "God hasn't abandoned him, or you."

"Then prove it. They say you cast out demons. Do it now."

"You love him, Victor. You know love. Do you see it in yourself?"

I thought my head would explode. I had to have the dark. "Why else would I call you?"

Joshu went to Paul. He laid his hands on Paul's naked shoulders and kissed his cheek. "Come out of him," he whispered.

Paul gazed at Joshu with recognition, then smiled at me.

Struggling to my tomb, I tried to lift the tablet into place, but I was too weak. *This is the end*, I thought. *I'll never leave this grave again.*

Then Joshu entered the niche. The tablet rose before him, cutting off my view of his face, and slid into position.

CHAPTER TWENTY-THREE

PAUL

A trace of light lingered in my room when I woke up, and the monastery bell tolled 6. I'd slept peacefully all day. No more nightmares, no more pressure on my head, and no more violent urge to lash out.

Lying in the darkening room reminded me of one late afternoon when I'd woken up as a little boy after a long nap. Pots and pans clanked in the kitchen as Alice made supper, and the aroma of onions and frying meat filled the house. Dad hadn't come home from work yet. He'd probably stopped off at a beer joint. I could hear Becky setting the table. Earlier that afternoon, Alice had crawled into bed with me to read a story from a Childcraft book. It was about a little boy who accidentally killed a beautiful spoonbill when he fired his father's gun. I'd never seen a bird like that, but a picture appeared in the book and its beak did resemble a spoon. When the bird plummeted from the sky, it landed near tall grass, its wings spread and its eyes closed. On the last page of the story, the boy looks up and sees a cloud shaped like the bird drifting across the sky. I cried and Alice put her arms around me until I fell asleep. When I woke up in the dusk, I remembered the sadness but felt safe and loved.

That's how I felt in my cell. I remembered the awful images, the monks gathering around my bed, my hateful shouts, the burning fever. I remembered trying to hurt Victor. But I also remembered the moment of release, which was like a warm embrace. I associated it with a picture of Jesus I'd seen when I was little. He held a child on his lap, and several other children gathered around him. Yet I knew I wasn't an innocent child, and I knew my release didn't make me one. The great thing about it—about the love I felt—was that it was even better than a mother's love. It was a love that saw me exactly as I was and that got stronger instead of fading. If this Jesus was Joshu, I could understand Victor's obsession.

Victor would be up soon. He would come looking for me. So would Father Claudio, who'd checked on me at dawn and gone away relieved. I got up and dressed, my balance fine, every muscle moving with ease. As I crossed the cloister, the gentle chant of vespers rolled from the church, like a quiet lake lapping the shore.

Down in the city, I walked along the busy Corso, past shops with bright lights in their windows and restaurants filling the street with the aroma of garlic and oregano and fresh bread. A winding back street took me past the open doors of a Jesuit church, where people were attending mass. Baroque ornamentation gleamed on the high altar, and carved panels in the ceiling were gilded like my illuminations.

At the Colosseum, I turned down the path descending to the Forum. The site sprawled in the dark like a cemetery that had been bombed, tombstones and funerary statues scattered about and columns and broken walls of mausoleums left standing. I sat down on the ruined steps of the Basilica Julia, where Victor and I had sat before, and waited for him.

Before long, his silhouette appeared near the massive arch of Septimus Severus. He hesitated, even after he discerned me sitting in the darkness. Of course he could see me perfectly, just as I saw him perfectly. But he stood there quite a while, his hands in the pockets of his leather jacket, before he moved toward me.

"How are you?" he asked, inspecting me. But he knew. I could see from the relief and excitement in his eyes that he knew everything already.

A thought came to me as I gazed up at him, standing in the ruins. This was his home, and he had been born there 2,000 years ago, 1,600 years before the first American city, nearly 1,900 years before my hometown appeared on the map. He seemed to read my mind.

"It was a magnificent city," he said, gazing around. "Columns and pediments and arches and bridges. Patricians gathered here. People filled the market. Carriages clipped along these avenues. It was alive."

"That's what the Dark Kingdom is like?" I said

He nodded. "Even better. It's Rome restored, with all its order and pride and power. But it's a Rome that will never collapse. Activity will never end—games, feasting, sex. Love."

I stood, opened his jacket, and then unbuttoned his shirt. He guided my mouth to his nipple. He caressed my head as I sucked. Then as I swallowed his blood, my quiet contentment changed to heat. A chemical seemed to blaze in my veins. My throat expanded to accommodate more of his blood. I wanted to take him into myself, to have him and to be him in the same moment. And I felt myself drinking in the centuries of his existence, with all of their disappointment, violence, determination, and passion. Through my mind flashed images of his bloody, terrified victims, of Justin, of an almond-eyed woman in a cinched tunic who must have been his mother. The images blurred into a bright disc that spun and spun until I thought my head would explode, before it shrank into a dot of light that evaporated.

When I opened my eyes, Victor continued to stand before me, his flesh as musky and solid as ever. Unlike Tiresia after she had transformed him 2,000 years ago, he showed no sign of shriveling like a mummy and crumbling to dust.

"You're still here," I said.

He smiled.

"You're not going, are you?"

"No," he said, touching my cheek.

"What will happen? What about the rules?"

"I don't know."

The noise of traffic receded into the distance. For that moment we stood in a silent, dark vacuum.

Equals now, we walked quietly along the Tiber, all the way to a spot on the bank near Trastevere where prostitutes brought clients. The evening was young, but under a cypress a woman's silhouette rose and fell on a supine figure. Victor put a finger to his lips, and we waited until her work was finished. The man paid her, buttoned his trench coat, hustled to a car parked on the street, and sped off into the night.

Victor nodded to me and we approached the woman as she slipped a sweater over her head. She seemed startled at first but then relaxed.

She said, "I don't do two at a time," pulling her long hair out of her sweater. "You'll have to take turns." Her pretty, middle-aged features were visible to us in the dark.

"That's fine," Victor said.

He pulled her gently to the ground, unbuttoning her jeans. Nuzzling her neck, he caressed her crotch. When she moaned, he sank his fangs into her throat. Her body stiffened. She tried to push him off, but he sucked hard, stealing away her consciousness in a matter of seconds.

I crouched beside him. I caressed her limp arm and brought my face to her throat. Victor withdrew his mouth and let me taste her blood. I drank slowly until the sweet, warm fluid filled my belly. When I drew away, he nodded to me. Clasping her head with both hands, I twisted it hard until I heard her spine crack.

Victor raised me to my feet. He kissed me, his mouth tasting of her blood.

We walked back along the river. When we reached Castel Sant'Angelo, a full moon hovered above the fortress like a white stone, glowing with wisdom.

32972344R00244

Made in the USA
Middletown, DE
24 June 2016